Mrs. Roosevelt's Confidante

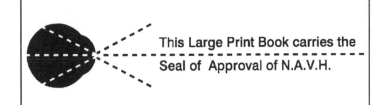

This Large Print Book carries the
Seal of Approval of N.A.V.H.

A MAGGIE HOPE MYSTERY

Mrs. Roosevelt's Confidante

Susan Elia MacNeal

KENNEBEC LARGE PRINT
A part of Gale, Cengage Learning

GALE
CENGAGE Learning·

Farmington Hills, Mich • San Francisco • New York • Waterville, Maine
Meriden, Conn • Mason, Ohio • Chicago

GALE
CENGAGE Learning

LIBRARY OF CONGRESS CATALOGING-IN-PUBLICATION DATA

MacNeal, Susan Elia.
  Mrs. Roosevelt's confidante : a Maggie Hope mystery / Susan Elia MacNeal. — Large print edition.
    pages cm. — (A Maggie Hope mystery) (Kennebec Large Print superior collection)
    ISBN 978-1-4104-8245-7 (paperback) — ISBN 1-4104-8245-6 (softcover)
  1. Women spies—Fiction. 2. Cryptographers—Fiction. 3. Roosevelt, Eleanor, 1884–1962—Fiction. 4. World War, 1939–1945—United States—Fiction.
  I. Title.
PS3613.A2774M77 2015b
813'.6—dc23   2015031254

Published in 2015 by arrangement with Bantam Books, an imprint and division of Penguin Random House LLC

Printed in Mexico
4 5 6 7 8 20 19 18 17 16

In loving memory of
Edna "Miss Edna" Wilkerson MacNeal
June 20, 1931–October 21, 2014

SOUTHERN NEGRO SPEAKS

I reckon they must have
Forgotten about me
When I hear them say they gonna
Save Democracy.
Funny thing about white folks
Wanting to go and fight
Way over in Europe
For freedom and light
When right here in Alabama —
Lord have mercy on me! —
They declare I'm a Fifth Columnist
If I say the word, *Free.*
Jim Crow all around me.
Don't have the right to vote.
Let's leave our neighbor's eye alone
And look after our own mote —
Cause I sure don't understand
What the meaning can be
When folks talk about freedom —
And Jim Crow me?

Langston Hughes, 1941

DECEMBER

1941

SUNDAY	MONDAY	TUESDAY	WEDNESDAY	THURSDAY	FRIDAY	SATURDAY
Full Moon 3rd / Last Quar. 11th / New Moon 18th / First Quar. 25th	1 335	2 336	3 337	4 338	5 339	6 340
7 341 Pearl Harbor	8 342	9 343	10 344	11 345	12 346	13 347
14 348	15 349	16 350	17 351	18 352	19 353	20 354
21 355	22 356	23 357	24 358	25 359	26 360	27 361
28 362	29 363	30 364	31 365			

Merry Christmas

Happy Motoring

1941

PROLOGUE

"Franklin!" Eleanor Roosevelt demanded in high-pitched, warbling tones just short of dulcet, "why didn't you tell me Winston Churchill's coming to the White House?" It was morning and she opened the door of the President's bedroom without knocking. She stood next to the Presidential flag, hands on hips, glaring.

She was a slim, tall, middle-aged woman who seemed constantly in motion — except for rare moments such as this. Her thick gray hair was pulled into a low chignon. She was already dressed for the day, wearing a simple suit and low-heeled shoes. A triple strand of pearls encircled her neck.

President Franklin Delano Roosevelt, armed with newspapers, mail, and messages, was taking breakfast in his narrow, white hospital bed. The room was furnished with a heavy, dark wardrobe, a mahogany bureau, and an old-fashioned rocking chair.

On the walls were watercolor paintings of clipper ships, an oil portrait of Isaac Roosevelt, and a framed certificate of his membership in the New York Marine Society. The ornate Victorian fireplace was carved with vines and grapes and showcased a collection of miniature pigs, as well as silver-framed photographs. A stocking with the name FALA embroidered and trimmed with golden bells hung from the mantel.

The President was recovering from a sinus infection and his usually clear eyes were ringed and red. The morning headlines for December 22, 1941, were far from reassuring: 80 JAPANESE TRANSPORTS APPEAR OFF LUZON, U.S. SANK OR DAMAGED 14 U-BOATS IN ATLANTIC, and HITLER OUSTS ARMY HEAD — SEIZES FULL CONTROL. Not to mention the continuing fallout from the attack on Pearl Harbor, fifteen days earlier.

In papers around the nation, there was speculation about a Japanese attack on San Francisco, fears of a Japanese terrorist attack with suicide agents in Washington, D.C., and rumors of Nazi U-boats patrolling the East Coast with an eye on Montauk, Long Island, and Boston. And there was news about citizens of Japan living in the United States arrested under the Enemy

Alien Act and sent to "immigration detention centers."

The true and staggering amount of devastation the Japanese attack at Pearl Harbor had wrought on the U.S. Navy was still not being reported to the newspapers — and so was still unknown by the average Joe, who heard only about a "heavy loss" of ships and planes and a death list that remained "incomplete."

Fala, the Roosevelts' small black Scottish terrier, was also taking breakfast in bed. The curled-up dog accepted the tiny pieces of bacon the President fed to him. Behind Roosevelt and the most famous dog in the land was a shelf with a half-finished model ship, various medicine bottles, nose drops, bits of paper, pencil stubs, a stack of books, an ashtray full of cigarette butts, and three telephones. Outside, fog obscured the dying rose garden.

At fifty-nine, Franklin Roosevelt was a tall, robust man — except for his legs, which were paralyzed by polio. He had a large, oblong face with a jutting jaw and silver pince-nez spectacles balanced on the bridge of his nose. He kept his Camel cigarette in an ivory holder between his teeth. In public, he always held it up at a jaunty angle, but in private, the angle of his cigarette holder gave away his mood, much like Fala's tail gave away his. This morning, the President's cigarette hung loosely in his mouth, pointing to the floor. The President wiped at his nose with a monogrammed linen handkerchief. He'd known the British P.M. was coming ever since the attack on Pearl Harbor, but for security reasons had kept the news to himself.

"Well, one of the first things we must do is remove all the art depicting the War of 1812," said Mrs. Roosevelt. "Keeping those paintings up would be a horrible gaffe."

The President reached down to stroke Fala's spiky ears. "Yes, dear." As the dog wagged his tail, hoping for more bacon, Roosevelt sneezed. "Oh, spinach!" he exclaimed. "I can't shake this lousy cold."

"Bless you." The First Lady entered, long arms folded across her chest. "I think we can keep the Revolutionary War paintings. But perhaps take down George Washington."

"President Washington?" the President echoed, giving a good blow. "Keep him up. Churchill has high respect for the Founding Fathers, so I've read. And even if he doesn't, Washington's still our first President. As the British learned in 1776 — and the Axis powers will discover soon — the American spirit is indomitable."

Franklin looked at Eleanor over the wire rims of his spectacles. "The Prime Minister's a guest, yes — and now our ally — but we're going to be negotiating quite a few things while he's here, including the fate of the British colonies. Might not be a bad idea to remind him who won the Revolutionary War." He slipped another morsel of bacon to Fala, who wagged his tail in appreciation.

"But why didn't you tell me *earlier,* Franklin? And I can't find Mrs. Nesbitt anywhere. What are we going to serve on such short notice? She's a mediocre enough cook as it is. If only I'd known . . ."

There was the heavy drumbeat of footsteps, then a knock at the open door. It was the President's chief butler, Alonzo Fields, a dignified colored man, well over six feet tall and nearly three hundred pounds. Roosevelt noticed him waiting at the door and lowered the emotional temperature.

"Now, Eleanor, all that little woman would do even if she were here is to tell Fields what we can tell him ourselves right now." He looked to his butler. "Fields, have your staff prepare bedrooms for the Prime Minister and his party. And if you see Mrs. Nesbitt, tell her to find Mrs. Roosevelt at once — we'll need dinner for twenty at eight, nine at the latest."

"Yes, sir."

Eleanor blinked. "My word, Franklin, I don't think you realize how much work a visit from a foreign dignitary takes! And even with Tommy on Christmas vacation, Blanche didn't show up for work today. She didn't even call — it's not like her." Malvina "Tommy" Thompson was the secretary who usually took dictation for the First Lady's "My Day" newspaper columns. Blanche Balfour had been brought in to temporarily replace her.

"I'm sure Blanche is fine. And let the staff take care of everything. It's their job."

Fields had waited. "Anything else, sir? Ma'am?"

"Thank you, that's all," said the President. Fields left, his tread heavy on the hall floor.

But Eleanor was still fretting. "As First Lady, it all reflects on me, you know. And in addition to my column, I have a press conference today —" She began to pace at the foot of the bed, from one end of the worn Persian rug to the other.

"I know you'll do a bang-up job, Babs."

His use of her nickname softened her edge a bit. The President kept his eyes on his newspaper, but the First Lady would not be put off. "And Franklin —" She stopped pac-

14

ing to look at him. Already a statuesque woman, she towered over the man sitting up in bed. "Have you had a chance to read my letter to the Governor of Virginia, regarding the impending execution of Wendell Cotton?"

The President sighed. "If you haven't noticed, dear, we're at *war.* I have more on my plate with the Japs and the Huns than I know what to do with. And now, with Winston coming . . ."

"A man's life is at stake!" Franklin Delano Roosevelt was President, but Eleanor Roosevelt was the matriarch of the family and a political powerhouse in her own right. Not only was she the President's eyes and ears for places his wheelchair couldn't take him but she exerted a moral influence of her own.

"I know." Roosevelt looked up at his wife. "But I can't rile up those boys from Dixie right now, just as we're entering this war. We all need to pull *together* to win — North and South. I can't afford to antagonize a nation that only recently wanted to throw me out of office and elect an isolationist."

"Shouldn't your 'together' include men like Wendell Cotton? What about the Negroes?" Eleanor perched at the foot of her husband's bed. "This is their war, too, you

15

know. How can we fight for democracy if our own armed forces are segregated?"

"You know what they say about us down South — 'She'll kiss the Negroes, he'll kiss the Jews, and they'll stay in the White House as long as they choose.' I simply can't risk alienating Dixie, especially now that we're in the thick of it."

The First Lady gave a sad, disapproving look and shook her head. "Unless we make this country worth fighting for by the Negroes, we shall have nothing to offer the world at the end of the war."

Fala looked up for more bacon, which Roosevelt fed to him before replying. "I'm not President New Deal anymore, Babs, I'm President Win-the-War. Any further domestic progress is going to have to wait until this war is over. If I make any sudden changes to the status quo in regard to the coloreds, certain people will lash out. I need to keep this country together. I'm doing the best I can." He looked out the window — the milk-glass winter sky was overcast and threatened rain — then back to the headlines.

The First Lady knew when the President had had enough. "I'm going to put Mr. Churchill in the Rose Bedroom. What do you think?"

"Perfecto, my dear." He didn't look up, but his voice was a few degrees warmer.

Mrs. Roosevelt's gaze went to the cluster of photographs of their children on the mantel. They were now grown and wouldn't be home for the holidays this year. "It's so strange to have Christmas with the country at war. And without the boys and Anna," she added. Their son James was in the Marines, Elliott was in the Army's Air Force, and both Franklin Jr. and John were in the Navy. Their daughter, Anna, was living in Seattle, while her husband and their son-in-law, John Boettiger, was stationed in England. "And without your mother, too, of course," Eleanor added. The President's mother, Sara Delano Roosevelt, had died that September.

The President nodded. "And your brother." The First Lady's brother, Gracie Hall Roosevelt, had also died in September. Roosevelt cleared his throat. "Well, I have the feeling the atmosphere will be considerably energized when the Prime gets here." He signed a few documents with a flourish, then looked up at his wife again, the spark back in his eyes. "You have no idea how much energy he has."

"Is that what you call him? 'The Prime'?"

"Indeed."

"Well, then I'll do everything to get ready for him and his staff." She rose, smoothing her skirt. "We'll put him and his detective and valet up here, and as many of the others as we can, and the rest can stay at the Mayflower — I'll have Mr. Fields call over. And what do you think he'd like for dinner tonight when he gets in?"

"I'm sure anything you choose will be splendid, my darling. Just make sure to have plenty of wine and scotch on hand. The Prime likes his hooch. And of course I'll make Martinis for Children's Hour."

Eleanor turned away to hide her grimace. Her father had been an alcoholic; alcoholism had just claimed the life of her brother. She rarely touched spirits herself, indulging in one of her husband's Old-Fashioneds only once in a blue moon. "I'll see what I can do."

The President tugged once on a frayed needlepoint bellpull to summon his valet. "I'm going to the airport to greet Winston and his crew."

"You're going yourself?" Eleanor couldn't conceal her concern. "Can't you send someone else and then greet him here? You're just getting over that nasty infection."

"The Prime and his staff have been on a

ship dodging Nazi submarines for the past ten days, and they've only just docked in Boston. I think the least I can do is to show up at the airport."

Eleanor turned to go but stopped in the doorway. "Well, if you see any of the staff, let them know I'm looking for Blanche — will you please, dear?" Then, "I'm worried about her. She hasn't been herself lately. She seems a bit . . . off."

Roosevelt grinned, one of those megawatt grins that routinely made the newspapers' front pages. "Babs, if I see Blanche, I'll be sure to send her your way."

When the First Lady had left, the smile vanished. The President sneezed, then wiped again at his nose. He checked his datebook. Under the day's date, December 22, 1941, he had written: R S F G H V N R Q U Q R X X M N V F. The code was one he'd developed in his days as an undergraduate at Harvard and had used ever since, occasionally changing the key for security reasons.

He gazed out the window at the gardens veiled in fog and picked up the telephone receiver. His gold signet ring — with a single bloodstone and the Roosevelt crest — on his left pinkie finger glinted in the glow from the bedside lamp. "Tell Frank

Cole to come to my office," he ordered. "Immediately."

"Come on, Davy! Attaboy! You can beat that big ol' Goliath, I just know you can!"

Wendell Cotton sat on the hard bed of his jail cell and watched his cellmates — a mass of fat, brown, shiny cockroaches — swarm at the bread crumbs he'd put down for them. They'd been his companions since his arrival, although they were uninterested in him until his meager meals arrived. To assuage his boredom and his loneliness, Wendell had organized cockroach races, using bread crumbs as prizes.

Two champions had emerged, and Wendell could tell them apart. The bigger cockroach was Goliath, the other one David. Although Goliath usually won, there were some days — like today — when David gave the big guy a run for his money. Wanting to be fair, Wendell saved crumbs, as consolation prizes, for the also-rans as well.

The roaches were his friends. His only friends. They helped him with his nerves, distracted him for a few moments. But it was impossible to forget he was in his tiny, solitary cell on Death Row at Thomas Jefferson Prison in rural Virginia. The glow that passed through the high, barred window was dim; it didn't so much shine as seep through the filthy glass. What light there was shone down on a narrow bed covered with a gray blanket, a washbasin, and a toilet.

Singing helped pass the time and made the loneliness more bearable, too. As the roaches gobbled their feast of crumbs, Wendell wrapped his thin arms around himself. He swayed and sang, in a voice surprisingly deep for a fifteen-year-old:

I have had my fun, if I don't get well no
   more
My health is failing me, and I'm goin' down
   slow
Please write my mother, tell her the shape
   I'm in
Tell her to pray for me, forgive me for my
   sin . . .

Sometimes the sunlight touched his face and illuminated his features — large, dark eyes with thick lashes and a dimple in his chin. He had the look of a boy who'd been forced to assume the responsibilities of a man much too early in life.

"Shut the devil up!" came a querulous voice from a cell down the hall.

It was the Row's only other prisoner,

Jimmy Walker, an older white man — bent over and gnarled, like a twisted tree. Jimmy was also scheduled to die. In Virginia, although segregation existed everywhere else, it didn't on Death Row.

"We all niggas here, boy," Walker had called out between the bars when he'd first seen Cotton walked in by four guards, white men in gray uniforms, their key rings jangling with each step. Cotton's callused hands were cuffed and his long bare feet shackled. "We in nowhere-land. Like the Land of Oz. Like ol' Cooter Brown."

Both men flinched when they heard the gate to the Row being opened. The newcomer was the preacher from Ebenezer Missionary Church, Ezra Johnson. He was a short, stocky man, his black hair touched at the temples by white, his face and hands marked with vitiligo, making his skin a patchwork of pink and colored. Reverend Johnson took a stool and set it down by the iron bars of Cotton's cell. Then he sat, Bible in hand.

"Thank you for comin', Reverend Johnson," Wendell said from his narrow bed, "but I pray to Jesus my whole life by myself — and I don't need no preacher to pray with me now."

"It's all right, son. We can just talk if you want."

Wendell threw another crumb across his cell. The roaches scuttled after it.

The reverend stared at the roaches' feeding frenzy. "What's that you're doing?"

"Races. I reckon they're just as bored as I am, bein' stuck in here. So I thought I'd give them something to do. Somethin' to eat."

Reverend Johnson nodded and reached through the bars to grasp the boy's bony shoulder. "I'm here for you, son. Whatever you need."

"You don't need to absolve my sins. Besides, I didn't do nothin' — nothin' that weren't self-defense. And God don't seem fit to care these days."

"Did you write that letter I asked you to?"

"I did." Wendell slid a piece of paper, almost transparent from folding and refolding, through the bars.

Reverend Johnson read Wendell's large, childlike handwriting silently:

Like the song says, I been buked and I been scorned. I been talked about, shos yor born.

But even though there be trouble all over this world I believe in God I have asked

God to forgive me. Even during these hard times I aint goin to lay my religon down. I don't know if He's heard my prayers, but I reckon maybe because he's God and He knows all. He's my judge, not the judge and jury of Virgina, and not the peeple. The Governor and the Courts don't know all the facts.

Seems to me that some people get to make mistakes and have them forgivan, no problem. Some people get lots of these chances.

And then there's some people that get no chances.

Do one thing wrong and its the electric chair for you.

I always worked hard to provide for my mother But he stol from me. Never work for a pore man or else he'll steel whats yours, I say.

And now it means I die Every second means I am closer to my our of death. I'm getting ready to put on my long white coat and meet my Maker.

But I appreciate every step you good people do toards helping me I am a poor laboring boy All I want is one more chance at life.

"You really think that'll go in a newspaper

24

after I'm dead?" Wendell asked.

"Is that what you want?" Reverend Johnson replied.

"I'd like my side of the story told, sure." Wendell shook his head. "You church folk be crazy. Why you do it? Visit us dead men walking?"

The Reverend slipped the paper into his jacket pocket. "I want to bring you comfort, Wendell. And there is still hope for you — for a retrial. This time by a jury of your peers, not white sharecroppers who can afford the poll tax."

Wendell sighed and rubbed the back of his neck. "I know Miz Andi been tryin' her best." Miss Andi was Andrea Martin, assigned to his case by the Workers Defense League to stop the execution.

"Miss Andi's been working day and night, and your momma too, to get you another trial. Miss Andi has some friends, who might help — friends in high places."

Wendell's face hardened. "Like who? Who gonna listen to some high-yalla Negro girl who dresses like a man and wants to go to law school?"

Reverend Johnson stood. "Mrs. Eleanor Roosevelt, for one. Miss Andrea's been in almost constant contact with her and her office. She's the First Lady of the United

States — that's a heck of a big deal."

"That and a nickel'll get you a Coca-Cola." Wendell snorted, tossing another crumb to the roaches to watch them scurry. "She ain't the Governor."

"No, but the President has pull with the Governor — who still has the power to pardon you. Miss Andi's trying to get Mrs. Roosevelt to ask her husband to intervene on your behalf. To have a word with the Governor, so he'll stay your execution. Maybe even get you a retrial. A *real* trial this time."

Wendell crossed his arms over his boyish chest. "Miz Andi's wastin' her time. Ain't gonna do me no good."

"I want to read you part of a letter Miss Andi sent me," the Reverend Johnson said. *"Tell Mr. Cotton that we want him to feel encouraged and to know he has thousands of friends all over the country. Tell him to keep well and strong because he has a tough job ahead of him. And please tell him that many people are praying for him."*

Wendell looked toward the light struggling to pass through the grimy window. He blinked, hard. "Tell Miz Andi that I'm more than glad to hear from her and to know I have some friends out there." He turned his face to the preacher, his eyes catching the light. "And please tell her to work fast. I only got one week left."

Blanche Imogene Balfour was hungover.

It was late afternoon, and fog stalked past her windows as daylight bled out. Her apartment's bedroom windows overlooked Massachusetts Avenue, and in the gauzy mist one car nearly struck another, causing a screech of brakes and then a long, loud battle of horns. As the ten-year-old in the apartment next to hers began to practice scales on the piano with one key out of tune, Blanche winced and clamped a pillow over her head.

Her head hurt, but she didn't mind. The pain helped her forget her real pain, the pain of the fight she'd had with her boyfriend, her "beau," as she called him. On the night-stand was a bottle of Old Crow bourbon and a Waterford lowball glass — as no lady descended from General Thomas Jonathan "Stonewall" Jackson, no matter how impoverished, would ever drink straight from the bottle.

Blanche raised her head and peered at the clock in the fading light — almost four. She groaned.

She'd wasted a full day in bed and hadn't even called in to Mrs. Roosevelt. Working for the First Lady was better than her usual job, behind the perfume counter of Lansburgh's department store — and, because it was the Christmas season, the endless gift wrapping.

Blanche pulled the pillow away and sat up. The room spun a bit. Even as tears filled her eyes, she tried to focus by staring at the marble fireplace. The place of honor above it was held by a reproduction of Edward Caledon Bruce's oil painting of Robert E. Lee, framed in dull gilt gesso. Lining the mantel were two silver candlesticks, a bit tarnished, from her great-grandmother. There was her old beaded leather Pocahontas doll and a Bible that had once belonged to Richard Henry Lee.

There was also a collection of silver-framed photographs — from Cotillion, from Apple Day, from Family Weekend. A postcard of Sir John Everett Millais's *Ophelia* that a former sorority sister had sent her from London. And her framed diploma from Mary Baldwin College, with her signed honor code pledge.

But those days were long ago, before her daddy had died. Before the money had run out. Like so many others in the Great Depression, they'd been rich until they weren't.

Blanche rose and staggered to the pledge, which she'd signed in violet ink as a freshman.

Believing in the principles of student government, I pledge myself to uphold the ideals and regulations of the Mary Baldwin College community. I recognize the principles of honor and cooperation as the basis of our life together. I shall endeavor faithfully to order my life accordingly. I will not lie . . .

But she had lied.

Or almost lied. Suddenly, her breakup with Byrd paled in comparison to what they'd planned to do.

Even though she was a Southerner to her core, she was no liar. She was no stool pigeon. And she wouldn't do anything to harm someone like Mrs. Eleanor Roosevelt. Even if the woman was an ugly Northerner with buckteeth and an overfondness for Negroes and Jews.

Holding on to the wall, Blanche made her way to the bathroom. She caught sight of herself in the mirror. She looked terrible — ashen, with deep purple shadows under her eyes, tears trickling down her cheeks. She opened her medicine cabinet, took out a bottle of doctor-prescribed sleeping pills, and poured them all into her palm. *I just — I just can't do what Byrd asked me to do. And I don't want to go on living without him.*

Blanche looked at her reflection as she raised the pills in her hand to her mouth, as if watching a film. Then, *I can't,* she thought, racked by sobs. She flung the pills into the toilet and flushed, then turned back to the mirror. "Would Scarlett O'Hara ever give up?" she asked her reflected face. "Certainly not. No — this will *not* do. I'll tell Byrd I've changed my mind. If he loves me, truly loves me — and I know he does — he'll understand why I just can't do it."

Blanche drank a glass of water from the tap, then washed her face and patted it dry.

She went to her telephone and dialed. She knew he'd still be at work. "Mr. Byrd Prentiss, please. Yes, his fiancée."

"Why, hello there, darlin'," Prentiss said when he picked up.

Blanche didn't mince words. "I can't do this."

"Now, we talked about this, sweetheart," he said in a voice one might use to gentle a wild horse. "You know exactly what the plan is. Just follow the plan."

"I'm not going to lie, Byrd," she hissed. "And I'm not going to have my good name

30

associated with that . . . balderdash. My reputation would be ruined."

There was a pause and a crackle over the telephone line. "Darlin', I'll come over when I get through here. You just sit tight. We'll get this all fixed up in a jiffy."

Blanche knew Prentiss's wheedling tones all too well and hung up the receiver. She turned her clawfoot bathtub's hot-water faucet, plugged the drain, and let the water rise, throwing in a generous handful of honeysuckle-scented bath salts. The air filled with steam and fragrance. As the tub filled, she poured herself another glass of bourbon, taking it into the bathroom with her.

She dropped her peach silk bathrobe on the tiled floor and stepped into the hot water, leaning back and letting it wash over her. She closed her eyes, then reached for her bourbon on the small rattan table with the potted fern.

Blanche didn't know how long she was in the tub, sipping bourbon and replenishing the hot bathwater using her foot on the brass cross handles.

By the time the man wearing leather gloves entered, she was drunk and relaxed and didn't even have the wherewithal to scream as he put his hands over her mouth,

31

muffling her cries for help. He shoved her head under the scented water and didn't let go. She struggled, frantically trying to claw at him, but he was too strong.

When at last Blanche's slender body was still, the man took her straight razor from the side of the tub and slit her wrists.

The water turned red.

The man placed the razor in her hand and closed her fingers over it, then released it, letting it splash into the bloodied water.

He moved to her bed, taking off his gloves and shoving them into the pocket of his coat, then picking up the telephone on the bedside table. He turned the dial with one finger, spoke to the operator, and was put through. "It's done."

There was static on the line and a few clicks.

CHAPTER ONE

"I'm back!" announced Maggie Hope.

Her cheeks were pink and eyes bright as the Prime Minister's jump flight from Boston approached the airport in Virginia. Her heart filled with joy as she saw Washington, D.C., glowing below through the fog. All those in the plane were transfixed with delight to look and see the amazing spectacle of a city lit up. For all of them who had endured over two years of blackouts, the sight of lights at night was precious, symbolizing freedom, strength, and hope.

"So, how does it feel?" asked David.

As the wheels of the plane touched down on the tarmac she cried, "Tops!" over the noise, her heart racing. And it *was* great — fantastic even — to be back. And not just in the United States after three years away, but her old self again — or at least a new version of herself.

"Back to being our plucky ingenue, I see,"

David said, reading her mind.

Maggie glared. "Pluck you."

He laughed. "Jumping Jupiter, it's good to have you with us again, Mags. Don't you agree, John? The three musketeers from the summer of 'forty reunited! We few, we happy few . . ."

John, slim with broad shoulders, impeccable in his blue RAF uniform, glanced up from his side of the aisle. "We band of blasted . . ."

"John —" Maggie warned.

He had been busily sketching in a leather-bound notebook on his lap. As the plane taxied down the runway, he looked out the window.

"No, *no* Shakespeare tonight — I must have American poetry!" David cried, ignoring their dour companion. "We're in America now! And the good old U.S. of A. has finally deigned to join us in our fight against the Nazi war machine." He smirked as he straightened his tie. "You Yanks — always late to a good war . . ."

Maggie put a gloved finger to her lips. "Not exactly the most politic way to begin our stay, now, is it?"

David sighed. "All right then, back to poetry — Emily Dickinson! Ralph Waldo Emerson! Walt Whitman! *'I sing the body*

34

electric . . . I celebrate the me yet to come . . .' "

Maggie beamed, for she, too, felt joy. Even though war continued to rage, there was reason to hope. After the attack on Pearl Harbor, just over two weeks ago, the United States had finally joined in the fight alongside the British. And as for her own personal battle, against the Black Dog of depression, as Winston Churchill called it, she had won, if only for the moment. And living in the moment was what counted now.

She slipped a silver powder compact from her purse and peered into its mirror, applying red lipstick. It was the lipstick that contained a hidden cyanide pill in the base, which she'd carried on her mission to Berlin as an SOE agent the previous winter. But even those memories were easier to deal with now. From habit, her hand went to her side, where the bullet used to be. But the bullet was gone, surgically removed by a vet in Scotland. *You've come far, Hope,* she thought.

Maggie Hope was assigned to Winston Churchill's trip to visit the United States and meet with President Roosevelt as, ostensibly, the P.M.'s typist. It was a job she'd once held, during the Battle of Britain, in the summer of 1940. But the reality was that she was now a Special Operations Executive, responsible for spying and sabotage behind enemy lines. At twenty-six, she was one of the most senior agents.

She, with the Prime Minister, his private secretaries David Greene and John Sterling; Lord Beaverbrook; his personal detective, Walter H. Thompson; and his beleaguered valet, Inces, had all left from Scotland on December 8. As part of Mr. Churchill's entourage, she'd boarded a blacked-out train in London and traveled to Scotland, then crossed the Atlantic Ocean on the HMS *Duke of York,* dodging Nazi ships and submarines, and finally arriving in Boston.

It was just past sundown, and the lights were obscured by fleecy fog. Overhead, clouds wrapped the moon in gauze. As they all looked out the small windows, she could see the P.M. approach President Roosevelt on the tarmac.

"The President is in a wheelchair!" she whispered to David and John, shocked. "President Roosevelt is in a *wheelchair!*"

President Franklin Delano Roosevelt was indeed in a wheelchair. An aide in naval uniform stood behind him. The President wore a dark coat over a gray double-breasted business suit, the cuffed legs of which exposed iron leg braces. The snap-brim of his fedora was turned up at a jaunty angle, matching that of his jaw and the cigarette holder clenched between his teeth.

She watched as the Prime Minister bent to shake the President's hand. The P.M., his face flushed with excitement and cold, had arrived in a navy-blue pea jacket from the Trinity House Lighthouse Service and a yachting cap, variations of which he'd worn on the ship during the journey over. He carried a cane equipped with a flashlight for blackouts.

"Oh, that's right — you didn't come to the Atlantic Conference with us. Polio," John said bluntly, as he put a few finishing touches on what he was drawing.

Maggie blinked, then nodded. She'd known FDR had contracted polio but had no idea the extent of his paralysis. She rose and craned her neck past David to see what John was drawing, but he closed his notebook with a snap. "What are you working on? Why won't you let us see?" she asked.

"I'll let you see it when it's ready to be seen." John slipped the book into his attaché case.

"Cryptic as ever," Maggie said, but smiled. As they stood and moved into the aisle, she stopped and reached up to fix his tie, brushing some imaginary lint off his lapels.

They'd almost been engaged to be married when John's plane was shot down over Germany in the autumn of 1940 and the RAF had pronounced him "missing, presumed dead." Miraculously, he'd made it back to England alive. But due to his extensive injuries, he wasn't allowed to fly again and had resumed his former job as one of Churchill's private secretaries.

David was already halfway down the aisle. "Come on, you two!" he called. He was bundled into his tweed coat, a striped Magdalen scarf wrapped tightly around his throat. Where John was tall and dark and somewhat dour when he wasn't smiling, David was shorter and fair-haired, with respectable round silver spectacles not quite hiding his often outrageous facial expressions.

Maggie adored David and was honored when he let her know his secret — that he was "like that." He lived with his lover, Freddie, in London, while the two men posed for the world as roommates, driven together by London's wartime housing shortage. "It's your homeland after all, Mags. Aren't you going to drop to your knees and kiss the hallowed Yankee ground?"

Maggie stuck another pearl-tipped pin in

her hat to affix it to her thick red hair. "I think it's a wee bit cold for any ground kissing, thank you. And we're in the Commonwealth of Virginia, by the way — the land of Dixie, not Yankee territory."

"But it's all the good ol' U.S. of A., yes?"

If only it were that simple. . . . Even though she was giddy to be back, the homecoming was difficult for Maggie. The United States had been attacked. And now she was back home, but certainly not the same person who'd left. Or was London home? Where did she belong?

Aunt Edith was the only real parent she had. She didn't really know her father, Edmund, much less her Nazi mother, Clara. And her sister — half sister, Elise — was convinced she was a monster. Were John and David and her best friend, Sarah, her family now?

As Maggie picked her way down the steep steps from the plane to the tarmac, a cold, wet wind blew, and she clapped a hand to her hat to keep it in place. She shivered in her blue wool coat. Surreptitiously, she glanced in all directions, checking the perimeter for any threats. *All clear.*

"Ah, so this is our largest colony," John deadpanned, glancing around. He looked over to Maggie, his face lighting up — and she felt as though her heart skipped a few beats.

In the cold haze, the Prime Minister continued to speak with the President and Lord Beaverbrook, eager and happy as a child. Then President Roosevelt was lifted like a child by his aide and placed into a large black limousine. The other men got in, and it pulled away. A second sedan waited for them in the misty air, engine running.

"Miss Hope?" John said, gesturing for her to get into their car first. He and Maggie exchanged a secret look.

"Why, thank you, Mr. Sterling."

But David pushed ahead. "I want the window seat!"

Maggie and John climbed in beside him, Maggie in the middle. The driver closed the door with a resounding *bang.* Inside, it was almost too hot, but as they headed to Washington through the hazy darkness, the three weary travelers luxuriated in the warmth. The radio blared the Andrews Sisters' "Boogie Woogie Bugle Boy," and David poked at Maggie. "So, is there 'no place like home'?"

"If only I could have clicked my heels three times to bring us here. Would have saved endless bouts of seasickness." She peered out the window. There were a few lights from houses, even Christmas tree lights. Not to mention the traffic signals, their garish glow piercing the velvety fog. The United States was also at war, but it looked nothing like London's complete blackout.

"We're so close to the shore — aren't they worried about sneak attacks by German submarines?" Maggie said. She gave a low laugh. "The ARP wardens in London would have heart attacks if they saw all this light! Goodness, I'd forgotten what headlights look like lit up, without those slotted covers."

"Are they daft?" John asked. "Aren't they worried about bombs?"

"There's not really anywhere close enough to launch an airstrike here on the East Coast," David mused.

"Yes, well, no one thought the Japanese could launch an airstrike on U.S. territory, either, and now look at Pearl Harbor," Maggie countered.

"True, true," David admitted.

"And all the light — not to mention the radio signal — is making it awfully easy for Nazi U-boats to find things in the dark. And don't tell me they're not out there, lurking." Maggie shivered into her coat, staring out at the veils of fog.

"Jumping Jupiter, it's Paris on the Potomac!" David exclaimed as they entered the city of Washington, referring to the wide boulevards and neoclassical architecture of the capital along the river, magically lit by the hazy glow of streetlamps. "It's just like the opening montage from *Mr. Smith Goes to Washington!*"

John nodded, dark eyes taking in everything. "Part French, part Federalist, part Daniel Boone."

The radio station segued into Billie Holiday's "God Bless the Child." As they passed the darkened Capitol dome, they also saw posters pasted on walls: REMEMBER PEARL HARBOR! ENLIST NOW! and BUY WAR BONDS!

Stopped at a traffic light, Maggie read a humble flyer affixed to a streetlamp: STOP WENDELL COTTON'S EXECUTION! it read. ONLY 8 DAYS LEFT! PRAYER MEETING WITH MOTHER COTTON AND ANDREA MARTIN! The flyer was illustrated with a photograph of a young colored man in a striped prison uniform.

On a bridge near the Lincoln Memorial, machine guns had been mounted, and soldiers patrolled. Outside the Jefferson Memorial, helmeted guards carried rifles

42

with bayonets. Temporary wooden housing had sprung up on the Mall for the sudden influx of war workers.

In the city, flags flew everywhere, while brightly lit shop windows were juxtaposed against darkened government buildings. Billboards importuned: WAR WORKERS NEED ROOMS, APARTMENTS, HOMES — REGISTER YOUR VACANCIES NOW. The sidewalks seemed crowded with soldiers and sailors in uniform. Posters proclaimed, VICTORY GARDENS WILL HELP US WIN, and THE U.S.A. PICKS CHEVROLET. As their car passed a newsstand, the *Washington Post*'s headline screamed: HONG KONG DOOMED. Next door, letters on a marquee spelled out KATHLEEN, STARRING SHIRLEY TEMPLE.

David whistled between his teeth, taking in a brilliantly illuminated department-store window. "Washington used to be a hardship post, you know," he told them. "Terribly hot and humid in the summer. Now it's like coming to Oz, isn't it? You know, England is all black-and-white and now we've arrived in the land of Technicolor. Oh! And what do you most want to eat while we're here?" he asked Maggie and John.

They'd all been living on rations for ages. "Hamburger, cooked medium-rare, extra-crispy French fries with lots of ketchup, and

43

a Coca-Cola with ice — *lots* of ice — from a diner. And chocolate ice cream," Maggie proclaimed.

"No New England clam chowder? Boston baked beans? Lobster roll?"

"We're in Washington, not New England, silly. This is the border between the North and South. Think Maryland crab cakes, biscuits and gravy, and shrimp and grits."

John raised an eyebrow. "What's a grit?"

Maggie gave a sly look. "Ah, *haute cuisine américaine.*"

David wasn't listening. "I want to try this 'moonshine' I've been hearing about. And peanut butter and jam on toast. And apple pie." A panicked look crossed his face. "You don't think they're rationing at the White House yet, do you?"

"Apple pie." Maggie sighed. "With cinnamon and nutmeg. And coffee with cream *and* sugar. And a steaming hot bath, more than five inches deep — bliss!"

"What do you want from Father Christmas — er, Santa Claus?" John asked as they passed yet another gaily decorated department store. "Fruitcake?"

Fruitcake, right, Maggie thought. *Surely he's joking — and thinking of something just a bit more romantic?* "I'm picking up a new toothbrush while we're here," Maggie declared. "Mine's completely worn down. And an enormous fresh cake of soap. Silk stockings — I hear they're having a run on them now — no pun intended."

"Ha! Well, it would be quite lovely of Santa to remember a nice Jewish boy, but I wouldn't say no to a bottle of bourbon," said David. "What about you?"

John considered. "Reams of paper." The rationing of paper had been hard on him. "More pens and notebooks."

Maggie didn't know exactly what he was working on, but she'd glimpsed a number of sketches. "Our own Leonardo da Vinci. But I'm getting you books — by American authors. You're both far too parochial in your reading choices."

As they talked about Christmas, their car approached the White House through the murky darkness. Blackout curtains hung at each window. Sentry boxes were set up at driveway entrances and along the perimeter fences. Police patrolled where only weeks before onlookers had promenaded. The wrought-iron gates to the once-accessible White House were now closed and locked. These days, anyone who wanted admittance had to show a "pass with picture engraved on it."

And then there were the soldiers — guards

brandishing M1 rifles with bayonets affixed. All carried full field packs and wore steel helmets. Guard towers had been built, and one-inch steel cables ran every which way, controlling the flow of foot traffic. Fifteen days after Pearl Harbor, the White House was in full lockdown.

"My God," Maggie breathed. "Washington's a war zone." After passing the guard booth at the northwestern gate, their car headed along the sweeping semicircular drive up to the entrance. There were antiaircraft batteries on the roof and sandbags surrounding the front door. "Limestone cut by Scottish masons and then built by slaves," Maggie said. She realized as they pulled up under the portico that the White House's luminous whitewashed frontage was cracked and peeling. Still, it was beautiful.

I'm back, she thought again. And then, with surprise and delight — *and it feels right.*

As the Prime Minister and his party were making their way to the White House, Presidential Press Secretary Steve Early had announced to the press corps the arrival of an "important visitor" at 6:45 p.m., and they were out in force, jostling their way to the front of the line, muttering guesses about who it could be, their breath making

46

indistinct clouds in the cold. "Bet you a dollar it's Churchill," said Ron Kantor from *The New York Times.*

Kurt Schmidt from the *Chicago Tribune* belched. "Ha! Betcha it's only Beaverbrook. Isn't Churchill a bit long in the tooth for the boat ride?"

Thomas O'Brian, a recent Harvard graduate originally from Buffalo, New York, was covering his first Presidential press conference, bouncing on the balls of his feet with excitement. He was young, with blue eyes so dark they were almost black, wavy golden-brown hair, and a smattering of freckles across the bridge of his nose. He was long and lean and filled with sharply focused energy. "But then why all the secrecy? I think you're both wrong. I say Molotov." Vyacheslav Mikhailovich Molotov was Russia's Deputy Chairman and had brokered the Molotov-Ribbentrop Pact in 1939. "But whoever he is, I wish he'd hurry up."

But the "important visitor" and President Roosevelt were running late. "Before the President and his special guest arrive," the Press Secretary intoned, "I'd like to remind you of the Censorship Act." There was a collective groan through the press corps but not a murmur of disagreement. The Censorship Act was another name for the First War Powers Act, approved days before, increasing the Executive Branch's power — including the President's ability to gag the press.

Just as Early was finishing, the line of long dark sedans pulled up through the haze to the porte cochere. There was a rap at the window of Maggie, John, and David's car. John rolled down the window, and the assistant press secretary told them, "The President will get out first and will be helped into position. Then the Prime Minister will join him. They'll be photographed. Then, when they're done, you'll follow behind."

"Ten paces behind or just a few steps?" David muttered when the assistant press secretary had left. "Shouldn't we be up ahead? Perhaps sprinkling rose petals?" Maggie elbowed him, but the three fell silent when they saw President Roosevelt taken from the sedan by a naval aide and thrown over the aide's back in a fireman's carry. Maggie smothered what would otherwise have been a gasp behind her hand.

Tom O'Brian put his camera up and prepared to take a picture. But Kantor reached out and forced the camera down. "No," the *New York Times* reporter admonished. "Never. We *never* photograph the

President unless he's standing and ready or seated. Then and only then."

Tom flushed and nodded. He, along with the rest of the press corps, waited for the President to be secured in position.

Once Roosevelt was standing with assistance on the South Portico, Winston Churchill emerged from the car, blue eyes twinkling with excitement, flashing the V for Victory symbol.

"Oh, merciful Minerva," David sighed.

Maggie was confused. "What? They adore him!" There was an explosion of flashbulbs and camera clicks as the Prime Minister made his way to the President.

"If I've told him once, I've told him a thousand times," David said, "the V sign with the palm out means Victory, but the V sign with the palm facing in means —"

"— er, means something else entirely," John finished.

The President had a cane in his right hand, while his left tightly gripped the arm of his naval aide. Churchill stood alongside, beaming, drinking in the flashes of light and the applause. As he and the President bantered with the press and posed for photographers, the Prime Minister hid his cigar behind his back.

Maggie shivered in the damp air, knowing

how much this moment meant to the P.M. — to all of them.

President Roosevelt was now officially, and publicly, on their side. At last there was more than a remote possibility they would win. It had been a long and lonely fight, but at least Britain wasn't on its own anymore. When the photographs were finished, the assistant press secretary came to get Maggie and the rest of the party. "Follow me," he instructed them.

David nodded to an ancient oak. "A beautiful tree."

"Yes, one of the ones you Brits didn't burn in 1812," retorted Maggie with a wry smile. While she wasn't yet sure if the United States was home or not, it felt good to be on familiar ground for a change. In London, she'd often been the odd one out because of her nationality and upbringing. But not here.

She intended to do her all to help the Prime Minister succeed in this mission. Just above their heads, she knew, parts of the White House had been painted over to cover the scorch marks made by the fire the British had set to it in the War of 1812, nearly burning it to the ground. Then, the two countries had been bitter enemies. Now they were allies.

While the rest of the reporters were rushing off to file their stories, Tom O'Brian spotted the redhead in the Prime Minister's entourage. "Maggie? Maggie Hope?" he called. But she didn't hear him.

"You know that girl with all that red hair?" Kantor asked. "She's a looker."

"I used to. Used to date her roommate at Wellesley when I was at Harvard, as a matter of fact. And we played together in a string quartet."

"Should have dated her instead, Mozart." Kantor tilted his head, considering. "But you have an in with someone on the Prime Minister's staff. That could be useful."

"By now she must be married. And I'm sure she's just a secretary."

"A drink with a pretty girl, married or not, at the Round Robin never hurt anyone. Besides, aren't you off to basic training in two weeks?"

"I am. Fort Bragg, and then wherever the U.S. Army sees fit to send me." Tom grinned. "You'd better believe I'll try to chat her up before I ship off."

"Welcome to the White House, Prime Minister!" Eleanor Roosevelt trilled as her husband and the P.M. entered with a gust of frigid air.

The P.M. blinked, shocked by the First Lady's impressive height. He bowed low before her, kissing her hand. "My lady."

Mrs. Roosevelt blushed. Then she addressed the group in her high, birdlike tones. "You all must be exhausted," she exclaimed. "Such a long trip — and the Atlantic is a shooting gallery these days."

And all at once, they were off on a tour of the White House, given by the First Lady herself. The first floor was impressive, filled with handsome dark wood furniture, dotted with oil paintings framed in gold. The travel-worn British worked hard to keep up with Mrs. Roosevelt, whose long legs and incisive stride kept her well ahead of the weary newcomers.

With her sensible shoes and toothy smile, the First Lady led them quickly through room after room — her skirts flapping, her hair pulling loose from its chignon, a shine on her nose. She was the opposite of the elegantly English Clementine Churchill, Maggie decided, but she couldn't help but be impressed by Mrs. Roosevelt. She'd always admired her, her writing, and her charitable works, but now she felt certain that if she had the chance to know this remarkable woman better, she'd like her as a person.

The President and Mr. Churchill took the rickety elevator up to the second floor while the rest of the group headed for the stairs. For all the grandeur of the public rooms, the private space was dingy and in need of repair, rather like a grand hotel that hadn't been kept up over the years. The threadbare Chinese carpets held the faint odor of dog. The floors squeaked underfoot, the ceilings had water stains, and the walls were chipped and yellowed.

"Sorry about the mess, but we haven't redone anything since the Depression," Eleanor explained. "Could hardly justify it, with everyone else suffering so much." Which made Maggie like her even more.

The First Lady's sitting room held an overstuffed sofa, wing chairs with tasseled cushions, and a few substantial Dutch Colonial pieces. The walls were painted in fresh cream and covered by black-framed photographs — hundreds of them, of family, friends, ancestors, sights from travels around the world. There was a radio in one corner and a desk in the other. Books were everywhere, and they could all hear the faint *clank* of a radiator. "As you can see, this is my office," Eleanor announced. "My bedroom's through there, that's Lorena Hickok's room, and there's also an indoor swim-

53

ming pool fifty feet under the West Terrace, if you'd like to use that while you're here. Franklin swims every day — swears by it. Oh, and here's Franklin's study!"

The President's private office was painted battleship gray and glossy white, softened by puddles of light from glowing green Tiffany lamps. Tall mahogany bookcases were crammed with models of ships. A massive oak desk stood in one corner, its blotter covered in stamps and collectors' albums. Burning logs popped and crackled behind the grate of a marble fireplace, and a shabby Persian rug was spread in front. Layered on top was a lion-skin rug, head intact and fangs gleaming. "From Ethiopia's Emperor Haile Selassie," the First Lady explained. "We call him Leo the Lion."

"The first shot against the Empire," John muttered under his breath.

The President was already holding court, seated in a streamlined wheelchair made from a regular dining chair. He was in position behind a small brass cart, mixing drinks, Fala at his feet. Churchill, looking every inch the English bulldog, made his way around the room, hand extended, saying, "How-de-do? How-de-do?" Fala was busily inspecting the Prime Minister's shoes and trousers, then sat back on his haunches

54

as if to say, *Yes, he passes my inspection.*

"Welcome to Children's Hour!" the President called to Mrs. Roosevelt's small tour group as the P.M. stooped to rub Fala's furry head. "It's my tradition of having cocktails at the end of the day!" he explained. "And today I daresay you all deserve one." He looked sideways at Churchill. "Or perhaps two." The bar cart was crowded with different-colored bottles of gin and French vermouth, Kentucky bourbon, Tennessee whiskey, rum, tonic, and various bitters. As the President took a sip from his glass, he closed his eyes in delight. "Oh, yummy — that's good."

Maggie took in the scene before her. She knew all too well that the Prime Minister's usual drinks were sherry, whiskey, brandy, and champagne — and only rarely a Martini, but with no vermouth, only "a bow toward France." As she saw the generous amount of vermouth Mr. Roosevelt poured into the jigger to mix with his gin and how graciously Mr. Churchill accepted the cocktail glass from the President's hands, she realized for the first time exactly how much the Boss would sacrifice to get on with the American leader.

John nodded in approval. "An Anglo-Saxon alliance, to meet the problems of the world. Well done."

President Roosevelt flashed his thousand-watt toothy grin. "Forgive me if I don't get up," he joked, then wheeled himself over, Fala following with a wagging tail. "My adviser Harry Hopkins, you already know, of course," he said, indicating a gaunt, chain-smoking man. "And this lovely lady is Grace Tully, my secretary — and Lorena Hickok, Eleanor's friend. Oh, and let me introduce Frank Cole, my right-hand man."

Frank Cole was a thoroughly average-looking man with wide-set eyes behind heavy black-framed glasses and a rumpled suit that suggested moneyed eccentricity. Giving him a long look, Maggie realized there was something off: one of his eyes was a bright green, while the other was a true hazel. "Who's Frank Cole?" she whispered to David when she could.

He sipped his Martini and nearly choked. "Heavy on the vermouth and — horrors — I believe a splash of Pernod." He shook his head. "Frank Cole is the economic specialist for the State Department who then became a rather successful journalist. Outspoken supporter of the New Deal and the Roosevelts. And, from what I hear, FDR's odd-job man."

Maggie took a small sip of her drink,

which had two Spanish olives speared to a toothpick with tiny U.S. and U.K. flags. She peered at the fine print: MADE IN JAPAN. *Oh, dear.* "Odd-job man? What sorts of jobs?"

David shrugged. "How should I know?"

"But what about Mr. Hoover?" Maggie pressed as the First Lady pulled out a record and placed it on the phonograph.

"No, Cole has nothing to do with Hoover. He answers directly to the President."

As the record crackled and then began, Marian Anderson's rich contralto voice filled the room, singing Handel's "And He Shall Feed His Flock." More guests arrived — including General Sir Alan Brooke, Chief of the Imperial General Staff — and the President exclaimed, "Oh, how perfectly grand!" As Fala shook hands with all of them on command, a waiter wheeled in a silver trolley, piled high with caviar and toast points, a carved roasted turkey, smoked clams, sliced green apples, and cheeses.

Mr. Roosevelt looked around the room and, spying empty glasses, called out, "How about a little dividend? Another sippy?" He began to make more cocktails, this time something called a Haitian Libation, made with rum, orange juice, egg whites, and brown sugar. "Ah, the sweet music of the shaker!" he called. "Who'd like to try one?"

Despite the President's questionable cocktails, Maggie did find herself liking him. It was impossible not to admire his unflagging energy, his irrepressible confidence, his effervescent charm. As more drinks were poured and plates were passed, she seized the chance to look around his private office. The room was large, but still warm and homey, stuffed full of clutter. A black-and-white Ansel Adams photograph of the Rocky Mountains hung in a place of prominence.

David and John perched next to Maggie with their cocktail glasses. David bent over to whisper, "Do you think they're going to serve us hot dogs for dinner? I hear that's what they offered the King and Queen when they visited."

"Hot dogs are a picnic food," Maggie replied sotto voce. "*Not* likely to be served at the White House in December. Although we can try to get you one from a street vendor."

"I'd like that," David returned courageously. "I've never had one, you know."

As Roosevelt and Churchill chatted and laughed, John murmured, "What kind of accent does the President have?"

"Hudson Valley Lockjaw — Dutchess

County via Amsterdam," Maggie whispered back. "With just a faint tinge of Old Money."

"Old . . . by American standards." John took a sip of his Martini and nearly choked.

"There, there." Maggie patted his back. "I know it's a lot to get used to — landing in a foreign country." John was silent.

"Rather heavy on the vermouth" was all he would say.

"So, Mr. Cole," said the Prime Minister, standing nearby. "What is it exactly that you do?"

"This and that," Cole replied. "I'm a newspaper columnist by trade, but I do enjoy being Man Friday to the President."

Churchill studied him. Then he raised his glass. "If that's your story, Mr. Cole, then stick to it."

When Children's Hour was over, Mrs. Roosevelt showed Lord Beaverbrook to one bedroom, the P.M.'s detective to another. David was led to the small Blue Bedroom. The detective and Churchill's valet shared a dressing room adjoining the P.M.'s quarters.

"And this is the Monroe Room," the First Lady explained to Churchill, never breaking stride. "In preparation for your arrival, we've had it emptied of furniture to serve as your map room."

The P.M. nodded. "Excellent, excellent."

"And this is my favorite — the Rose Bedroom, where King George and Queen Elizabeth stayed when they were our guests a few years ago. I do hope you like it, Mr. Churchill."

"It's perfect, my lady." The Prime Minister beamed at her.

"And Mr. Hopkins's room is there." She gestured to a door across a hallway lined with great piles of Christmas presents. "Mr. Sterling," the First Lady said to John, "you'll be staying at the Mayflower Hotel. And you, as well, Miss Hope."

When John reddened, Mrs. Roosevelt was quick to add, "In separate rooms, of course."

"Yes, ma'am," John said. Maggie was amused to see him, for once, embarrassed.

"Please take time to relax and freshen up. We will be having tea in the Green Drawing Room at eight-thirty. Miss Hope and Mr. Sterling, please come with me. I'll have a car take you to the Mayflower. It's quite close by."

As the elevator chimed and the white-gloved elevator man held the door, Maggie heard the Prime Minister mutter to John, "I do hope she'll serve something stronger than tea. And there will be something besides American Martinis."

Maggie smiled.

CHAPTER TWO

Though the neoclassical Mayflower Hotel was considered the grand dame of Connecticut Avenue, her rooftop now bristled with lookouts against aerial attack. The doors and windows, and even the massive skylights, were fitted with blackout shades. Still, inside, it was elegant and opulent — the lobby's gilt mirrors shone, marble gleamed, and chandeliers shimmered. At the front desk, amid the towering potted palms and monumental Sèvres vases, Maggie and John were each given a heavy iron key engraved with the Mayflower insignia. The concierge added with a wink to John, "They're adjoining."

Leaving the luggage for the bellhop, John and Maggie took the elevator up to their rooms. "Well, that was a bit awkward," she remarked into the silence.

John took her hand. "He's an idiot."

"I know. It's just that it's been so difficult

the last few weeks. Not having any time . . . Of course, we've had a few other things on our minds . . ."

"Such as the attack on Pearl Harbor. And getting the Boss across the ocean in one piece."

Maggie grimaced. "Goodness gracious, if I had to watch *Blood and Sand* one more time — I can tell you every line from that film . . ."

The bell chimed and the doors opened. "It's been a strange few weeks," John agreed as they walked down the empty hallway, enjoying the temporary solitude.

"Oh, please," Maggie protested, smiling. "It's been a strange few *years.*" At their respective doors, she stopped and looked up at him. "I don't want to rush."

"I understand."

"But, you know, I don't want to wait too long, either . . ."

"I —"

They were interrupted by the bellhop, a rake-thin man in a gold braid-trimmed uniform. "Your luggage!"

"Fantastic," John muttered as they both turned to unlock their doors.

Maggie's room was bright and cheerful, with dark Federalist-style furniture, chintz curtains, and a view of Connecticut Avenue.

After tipping the bellhop, she unpacked her suitcase, putting her things in drawers or hanging them on padded satin hangers in the closet. Then she made her way to the bathroom, where she drew a full tub of steaming water, throwing in the complimentary bath salts. Hot water wasn't rationed in the United States, and Maggie intended to take advantage while she could. After she'd taken her bath, and dressed in a pale blue evening gown and satin pumps, she heard a knock at the interior door. She opened it. "This is most improper, Mr. Sterling."

"There are no kettles in the room," John announced, making his way in. "Positively barbaric."

"No, kettles in hotel rooms are not de rigueur here. I'm sure you can ring for tea, if you really want it."

"Forget the tea," he replied, taking in her gown. "Why, Miss Hope, you're looking quite beautiful. And I do believe that's a saucy expression on your face." He raised his hand and traced the line of her jaw with a fingertip.

"You're looking quite handsome in your dress uniform, Mr. Sterling," she managed, her heart thudding. They lunged at each other. Eventually, they broke apart, each breathing with difficulty. "We should go,"

John said, looking at his watch.

"I'll get my gloves and wrap." They smiled at each other, silly smiles. "You should go back to your room," she added, straightening his tie. "It wouldn't look right for us to exit together."

"The things I'm thinking of, Miss Hope, have nothing to do with looking right."

"Go," she urged, pushing him through the door. "We'll continue this later."

"Promise?" he asked, looking more like a little boy than a brooding Brit.

"I promise," she breathed, raising herself up on tiptoes to kiss him. His cheek smelled of shaving soap. "Now, *go!*"

After tea and Bourbon Orange-Blossom Specials in the Green Drawing Room, dinner was served. The neoclassical State Dining Room, with its elaborate cornices, was lit by grand silver-plated chandeliers and tall beeswax candles in ormolu candelabras. The long table was covered in spotless linen and set with the President Franklin Roosevelt blue-banded service and Grover Cleveland's gold cutlery, and decorated with golden fruit bowls and vases brimming with white roses and holly berries. Lord Beaverbrook and Ambassador Lord Halifax were in attendance, as well as Secretary of

State Cordell Hull and Mrs. Hull, Undersecretary of State Sumner Welles and Mrs. Welles, Harry Hopkins, General Dwight Eisenhower, General George Marshall, and Admiral Ernest King. From a large golden frame, an oil-painted Abraham Lincoln stared moodily into the middle distance.

Colored waiters in black jackets and bow ties, and maids in black taffeta dresses with white organdy embroidered collars and cuffs carried in silver platters of broiled chicken and root vegetables for the guests. As they waited to be served, candlelight glinting off the silver and crystal glasses, David asked, "Mrs. Roosevelt, I'm curious — why is your staff made up entirely of darkies?" Maggie kicked his shin under the table. "Ow!"

But the First Lady was unperturbed. "We had to let some staff go, during the Depression." She looked to her husband. "Franklin and I thought there were better chances for the white servants to find jobs. And so we kept the colored servants. 'Colored,' by the way, is the preferred expression."

David nodded, chastened. "I'm terribly sorry."

"Oh, you're not from here, I can understand. Why, I myself used the term 'darky' until just a few years ago. A lovely young colored woman by the name of Miss Andrea Martin let me know in no uncertain terms that 'darky' is a hated and humiliating word."

Maggie looked up at the servers, their brown faces unmoving, dark eyes impassive. What were they really thinking? And what did they think about what was being said about them?

The First Lady continued. "I listened to Miss Martin, of course, and even though my great-aunt used it as a term of affection, I learned that not everyone heard it that way." She smiled, exposing large teeth. "I'm afraid I'm very much a nineteenth-century woman in the twentieth, but doing my best to come up to speed."

Maggie noticed a chip in her water glass and didn't drink from it. Mrs. Roosevelt noticed Maggie not drinking and called for another goblet — then told the assembled guests, with a perfectly straight face, "It seems that the President has taken a nibble from the glass."

"Of *course* I eat glass every evening," Roosevelt retorted. "Keeps me 'sharp.' " He roared with laughter.

"But you went all the way to the airport — you must be pretty tired?" Frank Cole asked the President. Maggie flinched; surely that was an inappropriate question. But as Mr. Roosevelt grinned, Maggie could feel the strength of the bond between the two men and decided it was not impertinence that made Cole ask but a true concern for both the President and the man.

"I'm quite well, Cole," FDR assured him. "Winston in person is quite different from Winston on the page and on the telephone, you must realize," he joked, winking at the P.M.

"Hear, hear," the Prime Minister said, raising a goblet.

After dessert of apple cake and vanilla ice cream, the President raised a coupe of champagne. "I have a toast to offer," he told them. "It has been in my head and on my heart for a long time . . . and now it is on the tip of my tongue — *'To the common cause.'* "

Everyone lifted his or her glass. Maggie blinked back a sudden prickle of tears, knowing how long and desperately the P.M. — all of them — had waited for this moment.

"To the common cause!" the guests echoed, their faces bright in the candlelight.

It was past ten o'clock. It had been a long day. As the waiters began collecting plates, silver, and glasses, and Cole said his good nights, the President turned and nimbly wheeled his chair toward the green-carpeted Oval Office, with Churchill, Beaverbrook, Halifax, Hopkins, Welles, and Hull trailing like ducklings in his wake, and Maggie bringing up the rear.

In the Oval Office, as George Washington's blue eyes kept watch from the Gilbert Stuart painting, the men took seats on leather chairs salvaged from Theodore Roosevelt's yacht *Mayflower.* A general discussion began, as prologue to meetings scheduled for the next morning and continuing throughout the week: strategic debate about defeating the Axis powers and creating a successor to the League of Nations, decisions about the borders of the Soviet Union, where to place emphasis on rolling back Axis fronts, and decisions about production and financing of weapons.

Maggie joined them to take notes in shorthand, while John and David went to set up the P.M.'s maps in the Monroe Room. She was too busy to look around at the Oval Office for long, but she did register the President's massive carved *Resolute* desk, the blue-green rug, and the bottle-green velvet drapes.

The Prime Minister's first question was direct: "Will the President concede to public desire to go directly after Japan? Or focus first on Nazi Germany?" Churchill pronounced "Nazi" in his idiosyncratic way, *Nazzi*. Maggie knew that while the Prime Minister realized that distances and resources made going after the Japanese first impractical, despite the crushing blow to Pearl Harbor, he wanted to make absolutely certain he and FDR were on the same page: beating Nazi Germany. And, knowing the President's wily ways, the P.M. wanted to make certain Mr. Roosevelt gave his word — in public.

"My dear Winston," the President replied, "the priority is Europe, of course." For the first time since they began their journey, Maggie saw the P.M. relax just the slightest bit. "Hitler's losses in Russia are the crucial fact of the war at this time. He now faces a winter of death from the elements, if not also the enemy — not to mention an enormous forfeiture of equipment."

"They're freezing on the Eastern Front," Hopkins said, fetching something from the President's desk. "I hear they're having a coat drive in Germany for the soldiers — not even trying to hide it."

The President nodded. "Hitler hasn't reached Moscow yet, and, quite frankly, I don't think he's going to."

Hopkins walked back slowly, as if in great pain. He spread a map of the world with its vast turquoise-blue oceans across the table. Maggie viewed this from her chair against the wall, pad on her lap, realizing she was witnessing history as it was being made.

"Germany is the prime enemy," Roosevelt said, pointing. "Once she's defeated, the collapse of Italy and defeat of Japan will follow, as night the day."

"Germany first!" Churchill agreed. "Our main objective for 'forty-two should be the occupation of the entire coastline of Africa. Taking back the coast will reopen the Mediterranean route for shipping to the Middle East and the Far East, and start to tighten a ring around everything the Germans now control there. We'll put three divisions in North Africa — more if necessary. And, of course, I want American forces involved as quickly as possible."

"Perfecto!" the President exclaimed. "And then on to Germany and blockade them." A finger traced the path on the map.

The Prime Minister nodded. "By 'forty-three, the path will be cleared for us to make our way back to the continent, where we will attack the Nazis and liberate Europe!"

"To nineteen forty-two!" the President cried, raising a tumbler. "A year of toil, a year of struggle, a year of peril — and a step closer to victory."

The Oval Office emptied, Churchill wheeling the President to the elevator as a mark of respect. His chivalry made Maggie think of Sir Walter Raleigh, spreading his cloak before the Queen.

When the President was finally dressed in his monogrammed silk pajamas and in bed with Fala at his side, he looked through his messages. Grace Tully — one of Mr. Roosevelt's secretaries, who'd taken on even more duties recently when her superior, Missy LeHand, had suffered a heart attack — handed him memos. When he saw one in particular, the President frowned.

Miss Tully, attuned to his moods, asked, "What is it? What do you need?"

"Get me Frank Cole," Roosevelt snapped. He yanked a cambric handkerchief out and blew his nose with a loud honk.

She did, picking up the receiver and dialing a string of numbers. Fala sprang up at the President's tone and watched the dial rotate. "Hold for the President, Mr. Cole," Miss Tully said; then she passed the receiver to FDR.

There was a hiss and a crackle on the telephone line. "Cole here."

72

"Thank you," the President said to Grace Tully, who knew that was her cue to leave.

He waited until she closed the door behind her. "What the hell's going on, Cole?" Fala, sensing his master's displeasure, looked on with anxious black eyes.

"Sir, the situation with Blanche Balfour — it's resolved."

The President whistled through his teeth, his hand dropping to pet Fala absently. "She's not going to go to the press with her crazy story?"

There was a long silence. "I assure you, Mr. President, Miss Balfour will *not* be going to the press." Cole's tones were clipped.

The President sighed and stroked Fala, who snuggled in, relaxed now. "At least it's not about Lorena Hickok."

"The 'She-man'? No, sir. There's been nothing on her. Nothing on Joseph Lash, either, thank God. Mr. President, if you'd like to know the details about Miss Balfour —"

"Cole," the President interrupted, "you're on my payroll to get things done. Things I don't need to be bothered with. As far as you're concerned, in situations like these, I don't need to know the details. That's why I call you the Cleaner."

73

There was a pause. "Yes, sir. Good night, sir."

The Prime Minister's upstairs quarters had already been turned into a war room, with the walls covered in huge maps with colored pushpins indicating the positions of British ships and troops, and a shelf of scrambler telephones. Maggie asked, "Do you have everything you need, Mr. Churchill?"

The P.M. waved a hand through a fog of thick blue cigar smoke. "Have that giant butler send up more scotch."

Mrs. Roosevelt knocked at the open door and then stuck her head in. "Everything all right?" Her tone seemed pitched even higher than usual.

"We're fine, ma'am. Thank you." Maggie looked closer at the First Lady. Her face was pale as a photograph that had been left out too long in the sun. "Are you all right, ma'am? Do *you* need anything?"

"I know it's silly, but I'm worried. My secretary didn't call in today. She's still not answering her telephone, and her doorman hasn't seen her. I think I should go and check on her."

Churchill spoke from behind his curtain of smoke, like Oz the Great and Powerful. "Use Miss Hope," he said, jabbing in Maggie's general direction with his cigar.

"Oh, no. I couldn't possibly . . ." Mrs. Roosevelt protested.

"She's an excellent secretary, and helpful in all sorts of . . . situations. Take her with you!" He waved at the smoke with the cigar. "I must insist!"

As if I were a piece of office equipment, Maggie thought. She and John locked eyes. This was *not* the plan. Not the plan at all.

"Well," said the First Lady, "maybe we should go to Blanche's apartment, Miss Hope."

" 'Apartment' means 'flat,' " Maggie whispered to the P.M.

"I know what 'apartment' means, Miss Hope!" he boomed. "I've been to America before — nearly run down in New York City back in the day, I'll have you know!" Then, in a gentler tone to the First Lady, "Well, Mrs. Roosevelt, Miss Hope is a woman of many talents. Perhaps she can accompany you, checking on this Miss . . ."

"Balfour," Maggie prompted.

Churchill glared. "Balfour, yes."

"Of course I'd be happy to help you in any way, Mrs. Roosevelt. Is there anyone you'd like me to call? One of your husband's detectives?"

"Call?" If possible, her voice rose even

75

higher. "No, no, I'm sure I'm just being a nervous Nellie. Perhaps she's ill? Maybe she needs soup? I could have Mrs. Nesbitt prepare some . . ."

Maggie saw John's look, his eyes dark. Well, their special evening would have to wait just a bit longer. "Would you like me to alert the Secret Service that we're leaving, Mrs. Roosevelt?"

"I've already arranged to have the car brought around, just in case. And, Miss Hope, I rarely travel with the Secret Service." The First Lady smiled, an expression that revealed what some might consider overly large teeth but was all the more beautiful for its sincerity. "Not only do I drive myself but I have a concealed weapon permit, and I always carry a gun."

Her normally pleasant expression turned fierce. "Franklin says I'm a crack shot."

"Public Enemy Number One is off and running!" Eleanor Roosevelt sang to Maggie on their way out. "It's J. Edgar Hoover who calls me that, actually — the Secret Service has named me Rover. Of course, Public Enemy Number One is better than Negro-loving Bitch. Have you heard that the Ku Klux Klan has a bounty on my head?"

"No, I haven't. Would you like me to

drive, ma'am?" The Secret Service had pulled up an anonymous-looking black sedan, then left it running, with the door open. It had been awhile, but Maggie was sure she could still remember how to drive on the right-hand side of the road.

"Oh, heavens, no." Once they'd settled into the car's leather seats, Mrs. Roosevelt pulled out of the gravel drive. "Are you comfortable, Miss Hope?"

"Yes, ma'am." *As comfortable as anyone could possibly be in this rather unusual situation.* "Thank you, ma'am."

Blanche's apartment was a faux-Tudor building on Massachusetts Avenue at Twelfth Street, now covered in cottony fog.

Mrs. Roosevelt was about to pull into the hazy circular drive that led to the main entrance when Maggie asked, "Maybe we should park on the street, ma'am?"

Mrs. Roosevelt looked surprised. "Yes, yes, of course, Miss Hope. That's an excellent suggestion."

They parked on Twelfth and then walked to the building, made of brick and covered in gargoyles, including one sticking out a forked tongue. A horse-drawn cart passed, the *clip-clop* of the hooves echoing in the hazy darkness, and the raw air smelled of horse and woodsmoke. Mrs. Roosevelt headed to the front door, replete with uniformed doorman, but Maggie had other ideas. "Let's use the side door — er, if you don't mind. Ma'am."

Mrs. Roosevelt gave the younger woman a curious look, then nodded. They waited until one of the cleaning staff exited, then held the door and walked in. Inside was the same Tudor architecture as the exterior, and Maggie was reminded of her years in Claflin Hall at Wellesley College. "What's her apartment number?" she asked as they stepped into the wood-paneled elevator.

"Seven fourteen."

The elevator arrived at the seventh floor, and they walked to 714. Maggie knocked. "Miss Balfour?" Then, even louder, "Blanche Balfour? Blanche?"

Nothing.

Still in her evening gown and long gloves, Maggie plucked a hairpin from her bun. A Glaswegian safecracker, lock expert, and master criminal had once taught her how to pick a lock at spy-training camp in Scotland. Seconds later, the lock sprang open with a smart *click*.

The First Lady's eyes widened. "You're a woman of many talents, Miss Hope."

You have no idea. "Please allow me to go

first, ma'am."

The heavy oak door creaked open. Inside, the apartment was deep in shadows. Maggie, with Mrs. Roosevelt at her heels, walked past the efficiency kitchen and through the living room.

"Blanche? Blanche?" Maggie pushed open the door to what she supposed was the bedroom.

The room reeked of bourbon, and the bedclothes were tangled. A light glowed from underneath a closed door.

"Blanche?" Maggie called. She opened the bathroom door. There, in a bathtub of blood, lay a young woman. Maggie took in the scene, the girl's staring, glassy eyes. "Oh, no . . ."

"What? What is it?"

Maggie turned. "I'm so sorry, ma'am, you don't want to see —"

But Mrs. Roosevelt pushed past her. "Oh, God," she whispered, taking in the sight. "Poor Blanche," she murmured, putting one gloved hand to her heart. "The poor, dear girl . . ."

Maggie was immediately aware of the possibility of scandal — the First Lady in the apartment of a girl who killed herself? *No, no. Can't have this. Must clear out immediately.*

"Mrs. Roosevelt," she said in a soothing voice, "I need to call the police. I'll tell them — anonymously, of course — what we found. And then you and I are going to leave from the side entrance. Quickly. Do you understand, ma'am?"

The unflappable Mrs. Roosevelt seemed smaller and almost frail. "She's dead," she murmured in disbelief.

"She is. And the best thing we can do is call the police and then leave."

Mrs. Roosevelt sank into a chair, clutching her handbag. "I just can't believe it."

"Mrs. Roosevelt!" Maggie cried, then softened her tone. "Please don't sit down. You may leave evidence."

Mrs. Roosevelt nodded and rose as Maggie moved to the bedside telephone. She picked up the receiver. "The police, please. Yes, I'd like to report a death," she said over the clicks and static. "At nine twenty-six Massachusetts Avenue, apartment seven fourteen." She hung up without waiting for any reply.

"We need to leave now, ma'am," she said. "Wait —" On the desk was a pad of yellow legal paper, the first page blank. A quick glance in the desk's wastepaper basket proved it was empty. Maggie took the entire pad and tucked it under her arm.

"What's that?" the First Lady asked. "Is it all right to take it?" Sirens wailed in the distance.

"Mrs. Roosevelt, with all due respect, we need to leave *now.*"

At the car, Maggie looked at Mrs. Roosevelt and saw that the woman's gloved hands were shaking. "Oh, spinach!" the First Lady exclaimed as she tried to fish the keys out of her handbag, only to drop them.

"Ma'am, would you like me to drive?"

Eleanor Roosevelt looked at Maggie with gratitude. "Thank you, Miss Hope," she managed. "I suppose I'm in . . . shock."

Maggie slid in behind the wheel. She waited, thoughts roiling, as the First Lady settled herself in the passenger seat and then handed her the keys. *I wish I had words of comfort,* Maggie thought, as she drove back through the thick fog to the White House in painful silence.

Only when they were safely ensconced in the First Lady's second-floor study did Maggie ask, "May I please have a pencil?"

"Of course." Mrs. Roosevelt procured one from her desk.

Maggie took it and began shading the top sheet of paper on the pad she had taken from Miss Balfour's apartment with the pencil lead.

"What are you doing?" the First Lady wanted to know, peering at the empty page.

Maggie, biting her lip and engrossed in her task, didn't answer. But what she was up to became increasingly clear as she continued to shade the paper with the side of the lead. As if by magic, writing began to appear on the page.

"Oh, I see," Mrs. Roosevelt murmured. "It's the last thing Blanche wrote."

To whom it may concern:

I'm so sorry, but I just couldn't take it any longer.

The First Lady of the United States of America, Eleanor Roosevelt, has — I'm ashamed even to say it — tried to kiss me. And, I blush to write this, more. When I refused her advances, she swore she would ruin my good name in Washington and that I'd never find respectable work again.

Please know I am a lady, of upright morals and character. I had hoped to marry, to have children.

But now there's no chance. Mrs. Roosevelt has ruined everything. Since I have nothing left, the only answer is to end my life.

Sincerely yours,
Blanche Imogene Balfour

There was a hush as Mrs. Roosevelt read the note, then struggled to take in its implications. She sank into the sofa. "This isn't true," she murmured, her face ashen, letter in hand. "Not at all. These are lies. *Lies!* I was never anything but kind to that girl."

Maggie stared into the First Lady's eyes. All she saw was pain and distress and she believed her. Still, it had to be asked: "Then why would Blanche write those things about you?"

"I don't know! None of it ever happened!" The First Lady looked at the paper again. "Do you know, I don't believe this is even her handwriting. Blanche didn't write this. She couldn't have!"

"Do you have an example of Blanche's handwriting?"

Mrs. Roosevelt rose and went to her desk. She rummaged in the papers. "Here," she said, handing a sheet to Maggie. "Here's a list she made."

Maggie studied the two handwriting specimens. "The penmanship's similar. But I wouldn't call it a match. Still, there's no way to say it's *not* a match either. All right, let's think this through logically. Blanche is dead. It looks as if she slit her own wrists — sorry, ma'am — in the bath. But she would have written the note first and left it. If that's the scenario, what happened to the actual note?"

"Maybe she decided against keeping it?" the First Lady suggested, sitting on the sofa. Maggie sat beside her. "Maybe she crumpled it up and threw it away?"

Maggie shook her head. "No, the wastebasket was empty."

The First Lady slumped back. "Then where's the original note? What happened to it?"

Maggie's mind raced. If news of Blanche's suicide and the contents of the note got out, it would cause a horrific scandal, and would weaken President Roosevelt's standing in the U.S. and in the world. It would hinder the vital newborn union of the United States and the United Kingdom. It would cause Hitler and his crew to gloat about the "degenerate" Americans. It would give critics excuses to pull away from the Roosevelt Administration during a time of crisis. She thought of Mr. Churchill, how hard he had worked, how much he had suffered to make sure this meeting would come off well. How much it meant to him, to all of them, to the British people.

"All right," Maggie said, "let's say, for the sake of argument, that Blanche wanted to frame you and left an incriminating note before she killed herself. Do you think she was a lone vigilante? Or could she have been working with someone else? A group? Do you have enemies?"

"My dear girl, we could start with the head of the FBI himself, J. Edgar Hoover, and then come up with a list of thousands."

"Well, then, is there anyone in particular you may have antagonized recently?"

Mrs. Roosevelt gave a squeak that might have been a laugh. "Not any more than usual. But then again, I always seem to be offending someone or other. I never thought of that as a terrible thing before, though. I always say, 'Do what you feel in your heart to be right — for you'll be criticized anyway.' In other words, Miss Hope, you'll find, if you haven't already, that you're damned if you do, and damned if you don't." She sighed and dropped the piece of paper to her lap. "I'm not the most popular woman in many circles, particularly down in Dixie. Most particularly with the Kluckers."

"The Kluckers?"

"The Ku Klux Klan, Miss Hope."

For a fleeting moment, Maggie felt a connection with the older woman. Ever since she'd arrived in London, three years before, it had been one "damned if you do, damned if you don't" situation after another.

Then she cleared her mind, as she had been taught, and returned to the case at hand.

Maggie had seen that the President and Mrs. Roosevelt did not share a bedroom. She had seen the proximity of Lorena Hickok's bedroom to Mrs. Roosevelt's. Maggie's own aunt Edith was a lesbian, living with her lover, the two of them posing as spinster roommates. Maggie knew how these deceptions went. She wanted to ask Mrs. Roosevelt, *Is there anything else that one of your enemies might have on you?* but she decided against it.

"Please," Maggie insisted, taking the notepad from the First Lady's white-knuckled hands, then ripping off the offending sheet. "Allow me." She crumpled the note into a ball and threw it into the flaming coals, where it burned, then turned to lacy ash. Then she asked, "I wonder if someone else could have seen the note and taken it to protect you?"

"No," said the First Lady decisively. "No. Where *is* the original copy of the letter? The person who has it could easily blackmail me. . . ." She put her head in her hands.

"Someone may have taken the note," Maggie suggested. "But whether it was to protect you or not — is . . . inconclusive. Only time will tell. May I see everything Blanche was working on for you here?"

Mrs. Roosevelt nodded to a small desk in one of the corners. "Everything's there, just as she left it."

Maggie went to the desk and turned on the light, which cast a small golden glow, then went through the files. There were drafts of Mrs. Roosevelt's "My Day" newspaper columns, both in shorthand and in type. There were many letters. There was a flyer for a rally protesting Wendell Cotton's execution. On the back was what looked to be Blanche's handwriting: *If an offender has committed murder, he MUST die. In this case, no possible substitute can satisfy justice. For there is no parallel between death and even the most miserable life, so that there is no equality of crime and retribution unless the perpetrator is judicially put to death. — Immanuel Kant*

Mrs. Roosevelt finally raised her head. "You're not just a typist, are you?"

Maggie put down the flyer and walked back to the older woman, remembering the frustration of, once upon a time, being "just a typist." Still, those days had been much simpler. She almost missed them now. "No. No, ma'am, I'm not."

Mrs. Roosevelt's blue eyes lifted to hers. "Who *are* you, then, Miss Hope?"

"I'm . . ." *Well, that's the question, isn't it?* ". . . someone who . . . helps. And, ma'am, may I suggest a cup of tea? It's something I've learned during my time in Britain — just how restorative tea can be. I suggest peppermint. Or perhaps chamomile, at this late hour. Despite the events of the day, ma'am, you must try to get some sleep."

Chapter Three

"Before a blackout, all lights in this hotel will blink three times at intervals of five seconds, and then again after five minutes. All hotel guests must stay away from the doors and windows. There will be no transportation during actual raids."

The manager of the Mayflower Hotel was a small man with a bullish face, dressed in a pin-striped suit. He strained to make himself heard over the chatter of guests, the click of high heels, and the silvery sound of ice in the barman's cocktail shaker. No one in the magnificent marble and mirror lobby of the Mayflower Hotel paid the slightest bit of attention to him.

Certainly not John Sterling, who was still waiting for Maggie on a love seat in the hotel's promenade. He was scribbling away in a leather-bound notebook, beneath an Aubusson tapestry and to the left of a large potted fern. In his Royal Air Force uniform, he drew admiring gazes from the ladies, and respect and envy from the men leaving one of the ballrooms. His long legs were stretched in front of him, crossed at the ankles.

While convalescing from his injuries, John had prayed to recover and rejoin the RAF as a pilot. He loved flying — the freedom, the excitement, the sense of being a knight-errant of the skies. But by crashing over Germany on his first long-distance mission, he felt he had failed his country, his King, the Prime Minister, his family and friends. And worst of all, he felt he had failed himself. It was fine to go back to work as a private secretary for the Prime Minister while he was recovering, but he was determined to redeem himself and return to the sky. The doctors had told him that in time his vision would improve and the headaches would become less frequent, but they were dubious about his return to the air. He couldn't pass the physical. For the time being, at least.

Having a father who was an MP and a mother who wrote and illustrated children's books, and having survived the barbaric traditions of Eton and then Magdalen College at Oxford, John was a part of the old-boy network. He knew its rules and rituals intimately and could partake in the camaraderie. But he hated it. Despite being a scholar and a star athlete — he had excelled at squash and tennis — he'd never quite felt at home among his peers. He wasn't an upper-class toff and had no wish to be. He wanted more.

The closest he'd felt to belonging was when he'd joined a writing group at Oxford, the Inklings, an ad hoc literary discussion group, specializing in the fantastic. The Inklings met weekly at a pub, the Eagle and Child. The company was mostly Oxford dons — J. R. R. Tolkien, C. S. Lewis, and Charles Williams — but also a few students, including Tolkien's son Christopher. John was one of the regulars and had developed a number of illustrated stories. He'd put writing fiction behind him when he started working for Winston Churchill in the mid-thirties. But the boredom of convalescence had helped him remember some of his old imaginary friends. He wasn't keen to show anyone yet, but he was working on a new idea, a story, this one featuring characters RAF pilots were all too familiar with — Gremlins.

He checked his watch; Maggie was officially late. He went back to his notebook — inside was a story he'd been working on, about Gremlins in airplanes. Gremlins were often joked about in the RAF: Anytime anything went wrong with a plane, "the Gremlins" were blamed. These mischievous creatures were believed to sabotage planes out of spite.

The idea for a story about Gremlins helping an injured pilot overcome his weaknesses and fly again had come to John during a fever dream in the hospital. Gremlins and their mythology had become an obsession. He'd filled notebooks with drawings of the creatures. It was a deliberate distraction. From Maggie. After they'd reunited, he'd learned that she had fallen in love with someone else. That she'd slept with someone else. The woman he'd proposed to marry had so quickly found the strength to carry on. And yes, while he logically realized it made sense under the circumstances, he still felt abandoned by the one person he'd believed would never give up on him.

He didn't look up as the woman approached, although all other heads turned. Nearly six feet tall, she was slim, graceful, and stunningly beautiful, with delicate features, wide-set eyes, and glossy, raven-black hair cut in a severe pageboy. She wore a red crepe evening gown, draped and pleated like a Roman goddess's chemise, accented with exotic gold jewelry.

The hush the manager hadn't been able to command with his air-raid announcement fell over the lobby, and the woman smiled, cool and gracious, as a society photographer took her picture with his bulky camera. Her glorious face glowed in the incandescent flash as she found the light and posed with ease.

Head held high, she made her way down the promenade, her friends trailing in her wake, stopping at John's crossed legs, which blocked her path. A look of annoyance flitted across her face, but when she saw the uniform and the man wearing it, it vanished. "Why, aren't you tall, dark, and most likely incorrigible?"

John looked up. He blinked, concentration broken by her scent of Shalimar. Hastily, he moved his legs. "Sorry, ma'am."

"Ma'am," the woman said, "but I'm a widow." She motioned to the rest of her party. "Look, he's in uniform — how dashing." One of the accompanying women was shorter, dressed in a too-tight yellow satin gown, topped off by oversize round glasses, which gave her an owlish appearance.

"Do we think he looks like Henry Fonda?" the first woman mused.

The shorter woman pursed her lips and

observed John through her spectacles. "Mmm — perhaps more of a Gary Cooper."

Ignoring John's discomfort, the taller woman eased herself down next to him, one gloved hand playing with her golden necklace. "And all alone."

He closed his notebook. Writing time was obviously over. "I'm waiting for someone," he explained.

"It speaks!" the woman in red exclaimed, and the rest of her party chuckled in amusement. "And with such a lovely British accent. We American girls adore that accent, you know. Did one of ours stand you up?"

"Yes. I mean, no. I mean —"

"I can't believe someone would leave a man as handsome as you alone in a hotel lobby, can you?" she said, looking into John's eyes.

The woman in yellow peered from over the top of her glasses. "Shocking. Absolutely shocking."

"What's your name, sir?" the first woman purred.

"Flight —" He cleared his throat. "Flight Lieutenant John Sterling."

"Oooh, a lieutenant!" The men in the party began to look uncomfortable, their dinner jackets paling in comparison to John's uniform, regardless of bespoke Jermyn Street origins and tailoring. "We honor you." The woman in red made a mock hand salute. "Did you see battle, Lieutenant?"

John didn't like her manner, and he didn't like her tone. He was brusque. "Yes."

The woman in red snapped her fingers, and a concierge appeared. "Drinks all around," she commanded. "Brandy for this young war hero and for the rest of us to toast his good health." More chairs were procured, and the rest of the party took seats. They realized when their leading lady's attention was captured.

"You must forgive me, Lieutenant," she said, her husky voice soft in his ear, "but I insist. You see, we've only heard about the war in Europe. There's no — ah, what's the word? — 'rationing' here. So to see an actual war hero in our midst —"

John felt his ears burn. "Ma'am, I'm not —"

"My name is Mrs. Regina Winthrop Wolffe," she interrupted, still playing with her jewelry. "And this lovely creature is Mrs. Evelyn Astor Thorne." Then the brandy appeared, in heavy cut-glass snifters, and they all drank, raising their glasses in John's direction.

He couldn't help but stare at the gigantic diamond dangling from a gleaming chain around Evelyn's sagging neck. She caught him looking. "Don't touch it — bad luck, you know."

John tried not to laugh at her brashness. "I wouldn't dream of it, ma'am."

"Oh you're adorable." Evelyn turned to Regina. "He's absolutely adorable! I'd like to put him in my pocketbook and take him home with me."

"I saw him first," Regina said, pouting her crimson-painted lips. "A toast to our new friend, Flight Lieutenant John Sterling," she declared.

They all raised their glasses again. One man, pasty and thick through the middle, with thinning hair, began in a querulous voice, "Although I've said and said again I was always against this war —"

They'd obviously heard this line before. "We know, but since Pearl Harbor, all bets are off," another man said.

The first man persisted. "Churchill's in town now, you know — glad-handing with Roosevelt. The British scare me."

"I work for Prime Minister Churchill," John said, emphasizing the title. "That's why I'm here."

"How perfectly splendid," crowed Regina, smoothing over the edges. "Even Lindbergh's come around since Pearl Harbor, you know."

"Well, good for Lindy," came the man's sarcastic reply, "but *I* haven't. I'm against the British now, yesterday, and tomorrow. And I'm for America first, last, and all the time." The brandy gave his voice strength and too much volume. Other guests in the hotel's lobby turned to stare. "And I resent that Roosevelt is using Pearl Harbor as an excuse to drag us into this damn war! Sorry for swearing, ladies."

John had endured enough. "So says Goebbels," he retorted.

"Ooooh, he got you," Regina cooed. "Nicely done, Lieutenant Sterling."

But the man wasn't finished. "The British are too clever for their own damn good — and I don't want any more of this 'Winnie and Franklin' nonsense I've been reading about in the papers."

John's eyes glinted. "So says Hitler."

The silence was deafening, even as around them the lobby continued to buzz with energy.

A shy, short, slight man in his forties with steel-rimmed glasses changed the subject. "Please let me introduce myself, Lieutenant." He extended his hand. "My pen name is C. S. Forester, but do call me Cecil. Since we're all pulling at the same oar now, I'd like to interview you about your experience in the RAF. Do you have any good stories, perchance?"

John glowered. "I crashed just outside of Berlin, lived, hid, and managed to escape and get back to London. End of story."

Forester sat down on John's other side and clapped a well-manicured hand over his heart. "How thrilling!" he cried, as the ladies murmured their approval. "I think it might make for an exciting piece in *The Saturday Evening Post,* if you're so inclined. Since the United States has only just entered the war, bona fide heroes are in short supply. You're that rare bird on this side of the Atlantic, Lieutenant, someone who's actually seen combat — and I'm sure your story will stir the hearts of patriotic Americans."

The isolationists snorted at this, but Forester and John both ignored them. John recalled that the newly created British Information Services was recruiting famous British authors, from H. G. Wells to Somerset Maugham, to do propaganda work and write stories to rally support for England in the American press.

He had acted as a liaison between the Prime Minister's office and BIS, which was trying to develop more tear-jerkers along the lines of *Mrs. Miniver,* a bestselling novel based on a *London Times* column that told of the hardships suffered by an English-woman and her family during the Blitz. And then there was Helen MacInnes's thriller *Above Suspicion,* a chilling story of Gestapo agents who hunted a courageous British academic and his wife across Europe.

Ego aside, John realized that a human-interest story like his might appeal to the American public and make them sympathize with the British struggle.

"You know who he is, don't you?" Regina murmured to John.

"Er, afraid not, ma'am."

"Call me Regina, I insist. And he's the same C. S. Forester who wrote the Captain Horatio Hornblower novels — you know, about navy life in Admiral Nelson's day."

John straightened. Like most of his coun-trymen, he'd devoured the Horatio Horn-blower novels when he was younger. Forest-er's novel *Payment Deferred* had been turned into a hit play in the West End, had run on Broadway, and was being made into a film. *That* C. S. Forester.

John turned back to Forester. "I — I can jot down something by tomorrow, sir, if you'd like. Of course I'll have to ask permis-sion —"

"Fantastic!" exclaimed the author. "Just notes are fine, you know. But specific details are crucial."

"I have the perfect idea," Regina cooed. "Come to dinner at my place tomorrow, Lieutenant Sterling! It will be loads of fun, and you can give Cecil your notes then."

"I — I'll have to ask —"

"We won't take no for an answer," Regina interrupted, rising in a swirl of perfume.

"We won't!" echoed Evelyn, who struggled a bit in her chair to stand.

"We'll see you tomorrow then, for cocktails and dinner. I'll have my butler send around a formal invitation to you in the morning at the White House. It will be fabulous." Regina extended her hand, and John took it. Then she bent down and said in a throaty whisper, "Ta till then."

And in a cloud of brandy fumes, they were gone.

John checked his watch. It was beyond late. He'd been up since he couldn't remember when. He'd have one more drink and give Maggie until then — and then he was going to bed.

Even if it meant going to bed alone.

CHAPTER FOUR

The grand piano in Chatswell Hall's former drawing room was out of tune.

The north London weather had had its way with the instrument. Still, even an out-of-tune piano couldn't ruin the power of Tchaikovsky's Piano Concerto No. 1. A man — dark and lean, a black eye patch over his left eye that gave him the air of a pirate — sat at the keyboard, graceful, long-fingered hands flying over the black and ivory keys. He wore flannel trousers, a shirt and tie, and a blue cardigan — nothing military about him except his perfect posture. His good eye was closed as he lost himself in the beauty of the music.

There was the thud of boots approaching on the parquet floor. "Heil Hitler!" Then, "You can't play that!" The newcomer was tall and broad, with sleek, graying white-blond hair and thighs like tree trunks. He was dressed in full Nazi uniform. Medals of all shapes and sizes adorned his barrel-shaped chest, while the Knight's Cross with Oak Leaf Cluster was pinned at his throat.

The man playing the piano didn't stop or even open his good eye. "I don't see why not," he answered in a reasonable tone.

The blond man scowled. "You must not play Tchaikovsky. It is *forbidden.*"

The man at the piano opened his eye. "Forbidden by whom? I must remind you, we're not in Germany anymore, General Kemp. No damn Nazis sniffing around. Well, except for you, that is."

The hulking blond rubbed at the back of his neck as he sat on a moth-eaten velvet sofa opposite. "It is unseemly, General von Bayer."

Von Bayer played to the end of the movement and then stilled, listening to the last chords fade away into the twilight.

"It doesn't matter where we are," Kemp persisted. "As German officers we must conduct ourselves with dignity and decorum, even if we're being held prisoner in Britain. The Führer would be appalled at your playing the music of a Russian, no matter where we're imprisoned — *especially* now."

"Unlike you," von Bayer retorted, "I am a German, but not a Nazi. I'm a Bavarian, not a Prussian. And besides, I like Tchaikovsky — he was an aristocrat, not a Bolshevik."

"He was a homosexual!"

Von Bayer shrugged. "Nobody's perfect."

"We are both German generals —" Kemp began.

Von Bayer sighed. "We're both *captured* German generals, imprisoned in England. A gilded cage, though, you must admit. Certainly much better accommodations than any currently imprisoned British generals are enjoying."

"True, true," Kemp agreed. "I've just written a letter to my wife, with the following advertisement for Chatswell Hall." He took a piece of paper from his uniform's breast pocket and unfolded it. "How does this sound? *Park Sanatorium: First-class accommodation, running hot and cold water at all hours of the day, also baths on the premises. Four generous meals daily, first-class English cuisine. Regular walks under expert guidance. Large library of carefully chosen literature of all countries. Table-tennis tournaments, billiards, chess, and bridge circles. Instruction in art and handicrafts. Alcoholism cured without extra charge. Moderate terms, varying according to social position. Best society assured at all times!*"

Von Bayer's lips twisted into a grim smile. When he had arrived at Chatswell Hall, the only other "guest" was Kemp, who'd been captured five months previously. Both men were the same age, both highly decorated generals. Each had commanded a panzer division in the Middle East.

And their accommodations *were* luxurious, if chilly. At present, they were in the canary-yellow drawing room, just one of the many large rooms at Chatswell Hall that smelled of must and rooms too long closed without fresh air, leaving molds and mildew to thrive. The Hall itself was a Tudor brick mansion with half-timbers, set on extensive grounds with gardens, located in the ancient woods near Cockfosters, on the edge of London.

Of course, Chatswell Hall had been taken over by the British government since the war and given over to the long-term internment of captured high-ranking Germans, so it was now bordered by barbed wire and patrolled by Coldstream Guards. The rooms where the prisoners were allowed had bars on the windows.

Still, it had undeniable charm: superb Tudor architecture with turrets, depressed arches, and curved gables, as well as a tennis court, pond, and maze. The prisoners had regular meals, hot running water, a library of leather-bound books, a wireless, current newspapers, a study for painting and music, and a dining room. On the third floor, as Kemp had noted, was a room with both table tennis and billiards. Laundry and sartorial issues were attended to by a London tailor who visited every few days. Lord Abernathy was the camp's overseer, but he called himself their "entertainment director" with a sly wink, as if they were all passengers on the *Titanic.*

"Shall we have a drink then? It's after six." Kemp rubbed his hands together for warmth, then moved to the bar trolley, which boasted an assortment of bottles. He mixed two Martinis, noting, "I'd make some for our other 'guests,' but I'm never sure if or when they'll appear." There were no cocktail glasses, but they did have mismatched teacups, mostly intact.

There were five prisoners at Chatswell Hall. Von Bayer and Kemp, of course. Then there was General Holzer, who had all his meals taken to him on trays, never left his room, and sketched only pastel nudes. And General Janz, who also never mingled with the other prisoners, preferring to devote all his time to translating *Faust* from German into ancient Greek. And now there was a new prisoner, a former high-ranking Abwehr spy chief, who had yet to appear in any of Chatswell's public spaces.

"This 'prison' is insanity," von Bayer declared, lifting his hands from the ivory keys and coming around to accept his cup. "Here, there is peace, beauty, and tranquillity. But out there" — he gestured to the window and the world beyond and sank down on one of the wing chairs, covered in a faded print of blowsy roses — "there is only war, devastation, and death."

"You're in a melancholy mood, General von Bayer." Kemp drained his red willow teacup. "Never fear — all will be well. The nation that produced Luther, Kant, Goethe, and Beethoven will never die. Love for the Fatherland is the religion of our time. Use my example — love Hitler's Germany with all your heart, so that the struggle continues to a victorious end. And never allow yourself to be alienated from this love of country by pacifism and weak talk."

Although the blackout curtains had been drawn over the mullioned windows, fringed silk lamps were lit, their light throwing dark shadows up onto the walls like those of Plato's cave. A large tapestry of the hunt softened one of the wood-paneled walls. A small fire struggled behind brass andirons.

Von Bayer cocked his head. "National Socialism is based on contempt for the individual, scorn for freedom, and disdain for free speech. At this point, Nazi Germany's victory would become a defeat for all people." He took a sip of his drink. "I can't predict when the war will end, but I believe one thing: now that the United States is fighting alongside Britain, and our troops are still fighting in Russia with winter closing in — the year 1942 will bring us a good way back along the road to Berlin, Rome, and Tokyo."

Kemp frowned. "You're negative. Negativity is traitorous. It's un-German."

"It's realistic."

The fair-haired general replenished his teacup. "Do you remember that awful propaganda film they made us watch back in the day — *Warriors Behind Barbed Wire?*"

Von Bayer picked lint off his trousers. "I used to nap during the films. They were dreadful."

"I think about it sometimes. It was all warnings not to talk, if captured. 'The enemy is always listening,' et cetera, et cetera . . ."

"First of all" — von Bayer gestured around him at the drawing room — "there's no barbed wire here. At least, you can barely see it from the windows."

"True, true," Kemp admitted. "The British are — while misguided and backwards — a civilized people. They know how to treat high-ranking Germans. And, really, that film was utter stupidity. We're officers, for God's sake. Not children, after all. We have every right to talk about political affairs."

"No, you're right. We're officers — with experience of life, with differing points of view — this is not the same as gossiping young lieutenants," von Bayer agreed. "Besides, the British have such good intelligence they don't need to listen to us old chatterboxes."

There was the staccato beat of high heels on the oak parquet floor in the hall, and then a woman's husky voice at the door said, "Old chatterboxes? Speak for yourself, darling."

Clara Hess draped herself in the doorframe. She was bright-eyed and platinum-haired, with a long, lean figure like Marlene Dietrich's that made even her simple wool dress look as if it had been designed especially for her by Coco Chanel. The only flaw in her exceptional beauty was her eyes, one of which aimed higher than the other.

The two men stood as she sauntered in.

"Heil Hitler!" said Kemp and saluted.

"Heil Hitler," she replied in her husky voice.

Von Bayer made a weak attempt at the Hitler Gruss, and Clara laughed. "Let's just assume the salute while we're all in here, shall we? Otherwise, we may pull shoulder muscles." Aware of the men's eyes on her, she continued. "Did you know that three hundred years ago, a prisoner condemned to the Tower of London carved on the wall of his cell *'It is not adversity that kills, but the impatience with which we bear adversity'*?"

Clara sat on a cracked leather sofa and stretched like a cat. Von Bayer resumed his seat, while Kemp went to the bar cart. From above the fireplace, the vitreous black eyes of a mounted stag's head stared down. "That's an apocryphal story, Frau Hess," Kemp scolded, mixing her a Martini in a teacup festooned with clematis and yellow carnations.

"No, I was there, in the Tower of London. I saw it myself."

Von Bayer whistled. "I didn't know that. What else have you been hiding from us?"

Clara fixed her gaze on him. "Well, we only met a few weeks ago, General. I do have a few secrets left."

"Three weeks for you. But some of us

have been here since nineteen forty. Almost two years for me," said Kemp. "And nearly that for von Bayer."

"You poor darlings," Clara purred. "This," she said with a gesture that encompassed the room, the house, the surrounding land, "is vastly superior to the Tower of London."

"Prost." The three clinked teacups.

Von Bayer sighed. "Every day this war continues is a crime. Hitler belongs in a padded cell."

Kemp stamped one gleaming boot in exasperation. "I always say, no matter how many faults this system has, no matter how wrong it is, I served under this system. I fought under this system. My soldiers fell under this system. So I cannot, the moment things go wrong, say to hell with it. No. I remain loyal and true — to Hitler."

"There we disagree." The alcohol had warmed von Bayer's blood. "I regret every bomb, every scrap of material, every human life that's being wasted in this senseless war. The only gain it will bring us is an added ten years of gangster rule." He looked to Clara, whose hair shimmered in the firelight. "And what do you think, Frau Hess?" She had been cagey about her politics since arriving.

"Oh la — the same argument." She picked

up a deck of monogrammed cards with gilt edges, the owner's name lost to time. "Bezique?"

"It's a game only for two people," von Bayer pointed out.

She shuffled. "Euchre, then?"

"A game for four."

"Well, the three of us must be able to figure out *something*," Clara said. "Who'd like to hear me sing? General von Bayer, would you accompany me?"

"It would be an honor." And for him it was. Before her career with the Abwehr, Clara Hess had been a renowned soprano, specializing in the works of Wagner and famed for her portrayal of Kundry in *Parsifal*. It was well known that she had been one of Hitler's favorite singers. It had also been rumored she'd had an affair with Joseph Goebbels.

Clara walked to the piano and draped herself in the crook. With a long, red-painted fingernail, she beckoned to von Bayer. "Play for me, darling. 'Lili Marlene.' "

Von Bayer obeyed. He went back to the piano and spread his fingers over the keys.

She took a deep breath, and began. Her voice — once silvery soprano, now a burnished bronze mezzo — lingered on the melody, caressing the doleful lyrics.

When the last notes had faded away, both men had tears glittering in their eyes.

Clara reclaimed her seat. "And who's *your* Lili Marlene, General von Bayer?" she asked her pianist. "Who's waiting back home for you?"

"My mother, God willing."

"Oh, a bachelor!" She turned to the other man. "And you, General Kemp?"

Although his medals glinted, the blond looked uncomfortable. "I have a wife back in Berlin, but she and I — well, we were living separate lives long before we were separated by war."

"I see."

"And you, Frau Hess? Of course we all know of your marriage to the great conductor Miles Hess."

She raised one perfectly plucked eyebrow. "My marriage to Herr Hess was a grand publicity stunt, dreamed up by our managers."

"What?" The generals knew the man she'd married. Both had attended concerts and operas Hess conducted before the war.

"He'd been caught in a hotel room with a young boy. Goebbels wanted the story to disappear. A huge wedding reassured everyone that Germany's foremost conductor of

Wagner liked beautiful blond Aryan girls."

There was a stunned silence.

"Oh, don't you dare feel sorry for me. We had a wonderful life, both together, as friends, with our various lovers on the side. It was ideal, really."

"Do — do you have any children?" von Bayer asked.

"I have a daughter, Elise Hess," Clara replied. "And . . ." She stopped.

"And?"

"And another daughter, Margaret Hope. From a previous marriage." She added, "To an Englishman." She stood and went to the blackout curtain, pulling it aside to reveal oriel windows with small, diamond-shaped panes of leaded glass. Outside was darkness pierced by starlight. She left the curtain open. "A small act of defiance against our British 'hosts,' " she announced.

"Where are your daughters now?" von Bayer asked.

"They tell me Elise is in Ravensbrück."

"I'm so sorry," Kemp said. "But they do keep the German political prisoners separate from the Jews, you know. They have much better treatment."

"I'm sure. And Margaret works for Churchill himself, if you can believe it. Such a disappointment, that girl. Both of them."

She sighed.

"We were just talking about what 1942 will bring for us," Kemp told her. "Von Bayer here thinks that, now that the Americans have joined the war, it's the nail in our coffin. While I remain loyal and true to the Führer, as befits a Prussian. What's your stand, Frau Hess?"

"I think Germany will have a few surprises in store for the so-called Allies in 'forty-two."

"So you've been saying." Kemp narrowed his eyes. "I know that you were in with Goebbels and his crowd before you were captured — is there something specific you know?"

"Oh, I think you'll be quite surprised when you learn what the Führer has up his sleeve. You've heard whispers of his so-called mystery weapons? Wait until 'forty-two." Clara sipped her drink. "Then the fun will really start."

Kemp leered. "Can't you tell us anything else, Frau Hess? You keep hinting at something. And you *did* work with the Abwehr for years."

"I'd love to tell you everything." The blonde revealed small, pearly teeth. "But then I'd have to kill you."

■ ■ ■ ■

"Shit! What do you think she meant by that? 'Mystery weapons'?" The microphones installed in Chatswell Hall's drawing room were excellent and could pick up everything, even the slightest whisper, which could then be heard distinctly up in the great house's attic.

When Chatswell Hall had been turned over to the British government, in 1940, and converted into a minimum-security prison, a staff of six was brought in to listen to the prisoners' conversations. Microphones had been concealed in lamp fittings, behind picture frames of gilt gesso, and in fireplaces, all over Chatswell Hall. MI-9's specially designed microphones reached everywhere. Nothing was out of range; even the trees were bugged. Conversations about the war were recorded, then transcribed, and then translated. The transcripts were stamped with TOP SECRET in red ink and sent on to Lord Cherwell and then, ultimately, to the Prime Minister.

Hidden away in the drafty, dusty attic of the Tudor mansion was the latest listening equipment. Under the sloped ceiling, the room looked like a telephone switchboard run riot. Making sense of the chaos were two young men — German refugees who'd escaped to Britain and were now specially trained as MI-9 monitoring officers. Both wore headphones, to listen in on the conversation in the drawing room below. Wavering yellow and blue needles measured the sound of the prisoners' voices.

"She's got nothing. Just trying to be dramatic — self-important bitch," declared the first, a dark-haired young man with a German accent, as he adjusted his earphones. His eyebrows were black and shaggy, and his cheeks were pitted with acne scars.

"Did you record it?" asked the second, rubbing his hands together against the cold. He was built on thicker lines, with fair hair and a deep dimple in his chin.

"Of course I recorded it — although I don't think it means anything," the first young man replied.

The second shook his head. "I think we should have it transcribed. Let's ask Captain Naumann."

Lord Abernathy wasn't really named Abernathy. And he was no lord. He was Captain Walter Naumann, an upper-level officer of MI-9. He was at Chatswell Hall in the role of Lord Abernathy to gain the prisoners' trust. His persona had been deliberately created; his "character" Lord Abernathy was a part-German distant relation to the royal family, and a friend of the Duke of Windsor and his American wife, Wallis Simpson.

In reality, however, Naumann was from a working-class background, had a Jewish mother, and, at least before the war, had specialized in character roles in amateur West End productions.

"We need to ask Captain Naumann what?" The prisoners' dinner was being served, and since Lord Abernathy was no longer needed, Naumann had made his way up to the attic. He was a tall man in his sixties, painfully thin, with silvery hair.

"Hess said something about what Hitler 'has up his sleeve' and 'mystery weapons.' What do you think?"

Naumann chuckled, wrapping a knit scarf around his throat. "She's a diva, that one. I wouldn't want to bother Lord Cherwell prematurely —" He gave a final tug at his scarf. "But go ahead — send it along, just in case."

"Yes, sir."

Naumann looked down his long, aquiline nose. "Do let me know if she says anything else on the matter."

When the older man left, the two with the headphones relaxed. The dark-haired young man, Arthur Chester, turned to his companion. "So what does your family think you do?"

The heavier, fair-haired Owen Rose chuckled. "They think I'm on patrol — security. What about yours?"

Arthur bit his lip. He had been born Teddy Schächter, a German Jew, and had escaped Germany before the war began. He'd Anglicized his name and joined the Pioneer Corps, serving in British army uniform. He was passionate about giving something back to Britain for saving his life. And also as retribution for what the Nazis had done to him and his family. "I left them in Berlin. I don't know where they are now. I imagine, if they're lucky, in a camp." There was a moment of silence. Then he added, "Sometimes one of the English says, 'Oh, how awful to fight your own people!' But they aren't my people anymore. They're the enemy."

Despite his background, Arthur did his best to distance himself from the prisoners' anti-Semitism. He always tried to stay professional in his speech and bearing, so that even when he heard about atrocities on the Eastern Front, he was able to remain detached. As Naumann always said, "What you're doing in the M Room is more important to the war effort than if you drove a tank or fired a machine gun — don't forget that."

Owen understood what Arthur was getting at. He had once been known as Heinz Rosenberg himself before changing his name and doing his best to lose his accent. "I'll get this conversation, including the Diva's mention of the so-called mystery weapons, transcribed and translated," he said. "And then we can send it to London for Lord Cherwell to decide." He chewed on his lower lip. "Wonder what they made of the last one we sent."

"Gimme," the Prime Minister ordered, seeing David pick up a folder that had been sent from London via the British Embassy in Washington.

David, used to the P.M.'s curtness, handed the page over. "Yes, sir."

It was two in the morning. And while everyone else at the White House was asleep, or at least in bed, Winston Churchill was working in his map room cum office.

Churchill's blue eyes, threaded red with exhaustion from the dangerous trip, the President's Martinis, and now the late hour, scanned the lines from Duncan Sandys and Lord Cherwell, also known as Prof. "Another memo from Sandys, hmm? And another one from Prof."

"Yes, sir. The reports we've been receiving about the prisoners held at Chatswell Hall in the last few days are vague. And the photographs of the possible rocket-making sites that are being developed at Danesfield House in Medmenham are inconclusive. In a nutshell, Duncan Sandys thinks attack by long-range rockets is a viable threat, and Lord Cherwell doesn't. Cherwell's been most outspoken on the matter."

"Heh," Churchill snorted. "If you read between the lines, Prof is saying it's bunk."

David permitted himself a small smile. "Yes, sir."

The two men had worked together for years. David had believed in Churchill even during the so-called Wilderness Years, when Churchill had spoken out about Hitler's rearmament of Germany in the House of Commons and been laughed at and called names. They'd been together as he became First Lord of the Admiralty, then Prime Minister. They'd been through the Battle of Britain. They'd been through assassination attempts and kidnappings. They had developed shorthand for what was most important. And their gruff, professional interactions were underscored by genuine affection.

Churchill looked at David. "You've seen these reports?"

"I have, sir."

"And what do *you* think about these alleged super-rockets, Mr. Greene?"

"I think the evidence Sandys cites looks credible. However, if we do as he suggests and bomb the hell out of the base at Peenemünde, we're taking away vital men and aircraft from defense."

Churchill sank back in his chair and slurped scotch and soda from his crystal tumbler. "But if it's true and we do nothing — and then London and the ports come under heavy bombardment from these flying things, we'll have to abandon our ultimate plan to land in France next year."

The P.M. blew smoke rings into the air and watched them melt away to nothing. "All right. I want Sandys to figure out if this rocket threat is indeed real. And — if so — what we must do to stop it. Let's make him Chairman of the — let's see — 'Defense Against Flying Bombs and Rockets.' Have him investigate this so-called super-weapon program."

David reached over for a pad of paper and

pen. "But isn't Sandys already Minister of Supply?"

Churchill grimaced. "He'll manage. We all do."

"What do you want him to do specifically?" David's pen hovered over the pad.

"The first task is to gather all the evidence on this so-called super-rocket program he can, and then present it to the War Cabinet."

"Yes, sir," David said, writing as fast as he could.

"And, of course, Prof should be a part of it. We need him for balance."

"Yes, sir."

"When you write to Sandys, make it directly from me. And ask him how his legs are. Don't want to seem like a complete martinet." Sandys had been wounded in action in Norway.

"Yes, sir," David said, remembering that Sandys was also the P.M.'s son-in-law. "Mrs. Churchill would be most pleased, sir."

"It's not enough I have to win this war. I need to keep my wife happy as well?" the P.M. growled.

"As we well know, it never hurts, sir."

The P.M. took a swig of his whiskey and soda. "Quite right, young man. Quite right, indeed."

■ ■ ■ ■

A soldier walked the perimeter of the Peenemünde compound, high walls covered with
barbed wire, his boots making crunching
sounds on the frosty ground. An Alsatian
barked in the distance. It was early morning, and the sun rose scarlet through the
pines and oak trees. Beyond the forest lay
marshes and sand dunes, and then the
Baltic Sea itself. The air smelled of evergreen and sea salt. The soldier tensed, sensing movement in the brush, but it was only
a squirrel. One of his fellows on patrol
called to him, "They're here! They're here!"
His breath made clouds in the icy air.

A sedan approached the last checkpoint,
long, black, and sleek, red Nazi flags on the
hood fluttering in the breeze, noxious yellow exhaust fumes trailing behind. It approached the main guardhouse, made of
concrete, painted in camouflage, and
swathed in barbed wire. The guards on duty
were expecting this man.

"Welcome, Herr Todt," the most senior
officer said, clicking his heels together. He
saluted. "Heil Hitler!" The senior officer
knew exactly who Fritz Todt was and why
he was there — Hitler's favorite architect

and Minister of Armaments and War Production for the Third Reich. Todt was a handsome man, with a straight nose and a strong jaw that compensated for his thinning hair. He was there for inspection, and at stake was the future of the entire Nazi rocket program. If it were shut down, all the men, including the guards on duty, would be sent to the Eastern Front.

Todt handed over his papers. "Heil Hitler!"

"Heil Hitler!" the guard said, saluting once again.

The gates swung open as the dogs barked, their hot breath visible in the frigid dawn.

Werner von Braun was sitting at his desk when the call came through. "Herr Todt is here, sir," his secretary announced. Her voice had an edge of panic to it. Everyone at the complex knew that all of the rockets had been crashing; they couldn't get off the launch pad without exploding, or they combusted in midair, or they veered, always to the right, to crash in the forest or the sea.

Von Braun's face was slick with perspiration. This was the day. He had everything to lose. "Thank you, Frau Meyer."

On the credenza behind him were models of rockets, each painstakingly crafted, each larger than the next. Boy's toys for a boyish-looking man. Next to them were a framed portrait of Adolf Hitler and a small Bakelite clock, ticking loudly.

Von Braun had a smooth, wide face, thick chestnut hair on the long side and worn combed back, and a crackling energy. At the age of just nearly thirty, he was the world's top rocket scientist and the reason they all were here, on this remote island just off the coast of the Baltic Sea. There were no signs, of course, for security reasons, but his kingdom was the Peenemünde Research Center on the island of Usedom, Germany. The research had grown so much in the past years that a small town had been built to support all the workers and their families. In addition to the rocket and fuel-making areas, there was a village train, shops, even a social club.

Von Braun loved rockets, and his goal, ever since he was a boy, had been to put a man on the moon. Now, all his boyhood dreams were coming true. Hitler had funded the rocket program to build a large-scale ballistic missile to destroy and demoralize the British. Von Braun's rockets, the Nazis hoped, would decide the outcome of the war.

Von Braun rose, wiped his sweaty palms

on his jacket, and went to greet Todt.

The rocket was enormous, over thirteen tons. It stood nearly forty feet high and five feet wide, covered in black and white panels, and was the world's first large-scale, liquid-propelled rocket. Men in dark coveralls and heavy black boots who worked in the massive rocket's shadow looked like ants as they made last-minute adjustments.

Von Braun, Todt, and other Nazi scientists and officers gathered in a concrete bunker under packed earth, a safe distance away, to observe the launch.

"We call this one *Washington, D.C.,*" von Braun told Todt.

Todt glanced at him. "I thought these were for use on London and British production sites?"

"For now." Von Braun's eyes were alight. "Tomorrow — who knows? We've started naming our rockets — *New York, Philadelphia,* and *Boston,* too."

While the workers ran for cover, the two men watched through periscopes as orange flames shot from the rocket's base. There was an earsplitting rumble and vibrations that rattled their very bones as the flames ignited. Against all rules of credibility, the *Washington, D.C.,* rose, slowly, slowly, then faster and faster. As it climbed higher, von Braun whispered, "It's broken the sound barrier!"

All at once, without warning, the rocket veered right — off course. It rolled and tumbled, finally crashing to the shore in a red fireball.

Von Braun's shoulders slumped.

One of the engineers said, "Sorry, Herr von Braun."

"Shut up," he hissed. Then, to himself, "The engines are underpowered. We still can't control them in flight."

"It's a fragile and expensive weapon." He heard the words inches from his ear.

He looked to Todt, and the two men locked eyes. Von Braun said, "Sir, we believe a rocket can reach the speed of five thousand kilometers per hour in only thirty seconds. Once we fix the rudders . . ."

Todt clapped the younger man on the back. "We will continue to fund the project, Herr von Braun. But not forever. I will be back before the new year to see your progress."

Von Braun's face paled, and the scientists and engineers looked down at their polished boots. "That's not very much time!"

"Yes, I know," Todt agreed. "But your project here is excessively expensive and taking a huge percentage of our resources — without anything we can use." His eyes narrowed. "And we need more men to fight in the East." He raised his hand. "Heil Hitler!"

Von Braun straightened and lifted his chin. "Heil Hitler!"

CHAPTER FIVE

The next morning, Maggie took John to a diner for breakfast. As bells pinged, a waitress called to the kitchen, "Two eggs, sunny-side up!" A radio in the corner played a tinny version of Glenn Miller's "Jingle Bells."

"There's so much food," John said in awe, surveying the Formica-topped table in front of them, piled high with plates. "I don't think I've ever seen so many eggs in one place in my entire life." It was hot and close in the diner, which smelled of grease and damp wool coats. Maggie had ordered for them — scrambled eggs, bacon, orange juice, and coffee with cream. A glass dispenser full to the brim with sugar stood on each table.

She nodded, taking a forkful of eggs, ignoring the din of conversation around her. All the booths, tables, and even the seats at the counter were full. "It's insane, isn't it?

Look, about last night —"

"I understand," John interrupted, reaching for his mug. "Mrs. R needed you."

"Well," Maggie continued, looking up through her eyelashes. "Maybe tonight?"

David slid into the booth with them before John could reply. "Knew I'd find you two here! Concierge at the Mayflower said he told you about this place."

Maggie and John exchanged a look of *so much for privacy.*

"Merciful Minerva, it's a real pea souper out there!" David declared, referring to the fog. He shrugged out of his coat and slapped a newspaper on the table. The headline was THE QUESTION OF JAPANESE AMERICANS.

"Old Man gave me the morning off, so I thought I'd tootle around Washington. Oh, heavens and little fishes, is that bacon? And so much of it! Mind if I have some?" He grabbed for John's strips without waiting for an answer. John smacked his hand, causing the strips to fall back to the plate.

Maggie grinned. "I thought you were Jewish."

"Not *that* Jewish," David said as he snatched a slice from John's plate and chewed, eyes squeezed shut in ecstasy. "Ambrosia! Food of the gods!" A waitress stopped at their table, her hips round beneath her uniform. Her bottle-blond hair was coming loose from under her gingham cap, a yellow pencil stuck behind one ear.

"Wattayawant, hon?" she asked, withdrawing the pencil.

David looked helplessly at Maggie.

Maggie patted his arm. "She asked you if you wanted anything. For yourself, that is. And she called you 'honey.' "

"Oh!" He looked to the menu. It was enormous. "Please tell her I'll need a minute."

"Tell her yourself!"

David looked up. "I. Need. A. Minute. Please," he said to the waitress. "Thank. You."

Maggie looked up at her. "Thanks."

"No problem, sweetie." The waitress leaned down a little closer to Maggie. "My brother's a bit slow like that, too. Bless their hearts."

Maggie suppressed a giggle. David, deep into study of the menu, didn't notice. "Jumping Jupiter, did you know they've crossed off hamburgers and written in 'liberty patties'? And they're calling spaghetti 'freedom noodles'? And what is this 'French toast'?"

"It's similar to *pain perdu*," Maggie said.

"I'll have that!" he declared.

"Great," Maggie said; she ordered. "And do you want coffee or tea?"

"*Don't* get the tea," John muttered.

"I'll have coffee, then — that Whitmanesque beverage of energy and freedom!"

"A coffee and French toast please," Maggie told the waitress. "Do you want bacon or sausage?" she asked David.

"You can have either?" He was shocked.

Maggie knew her friend's voracious appetite. "He'll have both."

"This isn't America," he declared, grabbing the creamer and flipping the lid. "This is *heaven*! Maggie, do you think there's any chance we could go to some sort of sporting event? Maybe a baseball game?"

She shook her head. "Baseball season's over, I'm afraid. As a Bostonian, I'm a loyal Red Sox fan. And I'm sorry to say that the Yankees won this year — beat the Brooklyn Dodgers."

"Won? Won what?"

"The World Series, of course."

David knit his brows. "Do any other countries play in this so-called World Series?"

"Er, no," Maggie admitted.

"I see. All right then — are there any sports we *can* see now? This so-called American football? Hockey?"

"Football's over, too. The Bears won."

"The Bears!" He rubbed his hands together. "I love it!"

"It's Christmas," Maggie explained. "So it's still hockey season. I'm a Boston Bruins fan, I'll have you know — but there aren't any games this week."

David looked disappointed.

"If you're keen on going to a sporting event, I'm seeing Aunt Edith on Christmas Eve day — holidays with her often feel like ten rounds in the ring," Maggie announced. "I'll be going before the Prime Minister's speech — I've already cleared it with him. We're meeting at Peacock Alley at the Willard for tea. Would you care to join?"

"As tempting as the offer is," David said, "I'll be with the Prime, as they seem to call him here — but I'll do my best. John, I'll see to it you can go." Though they were still best friends, David did everything possible to remind John who was now in charge.

"Oh, thank you so very, very much," John managed.

"Oh," Maggie said, realizing. "I need to get her a Christmas present!"

"Yes!" David said, as the waitress put down his plate and coffee mug with a bang. "Shopping! What fun! There are things here in shops that one can actually purchase!"

John sighed. "Last night I was invited to a party."

Maggie lifted an eyebrow. "Really? By whom?"

"Some ridiculously rich woman and her entourage. Of course I'll get out of it." He reached for Maggie's hand under the table. They clasped hands, smiling at each other.

"Oh, for Saint Peter's sake, stop it, both of you," David growled through a mouthful of sausage. "You'll put me off my breakfast."

They ate in genial silence, then David glanced up at the clock. "Suffering Sukra! Come on, we must dash! Get the bill, won't you, old chap?" he said to John.

John went to settle up at the cash register, and Maggie followed. As he paid, he murmured in her ear, "Tonight."

She reached for his hand.

"Come on, lovebirds!" David was at the diner's front door. "Chop, chop! Mustn't be late on our first day!"

Outside in the dreary, cold mist, a Salvation Army officer in dark blue uniform rang a bell and called for donations while a brass quartet played Vera Lynn's "The Little Boy That Santa Claus Forgot" behind her. Several colored men wearing wool caps leaned up against the brick wall of the alley, eating egg sandwiches. A young girl with coppery skin and a worn coat passed out flyers. "You can save an innocent life!" she called, as an exhausted-looking young mother pushed a carriage and a gray-haired man in a tweed hat walked his pug.

"Why are those men eating in the alley? Why aren't they inside?" David asked Maggie.

"Segregation," she responded, pointing at the WHITES ONLY sign in the window, next to an American flag. "They order at the kitchen door there, then eat in the alley. It's not so bad in Boston, where I'm from."

"Do you — they — you — have segregation in the North?" David's awe of America was evaporating.

They were interrupted by the girl, who handed Maggie a flyer. "Please come," the girl said, looking up at the trio with large eyes. "Hear Miz Andi and Mother Cotton speak about Wendell Cotton, and help them save him from the electric chair."

Maggie looked down at the thin piece of paper as David took several. "Thank you, miss."

John read as they walked through the polluted mist. "The electric chair?"

David shuddered. "I had no idea you Yanks were so savage."

"Yes, the death penalty. And Britain has it

135

as well." Maggie sighed. "Again, I'm from Massachusetts. It's not used as frequently there, and many of us hope they'll do away with it for good soon."

"But it's used more often here?"

Maggie glanced at the flyer and frowned. "In Virginia, where this man is scheduled to be executed, yes."

"In 'thirty-eight, the issue of the end of capital punishment was brought before Parliament," John noted. "A clause within the Criminal Justice Bill called for an experimental five-year suspension of the death penalty. When war broke out, the bill was postponed."

"What was Mr. Churchill's position on it?" Maggie asked.

"I've heard him say, 'Contemplate that if Hitler falls into our hands we shall certainly put him to death,' " John responded.

David added, in his best Churchill impression: " 'And the American electric chair, no doubt, will be available to us on lend-lease.' "

Overnight, the White House had been transformed into a winter wonderland. Walking in, Maggie, John, and David were met by the delicious smell of evergreens. A tub of box trees had been set up on the portico, while two tall pine trees stood guard on each side of the front door.

Inside, almost every surface was covered in garlands and greenery. All the windows of the lower floor had wreaths, and the front hall was resplendent with red poinsettias in carved stone tubs. The Blue Room and East Room, as well as the West Hall upstairs, boasted Christmas trees decked out with colored lights and shining tin ornaments. But the two world leaders — exhausted by their late night's work — were still asleep.

Their staffs were wide awake, though, and hard at work. In the Prime Minister's map room, David went over the P.M.'s "box." Momentarily free, Maggie read the flyer.

WENDELL COTTON is innocent!
Wendell Cotton is in Virginia today under sentence of death!
ANDREA MARTIN, a well-known writer and liberal leader, will speak.
Tuesday, December 23,
at 8 o'clock in the evening
Metropolitan Baptist Church,
1400 1st Street NW
(at the intersection of 1st and P)
ADMISSION FREE

There was a bellow through the thick oak

door. "Miss Hope! Hope! I must have Hope!"

Maggie recognized the voice instantly. "Coming, Mr. Churchill!" she called, scooping up the portable noiseless typewriter and taking it with her to the Rose Bedroom.

The P.M. was sitting up in bed, dressed in his favorite monogrammed silk pajamas and emerald silk robe embroidered with dragons. The satin-covered down quilt and linen bedclothes were hopelessly tangled, and newspapers littered the floor.

"Sit!" he barked at Maggie.

"Sir, I wanted to tell you —"

He ignored her and chewed on his unlit cigar. "For the War Cabinet," he said without a preamble, and began to dictate: "There was general agreement that if Hitler was held in Russia he must try something else, and that the most probable line was Spain and Portugal en route to North Africa . . ."

Maggie's typing was rusty, but she'd had a chance to practice on the trip across the Atlantic. And now it felt just like old times, when she'd typed for him on her noiseless Remington at Number Ten during the Blitz.

Churchill lit the cigar, inhaled, then continued: "There was general agreement that it was vital to forestall the Germans. . . .

The President said that he was anxious that American land forces should give their support as quickly as possible wherever they could be most helpful, and favored the idea of a plan to move into North Africa being prepared . . . with or without the Vichy French's invitation. It was agreed to remit the study of the project to Staffs. . . ."

When finished, he waved a hand, blurring the blue smoke. "Gimme," he demanded.

She handed the paper to him.

He read it over. "Give it to Mr. Greene and have him send it as a telegram." He looked at her. "How did it go last night?"

Maggie swallowed. "Sir, I went with Mrs. Roosevelt to Blanche Balfour's apartment. The young woman was dead — apparently committed suicide in the bathtub. She left a note — *allegedly* left a note — saying that Mrs. Roosevelt . . ." Maggie wasn't sure how to put it. "Mrs. Roosevelt's, er . . . attentions . . . had made her uncomfortable . . ."

There was a long moment as the Prime Minister's cigar burned. "What? What's that?"

This was no time for delicacy. "In the note, she alleges that Mrs. Roosevelt made sexual advances to her. And there's something else, sir. When I say I took the note, I mean I took a notepad that still had the imprint of a note. The note itself was missing. And no, it wasn't in the trash."

Churchill stood, his ankles thin and white, covered in ginger and white hairs. "Bloody hell!"

"Yes, sir. Someone must have snuck in after Blanche had written it and taken it. For what purpose, I don't know. But it hasn't been released to the press. Yet. Whoever took it either meant to protect the First Lady. Or to use it at some point for blackmail."

The P.M. nodded. "Two quite different scenarios."

"I called the police," Maggie continued, "anonymously, of course — and took the notepad. We left, and later I burned it in the fireplace."

The Prime Minister paced in front of the bedroom's mantel. "You did well, Miss Hope."

"Thank you, sir. And I don't think there's any truth in it, sir. The allegation, that is."

Churchill turned to the fireplace, watching the reddish orange flames dance. "Hmmm. And the actual note is, as far as we know, still at large."

"Yes, sir. Which is troubling. And I'm also concerned about the First Lady's enemies.

She has plenty, she says, starting with Mr. Hoover and ending with the Ku Klux Klan."

"Those damn fools who run around in white bedsheets?"

"The same, sir. And I came across a flyer for a rally supporting a man named Wendell Cotton's execution. Mrs. Roosevelt has been working to try to stop the execution. Maybe . . ."

The P.M. sighed. "If the First Lady is suspected of any impropriety, especially now, while I am in the United States, it will deflect attention from what the President and I must achieve. She would be discredited, he would be discredited, and then I — *Britain* — would be discredited by association as well. We are at an extremely perilous juncture in our relationship with the Americans — and the Roosevelts."

"Yes, sir."

The Prime Minister fixed his unwavering blue gaze on her. "And, what do you advise, Miss Hope?"

Maggie cleared her throat. She'd been up all night, thinking about it. "I'd start by investigating Blanche. What sorts of people she was involved with, including any ties to those supporting the Wendell Cotton execution — those who would want Mrs. Roosevelt silenced. I mean, it looks like an open-

and-shut case. But then, where's the note? It makes no sense. I'd like to investigate — there's something" — she tried to find the right words — "not right about this situation. And I need to find out what it's about, to protect Mrs. Roosevelt." She tipped her head in Churchill's direction. "And you, and Britain, by extension."

The P.M. nodded. "Good, good. I shall lend-lease you indefinitely to the First Lady then. Report to Mr. Greene while you're here, but I'll let the First Lady know that if she needs you, all she has to do is let you know. Now, off with you." He waved a hand.

"Yes, sir."

When Maggie reached the door, however, he called. "Miss Hope!"

"Yes, Mr. Churchill?"

"If we're to win this war — which I believe we shall — we *must* have the Americans' undivided support. We can't have a scandal distracting them." He stabbed the air with his cigar. "It is crucial to resolve this situation."

"Yes, sir. Thank you, sir."

As she turned to leave, there was a knock on the Prime Minister's bedroom door. "Come in!" he bellowed.

The massive Mr. Fields entered, blocking Maggie's way. "Now, Fields," Churchill rumbled, "we had a lovely dinner last night, but I have a few orders for you. We want to leave here as friends, right? So I need you to listen. There is to be no talking or whistling in the corridors — do you understand? That's of the utmost importance. And I must have a tumbler of sherry in my room before breakfast, then a few glasses of scotch and soda before lunch. And French champagne and ninety-year-old brandy before I go to sleep at night."

"Yes, sir," replied Fields, in his burnished bass voice.

"Breakfast," Churchill instructed, as he zipped up the dark blue jumpsuit he called his siren suit, "must include something hot — eggs, bacon or ham, and toast — and two kinds of fruit. I also expect prompt delivery of the red government dispatch boxes, coming from the British Embassy."

"Yes, sir." Fields bowed and stepped out of the doorframe, holding the door open for Maggie as she ducked past him. She shot him a quick smile of thanks, which he acknowledged with a raised eyebrow.

Maggie set the typewriter down on the nearest desk so she could hand David the typed pages. Fields passed behind her, gracefully moving around another, much smaller man who was dressed as a footman in scarlet livery, breeches, and white gloves. "A message for Flight Lieutenant John Sterling," the newcomer announced, proffering a gold-crested invitation on a silver platter.

John looked up from his work, annoyed. "I'm Sterling."

"Then this is for you, sir," said the footman. He walked over to John and presented the heavy envelope. John took it, aware all eyes were on him.

David whistled through his teeth. "All right. Get on with it, then."

John opened it and read the calligraphy. "It's an invitation to a party," he told them. "At Mrs. Regina Winthrop Wolffe's house."

"May I tell Madame you will be attending?" the footman asked.

"I'll — I'll need to ask the Prime Minister first."

"Of course," said the man in red. He turned on his heel to go. "I'll check in with you later today, sir."

"Oh, fantastic," John muttered as the man left.

Maggie had seen the exchange from across the room. "What's that about?"

"That ridiculous American socialite I was telling you about. Of course I won't go."

The First Lady popped her head in the

door. "Good morning," she managed, her face drawn. "I trust everyone slept well?"

The trio snapped to attention. "Yes, ma'am."

"Excellent," said Mrs. Roosevelt, with a smile that never quite reached her eyes. "I'm sorry our weather isn't better for you — all this damp and fog. Miss Hope, when you have a moment, I'd like to speak with you."

Maggie could only imagine the night the First Lady must have had. "Yes, ma'am. Right away, ma'am."

When Maggie stepped into Eleanor Roosevelt's study, a police detective was there, in plain clothes. He had black hair closely cropped, the body of a football player gone to seed, and eyes surrounded by deep crow's-feet.

"Miss Hope, this is Detective Timothy Farrell," Mrs. Roosevelt said. "Detective Farrell, Miss Maggie Hope, the Prime Minister's typist. Detective Farrell has been kind enough to come and inform me in person that Miss Balfour — Blanche —" Mrs. Roosevelt's voice broke.

"I'm sorry to say that Miss Balfour has been found dead," said the detective to Maggie in a gravelly voice, his oily hair gleaming in the lamp's light. Dandruff dusted the shoulders of his jacket, and he fiddled with the gold wedding band on his left hand. "Suicide."

"Oh," Maggie said, her mind whirring. "I never met her, of course — but I'm so sorry."

Detective Farrell handed her his card. "In case you come across anything," he said. He looked to Mrs. Roosevelt. "If there's anything else we can do for you, ma'am —"

"No, thank you." The First Lady's mouth was set in a grim line. "You've done your duty, Detective. Of course I'll write to the poor girl's mother immediately, to express my condolences."

As the detective left, Mrs. Roosevelt half sat, half fell onto a chair.

"In light of what's happened, ma'am," Maggie said, "I would be glad to offer my services for the duration. I've asked Mr. Churchill, and he says it's fine with him — all you have to do is come find me in his office if and when you need me."

Mrs. Roosevelt looked up. "Services as a typist? Or something more specialized, Miss Hope?"

Maggie met her gaze. "Whatever you need, ma'am."

The First Lady stared at her for a moment. Then she sighed and gestured for

Maggie to sit. "Thank you."

"Ma'am, was there a specific reason Blanche would want to cause a scandal for you? At this time? What could she have gained?"

The First Lady looked out the window, to the leaden sky. "If I'm discredited, Franklin's discredited. The country will be distracted by scandal. And the war effort will suffer."

Exactly what Mr. Churchill's worried about, Maggie thought.

"And who would benefit?"

"Any number of people. Franklin's hated by the so-called aristocracy. They think he's betrayed them — much of the South, who think he's too friendly with the coloreds and the Jews — he was hated by the isolationists, but since the attack on Pearl Harbor, they seem to have come around . . ."

Maggie nodded. "Tell me about Blanche."

"Blanche was a debutante, but her family lost all their money in the Depression, like so many. She was selling perfume in a department store before she came to us. Tommy suggested her. Then I interviewed her and found her perfectly competent. I'd hoped working at the White House would be a step up for her. And I'd thought perhaps here she could learn some additional skills."

"How long did she work for you?"

"About a month."

"What work did she do for you?"

"Really just typing up the 'My Day' columns. Running errands. Filing. You saw what she was working on last night."

"I looked through her papers last night, but may I see your correspondence from the time Blanche was working for you also?"

"Of course." Mrs. Roosevelt went to her desk and pulled out a thick manila file. Her pale face was grim. "One of the things I'm involved with is the case of Wendell Cotton. Have you heard of it?" She turned back to the younger woman.

"I have, in fact."

"On the surface it's a simple story — a young colored sharecropper, Wendell Cotton, shot and killed his landlord in a dispute over distribution of the shares of the crop. There's no doubt Wendell did the shooting, but it's unclear if it was premeditated or manslaughter. Or self-defense. After a quick trial, by a jury of white sharecroppers, Wendell was sentenced to death by electric chair.

"Now normally the story would have ended there, but it became a matter of national concern when Wendell fled to Ohio after the shooting to avoid capture — and the story was noticed by key organizations, such as the Workers Defense League and the National Association for the Advancement of Colored People. As they investigated, it became apparent that the incident involved more than a simple — if fatal — shooting.

"Wendell's a typical victim of planter justice, which has ground down the poor people of Southern states — both white and colored — for generations, Miss Hope. He was tried in a court presided over by a judge who made no attempt to conceal his anti-Negro bias, and condemned by a jury consisting of a businessman, a carpenter, and ten landlords. His peers, sharecroppers, had no place on the jury list, which was made up only of people who paid the dollar fifty Virginia state poll tax."

"I see," Maggie said.

"Wendell's come to personify all those to whom democracy is denied in this country. He's now a symbol of the deep-seated racial and economic injustice that still poisons our society."

"What's your exact involvement in the Wendell Cotton case?"

The First Lady rifled through the file. "Wendell's lawyer is at an impasse. At this point, there's no way to stop the young man's execution, except by a pardon from the Governor of Virginia. And since the Governor is — shall we say — traditional, Wendell's lawyer thought if Franklin asked the Governor to intercede, that might help."

"And did the President speak to the Governor?"

The First Lady pressed her lips together. "Franklin — the President — does not want to get involved."

"But —" Maggie tried to temper the look of shock on her face. "Why not?"

"Legally, the President has no authority over the case. But the Workers Defense League felt that if he could appoint a commissioner, the Governor of Virginia would feel obliged to postpone Wendell's execution pending the committee's deliberation and, at best, recommend a plea for clemency."

"That sounds reasonable."

"It does, doesn't it? But Franklin feels he's done enough with his support for Negroes through his economic programs. And now, with the war, he's wary of alienating powerful Southern politicians. So he's avoiding any direct involvement in any potentially sensitive racial issues, such as the federal anti-lynching law and attacks on disenfranchisement. And since the attack on Pearl Harbor, Franklin feels the country has more pressing concerns."

Maggie gnawed her lip. "And who is Miss Andrea Martin?"

"Andrea Martin — Andi — is a young colored woman. She's about your age, maybe a bit older. Born here in D.C., but raised by her aunt in Durham. She wanted to go to the law school at the University of North Carolina and they rejected her application — not a surprise, unfortunately, and her rejection did have the benefit of garnering a great deal of media attention. Now she's set her sights on Howard — although that won't be an easy road either, I should think. Black women have what Andi calls the 'Jane Crow problem' — all of the issues of being colored in our society and then the additional challenge of being female as well."

Maggie nodded.

"Andi was determined to attend a nonsegregated college for her undergraduate education, and she did, graduating from Hunter, in New York. After that, she worked with the National Urban League, selling subscriptions to its journal, *Opportunity.* She protested against segregated seating on buses last year and was arrested — if you can believe it — and jailed just south of Petersburg, Virginia."

"My goodness."

"Yes, she appealed with the help of an NAACP lawyer, but lost and spent time in jail — about a month, until the Workers Defense League paid the fines and got her released. After that, Andi wanted to pay the WDL back, so she took a job with them in New York. And then the Wendell Cotton case came up." The First Lady smoothed back her hair. "She was sent to Virginia with the WDL to help Wendell. She's been raising funds for Wendell's defense and trying to get as much public support as possible."

"And how do you know Miss Martin?"

"She sent me a letter months ago, telling me of Wendell's situation, and asking me to look into it. I did, and since then we've stayed in touch. Of course, it's tricky. I'm not the President, after all, and even he sometimes has his hands tied when it comes to the good ol' boy networks of the South. So I wrote to Governor King of Virginia personally, saying, 'Please look into the case and see that the young man has a fair trial.' It might not seem like much, but I felt stronger words would prejudice the Governor the other way."

Maggie nodded. "Do you have a copy of

the letter you wrote to Miss Martin?"

"Let's see," Mrs. Roosevelt said, going through the file on her lap. "Ah, here it is, yes — *'I've received a great many letters about Wendell Cotton,'* " she read. " *'If the facts stated by his defense lawyer are true, I hope very much that you will be able to go over the case very carefully, as it has created strong feelings among both white and colored people, and may not have only national but international implications.'* "

"Quite politic. And have you met with his lawyer?"

"No, he asked, but I felt that would be too much. And I would not allow the letter I sent to the Governor to be made public. Despite all that, however, the *Village Bee,* oh, let's see" — Mrs. Roosevelt went through the file again and pulled out a newspaper clipping — "ah yes, here we are: *'The First Lady has made gratuitous intrusion into matters that don't concern her. Let the President be warned that if he doesn't restrain his wife's sociological impulses he risks losing the support of the people of the South.'* " Mrs. Roosevelt blinked and pulled out another sheet of paper. "And this is the original letter Miss Martin wrote to me." She handed it to Maggie, who read:

MRS. FRANKLIN D. ROOSEVELT
THE WHITE HOUSE
WASHINGTON, D.C.

Dear Mrs. Roosevelt:

We respectfully urge and petition you to ask the President to appoint a Commission of inquiry to investigate the case of Wendell Cotton, the Negro sharecropper of Bloxom, Virginia. He is sentenced to die on December 28, 1941.

We believe it will be a national catastrophe if Wendell Cotton goes to his death, when millions of his fellow citizens are unconvinced that he was tried by a jury of his peers.

Your intervention, and that of the President, will help restore the badly shaken faith of our Negro minority in American democracy.

The best of the American people know that it is Hitler and his fascists who must be destroyed. Not Negro sharecroppers goaded into killing in defense of their own lives.

It is a dangerous situation. Did Wendell Cotton receive a fair trial? Is he being electrocuted because he's a Negro? This is the crux of our case.

IT IS IMPOSSIBLE TO EXAGGER-

ATE THE HARMFUL EFFECT ON RACE RELATIONS THAT THE EXECUTION OF WENDELL COTTON COULD BRING.

Thank you.

Yours sincerely,
Andrea Martin
Workers Defense League

As Maggie looked up, the First Lady was watching. "As incredible as it may seem, Miss Hope, the execution of a Negro sharecropper may lessen the chance the U.S. and allies have to win this war. I'm planning on attending a rally for Wendell tonight and then meeting with Miss Martin afterwards. Would you be interested in coming with me? It's after the Prime Minister's press conference."

"Yes, ma'am." *Could this be the link? Wendell Cotton's execution?* If Blanche Balfour was in favor of it and was trying to cause trouble for those attempting to have the execution stayed, could that be a motive for her allegations? Maybe Miss Martin knew something about Blanche — maybe Blanche had threatened her, or some other supporter of Wendell. Maggie wondered if she could speak with Miss Martin about Blanche after her talk. Then she remembered John and their plans. *Well, we've waited this long — it's just one more night.* She realized then that she felt the slightest bit relieved. *Are things going too fast?* "Thank you, ma'am. I'd be honored to join you."

At the Washington Office of the Governor of Virginia, on North Capitol Street, Byrd Prentiss flashed a wide smirk to the receptionist. Prentiss was the personification of Southern charm — young, tall, lanky, cleft chin, and a face just five degrees left of handsome. His muscles were earned hunting and playing polo, his tan from days out on his boat, *The Blackjack.* And he had the "good ol' boy" persona down — with just a hint of a drawl, a hearty handshake, a penchant for lavish parties liberally fueled by bourbon.

Prentiss had been the campaign manager for Governor King. On paper he was the perfect Southern aristocrat, son of a Virginia senator and one of the Sons of Confederate Veterans. He'd graduated from Virginia Military Institute and the University of Virginia, then the university's law school. Supported by his father's cronies, he'd tried for his father's seat.

And he would have won, if certain unsa-

156

vory personal details hadn't come to light. Details such as a fondness for cocaine, a fortune lost by gambling, and the frequenting of certain brothels.

Then there was the dead prostitute and Prentiss's inability to provide an alibi. And while old money could certainly silence the scandal, he couldn't continue his run — and so he left the campaign "for personal reasons." After a suitable time away from politics, he began to work for Campbell King's gubernatorial campaign.

In his second-floor office, he sat at a massive desk that had once belonged to Patrick Henry. Behind him was a large window looking out over Capitol Street. Mist blurred the edges of the view, bleeding away color. On the walls were mounted stag heads with glassy black eyes, a Hessian sword and scabbard, and a torn and singed Confederate battle flag hung in a gold rope-and-bead frame.

Prentiss called out to his pretty, young secretary. "Get me Governor King, won't you, doll?" He had gone through any number of bright and beautiful typists, graduates of the Madeira School, and called them all "doll."

"Yes, sir." She was young, slender to the point of fragility, with pale eyes and hair so blond it was almost white. She shivered in her thin dress; Prentiss didn't like his girls covered up in cardigans.

"And close the door for me, will you, doll?"

"Yes, sir."

There was the usual static and a few clicks on the line. "Hold for the Governor," said a switchboard operator; then came King's gravelly voice: "What?"

"Governor," Prentiss began, "the situation's been handled."

Governor King's tone was clipped. "Good."

"May I suggest you keep a close eye on the papers, sir? A certain scandalous letter that we've discussed will be making news any day now."

"Excellent. This should keep our friend Kissing Fish out of the Cotton execution. We *need* this execution. If I'm to look Presidential, we can't have this bungled."

"Yes, sir. Anything else, sir?"

"No." And before Prentiss could say any more, he heard a few more clicks on the line and then the connection was severed.

In 1941, the Executive Branch of the government of the United States of America was engaged in covert wiretapping.

The taps, mostly — but not exclusively — on telephones of foreigners from Japan and Germany, were carried out despite prohibitions by Congress and the Supreme Court. The legality of wiretapping was being debated publicly by the legislative and judicial branches, and there were any number of letters to the editor on the subject in all the major papers.

Despite the controversy, President Roosevelt had long been working on authorizing a program for the "surveillance of communications" within the United States, ostensibly seeking to prevent acts of domestic espionage. The President himself ignored the statute that forbade wiretapping and continued the program regardless of opposition from several high-level judges.

The President had issued a secret memorandum to Attorney General Robert H. Jackson in 1940 stating: *You are, therefore, authorized and directed in such cases as you may approve, after investigation of the need in each case, to authorize the necessary investigating agents that they are at liberty to secure information by listening devices directed to the conversation or other communications of persons suspected of subversive activities against the Government of the United States, including suspected spies.*

And so, in a small former cedar closet, on the third floor of the White House, Samuel Reynolds, an aide to Frank Cole, put down the telephone receiver. A tap on Governor King's office in Virginia had been authorized first, then one on Byrd Prentiss's office in Washington and, based on information gathered, on Blanche Balfour's telephone line.

Sam used an electrical recording device called a Dictograph to record Byrd Prentiss and Governor King's conversations. The Dictograph was a wooden console studded with buttons and dials, with a black handset on top. Inside the wooden console was a highly sensitive receiver, which allowed the Dictograph to record telephone conversations.

Sam was a recent Princeton alumnus, and his father, also a Tiger as well as the owner of the *New Jersey Eagle,* was a longtime friend of Frank Cole's, who had gotten him this job after he'd graduated the previous year. The young man was painfully thin and took to wearing multiple layers of sweaters in the winter both to give himself extra bulk and to stay warm. It was drafty and cold in the storage rooms of the White House, now taken over by any number of surveillance activities, and Sam found that a wool union suit and an extra pair of socks helped.

Just under the roof of the White House, Sam could hear the scratch of squirrels' claws as they scrabbled back and forth over him. He listened once again to the conversation and tried to piece together what it was about. Kissing Fish was Governor King's code name for Eleanor Roosevelt. And, of course, the Cotton execution was in the news. But a "scandalous letter"? That sounded bad.

Since the conversation had referenced the First Lady and the potential for public disgrace, Sam realized it was something to tell Frank Cole about. But not by a memo or telephone — of all people, he knew better than that. He'd take a taxi to Cole's office at the paper and deliver the news himself.

Sam's thin hands reached for his trilby hat and camel-hair coat, and a black-and-orange striped Princeton scarf on the hook behind the door. "This is not going to go well," he muttered as he put on his coat and hat and wrapped the scarf about his long, thin neck. Whenever he brought bad news about Kissing Fish, Cole was prone to yelling, his different-colored eyes bulging, the veins in his forehead throbbing.

He didn't want to go, but what choice did

he have? "Not going to go well at all," Sam muttered as he closed and then locked the closet door.

CHAPTER SIX

The P.M.'s press conference took place in what was known as the Press Closet, a small room just outside the entrance to the West Wing. The official reason for the conference was the formation of the Office of Defense Transportation under Joseph Eastman to coordinate the nation's rail, road, and water traffic. But rumors of Winston Churchill's appearance in the Capitol had already spread like wildfire through the press corps.

The Press Closet was a cramped and cluttered space, with tiny desks and battered chairs, the wood blackened by cigarette burns, and the walls and ceiling stained yellow by smoke. It reeked of tobacco, sweat, and whiskey. But despite the shabbiness, the atmosphere under the low ceiling was electric.

Roosevelt and Churchill were already in place. The debonair President wore a pin-striped suit with a black satin mourning band around his arm in honor of his late mother. Next to him sat the Prime Minister, his round face ruddy, in a navy blue suit with a blue-and-white-polka-dot bow tie, chewing on his cigar. Harry Hopkins, his long face drawn and sallow, stood to one side, leaning against a wall for support. Frank Cole stood beside him, his different-colored eyes inscrutable behind thick glasses.

Maggie and David stood against the stained wall as well. As the journalists all mumbled and smoked, the energy grew even more intense. Maggie was glad to see that Churchill still looked serene.

"We can't see!" came a shout from the back from Ron Kantor of *The New York Times.*

Tom O'Brian was beside him with his camera. "Shouldn't that be 'We still can't see, Mr. Prime Minister'?" Ron only smiled.

President Roosevelt looked to Churchill, beamed, and nodded. "Would you mind standing, dear friend? So those in the back can get a good look at you?"

The Prime Minister stood.

"Still can't see!" chorused the voices from the back of the Press Closet.

And so Mr. Churchill climbed onto his

chair, gesturing broadly and waving his cigar.

"Oh, dear Lord," David whispered to Maggie, tensed and ready to come to the rescue should the P.M. falter or fall.

But he did not.

And once they got a glimpse of him, the assembled reporters and photographers applauded and cheered.

"Go ahead. Shoot," the Prime Minister called grandly from his perch atop the chair, gesturing with his cigar.

One of the journalists in the back thrust up a hand. "Mr. Prime Minister, isn't Singapore the key to the whole situation out there?"

Churchill nodded — but, as a seasoned politician, refused to be led down that path. "The key to the whole situation is the resolute manner in which the British and American democracies are going to throw themselves into the conflict."

As he answered, the tension lightened. The P.M., schooled in the House of Commons, was used to public questioning, and the crowd felt his confidence.

A silver-haired man in the front row raised a hand. "Mr. Minister, could you tell us what you think of conditions within Germany — the morale?"

The P.M.'s blue eyes flashed. "Well, I always have a feeling that one of these days we might get a windfall coming from that quarter, but I don't think we ought to count on it. We need to go on as if they were keeping on as bad as they are, or as good as they are. And then — one of these days — as we did in the last war — we may wake up and find we've run short of Huns."

Laughter filled the smoke-filled room. Another reporter yelled out: "Do you think the war has turned in our favor in the last month or so?"

" 'Our' favor," David muttered. "Only been in the war two weeks and already it's 'our . . .' "

Maggie put a finger to her lips in warning.

But the P.M. beamed. "I can't describe the feeling of relief with which I find Russia victorious, and the United States and Great Britain now standing side by side. It is incredible to anyone who lived through the lonely months of nineteen forty. Thank God."

There was a murmur of approval. "Mr. Minister, can you tell us when you think we'll lick those boys?"

Churchill looked down to Roosevelt, confused. David groaned. "He means *beat*!"

a deep voice chimed in helpfully.

"If we manage it well," Churchill said with a nod and wink, "it will take only half as long as if we manage it badly."

Another roar of laughter, then, "How long, sir, would it take if we managed it badly?"

"That has not been revealed to me at this moment." The Prime Minister shook his head and wagged a finger. "We don't have to manage it badly."

"Mr. Prime Minister, do you have any doubt of the ultimate victory?"

Churchill stood even straighter on his perch and raised his chin. "I have no doubt whatsoever," he growled.

Tom called out in a clear tenor voice, "What about a Christmas message for the American people?"

"I'm told I'm to give that on Christmas Eve," the P.M. replied with a cheeky grin, "so I won't give it away beforehand."

Throughout the press conference, Mr. Roosevelt glowed with pride. When it was over, and all the requisite photographs had been taken, the President said, "Thank you, gentlemen." The crowd began to disperse.

"Hey, there's the redhead." Kantor elbowed Tom. "Now's your chance!"

"Maggie? Maggie Hope?" Tom called.

She stared for a moment, then recognition dawned. Of course she recalled him — Thomas O'Brian, with his square-jawed, all-American charm, and the Tom Sawyer–like glint of mischief in his eyes. "Why, Tommy O'Brian from Harvard — now here and larger than life!" She gave him a huge hug. "What are you doing in Washington?"

Tom had stepped out with Maggie's roommate, Paige Kelly, when they were both at Wellesley. He and Paige had met at Mass at the Church of St. Paul in Harvard Square and found much in common as Irish Catholics whose families both knew the Kennedy clan. Tom lived at Winthrop House, the only dormitory at Harvard that allowed Catholics and Jews, and persuaded Maggie, a viola player, to join their string quartet. "I didn't know that I'd recognize you without your violin tucked under your chin."

Tom grinned and raised his camera. "Reporter and photographer for the *Buffalo Evening News* now."

"That's right, you took photographs for the *Crimson,* I remember. And you had me convinced at one party that Buffalonians had fifty words for snow, like the Eskimos."

"But we do!" Tom laughed. "And I learned them all at Canisius High School. But what brings you to the White House, Maggie?"

168

"I'm, ah, Mr. Churchill's secretary. Well, typist, really."

He whistled through his teeth as they started to make their way out of the room. "How'd you get that job?"

"I moved to London after graduation with Paige. My grandmother died, and I needed to sell her house. . . . Well, it's a long story."

"I'd love to hear it. You were a math major, right? And a Red Sox fan! Can I take you out for a drink later so we can catch up?"

They reached a large plantation table in the corridor that had earlier been covered with men's hats. Now there were only a few left. Tom picked up his, a gray Stetson with a small enamel New York Yankees pin affixed to the band.

"And you're a Yankees fan." Maggie frowned with mock disapproval. "It's a wonder we were even on speaking terms . . ."

John appeared at her side. "Time for the Children's Hour upstairs," he announced, taking Tom's measure. John was taller, but Tom was more muscular.

"Oh, John — meet Tom O'Brian. He was at Harvard when I was at Wellesley. A decent enough fellow, despite his rooting for the Yankees."

"The *World Champion* Yankees," Tom corrected.

Maggie rolled her eyes. "Maybe this year, but we'll see about next. Tom and I played in Winthrop House's string quartet. Mostly Bach, a little Mendelssohn and Haydn thrown in for good measure."

"Maggie's an ace viola player. We had to recruit her from Wellesley and ply her with chocolate ice cream sodas from Bailey's."

"That's the problem with Harvard, as I see it," said Maggie. "All first-chair violins, but no violas."

"Say, do you remember the Winthrop Ball we all went to? You went with the cellist. What was his name? Oh, good Lord, that was the night Paige threw me over for Joe Kennedy."

"I remember! Do you ever hear from Joe? What's he doing?"

"He was at Harvard Law, but I hear he got his wings in the U.S. Navy — went across the pond to shoot down some Nazis. Still there as far as I know."

John did not look pleased.

"Well, it's perfectly grand to meet you!" Tom grabbed John's extended hand and pumped it with enthusiasm, then gestured to John's uniform. "One of 'the few,' huh?

I'm off to Fort Bragg myself after New Year's."

"Army?" John's expression thawed slightly.

"Army," Tom confirmed. "Still not sure if I'll be sent to Europe or the East."

John nodded. "Good luck to you." Then, to Maggie, "We need to go." He offered his arm.

"It was wonderful to see you again, Tom," said Maggie as she turned to leave and slipped her arm through John's.

"Yeah, you, too!" Tom called after her. "Maybe we can reminisce later?"

But she was gone.

"You're not actually going to meet up with that mick while you're here, are you?" John took a sip of the Whiskey Sour the President had mixed, grimaced, and put it down.

This evening, Children's Hour was being held in the White House's Green Drawing Room, with more guests than the previous night. The walls were covered in green watered silk, and there were enormous vases of red roses dotted with tiny white spirea blossoms on the tables. Poinsettias and holly as well as flickering tapers decorated the mantel of the fireplace, which was piled high with blazing logs. A pianist played "Winter Wonderland" in the background, while Lord

171

Beaverbrook and Ambassador Halifax conferred in one corner. Behind the bar cart, President Roosevelt used silver tongs to drop more chipped ice into his Chinese silver cocktail shaker. "Ah, sweet music!" he intoned over the din.

Maggie smirked — just a bit — and sipped her drink. "I'd like to, but there's really no time."

"Did you date him?" John was trying to look unconcerned but failing.

"No, we did *not* date. Tom stepped out with Paige, actually."

"Oh," John said. Their friend Paige, who'd been working for Ambassador Joseph Kennedy in London, had died during the summer of 1940. "Well, he seems like a decent chap."

"He was. Is," Maggie corrected. "Terrific violin player, too. Besides, I already have a date for tonight." But again, Maggie felt a wave of uncertainty. *It's all just going so fast. . . .*

"Hello, lovebirds!" David trilled. "Today has been a *great* day!"

Maggie clinked sour glasses with him. "Indeed." She sneaked a peek at Mr. Churchill. He looked nothing like the man from the press conference. He seemed unusually subdued and wan, his cheeks ashen. "Is the

Boss all right?"

"He saw a doctor last night," David confided. "We're on top of it."

Maggie nodded, watching as Churchill took a seat. "How did the meeting with the State Department officials go?"

" 'Worldwide strategy and worldwide supply — leading to worldwide victory.' " David raised his glass in a mock toast. He was about to take a sip when John warned, "Trust me — don't."

Harry Hopkins used a silver bar spoon with its long, twisting handle to clink his own glass — filled with water — and the room quieted instantly.

Mr. Roosevelt treated everyone to his dazzling grin. "Thank you, all," he said, raising his glass. "To the unconditional surrender of the Axis!"

"To unconditional surrender!" everyone echoed.

Mr. Churchill excused himself and made his way to the door. When he saw John, he paused. "Mr. Sterling," he intoned. "Mr. Greene told me about your invitation from Mrs. Regina Winthrop Wolffe. Enjoy yourself at your party tonight, young man."

John looked to Maggie and then back to the Prime Minister. "Thank you, Mr. Churchill. But I'm not going, sir."

"Not going? But you must!"

"I already have plans, sir." He avoided Maggie's eye.

"Then cancel them, my dear boy! As an RAF pilot loose among the elite of Washington, you are an invaluable asset!"

"Mr. Churchill." John tried to choose words that would make the P.M. understand. "They're the American equivalent of the Cliveden set." The reference was to a group of pro-Nazi British aristocrats who met at Cliveden, Nancy Astor's manor house in Buckinghamshire.

"Mr. Sterling." The P.M. dropped his voice and leaned in. "We are not only fighting a war abroad but fighting a shadow war with American public opinion."

John's mouth twisted. "I'm no whiskey warrior, sir."

"No, of course not. But we all must do our duty."

"Sir —"

"No, not another word. On the contrary, young Sterling, you *must* go. You're our secret weapon, spreading charm, glamour, and British goodwill throughout the District. Go!" He motioned with a finger for John to lean down and whispered to the younger man, "Lie back and think of England, if you must." And then he disappeared.

At that moment, Mrs. Roosevelt approached them. "Miss Hope, I'm leaving now to see Miss Martin's talk at the Metropolitan Baptist Church in Shaw. Are you still interested in going with me?"

She looked at John. John looked back at her.

Maybe it's for the best? "I'll get my coat, ma'am."

Sam Reynolds had gone to Frank Cole's office and was told on arriving that Cole was headed back to the White House. The young man retraced his steps, out of breath from his exertions when he reached the President's study, where the celebration continued. He found Cole in the throng and approached. "Mr. Cole, may I speak with you, please?"

Cole was talking with Hopkins, a bourbon on the rocks in hand. "Now?"

"Y-yes, sir," Sam said, his face flushed from his journey. He undid the horn buttons on his coat with cold hands. "It's important, sir."

The two men walked to the hallway. "News on the wire tap about ER," Sam whispered.

Cole ground his teeth. "What now?"

Sam looked around to make sure the corridor was empty, then leaned in. "Byrd's talking about a 'scandalous letter.' And to watch the papers."

Cole took a gulp of his drink. "That's been handled."

"Sir?"

"The letter's been handled. That's all you need to know."

Sam nodded, then looked longingly through the doorway at the crowd drinking and eating canapés. But Cole clapped the assistant on the back and turned him toward the door. "Now, back up to your listening post, young man."

In the taxi to Dupont Circle through the restless fog, John took out the article he'd written the night before.

After he'd met with Regina Winthrop Wolffe and C. S. Forester in the promenade of the Mayflower, he'd gone back to his room and spent a long night wrestling with his memories of his plane crash in Germany. The words had come more easily than he'd expected, and he'd gotten it all down on paper by dawn. He wanted to title the essay "A Piece of Cake" — after the term pilots used to describe each maneuver, regardless of how dangerous — but finally settled on

"Shot Down over Berlin." He'd typed it up while the P.M. was meeting with the press.

It was good.

He was proud of it.

But although he was pleased with what he'd written, he had mixed feelings about not actively serving in the RAF. He'd turned twenty-eight that September and felt guilt and disgust at being injured and left out of the battle so soon. Back in the office, working for Churchill, he'd been haunted by the thought of the friends in his old squadron who were still fighting. He realized that he should be grateful — the life expectancy of an RAF pilot was short, and he knew all too well how lucky he was to have survived a crash and to have made it out of Germany alive.

On the other hand, the idea that he might have to sit out the rest of the war as a civilian, trotted out for parties in his dress uniform and recounting old flying stories, was the height of humiliation.

He ground his teeth as he walked up the slippery steps of Regina Winthrop Wolffe's marble palace on Dupont Circle. Then he tucked the article into the jacket of his dress uniform and rang the bell.

John had done some querying and had been informed that Regina's parties were famous. Her guest lists were regularly reprinted in the "Town Talk" section of *The Washington Post,* and her palatial home — complete with ballroom, theater, ornate gardens, and greenhouses — had earned a reputation for being a gathering place of fifth columnists, appeasers, apologists for Hitler, right-wing Republicans, and Roosevelt haters. However, now that Pearl Harbor had been attacked, most had softened their tone considerably.

Inside, the drawing room's walls were painted cream and the Biedermeier furniture upholstered in pistachio silk. There was a plush eighteenth-century Aubusson carpet, an enormous crystal chandelier, and Monet water lilies — and at the far end of the room, a gilded Chinese Chippendale mirror hung over the mantelpiece. A grand piano stood in the bay window facing the terrace, framed by burgundy damask curtains. Masses of red roses and poinsettias made brilliant splashes of color everywhere. All this was overseen by Regina's stern Bavarian butler.

"Ah, there you are!" Forester called, spotting John getting a drink at the bar. Making his way through the guests, the author saw John's selection. "Ah, Macallan, neat — excellent choice."

"I have what you asked me for," John said, reaching into his breast pocket and retrieving some folded pages. He handed them to Forester.

The older man accepted them, then reached for his glasses. "You were meant to give me notes, young man, not a finished story!"

When he came to the end, he looked up. "Well, I must say, Lieutenant Sterling, I'm bowled over. Your piece is absolutely marvelous. I might want to tighten things up a bit here and there, but there's no doubt you're a gifted writer."

"Thank you, sir," John replied. "That's kind of you to say."

"No, no," Forester said, clapping John's shoulder, "thank *you*. I'd like to go over this, make a few edits, and then send it to my agent, Harold Matson. If he's as pleased as I am — which I predict he will be — he'll forward it to my editor at *The Saturday Evening Post*. As your literary agent, Matson will take fifteen percent, but in my opinion, he's worth every penny. For a beginner, they pay about a thousand dollars."

It took all of John's British public school upbringing not to gasp. Instead, he gulped his scotch. "I see."

179

Forester scanned the crowd. "Ah, someone I'd like you to meet." He caught the eye of a bright blonde holding a champagne coupe. She was tall and slim, with gilt hair, wearing ruby lipstick and a silver beaded gown. She glided over, smiling and nodding as she approached. "Darling, meet Flight Lieutenant John Sterling. Lieutenant Sterling, may I present Martha Gellhorn."

"How do you do, Miss Gellhorn," John said.

Martha laughed. Forester began to correct John, but she stopped him. "No, I like Miss Gellhorn. Sounds much better than Mrs. Hemingway." She extended her hand, and John shook it.

"Hemingway?" John said. "You're married to Ernest Hemingway? *The* Ernest Hemingway?"

"Yes, but hush, darling. I don't like to talk about it," Martha told him. "I'm a human being in my own right, if you don't mind. A war correspondent, no less. I covered the Spanish Civil War before we realized it was just a prelude to the one we're in now. Wrote about the Nazis in Berlin back in the thirties, too, you know."

"I was in Berlin, as well."

"Cheers, then." She raised her champagne coupe.

"It's strange, isn't it?" John asked. "To come back from war, where people were killing each other, and then find yourself in the middle of a cocktail mob in America?"

"Indeed," she agreed.

Forester interposed. "Flight Lieutenant Sterling has written a story about it for me, about his plane's crash and his escape from Berlin, Martha. We'll be sending it to the *Post*."

"You hit the ground then?" Her shrewd eyes studied John.

"Afraid so."

"How did you get out?"

"You'll have to read the story."

She smiled. "Touché."

"Darling, there you are!" Regina joined them, clothed in Balenciaga and a veil of clove-scented Mitsouko. "So thrilled you could make it!"

Forester raised his highball glass to John. "Our rising literary star."

"Wonderful, darling. Do you have the piece? May I read it?" She plucked it from Forester's pocket. "Well, well," she said, seeing a pencil drawing on the back of the last page. "What's this? A cartoon? You're a man of many talents it seems, Lieutenant Sterling."

"It's nothing," John mumbled, embarrassed, trying to rescue the paper from her. "Just a scribble."

"No, no, I *must* see," Regina insisted, laughing, the papers tight in fingers tipped with pointy, red-varnished nails.

—Baby G's

"It's adorable! But what is it?"

"It's — it's a Gremlin," John replied.

Her penciled eyebrows drew together. "Whatever is a Gremlin?"

"A sort of pixie," John explained. "A fairy, if you will. They like to sabotage aircraft."

"I've heard of them," Martha said, nodding. "British pilots were talking about them in Malta, back in the twenties."

Regina and Forester exchanged a look, and the lady of the house's smirk grew wily. "Are you thinking what I'm thinking?" she asked her friend.

182

"I am!" Forester said, rubbing his thin hands together.

John blanched. "Fear and common sense keep me from asking."

Martha wagged a finger. "Oooh, nothing good, most likely, knowing you two."

"Excuse me, darlings," Regina said, "I need to make a telephone call." She dashed off, leaving the ghost of her perfume behind.

Martha asked John, "So, what brings you to Washington?" And by the time John had finished regaling her with tales of crossing the Atlantic with Winston Churchill, Regina had returned.

She tucked her arm into John's and whispered in his ear, "How'd you like to take a little trip? To the West Coast?"

He blinked. "Trip?"

"I just called my friend."

"Who?" John's impeccable social mask slipped for just a moment.

"Someone rich, famous, and quite powerful. He says he wants to meet you."

"You told him about *me*?"

"Indeed — the handsome, injured RAF pilot — who draws gremlins. He thinks you have potential. Can you get to Los Angeles in the next few days? Never mind, of course you can. I'll have my boy make a few calls, get you on one of those flying tin cans. A few jump flights and you'll be there before you know it, Lieutenant."

"No one just 'flies across the country.' Unless you're Dušan Popov or the like, of course."

"Oh, darling," she said, shaking her head with pity at his ignorance, "if you're in our gang, you do."

As the butler announced, "Dinner is served," she winked. "I'll see you later."

Entering the enormous dining room, Martha leaned in to John and whispered, "And if you're lucky, you'll get a gold Tiffany key to her front door, as well. All her gentleman friends do."

CHAPTER SEVEN

While John dined in Dupont Circle, Mrs. Roosevelt and Maggie made their way through the fog in Mrs. Roosevelt's unmarked sedan to Shaw, one of the District's colored neighborhoods. Once she'd parked, they shook off the cold and damp and entered the Metropolitan Baptist Church.

On the walls hung American flags in all sizes, as well as enormous banners proclaiming SAVE WENDELL COTTON! ABOLISH THE POLL TAX! BROUGHT TO YOU FROM THE WORKERS DEFENSE LEAGUE, THE NAACP, AND THE BROTHERHOOD OF SLEEPING CAR PORTERS. The church was packed, buzzing with conversation, and a bit too warm from the crammed-together bodies. Several of the ladies fanned themselves. The air smelled of wood polish, Murray's pomade, and the jasmine fragrance of Emeraude.

"Thank you again for coming with me,"

the First Lady murmured to Maggie. Her throat and shoulders were wrapped in silver fox fur, and she nodded and waved to the crowd in greeting as she led Maggie to a pair of empty seats.

Before they could sit, however, a uniformed police officer stepped up. "I'm sorry, ma'am, you can't sit there," said the officer, who sported a neat ginger mustache. "That's for coloreds only."

"Oh, for pity's sake, Officer," said Mrs. Roosevelt, not at all amused. Her fox's beady glass eyes glared balefully at the man. "Where should we sit, then?"

He had the decency to blush. "The whites-only section is down there, ma'am. At the front."

"Fine." Mrs. Roosevelt and Maggie made their way to the whites-only section. The First Lady whispered to Maggie, "Watch this!" as she took two of the chairs from the white section and carried them in between that section and the colored one. The two women sat, apart, in color limbo. Maggie glanced over her shoulder. The mustached officer frowned but made no comment.

Once they'd settled in, Mrs. Roosevelt told Maggie, "You know, this is the first year since we moved into the White House that there won't be a child or a grandchild home for Christmas. Not that I have any right to complain, of course, with everything going on in the world. But I do like to keep busy. And now, with —"

The unspoken hung in the air. Maggie nodded. "I understand."

"No, you don't. But maybe someday you will."

"Ma'am?"

Mrs. Roosevelt put a finger to her lips. "Shhh, they're starting."

Reverend Earl Hillard introduced Mother Cotton, a tiny, middle-aged black woman with white hair, a wide face, and high cheekbones, who spoke about her son, Wendell — what he'd been like as a baby, growing up, how hard he'd worked from age twelve on to support her.

After warm applause, Mother Cotton sat and Andrea Martin rose to speak. She was taller than Mother Cotton, lighter-skinned and more angular, with glossy black hair pulled back into a roll. She was petite, and while her shoulders were delicate, she had swagger.

She spoke about the crime itself, about the charges brought, about the unfairness of the trial, about the poll tax and jury selection. "It's not just one man and his family," Andi told her enthralled audience, "although they're important too. No, it's the whole setup — the terrible problem of white and colored sharecroppers, of tenant farmers and landlords. Wendell Cotton is on trial, yes, but so is *American democracy!*" She was rewarded with thunderous applause.

After the talk, Maggie and Mrs. Roosevelt were escorted by Reverend Hillard to a back parlor for hot coffee and frosted gingerbread cookies, and to meet Mother Cotton and Andrea Martin. When they were all introduced, Maggie said, "Your talk was inspiring, Miss Martin."

Andi looked Maggie up and down. "Thank you, Miss Hope. But time's running out for Wendell."

"I was wondering if I could ask you some questions," Maggie persisted, "when you're done here."

Andi's eyes narrowed. "Are you a journalist?"

"No." Maggie looked to Mrs. Roosevelt and then back. "A supporter," she said finally.

"And how do you know the First Lady?"

Maggie felt as if she were being interviewed — which, she supposed, she was. "I'm on Mr. Winston Churchill's staff and here in the States with the Prime Minister.

He's, er — lent me to Mrs. Roosevelt as a secretary for the interim." Maggie decided not to mince words. "Because her secretary, Miss Balfour, died."

Andi studied Maggie closely. She was just as blunt. "Died? When?"

"Yesterday."

"How?"

"Alleged suicide," Maggie responded. "I'm sure it will be in the papers by tomorrow."

"Tragic," murmured Mrs. Roosevelt. "Miss Hope was kind enough to lend a hand."

Andi nodded, absorbing the news. Then, "I think we should talk. Are you hungry, Miss Hope?"

"Yes, yes I am, Miss Martin." *But where could the two of us — colored and white — have a meal together?*

Andi's eyes sparked, as if she'd read Maggie's mind. "Don't worry, I know just the place."

Maggie looked to Mrs. Roosevelt. "Of course!" the First Lady said, beaming. "I knew you girls would be fast friends! Just — be careful."

Byrd Prentiss was standing against the back wall of the Metropolitan Baptist Church, watching Mother Cotton and then Andrea Martin address the crowd. His face had become grim when he saw Eleanor Roosevelt enter. Obviously the First Lady wasn't backing down on her support of Cotton. And who was the redhead with her? A new secretary?

Prentiss watched as the two women tried to sit in the colored section, then smirked as they were moved into the whites-only area. He ground his teeth as they created their own place, in between the two. He could get a good shot at the First Lady's head from here, he thought, squinting one eye and looking at Mrs. Roosevelt's hat, towering over the others in the crowd.

That would solve our problems, he decided.

But it wouldn't, not really. She'd only become a martyr to the cause — and that was the last thing he needed if he was going to redeem himself in the eyes of his father, of Governor King, and of the voters of Virginia. He needed to make things right.

While Mother Cotton and Andi spoke, he closed his eyes and mentally recited the lyrics to his favorite songs: "Onward, Christian Soldiers" and "Stand Up and Be Counted." After he'd sung them both countless times in his head, blocking out the talk going on in front of him, it was finally over.

He made his way through the crowd, careful not to touch any coloreds by accident, peering into the room where the First Lady and the redhead spoke with Mother Cotton and Andrea Martin. He watched the First Lady leave and decided against following her.

But when the redhead and Martin left together, he was intrigued. Where were they going? What were they going to do together? He decided he would find out.

"Follow me," Andi said as she and Maggie walked out of the church and into the thick mist.

Maggie did, taking long steps to keep up with her new acquaintance. A young man with his coat unbuttoned and scarf undone called out to Andi, "Hey, sweet cakes, where'd you get that fabulous tan?"

Maggie was horrified, but Andi merely tossed back, "Birth!" and kept walking.

"Do you like jazz?" Andi asked Maggie, as they marched on in the murky darkness.

"Jazz? Yes, of course." Maggie, John, David, and their friends had often gone to the Blue Moon Club in London.

"Good." They came to a scarred wooden door, and Andi rapped three times, then coughed. Nothing.

"What is this place?" Maggie asked.

Andi banged three times again at the door, then gave another loud cough. Nothing.

One more bang and the door swung open. "Miz Andi! So great to see you!" said the man on the other side. He was in his twenties, colored, with a large forehead and high cheekbones. "And who's your friend?"

"This is Miss Hope, Odell. She's working for Mrs. Roosevelt." Maggie could hear music in the background and smell cigarette smoke mixed with rum.

He nodded. "Any friend of Mrs. R is a friend of the Music Box. Come on in, and I'll get you ladies settled."

"Thanks, Odell." They walked down a flight of steep steps to the building's basement. There was a long bar against the wall, a number of small tables ringed with café chairs, and a tiny stage at one end. The stage area was lit by Christmas lights in black Bakelite sockets tacked onto the walls, which made a colorful glow. The walls were decorated with American flags.

Three colored men played — one on drums, one on piano, and one on trumpet. They were riffing on Duke Ellington's "All Too Soon." On a tiny wooden floor in front of the stage, a few couples danced.

Andi led Maggie to a table in the back,

covered in a cotton flowered cloth with a mason jar of pink carnations and a candle stub with a gold flame that flickered in the dark. "We can talk here," Andi said as she slipped off her coat and sat. "Did you see *Birth of the Blues?*"

"We don't get a lot of first-run movies in London anymore," Maggie said, unbuttoning her own coat and sitting.

"Sorry — I forgot. We're at war now, too, of course, but it all seems so far away still. You were really in the thick of it, weren't you?"

Still am. "We're all doing our duty," Maggie replied — then, realizing how cold and British she sounded, she amended, "Did you like the film? *Birth of the Blues?*" She remembered reading a review of it. It starred Bing Crosby and Mary Martin.

Andi cocked an eyebrow. "I think that, for a movie about the blues, it had too many damn white people in it."

Maggie laughed, then became aware that people were staring at them. "Is something wrong?" she asked Andi.

"Wrong?"

"Is my hair sticking up? Is there lipstick on my teeth?"

Andi chortled. "They aren't used to seeing a white woman down here. And probably none of them have ever seen a white woman with hair that color. Is it natural? Or from a box?"

"Er, birth . . ."

"Ha!" Andi laughed. "Good for you. I'm going to the ladies'. You'll be all right, won't you?"

"Of course," Maggie said. She was seated near a table of men — middle-aged, dressed in dapper suits with ties and matching pocket squares, drinking mugs of beer. *What did colored men talk about on their own time?* she wondered as Andi disappeared — and decided to eavesdrop.

"I tell you, Bub, you missed it. By this time of year that window's closed. You're gonna have to wait another year."

The man lifted an icy mug. "Nah, I still got time."

"I'm telling you no, man. It's just not gonna work."

What were they talking about? Gambling, maybe? Moving money? Stolen goods? What window of opportunity had closed?

"I tell you, if you want flowers in the spring, you gotta put in the bulbs by September."

"But I heard if you're doin' the late-blooming flowers, like tulips, you can put them in later."

"Well, you can put 'em in all right if the ground's not frozen. And it's been a warm winter. As long as you gets them in before the frost — January, even — they'll bloom fine."

"I like my annuals," declared another man. "My marigolds is cheerful. I don't need no bulbs."

"Yeah, but there's nothin' like seein' those first crocuses comin' on up in spring. Oooh, and the smell of those hyacinths!"

They were talking about gardening. Gardening. Bulbs and perennials versus annuals. Marigolds and crocuses and hyacinths. Maggie suddenly felt ashamed of herself.

And then Andi was back. "Would you like a drink?" she asked.

"That would be great, thanks."

"Odell should be over soon." Her lips curved in a mischievous smile. "Do you like absinthe?"

"I've never had it," Maggie admitted.

Andi raised her hand and gave a signal to Odell, behind the bar. He nodded. In a moment, he came over with a tray holding a bottle, two Pontarlier glasses, a bowl of sugar cubes, and a carafe of ice water — as well as a small bowl of sliced pickles and a plate of deviled eggs.

"It's my own personal bottle," Andi explained. "Green Fairy. I brought a few back from Paris. Odell lets me keep them here."

Maggie was impressed. "You were in Paris?"

Andi searched in her handbag, taking out a slotted silver absinthe spoon. "Yes, a few years ago," she answered, using her napkin to clean it off. "Well, it's not Les Deux Magots," she sighed, "but it will do." She placed the sugar cube on the slotted spoon across the mouth of each glass and poured over the absinthe, until the drink turned cloudy. She handed one to Maggie. *"Santé."*

"Santé," Maggie replied. They clinked glasses. She took a sip.

"Do you like it?"

Maggie pondered. It was . . . interesting. "What is it? Fennel?"

"Anise, fennel, star anise, and wormwood. The wormwood allegedly gives it hallucinogenic properties. I personally doubt it, but it's all part of that 'green fairy' legend."

Andi put down her drink and took out a pack of violet Milos. The trio had segued into "Polka Dots and Moonbeams." "So, what's your favorite band?" she asked, pulling out a gold and black lacquered man's lighter. It sparked, and she touched her cigarette tip to the blue flame.

"Love Artie Shaw," Maggie said, biting

into an egg. "But, of course, there's only one Benny Goodman."

"Did you know that Benny Goodman doesn't do his own arrangements? All of the orchestration was done originally by a colored man — Goodman bought the orchestrations fair and square, but he's passing them off as his own. It's not right." Andi blew out smoke. She tapped her cigarette in the ashtray — ceramic with a painting of the Lincoln Memorial. "Smoke?"

"No, thanks." Maggie had smoked at one time, after her mission to Berlin, but had quit. "Oh, just one." Andi lit it for her.

The man on trumpet was improvising again, carving out his own variation on the melody, spotlight glinting gold off his horn. The papery sound and wistful tune made Maggie think about lost chances and lost loves, while dust motes sparked in the smoky air. *Is it too late for John and me? Too much water under the bridge?*

"He does amazing things with the trumpet," Andi remarked, nodding toward the stage. "In the wrong hands, the trumpet can sometimes sound thin, but his sound is full. He's writing music now, too — good stuff. Hey, aren't you going to ask me why I was in Paris?"

Maggie smiled and tapped off ash. "Why

were you in Paris?"

"I went on a two-week college trip — and then stayed for six months."

"Did you like it?"

"I loved it. I loved Paris." She took a long, wistful drag on her cigarette. "And Paris loved me. Man Ray told me I should be an actress. Matisse painted me nude. I learned how to drink absinthe with Hemingway. And I slept with Josephine Baker."

Maggie did her best not to drop her cigarette or jaw. Andi continued, "There's no Jim Crow in Paris — or in jazz or on death row for that matter, as I like to say. Everyone's simply a person there." She exhaled a long tendril of smoke. "The races can actually mingle in Paris, get to know each other. Although they didn't always know what I was. I was *l'exotique* there."

Maggie took another sip of her drink.

"You're not going to ask? Good for you, Maggie — but I'll tell you anyway — my mother was a light-skinned Negro, my father was Creole. So here I am, a . . ." — here Andi took a deep breath — "tragic mulatto, gray baby, sepia sister, high-toned gal, tallow woman, rooster red, tea honey with milk, cinnamon sugar, sallow gal, jazz baby, high-toned mulatta, high-yaller, half-breed, wild baby Creole, Cherokee, sugar-

198

cane, 'noble savage,' and — my favorite — American cocktail!"

"Brava!" Maggie exclaimed and clapped. The room seemed to be getting warmer. Maybe it was the absinthe.

"And where are you from?"

"Boston. Well, Boston and then London for the last four years."

"I was in London for a while," Andi said. The trio was taking a break, and Odell put on a Cab Calloway record and turned up the volume. "Stayed in Pimlico with some friends I'd met in Paris. There was one woman who said to me — I'm not joking — 'you know, you mustn't get sunburned or stay in the sun too long. People who live in hot countries have thickened skulls and can't think as well.' " As Calloway scatted to "Hep! Hep! The Jumpin' Jive" in the background, Andi rolled her eyes. "Really? Not as well as people who live in a permanent fog?"

Maggie laughed.

"So I said to her, 'I believe that all intelligence on this island was brought by the Phoenicians or Assyrians or Egyptians or wandering Arabs — who came with an advanced knowledge of mathematics and astronomy that you British are only just now beginning to understand. Do you think the sun affected *their* thinking?' "

"Oh, good for you. What did she say?"

Andi blew a smoke ring, pleased with herself. "Oh, she just poured more tea and began to talk about the weather."

Feeling a little dizzy from the nicotine mixed with the powerful cocktail, Maggie cackled with laughter. "Yes, the Brits are good at making tea and talking about the weather," she agreed. "Have you ever been to Boston?"

"I have. Boston's all right. Not utopia, of course, but it's the North, at least. Mother Cotton and I have been traveling around the country, trying to raise money for Wendell. Traveling and staying in the North and South is like night and day. Our country is schizophrenic."

Maggie raised her glass. "It is!"

They clinked again. "I'm the answer, you see?" Andi said. "The answer in one body. Black *and* white. Man *and* woman! Marcus Garvey thought we should all go back to Africa, but — really — what's someone like me going to do there? No, I'm an American, and I'm going to stand my ground. And, with my staying, I hope that people here might just understand the advantages of integration, amalgamation, intermarrying, intermingling — and taking the best of each

200

to make one human race. It's my profound hope that in the next century the concept of 'race' will be archaic." The young woman's expression was fierce.

Maggie nodded as the trio came back to the stage. She and Andi applauded. As they began their set with "Up Jumped the Devil," Maggie said, "I know. The stupid futility of killing so many people in the name of isms — Nazism, Fascism, nationalism, Communism, Zionism, Protestantism, Catholicism . . ."

"Would you like another absinthe?"

"Yes, thank you."

After refilling their glasses, Andi spoke again. "I'm not a fan of your Mr. Churchill, I'll have you know." She blew a string of smoke rings that grew lighter and more fragile before disappearing.

"Really? Why not?"

"How can Britain be a so-called champion for freedom in view of her history of colonization? Colonization that your Mr. Churchill personally fought for?"

My *Mr. Churchill*? Maggie thought.

Andi continued. "Nothing Hitler could do to England would be any worse than what Britain's South Africa and Australia are doing to the natives. Your Mr. Churchill is doing everything to preserve England's colonial empires *and* her exploitation of cheap colored labor."

"But let's put it this way," Maggie countered. "Which country would you rather live in? The United Kingdom — or Nazi Germany?"

"That's not a fair question!"

"You didn't answer it."

"I'd rather live in a free India under Mr. Gandhi," Andi stated bluntly. "And I do believe India will one day be free."

Maggie shook her head. "But what about the world we live in *now*?"

"Look, U.S. and U.K. imperialism and Jim Crow are two sides of the same coin. We colored folks have been criticizing European colonialism and theorizing about colored Americans as a captive colonial people for ages." She punctuated her words with jabs of her cigarette. "Don't you see that's how the Nazis compare with Dixie? We coloreds realized as early as 'thirty-three that Hitler was evil. If you read any of the colored papers, you'll see that we've been reporting on his persecution of the Jews since the mid-thirties. Moreover, we've repeatedly linked Jim Crow with Fascism."

Maggie took a sharp inhale. "Do you think Hitler got his ideas from Dixie?"

"Yes!" Andi ground out her cigarette in

the ashtray, obscuring the tiny painting of the Lincoln Memorial. "Not only is there Fascism in America but Mussolini and Hitler *copied* it from us. What else are Jim Crow laws but Fascist laws? And what were the Jim Crow laws inspired by? The ones that tried to separate and then exterminate the American Indians — the real Americans.

"To me, it's obvious Hitler modeled his laws against the Jews directly on the laws against the Indians, which were the basis for the laws against the coloreds after the Emancipation Proclamation. Did you know that Hitler is a great admirer of Andrew Jackson? The Indian reservations — don't they seem awfully similar to concentration camps? 'No Indians or dogs allowed' — doesn't that sound like the signs that Germany started putting up in the thirties?"

Andi took a shaky breath. "A review of Hitler's legal restrictions of the Jews ran under the heading 'The Nazis and Dixie.' How is it that white Americans can become so incensed over the ousting of Jews from German universities and yet not the banning of Negroes from American ones? They're killing Jews in concentration camps — but what about executing coloreds in American prisons? What about the death penalty? What about Wendell Cotton?"

Maggie watched as Andi lit another cigarette. "I'll take another, if you don't mind."

Andi passed her one and lit it for her. "There you go," she said, as Maggie took a deep inhale. "Look, I'm sorry, if I sounded . . ." She shrugged. "I'm just full of splinters most days. Most of us colored are, you know. But at least when I think of the First Lady, I have hope. White folk can't be all bad if you have Mrs. Roosevelt."

Maggie exhaled blue smoke. "Speaking of Mrs. Roosevelt, I'd like to ask you about Blanche Balfour."

Andi nodded. "I didn't know her well. I know Tommy, Mrs. Roosevelt's regular secretary, a bit better. I write a lot of letters on behalf of the Workers Defense League that Tommy passed on. And Mrs. Roosevelt has been kind enough to ask me to the White House to discuss things over the past year or so."

"Did you ever have any interactions with Blanche?"

"Not really," Andi said. "I only met her once. But I definitely got the feeling she resented the fact I met with Mrs. Roosevelt. She resented my being a *guest* at the White House, as opposed to my being a servant." A mischievous look played across her face. "Mrs. Roosevelt had her hang up my coat and fetch me a glass of water — Blanche made it very clear she thought such things were beneath her."

Maggie tapped burning ash into the tray. "Did she ever speak to you?"

"No, but if looks could kill . . ."

"Do you think she was a threat to Mrs. Roosevelt? Do you know if she was associated with anyone who might pose a threat?" Then, "Do you think she was a threat to *you*?"

Andi laughed, more sad than bitter. "Oh, honey, we colored folk get that look all the time — we don't pay it any mind. Blanche gave me the same look any number of white women have over the years. I didn't pay any attention to it."

"And you talked to the First Lady about Wendell Cotton?"

"Yes, Mrs. Roosevelt's sympathetic to Wendell's case, but, as she says, her hands are tied. There's only so much she can do. And it sounds like the President's not going to intervene. Speaking of Wendell, what did you think of the talk tonight?"

"I think the whole situation is horrible," Maggie said, crushing out her cigarette. "Is there anything I can do to help?"

"Not unless you can convince the President to intervene with the Governor and stop the execution." A thoughtful look passed across Andi's face. "Do you want to meet Wendell? It's easy to talk *about* him and think of him as some kind of abstract idea — but he's a real person, you know. A sweet boy, who had to grow up too fast."

Maggie had never considered the possibility of meeting someone on death row. "I —"

"We need people who understand our side of the story. Too many of our stories get twisted by the white press. We need witnesses. We need storytellers."

Maggie realized what she was being asked. "I'd be honored."

"How about Christmas dinner with Wendell? I'll be there, with Mother Cotton. The prison's relaxing the rules as the execution gets closer."

Christmas dinner in prison? "Count me in."

"Good!" Andi exclaimed, draining her glass. "And I'm not all gloom and doom, by the way. I don't believe God's left anything to chance. Personally, I believe that God's put me here in the middle, so that I can stretch across the world's divides. I can talk to everyone — and I think it's God's plan for me."

"That's beautiful," Maggie said, genuinely moved and also getting tipsy. "My sister —

half sister — was planning on being a nun. She's religious, too."

"Does your sister still live in Boston?"

She lives in Berlin and might already be dead or dying in a concentration camp as we speak. "No — it's a long story."

The band acknowledged applause and then counted down to "Take the 'A' Train."

"*This* is what's important in life — jazz." Andi threw her arms wide to encompass the club, the stage, all the stages across America where the music was played. "I could pout about all the pain and injustice, or I can listen to jazz. I'll choose music any day. And it's no accident the coloreds and the Jews are leading the way. Gives you hope, doesn't it?"

"Jazz is popular in London, too," Maggie told her. "But it's definitely American music. You can't be full of hate and listen. You can't hate and dance."

"Music will save us! Music and dance!" Andi grabbed Maggie's hand. "Let's be soldiers of music! Generals of jazz! Divas of dance!" She pushed her chair back and stood, pulling Maggie up with her. "Come on!"

They ran to the tiny dance floor as the trio swung into a song from *Sunday Sinners.* "I'll lead," Andi said as they began to jitterbug, stepping and turning, twisting and spinning.

"But I'm taller . . ."

"I'll lead," Andi insisted. "Come on — don't think, just dance!"

Prentiss watched the door of the Music Box through the smoky fog from the driver's seat of his dark green Lagonda coupe. He'd trailed the two young women from the church and waited, taking the occasional sip of bourbon from a monogrammed silver hip flask. Rats, searching for food, scuttled between the garbage cans by his car.

Maggie and Andi were walking arm in arm and laughing as they left the club.

Prentiss watched them and grimaced. Had they talked about Wendell Cotton? Had they mentioned Blanche?

He slipped out of his car and followed them up the alley in the shadows, their echoing laughter increasing his anger. He knew it was dangerous to follow them. He knew it was wrong. He knew it was just the kind of thing, like the incident with the prostitute, that could harm his political career, but he wanted to scare them. Just that, scare them. He pulled his hat down to cover his eyes.

Maggie and Andi had stopped at an intersection to let a car pass. "What's a white woman like you doing with a darky like that?" said a man's low voice behind them. Maggie turned. He was tall and broad and walked around them with long steps to block their way. A wide-brimmed black hat hid his face from the light of the street lamp.

"Let us pass," Maggie said, suddenly sober.

"You like jazz?" he said, his voice rough. "You like dancing with colored girls? What else do you like to do with colored girls? I know what you two are."

"Let us pass," Maggie insisted. She looked around. It was almost midnight. The street was deserted, except for a parked car opposite.

"You wanna dance with me?" He grabbed at Maggie's shoulder. "Both of you? Maybe you first, then her?" He licked his lips.

"Hold this," Maggie said to Andi, giving the shorter woman her pocketbook.

"I said, let us pass." She shook off the man's arm. She could feel the adrenaline racing through her. It had been too long since she'd been in a fight, and Maggie found herself almost enjoying it.

He lunged for her throat.

She kneed him in the groin. When he was doubled over in agony, she grabbed his head by both ears and pulled him back up to standing, then smashed his jaw with the heel of her hand, the force of her entire weight behind it.

"Ow!" the man cried, both hands going to his injured nose. He staggered, then fell to the pavement and stayed there, moaning.

Maggie looked back at Andi, who stood frozen, holding both their pocketbooks, eyes wide. "Run!"

The two women ran.

Maggie smuggled Andi into the Mayflower using the service elevator. Once they were safely in her room, the door locked behind them, Maggie asked the other woman, "Are you all right?"

"I'm fine — but where did you learn to do *that*?"

Maggie thought of the various spy-training camps she'd been to in England and Scotland. "Well, you went to Paris. I had my own . . . finishing school."

Andi peeled off her gloves, then unpinned her hat. "No offense, but you don't look like the type of woman who could do that. You seem the prim and proper type, more likely to clutch her pearls than knee a man in his —"

"Thank you, I think." Maggie laughed,

hanging up their coats. "Let's just say I'm full of surprises." She got two rocks glasses from the bar and filled them both with water from the bathroom sink. "Come on, drink up," she urged. "If we don't, we're both going to have horrible headaches tomorrow."

Andi was still standing, looking uncomfortable. "I'll just have some water and be going —"

"Nonsense," Maggie interrupted. She sat down on the sofa and pointed to the bed. "It's late. There's a crazy man out there with a grudge against us. And, let's be honest, you're not going to get a taxi. Stay here for the rest of the night and be safe. You take the bed, I'll take the sofa."

"You sure?"

"Of course."

Andi had just taken a seat on the edge of the mattress when there was a rap at the adjoining door and it swung open. John was shirtless and in pajama bottoms, and carried a bottle of champagne in a silver bucket. When he saw Andi, he froze. "I'm sorry — I didn't know you had a guest," he managed, taking in the other woman.

Maggie realized that she'd forgotten about their late-night date — but was it so bad to put it off another night? True, John was gorgeous in his near nakedness and adorable in his modesty, shielding his chest with folded arms and the ice bucket in a vain attempt to cover up. "I'm so sorry," she said, going to him and giving him a kiss on the cheek. "This is Andi Martin. Andi, please meet my . . . er, friend . . . John Sterling. Andi and I met at the rally for Wendell Cotton and went out to a jazz club. And then we were jumped when we left. I invited her to stay here, to be safe."

"Are you all right?" John's face was stern.

"We're fine."

"Your skinny little white girlfriend here has quite the street-fighting technique," Andi added. The two women convulsed in laughter, laughing so hard that tears came to their eyes and Andi began to hiccup.

"Yes, I've seen some of her moves," he deadpanned. Then, "Well, maybe another night then."

"Tomorrow," Maggie said. "I promise." He kissed her on the cheek, then turned and left.

"It's perfectly fine with me if you want to go to him," Andi said, kicking off her shoes. "Handsome devil."

Maggie looked at the clock and considered. It was nearly one. She went to the door and knocked. "John?" She knocked harder. "John?"

"I'm tired," he called through the door. "I need to get some sleep. You need some, too."

"All right," she said. "I'll see you in the morning."

There was no reply.

"What the hell is that?" Royal Air Force Captain Maximilian Evans muttered under his flight mask. He was flying his beloved Spitfire on a reconnaissance mission over the coast of the Baltic Sea.

The red morning sunrise glowed above the island of Peenemünde. Captain Evans flicked his eyes to the photograph of the plump blond woman wedged into the glass of the cockpit. "Sorry, old thing, I know you don't like it when I swear."

It was, quite literally, freezing in the cockpit of his plane — the temperature was minus fifty centigrade and the heat from the engines was being bled off to keep the cameras and film warm.

Because there were no weapons in Max's plane. Even though he was flying a Spitfire, as he had as one of "the few" during the Battle of Britain, his was a stealth mission. With Western Europe on the brink of defeat, Britain had once again turned to the iconic plane. However, this one was armed not with guns or bombs but with something that might keep them one step ahead of the Nazi war machine — an F-52 surveillance camera, pointed down through portholes in the fuselage. The multiple cameras shot straight down, producing overlapping vertical photos.

Max loved flying, and he loved his Spitfire. But he didn't like to be alone. And so he'd tucked a picture of his fiancée, Lady Sybil Bristol, in the crevice between the dashboard and the window, and he spoke to her often. "Nothing moves in Europe that we don't see, darling. And we're supposed to be looking for some kind of Nazi super-weapon. But, naturally, I have no idea what it is."

Below Max was an island. On the island were a huge factory and a surrounding village. But what caught Max's attention were three enormous cleared circles, made of what looked to be concrete. They were surrounded by equipment Max didn't recognize.

He flew over the sea, then turned his Spitfire around and leveled out for another pass, this time to take photographs. He flew a straight, level approach, so the plane's movement wouldn't cause distortions.

As he kept a low and steady course, the

cameras clicked and rolled. But Max's eyes were wide. "Holy fuck," he muttered. Then, to Lady Sybil's picture, "Er, sorry, darling."

CHAPTER EIGHT

The next morning, Prentiss had his secretary buy all the day's newspapers, including the *Buffalo Evening News,* from the paperboys on the streets and also the nearby tobacco store. And he had her fetch him an ice pack, which he pressed against his swollen nose.

Sitting in his office, facing the framed Confederate flag, he went through all of them, looking for any mention of the death of Blanche Balfour.

As he finished with each one that produced nothing, he threw it on the floor, then wiped his inky hands on his fishbone tweed trousers. In *The Washington Post*'s obituary section, in small print, toward the bottom of the page, he finally saw a mention of Blanche. It read:

BALFOUR. — Blanche Imogene, daughter of Donald and Hazel (Ellis) Balfour of Alex-

216

andria, Va., was born in Alexandria on Aug. 5, 1919. She died suddenly at her home at Washington, D.C., on December 22, 1941; aged 22 yrs. She was engaged to be married to Byrd Prentiss, also from Alexandria, Va. She is survived by her mother and two sisters, Stella E. Balfour and Violetta (Balfour) DeBolt, both of Alexandria, Va., as well as her maternal grandparents, George and Mary Wagner of Buffalo, N.Y. Memorial services will be held at her native Christ Church in Alexandria, Va., and interment made in the burial lot nearby. Services will be performed by Rector Pierce Van Deventer of Christ Church, assisted by associate Rector George Whitfield Klemmt.

" 'Died suddenly'?" There was no mention of suicide, no mention of any sort of letter, no mention of Eleanor Roosevelt — nothing. "Damn!" he raged, crumpling up the offending page and then flinging it at the wall. First Blanche had ruined everything by not wanting to go through with their plan, then the note implicating Kissing Fish had disappeared, and now it all seemed to have been for nothing. What the devil had gone wrong? And how would he redeem himself? He needed to pull this off. "Goddamn it!"

His secretary knocked timidly at the door. "Is everything all right, Mr. Prentiss?" the pale young woman asked. "Do you need more ice?"

"Get me the Washington correspondent for the *Buffalo Evening News* on the telephone," he roared, slamming his fist into the leather-tooled desktop. *"Now!"*

After a quick breakfast of bacon and eggs and coffee at the diner, Maggie and John walked back into the White House. The office was filled with red dispatch boxes from the British Embassy. David's desk was strewn with newspapers, as he was following the American media's reception of the Prime Minister's visit. Maggie went through them — there was a copy of *Time* magazine, its cover a painting of "Japan's Aggressor: Admiral Yamamoto." The *Los Angeles Herald and Express* had a large banner proclaiming MERRY CHRISTMAS! under which ran "exclusive photos of torpedoed seamen," and the *Los Angeles Times*'s front page announced FOE LANDS 75 MILES FROM MANILA! The day felt somber, despite the good notices in the papers for the Prime Minister's press conference and promising news from Russia.

Maggie looked out the window and shivered, drawing her cardigan sweater closer around her. The view was gray, and the leaden skies threatened rain. She went back to the papers. It was clear that the Allies were on the defensive, and would continue to be for some time. There had been Nazi spies — fifth columnists — arrested in New York City. There were calls for an inquiry into America's lack of preparation for Pearl Harbor. Wake Island was being invaded. The British were near surrender in Hong Kong, Malaya, and Burma. Australia was in danger.

Maggie searched through the newspapers until she found the one she was looking for, *The Washington Post.* She flipped to the obituaries and saw Blanche's. Maggie scanned the item. *Thank goodness,* she thought. There was no mention of suicide. And there was no mention of a note or anything regarding the First Lady. She breathed a sigh of relief.

The Prime Minister, dressed in a dark blue suit and chewing on a cigar, looked in on his staff. "I'll be in meetings most of the day with the President," he informed them on his way out the door. "The very fate of our British Empire hangs in the balance!"

he roared, his husky voice trailing down the hall.

"What does he mean?" Maggie said when Mr. Churchill retired. "Roosevelt's decided to go after Hitler first, not Japan. It's what the P.M. was praying for."

David sighed. "True, but to no one's surprise, the fate of the British colonies *is* a source of tension between our two fearless leaders. Otherwise, they're thick as thieves."

"Roosevelt's not fighting the U.K.'s war, he's fighting his own. He was brought in not by Britain but by the attack on Pearl Harbor." John, packing up papers to be sent back to London, looked dour. "Churchill wants above all to preserve the British holdings, which is anathema to Roosevelt." He set the last stack down on the desk. "And there you have it."

David was addressing files to be sent to the British Embassy. "Haven't you ever realized? The Old Man is obsessed with Empire. Obsessed! If he were talking about a chip shop in Salford, he'd find a way to mention how important its chips were to the Empire."

"But as the Boss said in the meeting, 'Empires just don't bargain.' "

David retorted, "And as Mr. Roosevelt said, 'Republics do.' "

"Britain's colonies are dissolving like a lump of sugar in Roosevelt's teacup." A muscle in John's cheek twitched. "Do you want to see the Empire destroyed? The Germans are already calling the Boss 'the Undertaker of the British Empire.' "

David remained calm. "I'd like to see self-rule in India and the other colonies. Mark my word, it will come."

John exploded. "But it's the *British Empire!*"

David tried to deflect with humor. "Honestly, I think it was the horrible food in Blighty that led to colonization," he said, in an aside to Maggie. "We invaded all these other countries because we were hungry for something besides mutton and turnips."

"I see the Boss as unwilling to commit Britain to principles that would undermine political ties, such as self-determination of India and elimination of the 1932 Ottawa Agreements," John said.

"But that's hypocritical!" Maggie protested. "If we're not careful, this alliance could be British colonialism in new form, with too much to do with Empire, and too little to do with democracy. As a citizen of a colony which fought for independence — and won — I can understand their frustration. South Africa, India, the Far East —

didn't the Atlantic Charter promise self-rule?" Realization struck. "If not, then Hitler's invasion of Europe and Japan's invasion of China are just a logical continuation of colonialism begun by the Spanish, Portuguese, Italians, and French. And . . . the British."

"Hear, hear!" David cried.

Maggie turned back to John. "The current collapse of the Far East because Japan herself is colonizing the British colonies sounds a bit like chickens coming home to roost, now, doesn't it?"

"Every man is free when he sets foot on British soil."

"Not if you're a colonial!"

"It's the end of the Empire," John insisted.

"And is that such a bad thing?" Maggie shot back.

"As Secretary of State for the Colonies, the Boss stated that within the British Empire 'there should be no barrier of race, color, or creed which should prevent any man from reaching any station if he is fitted for it.' " John's voice was rising.

"Yes," David retorted. "Yet he immediately qualified it, saying that 'such a principle has to be very carefully and gradually applied because intense local feelings are excited' — which was a flowery way of saying that its actual implementation should be delayed indefinitely. He's" — David looked around to make sure they were indeed alone — "absolutely inconsistent! He's like Dr. Jekyll and Mr. Hyde! The key to the Boss is to realize that he's Victorian — steeped in the politics of his father's period. He's never developed a modern point of view."

"I am an admirer of Gibbon," John countered. "And I support the British Empire for Gibbonian reasons."

"British rule in India is the most horrible of all spectacles," David argued. "The strength of civilization without any of its mercy."

"Don't you think that what's happening in India now is similar to what happened in the U.S. before the Revolutionary War?" Maggie asked.

"The situations are not the same," John said, a warning in his eyes.

"But they *are* the same! They're *exactly* the same! 'Britons never, never, never shall be slaves' as per 'Rule Brittania' — but it's perfectly fine to enslave others?" Maggie protested.

"It's because they're brown-skinned," David said to Maggie. "That is the difference — let's not tiptoe around it." The words hung in the air, suspended by ugliness.

The three were all breathing hard and glaring when Mr. Fields knocked and entered. "A note for Miss Hope," he announced in his burnished bass voice, handing over a missive. His face was impassive. Maggie hoped he hadn't heard what had just been said.

"Thank you, Mr. Fields," she said, smoothing back her hair and taking the envelope. "No silver platter and messenger for me," she added, trying to lighten the atmosphere.

"What is it?" John asked.

"It's a note from my aunt Edith, confirming tea this afternoon. To which you are both invited. Hint, hint."

"Ooooh, the infamous Aunt Edith Hope!" David exclaimed. "I'd love to come! Not sure if I can, of course — still lots of work for the Boss's speech at the tree lighting tonight."

"John?"

John had resumed sorting through stacks of correspondence from the Embassy. "I'll do my best," he said, without looking at either of them.

The Prime Minister returned, smelling of Blenheim Bouquet and cigar smoke. "Edith Hope? You're meeting your aunt?" he asked.

"What do you need, Prime Minister?" David asked.

"My glasses," the P.M. grumbled. David set off to find them.

"Yes, we're meeting for tea at the Willard Hotel, sir. We discussed my time off —" She'd mentioned having an afternoon to see her aunt to the P.M. multiple times, but he didn't always remember such things.

However, this time, he did. "Yes, yes," he said, waving a hand. "See your aunt, of course, as long as it's all right with Mrs. Roosevelt. Is this aunt of yours still British?"

"She's been an American citizen for over twenty years now, sir."

"Another one, lost to the colonies!" the P.M. griped. "Gimme —" he said to David, who had procured his glasses.

John cleared his throat and pulled at his collar. "Sir?"

The P.M. had put on his thick, gold-rimmed glasses and glared at John, his eyes magnified. "Yes? Speak up, Mr. Sterling!"

John gave Maggie a guilty look, then turned back to the P.M. "When you have a moment, sir, I have something I need to discuss with you."

"Yes?"

"In private, sir."

"Fine," he said, stomping out once again.

The three held their breath, but he didn't return.

"By the way," John remarked to Maggie and David, hands in his pockets, leaning against the map room's doorframe. "A piece I wrote might run in *The Saturday Evening Post.*"

"Really?" Maggie and David chorused. "What about?"

"Being shot down near Berlin."

"Gracious!" Maggie said. "I didn't know you were writing an article."

"Of course not! When do we have time to talk?" John looked pointedly at David. "In private?"

David shrugged. "There's a war on, you —"

"That's because there's no time!" John exploded. "There's no time for *anything* anymore!"

"Well, I'm very happy for you," Maggie said. And she was. "Will we at least have tonight?"

"Yes — yes, by God."

Maggie stepped closer. "Penny for your naughty thoughts, Lieutenant."

John's lips twitched. "You'll just have to wait and see, Miss Hope."

David sighed. "Heroic Hera — you two, there are things I don't need to know."

Maggie jumped when she heard the distinctive high-pitched voice. "I'm sorry you all have to work today." Mrs. Roosevelt peered into the room. "It's Christmas Eve day, and you're all so far away from home."

"Holidays and workdays are the same, ma'am," said David, giving Maggie and John a dark look. "Until this war is over, nothing else but work can be on our minds."

"Miss Hope, would you come with me to my office?" the First Lady asked.

"Of course, ma'am," Maggie replied.

Together they walked the hallway, stopping at the President's open door. There he was with the Prime Minister, engrossed in talk, poring over a map. Both men were flushed with excitement and animated, speaking loudly as they moved pushpins representing ships, submarines, and aircraft carriers around the blue-ink oceans.

"Sometimes when I see them together, they remind me of a boys' book of adventure. They're having a wonderful time, really." The First Lady looked sorrowful. "It's the male tendency to romanticize war, I'm afraid. I've seen it before. Uncle Teddy, that is, President Theodore Roosevelt, cared about environment and social progress — but then he got caught up in the Spanish-American War and that was the end of it."

Maggie's gaze went back to the two world leaders, ostensibly engaged in military discussion yet for all the world looking like two little boys playing soldier.

"Well, they're having a wonderful time with all this derring-do," the First Lady remarked as they continued down the corridor to her office. "I just hope not *too* wonderful."

Like the White House, but built on a smaller scale, the Virginia Executive Mansion was a white Federalist building with tall Grecian columns at the entrance. During the Civil War it had in fact been called the White House of the Confederate States of America. Thomas Jefferson had lived in a rented house on the land, but the current house wasn't finished until the eighteenth Governor of Virginia, James Barbour, moved in.

Prentiss didn't park his coupe in the circular drive but continued on through the filmy mist, behind the house. His meeting was in one of the abandoned buildings formerly used as slave quarters. The overcast afternoon had turned chill, and fog was beginning to roll in.

An old, paint-chipped sign announced SLAVE STREET, and Prentiss strode down the deserted oak tree–lined lane, the damp wind sighing in the branches and his brogue oxfords crunching on the gravel drive. The first building, like all of them, was a wooden shack made from rough-hewn logs, white-washed but weathered, with a sloping roof and a brick chimney. He walked up the steps and shoved open the creaky door.

Governor King was already there, smoking a black cigarillo, sitting on a three-legged stool in front of a simple brick fireplace. An old straw mattress, now infested with mice, was in one corner of the room, a broken spinning wheel in the other. The room smelled of tobacco smoke, damp, and decay.

King was a robust man in his mid-sixties, with long, drooping eyebrows, long, drooping bags under his eyes, and long, drooping jowls on each side of his mouth. He wore a fur-trimmed coat, and his gray eyes were shrewd. "What happened?" he demanded without preamble.

"I —" Prentiss began.

The Governor stood. The stool toppled. "No excuses."

"Sir, when I left her, she was dead. And the letter accusing Mrs. Ro— I mean Fish — was on her desk, waiting to be found."

"Then who took it?"

"Sir, I don't know."

Governor King dropped his cigarillo and ground it into the floor with his heel. "I saw the obituary in that Yankee rag of a newspaper. It was brief. Didn't mention Fish at all. And 'died suddenly'?"

"It was suicide," Prentiss insisted. "I know. I *know.*"

"How could you possibly know?" the Governor demanded.

Prentiss swallowed. "Sir, I think the less you know, the better."

"Well. I'm sorry for your loss."

"Thank you, sir." Prentiss's features settled in an expression of strength through sorrow. It was a facial expression he'd perfected ever since the killings began. First the ants, the flies, then the abandoned kittens. As he grew older he went after his Irish setter, Charlie. Then, at the University of Virginia, the prostitutes — which had gotten him into trouble — and now Blanche. Blanche was harder to kill, of course, but he needed to redeem himself. Had to. For his own sense of self-worth and also someday to get King elected President. And, then — in the coming years — to be elected to the highest office in the land himself.

Governor King lifted one eyebrow. "You think the police were Roosevelt sympathizers?"

"That, or the press didn't want to pick it up. Too tawdry."

King folded his arms across his barrel chest. "You need to do something."

"I know one of the reporters for the *Buffalo Evening News* is filing a story. Blanche's mother was originally from Buffalo, you know — we can use that to our advantage."

"How?"

"What if Blanche had given me, her beloved fiancé, another copy of the letter, in case she met with foul play?"

The Governor looked out the cracked and warped glass of the window. "I thought the girl committed suicide."

"What if it was a murder disguised as a suicide? The Fish or her husband had her killed to shut her up?"

"If you had another copy of the letter in your possession, to be opened in case of any kind of an emergency, then that would implicate Fish — not just as a lesbian, but as a murderer. Or at least put her on a list of suspects." The Governor gave a grim smile. "Why, this plan is even better than the original."

Prentiss looked at his heavy gold Rolex. "I can make it back to D.C. by tonight — and catch my journalist friend at the tree-lighting ceremony."

231

"Well, in spite of all your youthful tom-foolery," the Governor said, nodding, "you might just redeem yourself yet, boy."

Prentiss started, his face full of hope. "Yes, sir."

The older man walked closer to the window, watching the black branches dance in the mist. "We're doing God's work," he said, turning.

Prentiss took off his hat and bowed his head. "Amen."

The Governor did a double take when he saw the extent of Prentiss's bruised face. "What the hell happened, boy?"

"Kissing Fish has a new friend — a red-headed girl who came over with Winston Churchill. Fish took her to the Cotton meeting. Let's just say . . . she has quite a right hook."

"Stay out of trouble, Prentiss," the Governor said, shaking his head. "I'm warning you."

Prentiss clasped his hands behind his back. "I will, sir. I promise."

"Come on then, let's go back to the house before you leave — or else the wife will have a fit. Christmas Eve day and all that."

Prentiss noticed the change in the man's mood. "Will Mrs. King be serving her special eggnog this afternoon?" he asked, already knowing the answer.

King beamed. "Yes, with her famous bourbon whipped cream. And those little pecan cookies."

As the two men opened the door to step into the thickening fog, King clapped his arm around Prentiss's shoulders. "And I do believe there will be carolers!"

Maggie couldn't wait to see Aunt Edith, but first she had Christmas presents to buy. She didn't have much time, so she ran down the herringbone-patterned brick sidewalks in the raw damp, to where she knew there was a department store. She stopped for a passing group of schoolchildren, walking hand in hand and singing, *"Hi-ho, hi-ho, we're off for To-key-yo — to bomb each Jap, right off the map, hi-ho, hi-ho."* U.S. flags were everywhere, flapping from poles, tacked up to windows, graffitied on the sides of buildings, even chalked onto the sidewalks.

Breathless, Maggie made it to Woodward & Lothrop and wandered the floors, luxuriating in the piles of plenty, especially after witnessing the dearth of merchandise in the department stores in London. For women, the store had jewelry, slippers, quilted robes, and nightgowns. For men, there were arrays of smoking jackets, pajamas, White Owl cigars, shaving kits, and shirts.

In the housewares department, Maggie giggled at perhaps the best slogan of the season, for the Proctor toaster: "Merry Crispness." There were portable radios, as well as records by Nelson Eddy, Kate Smith, and the Dorsey Brothers.

But despite the massive quantities of items available on the shelves, Maggie chose only a few pairs of silk stockings, a bargain at $1.15 a pair. She realized she should probably buy everyone war bonds; that was the patriotic thing to do. As she waited for the cashier to ring up her purchase, she glanced around at other shoppers. The sight of a man in a fedora briefly caught her attention. *Haven't I seen him before?*

Maggie was stopped in her tracks by a mannequin wearing a pink silk negligee with a black lace bodice, not unlike the one Rita Hayworth had worn in a recent *Life* magazine spread. *Well,* Maggie thought, *my wearing it tonight might just take care of John's present.*

But after paying at the register, she realized the man in the fedora was still there, following at a distance. Reverting to training, Maggie ducked into a ladies' restroom, took off her coat, turned it inside out so that the blue lining showed, and draped it over her arm. She took a beret out of her handbag and covered her red hair with it, then added a pair of plain-glass spectacles. Realizing she had not been wearing makeup before, she painted on a red lipstick bow. Satisfied, she left, using the service elevator to get downstairs, then made her way out to the street.

She window-shopped in the mist, checking her reflection in each plate-glass window to make sure she wasn't being followed, relying on her training and instincts to spot anyone she'd seen before, or anyone covering his face with a hat or newspaper or umbrella. Satisfied at last that she'd lost the tail, she took yet one more precaution — darting across the street, getting on a bus, and sitting just behind the driver. A few blocks before the Willard Hotel, she got off. She took a roundabout way to the Willard, still checking reflections in shop windows, until she spotted a bookstore, a tiny one, sandwiched between two larger buildings.

The store was deserted, except for a huge ginger cat, grooming himself on a table of books. There was a lump in her throat as she reached down to pet him, thinking of her own cat, K, now residing at Number Ten Downing Street with the Churchills' menagerie.

A day in the life of a spy, she thought. Even though she might be trailed by God knows whom, she couldn't show up without Christmas presents.

For Aunt Edith, she decided on one of the year's most popular novels, *The Sun Is My Undoing,* by Marguerite Steen, about a slave trader's descent into madness. *Well, that should be serious enough for her.* For David, who was still obsessed with all things American, she chose Louisa May Alcott's *Little Women.* And for John, she picked up F. Scott Fitzgerald's *The Last Tycoon,* since he'd apparently never read an American novel. She also thought he might learn a thing or two. She paid at the register with her eyes on the front window, watching the passersby, but the street stayed empty.

When Maggie arrived at Peacock Alley at the Willard Hotel, damp and cold, parcels in hand, Edith Hope was already waiting. Fringed lamps lit the long, carpeted corridor, and the potted topiary trees were hung with tiny silver lights and glinting Christmas ornaments. A harpist in the corner played "Silent Night."

"My goodness!" Edith exclaimed, looking at the grown woman in front of her. "Margaret, is that you?"

Maggie realized she still had the beret and glasses on. She removed both and bent to kiss her aunt, who was sitting on a small, fat sofa, then sat down herself. Aunt Edith was older, she realized with a pang, with more gray in her hair and deeper lines around her eyes. Still, she was a handsome woman, with ramrod-straight posture and a regal bearing.

"You're looking well, Margaret."

"Thank you, so are you."

"It's been much, much too long." Aunt Edith sniffed. "I still don't understand why you couldn't have come home for Christmas. The trains are horrible this time of year, and with all the military on the move — I didn't think I'd get a seat."

Well, I traveled across the Atlantic Ocean, dodging Nazi submarines, Maggie thought, but she let it go.

"I'm so sorry, but because I'm here working for the Prime Minister, I don't have any time off to travel far." Maggie took a quick sweep of the room, just to make sure the man hadn't followed her. Other than a few hotel guests chatting in the lobby, she saw no one suspicious, certainly not the man in the fedora. "And you do look wonderful," she said.

"Don't flatter me. I look old," Edith

replied. She was dressed in a brown-and-white checked suit with a rust-colored silk blouse. She wore no lipstick or powder. On her lapel was a small blue enamel pin with the college arms of St. Hilda's, Oxford, her alma mater. Her shoes were sensible and low-heeled.

"How's Olive?"

"Olive's quite well. She sends her regards."

A waiter materialized. "Would you ladies like menus?"

"I'll have a pot of Darjeeling," ordered Aunt Edith.

Maggie smiled. "I'd like the cream tea."

Edith made a *tut-tut* sound. "All that fat and sugar."

"Which I haven't had for years because of rationing!" Maggie retorted. She tried a new tack. "How are your classes this term? Any young Marie Curies in the lot?" Edith was a professor of chemistry at Wellesley College.

"My students seem to be getting worse every year. I keep waiting for one of them to set herself on fire with a Bunsen burner."

"How has the war affected campus?"

"Everything is topsy-turvy. We have a semi-blackout on campus — to protect Boston Harbor. Even Mildred's leaving us to lead the WAVES — the new Women Ac-

cepted for Voluntary Emergency Service —
everything's an acronym now, isn't it? At
any rate, it's part of the U.S. Navy." The
Mildred in question was Wellesley College's
president, Mildred McAfee. "And everyone's knitting socks for soldiers. When I
lecture I can scarcely hear myself over the
clatter of those damn needles."

Maggie pulled out her own knitting, a
sock with "Victory" in Morse code around
the top. "I've been doing my bit, too."

Aunt Edith looked down her long nose. "I
know you're working for the war effort, and
you're to be commended for it —"

Here comes the "but," thought Maggie.

"But I did have such high hopes for you,
Margaret. I didn't want your extraordinary
upbringing and education to be for naught."

"I —"

"I hear some of the seniors are taking a
Navy correspondence course — Helen
Dodson, the astronomy professor, is teach-
ing it. After they graduate they'll go into the
WAVES — I hear they're also learning
cryptography. You know, it's not too late for
you to do something like that. And then,
maybe when this infernal war is over, you
can do something, well, *important* with your
life. I didn't raise you to be mediocre, you
know. I raised you to be extraordinary."

"I'm assisting the Prime Minister of Britain!" Maggie quieted as the waiter brought a tray with their tea and scones. They waited for him to leave.

"You type, you file," Edith said, checking to see if her tea had steeped. "Anyone could do that. And I'm sure it's exciting — all those young men, the threat of bombs . . ."

Maggie poured hers without looking and dumped in sugar and milk simply to be annoying. "Has *your* city been bombed recently?"

"I lived through the Great War —"

"The Great War took place in the trenches of France. Britain wasn't in the line of fire. The lives of British civilians weren't at risk every night." Maggie did the mental calculation. "Plus, you left for the U.S. in 1915 — you missed most of it."

Edith decided her tea was properly steeped. "Margaret, don't be dramatic." She poured tea into her fragile china cup. "I worry about the way you seem to define yourself through men. 'Mr. Churchill's secretary,' you keep writing. What about you? Why do you need to hide away in the shadow of a great man? Be a great *woman*!" She sighed. "I worry that all this is because I couldn't give you a proper male figure in your life growing up."

Oh, for pity's sake! Why can't she see?
Maggie thought, but she surrendered. "You know, you're right. And when this war is over, I'll try to be more . . . great. Greater." She slathered a scone with clotted cream and jam. "By the way, your brother — my father — you know, the one that I grew up believing was dead — says hello."

"Does he?"

"Well, no. I haven't seen him recently. For all our dramatic reunion, dear old Dad seems as odd and self-involved as ever."

Edith lifted the delicate porcelain cup to her lips. "I'm not surprised," she said in even tones.

When the waiter passed, Maggie caught his eye. "I'd like a glass of champagne, please."

"Yes, miss."

"Drinking already?" Edith protested. "It's not even six!"

I need a drink if I'm going to get through this damn tea. "I drink now. Everyone does in London. It helps make the bombing more tolerable."

"Well, if everyone jumped in Lake Waban, would you, too?"

Maggie gritted her teeth. "Maybe . . . if I felt like it."

"Your great-grandfather was an alcoholic,

Margaret," Edith intoned.

"I am not an alcoholic!" She started as the waiter put down the coupe.

"Margaret, please lower your voice," Edith scolded, her lips pursed. "Ladies never speak loudly in public."

"Speaking of relatives — maybe you could have mentioned that my father wasn't actually *dead*?"

Edith sighed. Maggie recognized the sound, one she remembered Aunt Edith using on chemistry students whom she saw as especially dense about an obvious — to her — equation. "It was a long time ago. And there are things one doesn't discuss with children."

Maggie could feel a muscle under her eye begin to twitch as her blood pressure rose. "I'm not a child!"

"Do drink your tea, Margaret. It's getting cold."

There was a painful silence, and the harpist segued into a Cole Porter medley. "Julia Ward Howe — now that was a great woman," Edith remarked. "She wrote 'The Battle Hymn of the Republic' while she stayed here, you know. It was after she met Abraham Lincoln." Aunt Edith sniffed. "Poor Julia. What would she think of the advantages you've had and the choices you've made?"

"I'm working with Eleanor Roosevelt! Now, *she's* a great woman —"

"But that's different from *being* Eleanor Roosevelt!"

Scanning the room, Maggie spotted David and John walking in. She breathed a sigh of relief. "Oh, thank goodness — I mean, look — here come my friends." When everyone had been introduced and the young men had ordered, the four sat in awkward silence, the two women on the sofa, the men in chairs across.

"So!" David said brightly, sensing the tension. "It's an honor to meet you finally, Professor Hope. Maggie's said so many lovely things about you."

"I highly doubt that."

"Well, that's wartime propaganda for you!" David replied with brio.

Maggie decided to take control of the situation. "What do you think of the death penalty, Aunt Edith?"

The older woman blinked. "The what?"

"There are posters all over town in support of Wendell Cotton, who's sentenced to die in Virginia. I went to a meeting last night, protesting his execution. I was wondering what you thought."

"The death penalty is incompatible with

human dignity. It is cruel and unusual punishment," Edith said, warming to the topic. "It is the weapon of white supremacy and a means of public lynching."

John frowned. "I believe each person is his own decisive moral agent."

Edith's eyes flashed. "You don't attribute anything to environment?"

"I think people need to be responsible for their actions. Especially when we're talking about taking another human life. We can't just let murderers go free. If we don't execute them, more murders will be committed that otherwise would have been deterred."

"Utter speculation," Edith snapped. "The death penalty is morally indefensible."

"Samuel Johnson wrote about the executions of children who stole loaves of bread and how their public hangings became fertile ground for pickpockets," David interjected. "No deterring crime there."

"It was Boswell quoting Dr. Johnson," corrected John. David looked uncharacteristically cross, but John didn't notice. "The death penalty served to deter those considering murder — who hadn't yet committed to a course of action."

"There's no difference in murder rates in states that have the death penalty and those that don't," Maggie argued. "Not only that, but the application of the death penalty is unfair. For example, Wendell Cotton was sentenced by a bunch of old white men who could afford the poll tax. They are hardly his peers."

"So you're saying you're against the death penalty because it's not fairly applied?" asked John.

"It's never going to be fairly applied," Edith stated. Maggie gave a grim smile — at least they were on the same page about *something.*

"Still," John persisted, "when I hear about an especially gruesome crime, I can't help rooting for the death penalty. How can you deny the pain of husbands and wives, and fathers and mothers who are left to grieve? They want vengeance. They want peace — the peace of knowing their loved one's killer is gone from the world. And I believe they should have it."

"But do you think our legal system should be in the business of doling out vengeance?" Edith asked. "Death, the ultimate punishment, for which there can never be any correction? There's shameful racism in our justice system that's a call for humility and self-awareness, not more death!"

David looked around at the angry faces.

"More tea, anyone?" he tried.

Maggie realized that it was indeed time to change the subject. "Oh, and I have presents for all of you! Sorry no time to wrap them, but as we say in Blighty — 'There's a war on, you know' — paper rationing."

"I've heard of *The Sun Is My Undoing*," Aunt Edith said, thawing slightly as she accepted her book. "*The New York Times* gave it a good review. Thank you, Margaret."

As David tried not to snicker at Maggie's being called Margaret, she handed him *Little Women*. "I know it may not look like your sort of thing," she said, "but it's as all-American as you can get, and one of my favorite books when I was younger."

"I shall treasure it always," assured David.

"And this is for you." She handed John F. Scott Fitzgerald's *The Last Tycoon*.

"An American author," he grumbled. "I don't read Americans. With an exception for Charles G. D. Roberts, but he's a poet, and Canadian at that. But I'll try your Fitzgerald." Under the table, Maggie pulled out her shopping bag, tilted it, and gave John a peek at the lingerie. His eyebrows rose in appreciation.

David glanced down at his watch. "So sorry to break up the party, Professor Hope, Maggie, but I'm afraid we must go. The

Boss needs us to hold his hand while he gets ready for his speech at the Christmas-tree lighting."

"Professor Hope, you must join us," John added.

Edith was not convinced. "I abhor crowds."

David winked at Maggie as he took care of the bill. "Well, ma'am, we'll make sure you have the best seat in the White House."

As Edith rose, he gave a courtly bow. "And, really," he asked, offering his arm, "how often does one have the chance to hear someone say that?"

CHAPTER NINE

In the District, it was cold and damp. As the sun set, the silver clouds became touched with orange and the air turned even more chill.

But that didn't stop nearly twenty thousand people from wanting to get a glimpse of the White House Christmas tree — this year on the South Lawn — and hear the President and Prime Minister speak. "No cameras, no packages!" the security staff called as people made their way through bare trees in the fading light, a crescent moon tangled in strands of fog. As the Marine band played "Joy to the World" and "Adeste fideles," choirs from a multitude of churches sang.

David was true to his word. Aunt Edith had a place near the guests of honor in attendance, including the prizefighter Joe Louis and Crown Prince Olaf and Crown Princess Martha of Norway. Maggie was busy with the P.M. but pleased that when she had a moment to check in on her aunt, Edith's eyes were wide and her mouth just slightly open. *Well, maybe a first-row seat at the White House is what will finally impress her,* Maggie thought, amused. She also did a quick scan for her follower from earlier in the day. But it was impossible to spot individuals in the throng.

There was an invocation by His Excellency, the Most Reverend Joseph Corrigan, the rector of Catholic University, then introductory remarks by the Honorable Guy Mason, Commissioner of the District of Columbia.

And then, what everyone was waiting for — Christmas greetings from the President and Mrs. Roosevelt. "Our strongest weapon in the war is that connection of the dignity and brotherhood which Christmas Day symbolizes," the President said, standing with the help of two aides. "More than any other day or any other symbol. And so," he said, flashing another irresistible grin, "I am asking my associate, my old and good friend, to say a word to the people of America, old and young, tonight — Winston Churchill, Prime Minister of Great Britain."

Mr. Churchill rose and walked to the

podium amid deafening applause, welcomed by the American people like a prodigal son. He positioned himself in front of a forest of microphones and waited, fingertips under the lapels of his coat, for the crowd to quiet. "I spend this anniversary and festival far from my country, far from my family," he intoned. "Yet I cannot truthfully say that I feel far from home. Whether it be the ties of blood on my mother's side, or the friendships I have developed here over many years of active life, or the commanding sentiment of comradeship in the common cause of great peoples who speak the same language, who kneel at the same altars and, to a very large extent, pursue the same ideals, I cannot feel myself a stranger here in the center of the summit of the United States."

It was a magical moment. David, John, and Maggie all caught each other's eye and nodded. They'd come a long way, both literally and figuratively, to get to this place, to this time, and they knew it had all been worth it.

In his plummy tones, Churchill continued. "I feel a sense of unity and fraternal association, which, added to the kindliness of your welcome, convinces me that I have a right to sit at your fireside and share your Christmas joys." He beamed. "And so, in God's mercy, a happy Christmas to you all."

There was wild applause and cheers and then a countdown. As the tree's colored lights sparked on, the crowd gasped, then applauded. The enormous evergreen glimmered in the darkness, and the band played "God Save the King" and "The Star-Spangled Banner." As the United States's national anthem was played, Maggie noted with amusement that Fala stood at perfect attention. And, when it was over, he flopped back onto the wool blanket in his basket.

Aunt Edith glanced back at Maggie and smiled. Maggie felt a glow of pride. And she felt, too, the bittersweet knowledge that she would never be able to tell her aunt the whole truth.

Byrd Prentiss was also at the tree lighting. He made his way through the crowd to the press section. "Thomas O'Brian? I'm looking for Thomas O'Brian, *Buffalo Evening News*?"

Tom had finished his last photographs. "I'm Tom O'Brian," he said.

Prentiss strode over and stuck out his hand. "Byrd Prentiss, Governor King's representative in Washington. We spoke by telephone earlier today."

Tom took the offered hand and shook.

251

"Yes, good to meet you in person."

"As I mentioned, we have someone in common," Prentiss continued. "My fiancée is — was — Blanche Balfour. Her mother was born there and her grandparents still live in Buffalo — on Bidwell Parkway."

"I grew up not far from Bidwell," Tom said, nodding. "I'm sorry for your loss."

"May we talk in private?" Prentiss led Tom away from the crowd, to a more shadowed section of the White House lawn. "I didn't want to say this over the telephone, but the thing is," he said, "I don't believe Blanche's death was a suicide. I believe it was foul play. In fact, I'm convinced Blanche was murdered."

Tom stared at him, trying to read his eyes. "What makes you think she was murdered?"

Prentiss lowered his voice. "Blanche knew she was in danger." He pulled out an envelope from the pocket of his camel-hair coat. "She told me to keep this, and open it only if something happened to her." He handed it to Tom. "Well, now something *has* happened to her. And of course I opened it and read it. What I found was, well, shocking."

Tom opened the envelope and began reading the note.

To my darling Byrd,

If you're reading this now, something terrible has happened to me.

For I believe myself to be in danger.

The First Lady of the United States of America, Eleanor Roosevelt, has — I'm ashamed even to say it — tried to kiss me. And, I blush to write this, more. When I refused her advances, she said she would ruin my good name in Washington and that I'd never find respectable work again.

I told her I'd never say anything. I told her that it would stay our secret. But if you're reading this, it means Mrs. Roosevelt has made good on her threat to make sure I couldn't tell a living soul about what happened — what she tried to do.

I will always love you, darling —

Your Blanche

Tom's eyes widened, even as he shivered in the misty cold. "My beloved fiancée was murdered," Prentiss insisted. "I believe by the Roosevelt Administration — to cover up a potential scandal."

"Holy . . ." Tom was speechless.

"Yes, it's the story of a career," Prentiss said. "*Your* career."

Tom reread the letter. "There's no date."

"She — she gave it to me the last time I saw her, on December twenty-first."

"And she died on the twenty-second."

"Yes."

Tom's dark eyes narrowed. "Why don't you take this to the police?"

"The police aren't interested in any potential scandal concerning the First Lady. But if Blanche was murdered —"

"Her name could be cleared of the suicide and her killer brought to justice. But . . . Mrs. Roosevelt . . ."

"Exactly."

Tom whistled. "It would be a huge story. Huge. And not the sort of thing a cub reporter from Buffalo usually gets to break." He gave a rueful smile. "So, why bring this story to me? Why not *The Washington Post* or *The New York Times* or one of the other big papers?"

"They're in the pockets of the Roosevelts," Prentiss said. "Look, I just want some justice for my poor Blanche. I want her family to know she didn't kill herself — that she would never have done such a thing. That she was a pure, honest, God-fearing woman. And I want the world to know that the Roosevelts murdered her. The Roosevelts' papers won't help me. But I'm hoping you can."

"May I keep this letter? At least for now?" Tom asked.

"Of course."

"I'll be in touch," Tom said, placing it in his suit's breast pocket.

"Thank you, Mr. O'Brian." Prentiss turned to walk away in the darkness. "I look forward to hearing what you discover. And reading the story you write."

That evening, Churchill and his staff joined the Roosevelts for Christmas Eve dinner at the White House, where instead of the British holiday favorite of goose, the P.M. dined on roasted turkey, oyster and sausage stuffing with sage, and cranberry sauce flavored with orange zest. Aunt Edith had been invited as well, seated between Lord Beaverbrook and Ambassador Halifax, and speaking earnestly with Eleanor Roosevelt about supporting women scholars in math and the sciences.

When it was time to leave, Maggie smiled at John and squeezed his arm. Then she suggested to her aunt, "Let's all take a taxi together, shall we? Where are you staying?"

Aunt Edith gave an owlish blink. "Why, with you, of course."

"With — with me?" Maggie managed. She

didn't dare look at John.

"Why yes, 'no room at the inn' — or at the hotels either with all the military personnel converging on Washington," her aunt replied. "So I left my suitcase with the concierge at the Mayflower. You and I can have tea and knit and listen to the wireless" — for the first time, the woman gazed at Maggie with something approximating maternal affection — "just like old times."

"Yes," Maggie said, refusing to think of the new negligee still enfolded in delicate silver tissue-paper wrapping in her shopping bag, "like old times. Perfect. Absolutely . . . perfect."

Clara Hess, General von Bayer, and General Kemp were in Chatswell Hall's wood-paneled library, listening to Goebbels's Christmas Eve speech on the wireless. They were enjoying a bottle of fine cognac that Lord Abernathy had given to them as his gift, sipping from their teacups while the fire crackled and popped behind the massive andirons.

"There are few presents under the Christmas tree this year," Goebbels's voice intoned. *"The effects of the war are evident there as well. We have sent our Christmas candles to the Eastern Front, where our soldiers need*

*them more than we do. Rather than produc-
ing dolls, castles, lead soldiers, and toy guns,
our factories have been producing things es-
sential for the war effort. . . . The great task
demands the same sacrifice from us! The
hardest demands are on our soldiers. The
same is true for all Germans abroad. They
often live in an entirely foreign, sometimes
hostile, world."*

Clara snorted. "Ha!"

Kemp raised his chipped teacup. *"Prost!"*

Goebbels continued, *"It should not surprise
us that we are not always loved as we defend
our right to life. Envy and distrust, hatred and
persecution often surround our fellow country-
men. We read about it occasionally in the
newspapers, but they experience it every day.
Today, they are at least connected to us by
radio."*

Clara and Kemp shared a wan smile.

*"Earlier we sang of peace on earth in our
songs. Now the time has come to fight for it.
Peace through victory! That is our slogan."*

Von Bayer rose and walked over to the
wooden wireless, turning the black knob to
shut it off with a loud click.

"But — but he wasn't finished!" Kemp
protested, nearly causing his cognac to spill
from the cup.

"Oh, but he is," said von Bayer. "That . . .

257

midget . . . is completely finished." He began to pace in front of the fireplace, his good eye blazing with rage. "It's a scandal! It's shameful! Regarded objectively, it's a speech of absolute despair. Do you two have a different impression?"

Kemp considered. "At the beginning, I thought something was coming. But the speech's goal was simply to urge the people to accept measures that are already in existence. And it was quite senseless not to close on the note of confidence in the Führer. *That* ought to have been the conclusion — but no, off he went yet again."

Clara's eyes were dim. "I'd hoped he was going to announce something of special importance, too."

Von Bayer continued to pace. "It's disgusting! It ought to have been a brief, concise speech, couched in serious terms, lasting half an hour at the most. But instead it was a typical beer-house tirade." He leaned against the marble mantel and stared into the dancing flames. "I am ashamed of the impression these fellows make on the world! Ashamed!"

He pivoted to face Clara and Kemp. "If I had the chance, I should like to speak directly to Goebbels. I've heard about how delightful and charming he can be, from people who know him well. But in these matters — no! A man who was there told me that he gave a lecture on the conduct of propaganda, and said his philosophy was 'The masses themselves are stupid, you can do what you like with them.' That's what Herr Goebbels thinks of people. Of our own people!"

"Yes, that's Joseph," Clara said, smoothing her skirt. She slipped off her shoes and tucked her legs under her.

Von Bayer refilled Clara's cup. "You know him, don't you?"

"I do." Coiled in her seat, Clara drew out a cigarette.

Both men nearly fell over themselves in their haste to light it, but Kemp got there first with his monogrammed lighter and flickering flame. Kemp turned on von Bayer. "But it is not the right thing to throw all the blame on the Führer." He narrowed his eyes. "Especially for those people who always used to cheer him the loudest."

Von Bayer's lip curled. "I can say, with pride, that I *never* cheered him."

"What?" Kemp looked horrified. "Above all there's one thing which we must not forget — that we have given our oath. After all, Hitler is our Führer. Goebbels is his right-hand man. And here you are, every day pulling them to pieces. If we adopt that attitude, then in time we shall become great friends of England and enemies of Germany." He raised a defiant fist. "We must continue to support our Fatherland!"

Clara took a long drag on her cigarette and blew out a curling wisp of gray smoke. "If only we hadn't started this tomfool war — it was so unnecessary. After we had Austria and Czechoslovakia, we should have stopped." She looked at the long shadows flickering up the yellow walls. "Everything was marvelous! The worst mistake we made in this war was not to invade England after the French campaign. Even if it had meant hundreds of thousands of casualties. And now the Russian campaign is costing us a million dead. And more."

"The Russian campaign . . ." Von Bayer resumed his pacing in front of the fireplace, watching the flames twist and flicker. "Well, it makes me sick."

Kemp poured them all more cognac, the liquid glittering amber in the firelight. "After all, our Führer wrote in *Mein Kampf* — never wage a war on two fronts —"

Von Bayer swung to face Kemp, his good eye bulging. "*Mein Kampf* was written by an ape who's ruined our people and our religion. There is hardly anything we haven't attacked — we've attacked the past, our religion, the Jews, France, England, Russia . . . And now we declared war on America. We've attacked anyone who doesn't share our same politics — and in a stupid, brutal way."

Kemp's face paled in shock. "But the Russians are beasts!"

Von Bayer stood, undeterred. "Our Gestapo competes with the Russians in their bestial actions!"

"That's the trouble," Kemp mused. "All the killing. If only all senior Army leaders had said, 'We won't participate in that mess! It is dragging the name of Germany in the mud!' "

Von Bayer slumped into one of the overstuffed chairs. "A few did, and they were never heard from again. The fact that such things were done by Germans will puzzle world historians for centuries," he continued, but his voice was now subdued. "History will hold the German Generals responsible for not protesting and laying down their arms."

"Come, it's Christmas," Clara said, eager to change the subject. "Let us drink a toast to the health of our glorious Führer."

Von Bayer drained the last of his cognac and threw his cracked teacup into the fireplace. It exploded like a grenade. "I refuse to toast that man. And I will not pretend that there is any hope of our winning this war. Especially now that America is in it."

Now Kemp was angry. "We Germans have been bled white. Don't forget we were swindled by those miserable Fourteen Points in the first place."

"That was a long time ago and another war. Now, I regret every bomb, every scrap of materiel, and every human life that is still being wasted in this senseless conflict. The only gain that the war will bring us is the end of the ten years of gangster rule. Every day the war is a crime. The men at the top must realize that. They must put Hitler in a padded cell. A gang of rogues can't rule forever. They ought to be hanged. In my opinion, the collapse of Germany is inevitable."

Clara's eyes narrowed. "If our homes are at stake, if our Fatherland is at stake, we must fight on. If we capitulate now, Germany will be wiped out once and for all, and we will all find ourselves in Siberia. The German people will be finished forever. Do you truly believe that a people like the English, with their supercilious and uncultured ways, should dominate the German people?" She rose and strode toward von Bayer. "That's a piece of insolence that we simply cannot accept. Our national pride won't allow us to be ruled by such swine."

She smiled, a sultry smile, and leaned in to him. "Besides, I still believe in the long-distance rocket."

"You're using the word 'rocket' now?"

Clara tilted her head. "None of these idiots are spying on us. Look at Lord Abernathy — he's practically one of us."

Von Bayer grimaced. "Still, you mustn't forget that a war has never yet been decided by a new weapon."

"And do you believe that such a thing will still come in time?" Kemp's eyes sparked with hope.

The blonde gave a catlike smile. "Yes, in the summer Goebbels told me in private that the rocket program was already in the final stages of completion — in Peen-emünde."

Von Bayer shook his head. "This business about a new weapon — I still don't believe it. You can't just produce a new weapon out of a hat."

"Not out of a hat," Clara corrected. "Launched into the sky!"

Kemp's eyes grew large, like a child's. "But will it come in time?"

Von Bayer stared as the former opera diva rose and walked over to Kemp, sitting on his lap, kissing him on the mouth. "Oh, it will," she vowed, stroking his hair. She whispered, "Lord Abernathy got me the bottle of Chanel Number Five that I asked for." She extended her slim wrist to him. "What do you think?"

Kemp took her hand and brought it close, closing his eyes and kissing her palm. "Merry Christmas," he murmured.

In the chilly attic of Chatswell Hall, Owen and Arthur were listening intently. They knew something important was being conveyed, and they had turned on the phonographs to record the conversation.

"There! Now that'll impress Lord Cherwell and the rest of the brass!" Arthur crowed as he watched the needles on the dials rise and fall.

Owen was not as sanguine. "Oh, she's just showing off. A rocket? Come now — that's something for novels and H. G. Wells wireless broadcasts. Not real life. Not real war."

"Look, she said 'rocket' and 'Peenemünde' — and they all seemed to know about it." Scowling, Arthur rubbed the back of his neck. "I wouldn't put it past those Krauts."

"Hey, *we're* Krauts!" Owen punched him

on the arm.

But Arthur didn't want to joke. "I may be from Germany, but I'm British now."

"Well, I'm German, but I'm no Nazi. And I'd like to go back someday — when they're gone."

"Not me. I'm staying here. I'm never going back." Arthur shook his head. "Look, I'll start the transcription . . ."

"Then we'll send it to London. Up to Cherwell and Sandys. And Churchill, of course."

Clara's drafty bedroom on Chatswell's second floor was the former great house's master suite. It consisted of a sitting room, a dressing room, and then the bedchamber itself. The rooms were paneled in dark-stained oak, with built-in bookshelves, now empty, and a massive fireplace. Murky oil paintings of hunt scenes hung on the walls.

Bored, exhausted by ennui, and also quite drunk, Clara flung herself on a moth-eaten velvet fainting sofa, spreading her arms wide and tipping her head back in a dramatic pose, worthy of the dying Violetta in Verdi's *La Traviata.*

It was then, looking at the room upside down, that she noticed one of the bookcases wasn't flush with the wall.

Chatswell was old, with the expected cracks in the plaster moldings, water stains, chipping paint, curling wallpaper, but this defect seemed different.

Clara squinted at it, considering, then rose and crossed the room to examine it further. Yes, the bookcase was definitely almost an inch askew. She pushed back on it.

Nothing happened.

Then she realized it wasn't the bookcase that was angled, but the wooden panel next to it.

She pushed on the right of the panel. Nothing. She pushed on the left. Nothing.

Clara wiped her dusty hands on her skirt, about to give up, when she noticed the paneling wasn't flush with the floor, either. She pushed on the top of the panels, just where the plaster started, and the wooden section began to move, opening slowly, on a secret hinge.

The blonde's eyes widened and her breath came faster. She opened the secret door all the way and peered inside.

It was cold and smelled dank. The walls were rough-hewn stone. There was something in the room, in the corner. In the dark, she could just make out a copper water jug and cup, now tarnished and mottled green with verdigris. Both objects were covered in spiderwebs.

Clara was well versed in British history, especially since she had once trained to be and then posed as a well-educated British woman during the Great War. She knew about Elizabeth's Protestantism and how the Queen had persecuted Catholics, especially after the Babington Plot. No priests were allowed to celebrate the sacred rites in private homes on pain of death. And so, in case of a surprise visit, homes owned by Catholics had built secret chambers — sometimes called priest holes — where communion wine, wafers, and vestments could be hidden and even the priests themselves could hide during a search.

She put in a change of clothing, thick-soled shoes, and a flask of water, and then replaced the panel exactly as she'd found it.

"Happy Christmas," she murmured.

CHAPTER TEN

Christmas Day, 1941. Maggie, Edith, and John waited on the wet pavement as the doorman stood in the street, raising one white-gloved hand and whistling for a taxicab. "Well, Margaret," Edith began, "I hope it's not another four years before . . ." Then without warning she threw her arms around her niece and squeezed. "Be safe, Margaret," she managed.

The taxi pulled up, and Edith waved off both Maggie and John. "I don't believe in long good-byes," she told them as the doorman opened the taxi door and she slid into the backseat. "Not good for the constitution." With that, she closed the door and started giving directions to the driver. And yet, Maggie was sure, as the sedan pulled away, that she saw Aunt Edith take out a handkerchief and dab at her eyes.

Maggie swallowed the lump in her throat, and then she and John began their walk to the White House — no one had Christmas Day off. The weather wasn't cold enough for a white Christmas, and overhead the sky remained leaden. They passed a group of rangy young men, up early, shouting and waving their arms with holiday exuberance. "Americans are so . . . loud," John observed.

Maggie knew exactly what he meant, but she wasn't in the mood. "The United States is vast. You haven't seen anything. There are mountains, plains, prairies. It's a big place. People need big voices." As they walked through Lafayette Park, she asked, "What was it you needed to talk to Mr. Churchill about?"

"Oh, that," John said, putting up his black Fulton umbrella as the raindrops fell faster. "Washington's weather — not so different from London's."

Maggie had spent enough time in Britain to know that when weather was invoked, it wasn't time to ask personal questions.

They arrived at the White House, passed through security, took off their wet things, and went upstairs to the map room. Their hands were chilled, their feet were cold, and the news that greeted them was grim. Wake Island had been seized by the Japanese. Even as the noose was tightening around their necks and defeat inevitable, the U.S.

soldiers still alive sent out the message "Merry Christmas from Wake Island. Send Us More Japs." The reports from the Philippines were dire. Hong Kong had fallen.

There was nervous speculation about who in the U.S. Navy might be court-martialed for nodding off behind the wheel at Pearl Harbor. Odds were high on Army General Walter Short and Admiral Husband Kimmel, both in Hawaii.

Still, it was Christmas. "Presents!" David exclaimed after Mr. Fields had served them coffee. He handed Maggie a book: *Total Espionage,* by Curt Riess. When Maggie saw the title, she rolled her eyes.

"Relax," David said, as if sensing her apprehension, "the woman in the shop said *everyone's* reading it this Christmas. And *Kirkus* — whatever that is — apparently gave it an excellent review."

David then handed John an enormous box, and he opened it. Inside was another, smaller box. He opened that one. Then another. Then another. Finally, wrapped in a bit of tissue paper, was a pack of spearmint chewing gum.

David beamed.

John looked dour. "Er, thanks, old thing." He went to some shopping bags he'd hidden under his desk and procured a rum-soaked fruitcake, wrapped in cellophane with a ribbon and a sprig of holly.

"Fantastic" — David laughed — "my favorite. Of course, if anyone else had gotten me a 'fruitcake,' I'd have knocked his block off."

John handed Maggie a wrapped package. It was also a fruitcake. "Oh, I simply adore fruitcake!" she said, smiling. But she didn't, really. She hated fruitcake, loathed it. And secretly, she was a bit disappointed. *Fruitcake? Really?*

Mrs. Roosevelt came in with Mr. Fields, who was wheeling a cart, to prepare them all a special breakfast, her own scrambled eggs in a chafing dish. As she plated the eggs with salt and pepper, she related, "I used to do this every year for the children, on Christmas morning. Of course, now they're all grown-up and away, so you'll have to permit me to fuss over you young people a bit." Maggie knew that the four Roosevelt sons were in the military. *What a strain it must be, always checking, always wondering, always worrying,* she thought.

As Mr. Fields set up a special folding table, they listened to a radio address from the King: *"I am glad to think millions of people in all parts of the world are listening to me now. . . . If skies before us are still dark and threatening there are stars to guide us on our way. Never did heroism shine more brightly than it does now, nor fortitude, nor sacrifice, nor sympathy, nor neighborly kindness. And with them, the brightest of all stars is our faith in God. These stars will we follow with his help until light shall shine and darkness shall collapse."*

"A wonderful man, your King," Mrs. Roosevelt said. "So brave that he and the Queen never left London. They visited us at Hyde Park a few years ago, you know — lovely people."

After they'd eaten the meal, complete with toast, butter, strawberry jam, and hot coffee, Mrs. Roosevelt blotted her lips with a napkin and stood. "I'll leave you now," she said. "Merry Christmas."

The two men stood when the First Lady did. David looked up at the clock and nodded when she left, then went to rap on the Prime Minister's door. "Sir? Sir, it's time to leave for the service."

"Come in!" Churchill's voice boomed. "Gimme —"

As David went into the Rose Bedroom to help the P.M., Maggie shrugged into her coat. "Aren't you coming?" she asked John, who was still sitting at the desk.

"Afraid not. I'm off in a bit."

"Where?"

His face was shuttered. "I prefer not to say at this point in time."

Really? First fruitcake and now obscurity? "Why, thank you, Bartleby the Scrivener."

"No, no, it's not that. It's just that . . . nothing is definite." He rubbed both hands through his hair until it stood on end. "I don't want to jinx anything," he implored. "Please understand."

"Well, tell me this, at least — are you going by car? Ship? Train?"

"Plane, actually."

"Airplane?" Maggie thought she'd heard wrong.

"Yes, airplane, with a series of jump flights — not anything direct, of course. I feel a bit like the narrator in *The Last Tycoon.* What was it she said? 'The world from an airplane I knew.' "

Maggie was impressed. "You read the Fitzgerald already?"

"Well, I made an exception for Fitzgerald, since it came from you. I'm about a third of the way through it. Since last night was rather free," he said with emphasis.

Maggie avoided his pointed look by buttoning her coat, then pinning on her hat. Yes, she probably could have sneaked off once Aunt Edith had begun to snore. But she still felt . . . conflicted. "How long will you be gone?" she asked.

"Just a bit. I —"

"Let me guess — you can't say." Maggie felt her heart crack just a little.

He rose and walked to her. "I'll see you soon," he said, standing close enough for her to smell the citrus scent of his shaving soap.

The door banged open. Churchill wore a dark blue topcoat and had a sprig of holly in his lapel. "Come!" he roared, striding through the office to the corridor, brandishing his cane like a saber with David at his heels. "Church! Mustn't be late!"

"I've got to go," Maggie told John.

"I know. I do, too."

They clasped hands. It was war; no one took for granted they would see each other again. "Well, bon voyage," Maggie murmured. "Please do let us know when you've arrived safely at your secret destination."

"I will," he promised, kissing her cheek.

The President and First Lady had decided to celebrate Christmas Day at Foundry Methodist Church. The First Couple rode in the first long black sedan with Harry Hopkins, while the Prime Minister, David, and Maggie followed in another just behind.

Together, they formed a queue of shiny automobiles driving past Lafayette and Farragut Squares to Foundry, a rusticated dove-gray granite church on the corner of Sixteenth and P Streets.

The mood in Churchill's limousine was grim. Maggie knew the news from Hong Kong wasn't unexpected, but the P.M. was still taking it hard.

As raindrops tapped on the car's roof, Maggie cleared her throat. "Mr. Churchill, I was wondering if you'd heard of the case of Wendell Cotton —" she began.

"Yes, yes, I've heard of it. Our Mrs. R seems to be quite involved."

"He's going to be executed."

"Yes," replied the P.M., staring out the window at people struggling through the rain.

"He didn't have a fair trial or sentencing. And so, I was wondering —"

David put a hand on her arm to still her, but Maggie shook him off. "Mr. Churchill, I was wondering if you might have a word with the President? To convince him to ask the Governor of Virginia for a stay of execution?"

Churchill shook his head without looking at her. "No." He pulled out a cigar to chew.

"No?" Maggie was shocked. "Why not?

It's the right thing to do!"

The Prime Minister's eyes met hers. "Miss Hope, do I need to remind you that we are at war? I must triage what is the 'right thing to do,' as you so naïvely put it, with 'what must be done.' As must the President."

Maggie remembered this was the same man who was willing to use chemical and biological weapons if he determined it necessary to guard Britain's coast. Still, she pressed on. "But an innocent man is going to die."

The Prime Minister's eyes blazed. "Miss Hope! Innocent men are dying all over this planet — a great number today, in fact — on Wake Island, in Hong Kong, in Russia. But from what I understand about this America of yours, we need both the North and the South — Dixie — fighting for us. We can't have the Southerners distracted by the President meddling in their business."

"But —"

"No, Miss Hope. The President would tell you the same thing. And I do *not* advise you ask him. Is that clear?"

In a small voice, she repeated, "A man is going to die."

"Yes. He will most probably die. Many men, and women — even children — will die before this war is over. But his death is not part of our battle, Miss Hope. Is that clear?"

India, Africa, China, the colonies. All those so-called brown people. And now Wendell Cotton, too. Maggie twisted her hands in her lap, pressing them together so tight that her knuckles turned white. Now she knew how Dorothy felt when she realized the Great and Powerful Oz was really just a little man behind a curtain.

"I said, Miss Hope, is that clear?"

Maggie stared out at the raindrops sliding down the window. "Yes, sir."

The Foundry Methodist Church was surrounded by government agents, armed with tommy guns and revolvers. As the parties emerged from the sedans into the rain, aides held large black umbrellas over their heads. Ron Kantor from *The New York Times* called out from a throng of journalists, "Mr. President! Why are you at Foundry? Why aren't you at an Episcopal church on Christmas morning?"

Roosevelt, pushed in his chair by his naval aide, caught his eye. "What's the matter with the Methodys, Mr. Kantor? I like to sing hymns with the Methodys," he called back cheerfully from underneath the tilt of his hat. "And it will be good for Winston to sing hymns with the Methodys, too. Just you wait and see."

Inside the thick stone walls of Foundry, there were lilies everywhere, in memory of the President's mother and the First Lady's brother, as well as evergreen boughs on the altar. The pungent scent was hypnotic. Roosevelt and Churchill sat in the fourth pew, as the minister prayed for "those who are dying on land and sea this Christmas morning" and for the P.M., who was leading "his valiant people even through blood and sweat and tears to a new world where men may dwell together, none daring to molest or make afraid."

As the service went on, Maggie struggled to make sense of balancing the deaths of many and the death of one. She came up with nothing.

While they were inside, the rain had tapered off. And when the service was over and they were stepping down the slick flagstone steps, she spotted Thomas O'Brian taking photographs. She hung back. "Go on without me," she told David. "I want to chat with my old college chum."

David shot Tom a dark look but replied, "Take the day off if you must," before he climbed into the car with the P.M.

"Merry Christmas, Maggie," Tom greeted

her, camera in hand. "May I take your picture?"

Despite the beauty of the service, Maggie's mood hadn't lifted. "I must confess, I'm not particularly jolly today." She glanced up at the tarnished silver clouds. "Not exactly classic Christmas weather."

"I don't think anyone's jolly these days," he replied. "So soon after Pearl Harbor, and with the news coming in from Wake. You don't have to smile if you don't feel like it." He took a few snaps, then asked, "Did you know Blanche Balfour, the woman who was working for the First Lady?"

"No, we never met," Maggie said. *Well, not while she was alive, anyway.* "I heard about her death. How horrible — she was so young, too."

Scattered drops began to fall. "I just wrote her obituary for the *Buffalo Evening News.*"

"Really?" Maggie's mind was clicking into high gear as she led the way to an overhang on the church's steps where they would be protected from the rain.

"Originally, we were told it was a suicide, but I had orders from my editor not to include that in the obit — to say 'death from natural causes.' "

"Is that typical?"

"With families from her social class, yes.

Any mention of suicide is considered taw-dry. But then, at the tree lighting last night, Blanche's former fiancé approached me. He thinks she was murdered."

"Murdered?" Maggie's heart skipped a beat. "Why does he think that?"

"First, he didn't believe suicide was characteristic of her," Tom replied. "No history of depression, no previous attempts. And she was newly engaged."

"Who is — was — Blanche's fiancé?"

"Byrd Prentiss, an aide to the Governor of Virginia. He's Governor King's D.C. liaison."

"And he thinks she was murdered." Maggie took that in. They watched as water gushed from a verdigris gutter, while pigeons taking refuge from the storm cooed in the eaves. A plump woman's umbrella turned inside out in the wind and she tried her best to protect her Christmas hat. A young man dashed by, a newspaper held over his head. And another man in a fedora sat in a parked black sedan across the street. *Why, hello, old friend.*

She turned her attention back to Tom. "Have you spoken to the police?" she asked. "Have they gotten the results of the autopsy?"

Tom looked down at her and tilted his

head. "Why do you ask?"

"Blanche died right before I came to the White House. And so I've been filling in for her, with the First Lady. Mrs. Roosevelt was . . . quite upset to learn of Blanche's death." She was careful not to say more. Certainly nothing about a missing letter.

"What was she working on?" Tom asked.

Maggie stalled. "Working on?"

"For Mrs. Roosevelt."

"Well, Mrs. Roosevelt has an extremely busy schedule, of course. Her 'My Day' column, press conferences, various charities . . ." Maggie took a deep breath — it wasn't news that Mrs. Roosevelt was involved with causes. "Mrs. Roosevelt's also working with Miss Andrea Martin to try to stop the Wendell Cotton execution."

"Bingo!" Tom exclaimed. "If Mrs. Roosevelt has the President's ear, which we all know she does, she could get him to speak to Governor King . . ."

"What's Governor King's relationship with the Roosevelts?"

Tom pulled his scarf tighter around his neck. "I don't know for sure, but King's a Southerner. Traditionally, men like that aren't too supportive of folks like the Roosevelts, even though they're Democrats. There's also talk that King wants the party's presidential nomination when FDR's term's up —"

"But," Maggie interrupted, "to the best of my knowledge, the President has no plans to intervene in Cotton's execution. King has nothing on him or Mrs. Roosevelt. So why would anyone want a secretary dead?" Well, when she was Mr. Churchill's secretary in London during the Blitz . . . but that was another story.

"That's the part I can't figure out," Tom said. "But the thing is, Byrd Prentiss showed me a letter —"

Maggie blinked. "A — a letter?" *Don't tip your hand, Hope.*

"Yes, a letter," Tom said. "He told me that the day before she'd died, Blanche had given him a sealed letter, to be opened 'just in case.' Well, when she was found dead, he opened it, of course."

"Of course," Maggie managed. *Another* letter? She felt ill.

"Yes," Tom said. He seemed to be having an internal struggle. Then he reached into his breast pocket and took out the letter Prentiss had given him. He handed it to Maggie.

She skimmed it, then went back to read it again, looking for every detail.

This letter was the same handwriting as

282

the letter she had discovered through her pencil-lead technique. And some of the phrases were the same. But it was *not* the same letter. The other note incriminating Mrs. Roosevelt was still at large. "Is this the original?" she asked.

"Yes."

Maggie was struggling to put the pieces together. *What if Blanche didn't do something she was supposed to? For example, she could have been sent to Mrs. Roosevelt's office to undermine her somehow, accuse her of sexual misconduct, discredit her. But maybe she couldn't do it. Or wouldn't do it. And then when she refused to go through with the plan, she was killed.* Maggie felt a cold touch to her spine and looked up at Tom. She thought of her last case, of a murdered ballerina in Edinburgh. "If Byrd Prentiss was her fiancé, I'd check to see if he has an alibi for the night in question."

"But" — Tom was momentarily speechless — "he's the one who came to me!"

"The murderer is generally someone close to the victim, Tom. I'm not saying he *is,* but you can't rule him out just because he was engaged to her."

"You'd make a damn fine reporter, Maggie Hope." Tom chuckled. "Er, sorry. Didn't mean to swear in front of a lady."

"Oh, believe me, I've heard worse. From you at rehearsals, if I remember correctly." She turned up the collar of her coat. "I'm thinking we should go to Blanche's apartment and look around, see if the police missed anything. And speak to Detective Timothy Farrell, in charge of the case. I met him at Mrs. Roosevelt's office, so he might actually talk to us. And I'd also like to see the coroner's report."

Tom's jaw dropped a bit. "Most girls I know would want to go to Christmas parties, you realize . . ."

"Tom," Maggie said patiently, "I'm not 'most girls.' So, on to Blanche's apartment — it's not too far from here." She marched down the stairs, leaving Tom to catch up.

"Wait." He looked shocked. "How do you know that?"

"Let's just say — how do they put it in your line of work? Ah, yes — I can't reveal my sources."

The streets were deserted, with people at home or in church. They dashed through the cold rain under Tom's umbrella to Blanche's apartment on Massachusetts Avenue, Maggie leading him through the side doors. She opened the lock, once again, with her hairpin.

"So, that's what they teach you at Wellesley College, huh?"

"Yes, lock picking — along with Shakespeare, French, and tennis," she muttered as the pin finally pressed against the catch.

Inside Blanche's apartment, Maggie retraced her steps. Of course, the police had been there. But they hadn't known about the letter. And she might have missed something the first time she was there. Back then she'd thought she was looking at a suicide. *But if it's murder . . .*

She and Tom looked through the apartment, going through bathroom cabinets, kitchen cupboards. Nothing. Then Maggie went through Blanche's small secretary desk. Nothing. She pulled out all of the drawers. In the bottom drawer, there was a box of stationery. Maggie opened it. Underneath Blanche's notepaper was an invitation addressed to her in engraved print: *We Celebrate the Newest Members of the Women of the Ku Klux Klan.* There was an address for a private home in Alexandria, Virginia, and then a photograph tucked inside — a group of young white women, smiling, in white dresses, carrying bouquets of roses. It looked like a graduation photo, except for the sharply pointed conical white hats they all wore.

"Look," Maggie said, handing Tom the invitation and photograph. "Blanche may have been part of the Klan."

"I didn't know there were women Klansmen, er, Klanswomen. Now, that's a disturbing thought."

"So, Blanche would definitely be supportive of Wendell Cotton's execution," Maggie mused, remembering Blanche's Kant quote as she put everything back in the desk the way she'd found it. "That's all there is," she said, rising and putting on her coat.

They went to the front door. "Wait," Maggie said. There was the door's lock, the one she had picked, but there was also a chain lock that could be fastened from inside the apartment. It was broken. "Look."

They both stared at the broken chain.

"But it could have been broken when she moved in," Tom pointed out.

Maggie shook her head. "This is a respectable building. They'd have replaced it before she moved in. What if someone *broke* in?"

"No way to tell for sure."

"Righty-o. Well, then, let's see if the police have any theories they might want to share."

At the Washington, D.C., police headquarters, even on Christmas Day, security was tight.

"Because of the attack on Pearl Harbor?" Maggie asked, looking at the lineup of officers with guns standing around the perimeter of the lobby.

"That," Tom said, folding his wet umbrella, "and also because of the demonstrations."

"Demonstrations?" Maggie repeated. "What demonstrations?"

"You've been out of the country for a few years," he said as they made their way to the receptionist's desk, leaving wet footprints on the stone floor. "So let me catch you up — security tightened in September, when there were some big marches and a rally here in D.C."

"Really?" Maggie asked. There had been few U.S. papers available in western Scotland, where she'd spent the autumn. "Why?"

"Police brutality against coloreds. The coloreds marched on the police this past summer because A. Philip Randolph, the founder of the Brotherhood of Sleeping Car Porters, wanted to challenge African Americans not being included in the armed forces and the nation's defense industry. Lots of folks demonstrated — and this was well before Pearl Harbor and war. Things got ugly."

"My God, I can imagine." At the front desk, Maggie said, "We'd like to speak with Detective Farrell, please."

The receptionist was a woman in her thirties, with henna-colored hair, a low-cut blouse, and a bad overbite. Some of the cherry lipstick she'd applied had migrated to her teeth. "Do you have an appointment?" she asked.

"My name is Miss Hope, and I work with Mrs. Eleanor Roosevelt." Maggie pulled out a card from her handbag. "Detective Farrell gave me this," she said, "when we met at the White House, and told me to come and speak to him if I learned anything regarding a particular case."

The receptionist's eyes widened. "I'll let him know you're here, Miss Hope. Right away, Miss Hope."

"Thank you for seeing us, Detective, and on Christmas Day, too," Maggie said as Farrell ushered them into a conference room to speak in private. He reeked of sandalwood cologne.

"Emergency-room doctors and cops don't get holidays off."

"This is Thomas O'Brian, from the *Buffalo*

288

Evening News," Maggie said by way of introduction.

"Anything for the First Lady," Farrell said, his oily hair gleaming under the fluorescent lights. "Now what can I do for you?"

"We'd like to see the case file on Blanche Balfour."

Detective Farrell's cheerfully expectant face fell. "I'm afraid that's not possible, Miss Hope. Those are private files."

"We have reason to believe that Miss Balfour was murdered," Maggie said.

"I'd be happy to review any evidence you may have."

Maggie smiled. "That's the thing — there are certain things we need to be discreet about, as you might assume, given who's involved."

Detective Farrell's cheeks began to redden. "I can't just hand over a file to a civilian — and a journalist —"

Maggie looked at him through narrowed eyes. "Give us Blanche Balfour's file and I won't tell your wife about the affair."

The detective gasped. "How did you know?"

"You have a band of light-colored skin on the ring finger of your left hand," Maggie said, "where a wedding ring would be, while the rest of your hand is tanned. I noticed in

Mrs. Roosevelt's office when we met that you slip your wedding ring on and off. And now you don't have it on, during a workday. Which makes me suspect that you're seeing someone during your lunch hour. And removing your ring while you do." She smiled sweetly. "You also just applied a prodigious amount of cologne."

Tom gave a low whistle.

"I'll — I'll get you Blanche Balfour's file," Detective Farrell said.

"Thank you, Detective. I certainly appreciate it," said Maggie.

"How did you learn to do that?" Tom asked as they left, making their way through the heavy raindrops back to the street.

Maggie had Blanche Balfour's file tucked tightly under her arm. "Do what?"

"Shake down that detective."

"Oh, that," Maggie said, looking to see if she could spot Mr. Fedora. "Just working on my Nora Charles impression is all."

"Right." Tom didn't sound convinced.

"Do you think this weather will ever let up?" Maggie said, changing the subject.

Tom took the hint. "With all this rain, you must feel like you never left England."

"We need to go somewhere dry to read this," she said, impatient, "but nothing's open on Christmas Day except churches."

"Churches, yes — and also Chinese restaurants," Tom said, raising his hand for a taxi. "Do you like dumplings?"

He took Maggie to lunch in Chinatown, Tao's on H Street NW, between Sixth and Seventh Streets.

It was warm inside Tao's and smelled deliciously of ginger and garlic. An article from *Life* magazine was pinned up on the wall, next to the flags of the United States and China: *"How to Tell Japs from the Chinese — Angry Citizens Victimize Allies with Emotional Outbursts at Allies."*

As Tom hung up their coats, Maggie read, *"LIFE provides a handy guide to distinguish friendly Chinese from enemy alien Japs."*

"Mr. Tom!" came a silvery voice from the back of the restaurant. Maggie looked up to see a petite and angular woman, her long gray hair fastened into a chignon and held with cloisonné hair combs decorated with kingfishers. On the collar of her dress was a small enamel pin with both the American and Chinese flags.

"Mrs. Tao!"

"Table for *two* today, Mr. Tom?" she asked Tom, fixing a questioning gaze on Maggie.

Tom gave her his most dazzling smile.

291

"Table for two, yes." As Mrs. Tao grabbed menus and led them to one of the tiny tables, he added, "May I say, you're looking exceptionally gorgeous today, Mrs. Tao?"

She rolled her eyes in mock exasperation, then gestured for them to take a seat at a table against a red-painted wall, near the plate-glass window. Outside in the rain, a yellow neon sign spelling CHOP SUEY blinked and buzzed. Maggie scanned the street. There was a dark sedan parked opposite the restaurant. At the wheel was the man in the fedora. She frowned.

"He's like that with all the girls," Mrs. Tao said as she handed Maggie her menu. "Mr. Tom," the older woman demanded, "are you going to let my husband cook for you today?"

"Mrs. Tao, it would be an honor for your husband to cook for us," he declared. "Is that all right with you?" he asked Maggie. "He makes some delicious dishes that aren't on the menu."

"Of course," Maggie answered. Mrs. Tao gave a satisfied smile and left them.

"I take it you come here often?" Maggie asked. "You certainly have Mrs. Tao charmed."

"This is the best restaurant in Chinatown. And I should know — I think I've tried them all."

A young waitress in black with a white lace apron brought them teacups and a silver pot, while Mrs. Tao brought a candle and lit it, with a significant look to Tom.

Maggie poured the steaming tea. It was jasmine — hot and floral. She took a sip; it tasted sublime. Feeling warmer, she looked around the restaurant. There were a few other people at the rickety wooden tables with green tablecloths. "I guess we're not the only people with this idea."

"Jews," Tom explained. "Jews eat Chinese food on Christmas Day too, because Chinese are among the only restaurants open. It's kind of a tradition now, I guess."

"Aha." Maggie pulled out the file and began to read as Tom sipped his tea. What she read was not luncheon-conversation appropriate, but she didn't care. When she was done, she looked up with wide eyes.

"What?" Tom asked. "Don't keep me in suspense."

"Blanche Balfour *didn't* commit suicide," Maggie said. "According to the coroner's report on the condition of her lungs, she was drowned first — and she fought against her attacker — and then, after she was dead, whoever it was slit her wrists to make it look like a suicide."

"If the girl was *murdered* —"

"Yes," Maggie said. "According to the coroner's report, Blanche was definitely murdered."

Tom's expression turned intent. "Well, let's just say that now I *definitely* want to solve this case. A girl whose mother was born in Buffalo . . . Did you know — her mother grew up in the same neighborhood I did, and her grandparents are still there, in the same house. Her family deserves the truth. *She* deserves the truth. Her memory, at least."

Maggie raised an eyebrow. "And a sex scandal would be an awfully big story for a cub reporter?"

"No!" Tom's blue eyes flashed. "I mean yes — but that's not why . . . My goal is to find out who murdered Blanche and bring her killer to justice. *Not* implicate the First Lady."

"Well, I'm relieved." Maggie cleared her throat. "May I keep this note? I realize that's asking a lot, but with the potential of a scandal . . ."

"How do you know Eleanor Roosevelt is innocent?"

"I — I know," Maggie said. "Really, I know. You'll have to trust me, just like you had to trust me in those tricky Beethoven passages." *How much to tell Tom?* "The night Blanche Balfour was murdered," Maggie began, "I'd just arrived at the White House. Mrs. Roosevelt was quite worried that Blanche hadn't come to work and hadn't called in. She couldn't reach her on the telephone. So I" — Maggie decided to omit the fact that the First Lady was with her — "went to Blanche's apartment. I knocked. And when she didn't answer, I — er — let myself in."

Tom took a sip of tea. "Since I've seen you do that in person, I definitely believe you."

"I found Blanche dead in the bathtub, with her wrists slit."

Tom nodded. "And it looked like a suicide."

"Yes. So I called for an ambulance and left. No one knew I'd been there. And I didn't find any suicide note. And there was nothing in the wastebasket. But there *was* a notepad on her desk. I took it with me and used a pencil lead to see what had last been written on it. Which was a suicide note — very similar to the one you showed me." She picked it up. "But not the *same* note."

"What about the handwriting?"

Maggie raised her shoulders then dropped them. "Inconclusive, in my opinion." She held the note to the small candle and watched as it caught fire, then disintegrated. *One less note,* Maggie thought. *One down, one to go.*

Tom looked on in shock and dismay. "You — you just burned my only evidence!"

"I know," Maggie said. "I'm sorry. I'm so sorry. And you'll just have to believe me when I tell you it's a matter of national, even international, security."

Tom looked at Maggie in amazement approaching fear as the waitress brought several dishes — fat dumplings, steaming noodles, and crispy-skinned sliced rare duck and rice.

Maggie first served Tom dumplings, then herself. "I think it's possible that Blanche wrote the first note — but then decided against it."

"Well, then," Tom said, still recovering, belatedly reaching for the duck, "why is she dead? If she decided *not* to kill herself and threw the note away —"

"Except she didn't, because it wasn't there."

"Then who killed her? And why?" Tom persisted, bewildered. "The note implicates the First Lady in her suicide. But she didn't actually kill herself. Then someone made it look like she did. But then the note's not there. It doesn't add up!"

"Also, since I've started working on the Blanche Balfour case, I've been followed," Maggie said, checking out the window. *Yes, Mr. Fedora's still there.* "The same man was outside the church this morning when we were talking, and he was there the night I went with Andi Martin to a jazz club. I think that's the man who tried to attack us as we left."

Tom's mouth dropped open. "Why would he attack you? Are you all right?"

"We're both fine." Maggie sighed. "I believe that someone may have killed Blanche Balfour and taken her suicide note in order to protect the First Lady. I don't think Mrs. Roosevelt knew about it, but it may have been done for her. To protect her. To protect the Roosevelt Administration."

Tom dropped his chopsticks. "You think someone on Roosevelt's staff *murdered* Blanche Balfour? And you think you're being followed by that same someone?"

"Let's just say I think it's a possibility." Maggie took a sip of tea.

They ate in silence for a few minutes, each lost in thought, desperate to piece together what they'd learned. "So, what are you doing for Christmas dinner?" Maggie asked finally.

"Going back to my sad little bachelor apartment with leftover noodles . . ."

"How'd you like to work with me? I'm meeting Miss Martin from the Workers Defense League tonight. We're going to spend the evening with Wendell Cotton and his mother at the Thomas Jefferson Prison in Virginia."

Tom speared a dumpling with his chopstick. "I'd like spending Christmas with you very much, Maggie. And I'd also appreciate the introduction to Miss Martin. But isn't prison an odd place to spend Christmas?"

"I know it's not exactly conventional, but believe me," Maggie said, as she maneuvered her chopsticks the way she'd learned to do in Boston's Chinatown, "I've had odder."

CHAPTER ELEVEN

While Mr. Churchill, David, and the rest of the entourage prepared to relish Christmas dinner at the White House, Tom picked Maggie up in his dented coupe. Together, they drove through the gloom to the Thomas Jefferson Prison in Virginia farm country less than an hour from Washington. The air was thick with fog and chill, but at least the rain had stopped.

The prison had a high barbed-wire fence with razor wire looped over it. Four guard towers staffed by men with rifles — one at each corner of the property. In the middle of a field of dead grass rose the prison itself. *It's like approaching the castle of the Wicked Witch of the West,* Maggie thought.

They parked in the muddy lot and then walked, stepping over puddles, to the main entrance. In the distance, a dog howled. One wire gate slid open for them, creaking and clanking, then another. "We're here to see Wendell Cotton," Maggie told the uniformed guard. "Meeting Miss Andrea Martin."

As the gates slammed shut behind them with a resounding *clang,* Maggie had a moment of panic, her heart beating fast. They were trapped.

But then the guard opened the next gate. He searched Maggie's handbag and patted them both down, then nodded toward a twisting brick path, overgrown with weeds. "That way."

A cold wind had picked up. *Follow the yellow brick road,* Maggie thought as she shivered in her coat. When her heel caught on a crumbled brick and she nearly stumbled, Tom grabbed her by the elbow. "Steady there," he said. He was very close. He smelled like shaving soap and wet wool.

"We're late," Maggie said, straightening and stepping away. "I mean, thank you. But I don't want to keep Andi waiting."

At the prison entrance, they were signed in and given badges. Andi sat waiting for them on a wooden bench covered in graffiti. She was wearing wool trousers and a jacket with large shoulder pads. Her hair was pulled back in a glossy roll. "There you are!" she exclaimed. "Merry Christmas!"

She and Maggie embraced. "Merry

300

Christmas," Maggie said. "Andi, please meet Thomas O'Brian, a friend of mine from college. Tom, this is Miss Andrea Martin."

"How do you do?" Tom said, shaking her hand.

"Please call me Andi. What do you do, Tom?"

"I'm a journalist," he said. *"Buffalo Evening News."*

"A journalist!" Andi beamed at Maggie. "Brava! You're a natural at this — bringing a journalist along. We can use all the publicity we can get." She looked to Tom. "Are you interested in writing a story on Wendell? Because anything you need, I'll help you with —"

"Just here as a friend of Maggie's," Tom interrupted.

"Well, we'll see what you have to say after you meet him," Andi said, leading the way down the tiled corridor. The air inside the prison stank of bleach.

There were more locked doors to be let through, and then at last they were in the visitors' room. It was small, with paint peeling off the walls and worn black linoleum underfoot. A heavy wire-mesh screen divided the room in two. A metal radiator hissed and spat in the corner, and a rusty ceiling fan squeaked overhead. They sat on folding gray metal chairs at one end of the scarred wooden table on one side of the mesh room divider.

"They ease up on the rules in the final days," Andi said as they waited, by way of explanation. There was the sound of a bolt being pulled, and then a guard led Wendell Cotton in. He was thin; the black-and-white striped prison uniform hung loosely on his narrow frame, and his hands were cuffed behind him.

"Please take the cuffs off," Andi instructed the guards, her voice low and strong.

After a glare and a stubborn pause, the guard produced a key. He unlocked the cuffs, and Wendell took the seat across the screen. They all stared at each other through the mesh as the fan continued to whir and clank overhead. "Hi, Wendell," Andi said. "Merry Christmas. These are my friends, Miss Hope and Mr. O'Brian."

Wendell ducked his head and attempted to smile. "Hello, Miz Hope, Mr. O'Brian. Thanks for coming, Miz Andi. And merry Christmas to y'all."

"How do you do," Maggie said, while Tom nodded.

"Tom's a journalist," Andi said. "Maybe he'll get some extra press for you."

302

"Ah, it's Christmas, Miz Andi!" Wendell chuckled. "Give the poor man a break! And you take one, too. Just for five minutes."

Andi laughed at this. "I know I can be a bit, well, intense sometimes."

"And I thanks you for it. I thanks you for comin'. Thank you all for comin'."

"How's your momma?" Andi asked, unbuttoning her coat.

"She fine," Cotton answered. "Well, not fine, exactly, but she be strong. She was here earlier, but I tol' her to go on home. She tired."

Andi nodded, her face grim. "Maggie came to see her and me at our talk the other day at Metropolitan Baptist."

Maggie nodded. "Your mother seemed . . . strong."

"She's a good woman," Wendell said, his large eyes meeting Maggie's. "I tol' my lawyer that I want them to send me to war," Wendell explained to her. "I could be like the Jap pilots who sacrifice themselves — what're they called?"

"Kamikaze," Maggie said.

"Yeah," he said. "Kamikaze. I could do that. I'd feel a lot better about doing that. Seems a waste to not let me get out and fight. This is America — this is my country, too."

Dinner was brought in on his side, a thin slice of what looked like fatty ham, collard greens, and a small square of corn bread. "Hope you don't mind me eatin,' "Wendell said. "I'd share, if I could." He poked at the meat. "Not that you'd necessarily want this."

Before he began, he closed his eyes. "Heavenly Father," he said, "please bless this food, and bless our friends and family. Especially bless those who've come to keep me company on this day, the day your Son was born. Amen."

"I've thought of Wendell Cotton as a public figure — it's good to be reminded he's a real person." Maggie walked beside Tom to the entrance of the Mayflower. The damp pavement, now freezing over in the cold night air, glistened in the hotel's lights.

"He seems like a decent young man," Tom said. "I don't know everything about his case, but I do know that jury looked suspicious. He deserves a retrial."

She stopped in front of the entrance as a doorman in livery held the door. "Do you want to get a drink?" she asked impulsively. "It's been a long and strange day. And it's still Christmas, after all."

"I thought you'd never ask."

Realizing all the Mayflower's bars were

closed, Maggie suggested, "I have a bottle of champagne in my room — is that all right?"

"Sounds good," Tom said, following her into the elevator.

"I mean, I don't usually go around asking men up to my hotel room, but it's Christmas —"

"And everything's closed. It's fine; as the good Jesuit priests of Canisius High used to say, we'll 'leave room enough between us for the Holy Spirit.' "

In Maggie's room, she hung up their damp coats, then pulled out the bottle of champagne John had left. The ice in the bucket had melted, but it was still chilled. Maggie popped the cork, then found two glasses. She poured. "Here," she said, handing Tom a heavy tumbler. "Not as pretty as a coupe, but it will do."

She sat in the striped wingback chair and he on the footstool. They clinked. "Merry Christmas," they both said at the same time. Maggie had a moment of sadness thinking of John. *This was supposed to be* our *champagne,* she thought. *I should be drinking it with him.* And then, *But he's not here. And it's Christmas. And Tom's an old friend. And I'm not doing anything wrong.*

Tom took a sip and looked around the

room. "This is nice," he said, then laughed. "Do you remember how I locked you out of your room one day, when I was dating Paige?"

"And I had a paper due the next day!" Maggie exclaimed. "I was furious with you! I could have cheerfully wrung your skinny little neck!"

"You were much too serious back then. You studied too much, worried too much. By the way, I never asked — how's old Paige doing these days? Married? Three kids? Summerhouse on the Cape?"

Maggie inhaled sharply. "You mean, you didn't hear?"

"No. Hear what?"

What to say? "I — I'm sorry to be the one to tell you. She's dead, Tom."

"Paige?" He blinked, struggling to absorb the shock. "Dead?" He shook his head. "But — but — she's so young . . . *was* so young . . ."

Maggie put her hand on his arm. "She was working for Ambassador Kennedy in London when the war broke out." Maggie couldn't tell him the real story, of course.

"Probably following Joe," Tom remarked.

"We reconnected when I arrived in London," Maggie continued. "We were flatmates for a while, actually, in my grandmother's house, the one I'd inherited, the one that brought me to London. But then, the Blitz . . ."

Tom put down his glass on an end table. "Paige . . . I just can't . . . She was so vivacious, so lively . . ."

"I know."

"How did she die? If you don't mind my asking."

Even if she wanted to tell Tom the truth about Paige's death, it was classified. "She died . . . in the bombing." Which was the truth, if not the whole truth.

"Paige." Tom tried to take it in. "I can't believe it." He looked to Maggie. "It's been hard for you over there — all of you over there — hasn't it?"

Maggie bit her lip. "It's been —" She tried to think of what Mr. Churchill would say. "It's been *challenging*."

"I'm glad Paige was with friends. When she died."

Oh, Tom . . . "Yes."

He spoke quickly, changing the subject. "How was your tea with your aunt?"

"However did you know about that?"

"I'm a reporter. I have my sources." He chuckled. "No, in all seriousness, I was coming into the Willard to have drinks with a friend and saw you."

307

"You should have come over and said hello."

"You had the two uptight Brits with you in addition to your aunt. I didn't want to intrude."

Only one is uptight. "Please," Maggie said. "Any and all distractions would have been welcome. It was rather awkward. She raised me to be the next Marie Curie, and I'm afraid I've let her down terribly."

"I was raised by a western New York congressman, and then didn't go into politics. Our holiday dinners back in Buffalo aren't exactly a barrel of laughs. Why do you think I'm here for Christmas?"

Maggie raised her glass. "They probably have a lot in common."

"I'm sure they do." Tom raised his as well. "To the professor and the politician."

They clinked. "Cheers."

"Still, your parents must be proud of you," she said.

He sipped his drink. "I'm sure they'd rather I'd married a nice Catholic girl right out of school, settled down, and had a bunch of kids by now. Gone to law school. Followed in my old man's footsteps." A more serious expression crossed his face. "Although, now with the war —"

"All bets are off." Maggie stifled a yawn.

"Sorry. It's been a long day."

"It has." He stood. "I should be going. Thank you for the drink."

Maggie rose, too. "My pleasure."

At the door, Tom put on his coat and scarf and pulled on his gloves. He leaned in, and his lips brushed her cheek. "Merry Christmas, Maggie Hope." The kiss was brief and chaste.

"Good night," Maggie said, watching as he walked down the hall, feeling something similar to disappointment. Then she shook her head, closed the door, and locked and chained it.

CHAPTER TWELVE

RAF Captain Max Evans's film of the new construction in Peenemünde was sent on to Danesfield House in Medmenham, in Buckinghamshire, England. Like Bletchley Park, Danesfield House was a great house located just outside London that had been taken over by the government for war work. At Danesfield, that work specifically was photo analysis.

The men and women there were trained to look for "anything odd or unusual" in the thousands of grainy aerial images set before them. Their mantra was "size, shape, shadow, and tone." They used black-and-white prints, rather than color, as the varying shades of gray in the shadows revealed more information about what was happening on the ground below.

In what used to be Danesfield House's ballroom, now filled with rows of military-issue desks and battered metal file cabinets,

Daisy Langston, one of the low-level photo analysts, was going over the prints made from Captain Evans's film with a loupe. She'd never before seen anything like the three enormous circles. "It's strange, that's all I know," she said to Beatrice Spencer, sitting opposite. She passed over the photograph.

The tea cart had just been by, and Bea was eating a Sally Lunn roll, but she wiped her sticky fingers on a cotton napkin, then took the photo. She squinted through her own loupe. "You're right. It's queer is what it is."

Much of the time, Daisy and Bea didn't know what they were supposed to be looking for; the two young women joked it was like looking for a needle in a haystack when you didn't even know what a needle looked like. But they'd worked at Danesfield long enough and seen enough aerial photographs of Europe that they'd both developed a keen instinct for what was "normal" and what wasn't.

"Let's take a closer look." Daisy grabbed for the stereoscope, which allowed her to see the photos in three dimensions.

Daisy was leggy and raven-haired, chosen both because her father was a Lord and because she had perfect vision — as did all the photo interpreters at Danesfield House, men and women alike. Like Bea, who had graduated from St. Hilda's in 1940, most were academics, mathematicians, and scientists recruited from Oxford and Cambridge. Finding the hidden details in photographs required not just excellent vision but also a sharp intellect and a creative mind. Seeing the image was one thing but working out exactly what it was, something else.

"Anything?" Bea asked. She was wide-shouldered and athletic, a former champion golfer, swimmer, and tennis player, with chestnut-brown hair and freckles.

"Here, look for yourself."

"What is it? Some kind of tube?" Bea crinkled her nose.

"Look, if you see it in 3-D, you'll see it's something standing. See, here's the shadow." Daisy and Bea knew that sometimes one could learn more from the shadow than from the object itself.

Bea looked with longing at her abandoned Sally Lunn roll but said, "All right, let's measure it, then." The "tube" was almost forty feet high. "It's a big pole sticking up in the air!" she exclaimed.

Daisy pushed back a lock of blue-black hair. "Well, what do you think it's for?"

"No idea. Large phallic symbol?" Bea joked.

"Ha! But, seriously, what could it be? A dummy, to cover up something else that's going on there? Why would they make a huge tube?"

Bea tilted her head. "If there's anything I've learned from this war, it's everything is about the almighty penis. Have you noticed? Guns, tanks, bombs . . ."

They were coming to the end of an overnight shift and feeling a bit giddy. Daisy convulsed in laughter. "Stop! Stop it!" She tried to collect herself. "I'll take it to Captain Mitchell. See what he thinks."

Bea giggled. "He'll probably see it as an homage to the all-mighty 'Fatherland' as well."

"Shut up, you!" Daisy barely got the words out through her laughter. "And I'll see you outside in five for our ciggy break."

The day after Christmas, Prime Minister Winston Churchill was scheduled to address a joint session of Congress. It had been a last-minute decision. Many of the representatives were out of town for the Christmas holiday. Nevertheless, the event was packed. After the Congressmen and Senators, seats went to the diplomatic corps and government bureaucrats. The public was barred, and sentries were everywhere. But the restrictions didn't stop hundreds of Americans from queuing in a long line along East Capitol Street NE in the damp weather, in hopes of catching a glimpse of the P.M.

With John away, Maggie and David had even more work to do, helping Mr. Churchill prepare for his speech. But he was unexpectedly amiable, relaxed even, as Maggie brushed the lint off the lapels of his three-piece pin-striped suit. "There, sir," she said. "Mrs. Churchill would approve." They left for the line of long, shiny, black sedans that would take them to the Capitol.

"It's big," David remarked as they walked up the white marble stairs, damp and slick, of the neoclassical building.

"Yes, one of the District buildings that survived the Brits in 1812." Maggie pointed to the top of the high dome. "*Freedom* is one of my favorite statues."

"A bit ironic as a topper for a building built by slaves, wouldn't you say, Mags?"

She sighed. "You have a point."

They walked with the P.M. to a small room behind the Senate Chamber, where they would stay until he was introduced. "Ah, the theater of politics," David murmured.

"Is he all right?" Maggie asked, alarmed, taking a closer look at Mr. Churchill. The Boss did look pale.

"I'll get him a glass of water," David told her.

Maggie cracked open the door to peek at the crowd. In the high-ceilinged chamber, all attendees had had their cameras taken away, but, for the first time, a live radio broadcast was allowed, and she could see the huge cameras present for newsreels.

At twelve-thirty on the dot, the event began. Maggie and David watched from the wings as the President of the Senate, Vice President Henry Wallace, called the vast room to order, then announced, "The Prime Minister of Great Britain!"

Churchill walked to the well, surrounded by a thicket of microphones. There he stood, fingertips under the lapels of his jacket, waiting for the crowd to quiet. As the audience turned their attention to him, he calmly took a leather eyeglass case out of his pocket and removed a pair of gold-framed spectacles, which he settled on his nose and ears.

He looked up, his steady gaze taking in the vast room, including the balconies, making eye contact with as many of the audience members as possible. The air crackled with anticipation. "I cannot help reflecting that if my father had been American and my mother British, instead of the other way around, I might have gotten here on my own," he began.

The Americans roared with laughter, and David and Maggie exchanged a relieved look. The Boss was fine. He was better than fine. He was downright *lovable.*

Churchill smiled, blue eyes sparkling, knowing he'd won them over. "I should not have needed any invitation," he continued. "But if I had, it is hardly likely that it would have been unanimous." Again, laughter erupted in the chamber.

"But here in Washington, in these memorable days, I have found an Olympian fortitude which, far from being based upon complacency, is only the mask of an inflexible purpose and the proof of a sure, well-grounded confidence in the final outcome."

He was interrupted repeatedly with applause and huzzahs.

He gazed over the crowd. "Now that we are together, now that we are linked in a righteous comradeship of arms, now that our two considerable nations, each in perfect unity, have joined all their life energies in a common resolve, a new scene opens upon which a steady light will glow and brighten."

He went on in that vein, finally concluding: "I will say that he must indeed have a blind soul who cannot see that some great purpose and design is being worked out here below, of which we have the honor to be the faithful servants. It is not given to us to peer into the mysteries of the future. Still, I avow my hope and faith, sure and inviolate, that in the days to come, the British and American peoples will, for their own safety and for the good of all, walk together in majesty, in justice and in peace."

When he finished, he was showered with applause. As he left, Churchill raised his right hand in the V for Victory sign. "At least he got it right this time," David muttered. The audience went wild, rising as one and stomping and cheering their approval as the P.M. waved and exited.

David and Maggie looked at each other, sharing the significance of the moment. An important battle had been won, even if it hadn't been fought with guns and tanks. They watched as Churchill shook hands with Vice President Wallace. "What's his schedule for the afternoon?" Maggie asked David as the crowd calmed and then dispersed.

"He's in meetings with Roosevelt and the top brass for most of the afternoon. Why?"

"If you don't mind, I have a few things to do for Mrs. Roosevelt."

"Go! Go!" David said. He was in a triumphant mood. "It's all under control here. By the way, I like your book. Thank you."

"You mean *Little Women*?"

" 'Christmas won't be Christmas without any presents,' " he quoted. "And I like this androgynous couple of Jo and Laurie."

Poor David. Don't get too attached.

Back at the White House, Mrs. Roosevelt was in her office. A fire crackled behind the screen, but it wasn't much use against the pervading damp. "Come in," the First Lady said to Maggie, beckoning. "And close the door, please, Miss Hope."

"Yes, ma'am."

The First Lady pulled out a file stamped with the words TOP SECRET in red ink. "I've spoken to Mr. Churchill about your security clearance."

Maggie's eyes widened. "Yes, ma'am."

"You have quite a . . . colorful background."

"Yes, ma'am." Maggie swallowed. "Mrs. Roosevelt, I have some news. Maybe you'd prefer to sit?"

"Oh my, is it that bad?"

Maggie decided to be blunt. "There was

another note," she said. "Allegedly written by Blanche. I destroyed it."

"What did it say?" the First Lady managed.

"It's similar to the pencil-rubbing one. It was given to a reporter by Byrd Prentiss, Blanche's fiancé. He said she gave it to him for safekeeping, 'just in case' anything were to happen to her."

Eleanor Roosevelt's hand moved to worry the triple strand of pearls around her neck. "A reporter?"

"It's all right," Maggie said. "I vouch for him. And I burned the note."

The First Lady's face creased. "But she committed *suicide*!"

"Well, that's what we assumed happened," said Maggie. "And that's what someone wanted whoever found her body to think. However, I was able to obtain her file from the police, and the coroner's report indicated all physical evidence points to a murder. Blanche was drowned, and, after she was dead, her wrists were slit. Someone wanted to make it *look* as though she'd committed suicide."

"Oh, my heavens. That poor child," the First Lady murmured. "But then where's the note?"

Maggie felt a surge of impatience.

"Ma'am, don't you see? What if someone knew she was going to accuse you? What if they murdered her and then took the note and destroyed it, in order to stop a potential scandal?"

The First Lady's face paled. "No," she stated. "It's not possible . . ."

"Byrd Prentiss is the D.C. liaison to the Governor of Virginia."

"Oh, yes." Mrs. Roosevelt nodded. "I remember him — just haven't heard that name in a while. Mr. Prentiss had a promising political career of his own, before he made a few missteps. Didn't realize he was working for Governor King now . . ."

"Ma'am, is there anyone — Mr. Hoover, perhaps? — who would go to such lengths to protect you? Your husband?"

Mrs. Roosevelt blinked away tears. Then she lifted her head and straightened her back. "No — there's not a chance Mr. Hoover could be involved, especially to protect me. He loathes both Franklin and me. He'd be absolutely delighted to see something scandalous take us down."

"Then, if I may ask, do you and your husband employ someone to" — Maggie tried to think of the most politic phrasing — "protect you both? Is that something perhaps Mr. Harry Hopkins also does, in addition to his other duties?"

"Harry?" Eleanor Roosevelt shook her head. "Not Harry. First of all, he's the most respectable man I know, with the most integrity. Moreover, he's recovering from stomach cancer. . . . No, not Harry. It couldn't be Harry."

"Is this" — Maggie didn't know how hard to press, but she went ahead anyway — "is this something you could speak with your husband about? Would it be possible to ask him?"

"No," the First Lady said. "No, no, Franklin wouldn't have anything to do with something so horrible."

Maggie wasn't convinced, but she nodded anyway. "There could still be a note accusing you out there somewhere, ma'am. Even if the President doesn't know yet, there's still a chance he may find out." She steeled herself. "I'm afraid that's not all, ma'am," she added.

"Oh, good God, there's more?"

"I've been followed since I attended the Wendell Cotton meeting at the church. By a man in a black coupe who wears a fedora. I haven't gotten close enough to identify him, but he's definitely been following me. I believe he tried to attack me the night of Andrea's speech at the Metropolitan

Church."

The First Lady put a hand to her heart. "Are you in danger?"

"Yes, ma'am. I can handle myself, and now that I'm aware I'm being followed, I can keep an eye out for this man. But I do wonder if he's part of the President's entourage. If you can't speak with your husband about any private security detail he may have in place, is there any way for you to check his files? Go through his papers? Er, I realize how that must sound, yet . . ."

"Part of the President's entourage? No!" Mrs. Roosevelt looked as though she might faint. "And go through Franklin's papers? Miss Hope, of course, *I* could never do that."

Maggie felt a pang of guilt for bringing the matter up. *How could I even have suggested it?* "I'm sorry —" She knew it was a transgression. And yet, it was quite possible that the President could be concealing evidence of a connection between his office and Blanche Balfour's murder.

Then the First Lady raised a hand. "*But* I can tell you that the President and the rest of his staff will be out tomorrow afternoon. And as I'm hosting a holiday tea at three in the Blue Room, I'll be keeping the entire household staff quite busy on the first floor." She looked to Maggie and winked. "If you should happen to be in the office tomorrow, chances are you'll have the second floor all to yourself."

CHAPTER THIRTEEN

As a former Royal Air Force pilot, John Sterling found flying as a passenger on someone else's plane an excruciating experience. Although a series of flights across the country was a luxury most people in the United States only dreamed of — and was reserved for only the richest businessmen, moguls, and movie stars flying on the studio's dime — he was nervous. He preferred being behind the controls himself.

John missed flying. He missed the RAF, and he missed feeling useful. But here he was — injured, not fit for service, now a passenger on someone else's plane. A civilian. One of what he and his crew used to call "the mundanes" — those who'd never felt the freedom of the sky.

Looking out the window to the plane's wing, he pictured a Gremlin. He pulled out his notebook and began to draw.

The lobby of the Los Angeles airport was plastered with vivid posters — REMEMBER PEARL HARBOR! DEFENSE BOND STAMPS — YOU BUY 'EM, WE'LL FLY 'EM, and KEEP YOUR TRAP SHUT — CARELESS TALK MAY COST AMERICAN LIVES — and everywhere John looked were soldiers in U.S. uniforms. At the terminal's entrance, a line of drivers held signs bearing the names of their passengers. John broke out in a chuckle when he saw his. It was bright white with unmistakable bubbly handwriting: *John Sterling.*

"I'm Lieutenant Sterling," John told the driver, a colored man with dark skin and a neat gray mustache, wearing a uniform and cap trimmed in gold braid.

"Yes, sir." The man grinned, taking John's suitcase as he did so. "Merry Christmas, sir. How was your flight?"

They passed by a group of U.S. officers. All saluted. John returned the gesture. "Flights, many flights," he replied. "And uneventful, thank heavens."

The driver's eyes took in the tall man's British military uniform and the haunted expression in his eyes. "Maybe uneventful's not such a bad thing these days, sir."

"Maybe not. May I ask your name?"

"Mack Hollis, sir." The man touched his free hand to his cap.

"A pleasure to meet you, Mr. Hollis."

"It's just Mack, sir."

"That's not how we do things in England."

"Well, sir, you may have noticed — you're not in England anymore."

Stepping outside, John was hit by a dizzying wall of jasmine-and-bus-exhaust-scented air, dry and heavy with heat. The sun glared down with an almost palpable weight; the sky above was a rich, sparkling blue; and palm trees grew hundreds of feet into the air, their ridiculous-looking fronds waving in the marigold sunlight. There were garish yellow and pink flowers in clay pots everywhere, women in brightly colored sundresses, their varnished nails peeping from open-toed sandals. A young boy dashed by, trailing a bouquet of rainbow-colored balloons. Everyone seemed bright-eyed, laughing, well fed. Utterly untouched by war — at least, war as they knew it in London.

"No, I guess I'm not in England anymore," John murmured as they approached the white Cadillac limousine.

Hollis chuckled as he opened the passenger door. "What do you think of Los Angeles so far, Lieutenant Sterling?"

John took a deep, greedy breath of California air before he slid into the sapphire blue leather interior. "I think . . . Well, I think that I have no idea why anyone would want to live anywhere else."

After driving dusty roads from the airport, Hollis finally pulled the Cadillac up Sunset Boulevard to the entrance of the Beverly Hills Hotel. The iconic sign was written in quirky cursive, and the stucco-covered Mediterranean revival hotel itself, hidden behind the palm trees and lush flora, was the startling color of a pink flamingo. Under the porte cochere, the ceiling was painted with stripes of cream and forest green. Wide-eyed tourists in island shirts with cameras lined the curb, no doubt hoping to catch a glimpse of the arrival of Bette Davis, Humphrey Bogart, or Howard Hughes.

"Here we are, sir," Hollis announced, opening the door.

John took a deep breath and stepped out onto the thick red carpet leading up the hotel's front steps.

The tourists and the magazine photographers, struck by his height and his uniform, flocked to him, snapping pictures. John looked hunted for a moment. But then he straightened his shoulders, flashed his best fighter-pilot grin, and gave the V for Victory sign.

Flashbulbs exploded like fireworks.

Hollis smiled, his amber eyes glinting in the reflected light. "Welcome to Beverly Hills, sir." As John passed through the pink pillars, he called: "A star is born!"

When the woman at the reception desk saw who'd made John's reservation, she threw a significant look to the hotel's manager, so it was he, and not the bellboy, who took John's luggage and escorted him back outside to his bungalow.

John and the manager navigated the winding paths of the hotel, the sultry air smelling of jasmine and oleander. Orange butterflies flitted among the hot-pink bougainvillea like rising embers. In the distance, a Mexican gardener tenderly pruned and watered the roses. BUY A BOMBER BREAKFAST! proclaimed one sign outside the restaurant; for a thousand-dollar bond, John saw, one could get a breakfast of ham, eggs, buttered toast, and the piano accompaniment of Eddie Cantor himself. At the Polo Lounge, people with tanned faces and heavy watches held court at leather banquettes.

The manager nodded. "The Sand and

Pool Club, sir." The water was a shimmering turquoise. The pool was ringed with oiled and bronzed bodies draped on lounge chairs, cushioned in the same green-and-white stripes found everywhere in the hotel. "If you like to sunbathe, sir, we have white sand imported from Arizona for the tanning section," he added.

John was rarely at a loss for words, but even he took a moment. "S-sand?"

"Many of our guests feel a beach tan is superior to a pool tan. So we had sand imported."

"I see," John said, stepping aside to let two beautiful women in tennis whites pass by.

"We're patriotic, sir, at the Beverly Hills Hotel," the manager explained. "After the attack on Pearl, we offered to drain our pool for antiaircraft enhancement. But the Army didn't see fit to take us up on it."

"Is the West Coast worried about an attack?"

"Oh, yes, sir. San Francisco has a complete blackout now. Those Jap subs are definitely out there, patrolling. They've sunk a couple of merchant ships and scuffled with our Navy — dirty yellow bastards."

When they reached John's bungalow, the lights were on, the windows were open, and the blinds were pulled back, so that the private garden with its perfect pink roses could be properly appreciated. The former pilot whistled through his teeth, taking in the suite's cream and beige living room, the well-stocked bar cart, and the open doors to the bedroom and marble bath, as the manager put down his suitcase. "Thank you," John murmured, slipping him some coins.

"Oh, sir — it's my pleasure," he said, pocketing the tip as he withdrew. "Would you like me to send a butler to unpack for you, sir?"

But John was already closing the door behind him. On the low coffee table was an impressive bouquet of flowers he couldn't identify, a basket of oranges, a plate of pink-frosted sugar cookies wrapped in rosy cellophane and tied with a gaudy satin bow, an ice-filled bucket of champagne, and an enormous box of See's chocolates.

John scooped up the bottle of champagne in one hand and with the other opened the door to his private garden, complete with potted palms. He sat down, stretched out his long legs, and opened the wine. It popped open and bubbled over, he thought wryly, exactly as if he were in a Hollywood movie.

Taking a swig from the open bottle, he sighed, leaned back in the chair, and took in the cerulean sky, the tiny yellow finches chirping in the lemon trees. In the distance, he could hear the faint sound of people laughing and splashing in the pool. He thought about Maggie, and how he'd love to share this with her.

He raised the bottle in mock salute. "Cheers, love."

At Danesfield House in Medmenham, Bea Spencer knocked at the open door of Captain Mitchell's office. "Sir, I have something you may want to see."

Captain Owen Mitchell gestured for her to enter. His metal military-issue desk seemed incongruous on the parquet wood floor and beneath the intricate plaster molding and the medallions on the ceiling. A picture of the King was the only ornament on the lavender-blue walls. Captain Mitchell was a middle-aged man, with thinning hair, gray, bushy eyebrows, and thick horn-rimmed glasses.

Bea walked in past a dead palm slanting in a Ming pot, handing over the photographs of Peenemünde taken by the pilot Max Evans.

Mitchell glanced at them and blinked. He

studied them for a moment, then ran his fingers through what was left of his hair. "And what am I supposed to be looking for, Miss Spencer?"

"There, sir, on the left." Bea pointed.

He picked up a loupe and peered. "Where they're extending the airfield?"

"No, sir," Bea replied. "The circles."

"That's a dredging operation, dear — drains, most likely."

"Sir, do you think it could be a launching pad — for a rocket? The memo from London asked us to continue to look into anything that could be rocket installations."

"That" — Mitchell jabbed a finger at the photograph — "has something to do with sewage, I'm afraid."

Beatrice stood her ground. "Then what *do* rocket installations look like? Sir?"

Captain Mitchell pushed his chair back from the desk. "Miss Spencer, no one knows, because we've never seen a rocket installation before. They might not even exist."

"Our instructions were to 'look for something unusual.' "

"What you're showing me is hardly unusual."

"See this shadow?" she persisted. "It shows that this — what looks like a pole —

is actually forty feet tall. Look, and then that building, there, could be the observation tower."

"It could," Mitchell countered, "also be a partially deflated barrage balloon."

Beatrice ground her teeth. "Sir, I believe it's a rocket."

Mitchell glared at her, then sighed. "All right. We'll get some more photographs, then." He took a closer look at Beatrice, his eyes running up and down her body. "And what do you happen to be doing for dinner tonight, young lady? How would you like to keep an old man company?"

Beatrice smiled. "Why don't you write the report on this, I'll file it, and then we'll talk?"

Captain Owen Mitchell didn't believe the forty-foot tube was a rocket launcher, but in order to secure Beatrice Spencer's company at dinner, he wrote a report, then sent it by motorcycle courier, with copies of the photographs, to Duncan Sandys. Sandys was Finance Member of the Army Council and the newly named Chairman of the War Cabinet Committee for Defense against German Flying Bombs and Rockets.

When Sandys saw the photographs, he immediately called a meeting of the War Cabinet.

It was almost ten in the evening on December 26 when the Cabinet members filed into the meeting room in the Cabinet War Rooms, minutes away from Number 10 Downing Street under the Treasury. This underground warren of rooms was hidden beneath a thick slab of protective concrete and served as their bomb shelter. Even though the ventilation system — called "air-conditioning" — was on and black fans mounted on the walls whirred, the space was hazy with smoke. The conversations of the men in uniform rumbled in the small space.

"The P.M. is in Washington, of course." Sandys spoke from the head of the U-shaped table, and the men quieted. Duncan Sandys was a handsome man, tall and lean, with prominent cheekbones, a high forehead, and a noticeable limp from a battle wound he'd received in Norway. "But he's asked me to look into German weapon development. In front of you are folders containing the latest intelligence. I believe that what we're looking at are rockets — forty-foot rockets on the Peenemünde site."

"Science fiction," Lord Cherwell muttered. A former physics professor at Oxford and one of Winston Churchill's oldest and closest confidants, he had only recently been named a baron. From his association with the P.M., he wielded considerable power in the War Cabinet, offering advice on science and technology, including the making of anthrax and other bioweapons.

"What was that, Lord Cherwell?" Sandys asked rhetorically as he folded his hands in front of him. While his face betrayed nothing, his knuckles had gone white. He and Cherwell had been battling about the rocket situation for years now. Sandys believed they existed and were a threat; Lord Cherwell did not. "Didn't quite catch it."

"I said," Lord Cherwell spoke with emphasis in his patrician, German-inflected accent, "it's all a load of science fiction. Maybe after the war you can carve yourself out a little career as an author, but for now, we need to fight the actual war — not one made up by H. G. Wells."

A few members of the War Cabinet thumped their palms on the table in support.

The men were exhausted, all of them. And while Hitler had currently turned his attention to Russia, and their Prime Minister was shoring up their new partnership with President Roosevelt and the United States, no one had any time or energy to waste on chasing untested theories.

"So, just because we don't have it — it's not possible for them to have come up with it?" Sandys arched an eyebrow. "The reason I called this meeting, gentlemen, is that we have *new* evidence in hand — photographic evidence — evidence that points directly to a German rocket-building program."

"Balderdash." Lord Cherwell glanced through his assembled folder, then pushed it aside. "Your 'intelligence' is not very intelligent. As a scientist, I know the weight of a warhead would be too heavy for any rocket propelled with cordite to lift. It's against the laws of physics."

"What if they've come up with some sort of new fuel?" Sandys queried.

"And again, I say, balderdash." The older man defied Sandys through narrowed eyes.

Sandys struggled to keep his temper. In the close confines of the windowless room, the stale, smoky air was beginning to heat up; beads of perspiration broke out on his forehead.

"Lord Cherwell," he said, "with all due respect, we have aerial photographs of Peenemünde from Medmenham. We have independent talk of 'mystery weapons' from one of our spy houses, Chatswell Hall. The

Germans are most definitely recruiting scientists from the occupied countries. And we have the Oslo Report. We also have three-dimensional confirmation of a forty-foot rocket."

"It could be a fake!" Cherwell growled. "To distract us from something else! Something we *don't* anticipate."

"Paranoia doesn't become him," whispered one of the members to another behind a raised manila folder.

Cherwell was undeterred. "The tubes in those photographs could be chimneys! They could be exhaust pipes! *My* best guess is that they're sewage drains!"

There was low laughter from the others.

Cherwell's face was strained. "Yes, by all means, let's squander the few precious resources we have left on the Nazis' sewage system!"

The room erupted, and Sandys let them go on for a minute before standing and commanding, "Quiet, gentlemen — quiet, please."

A hush fell over the room as the Cabinet members smoked. "I propose bombing what is most likely a German rocket installation," he said, "before they can get them off the ground."

"But that's exactly what they want us to

do!" Cherwell retorted. "And waste our bombs!" Then he backpedaled, just a bit. "Say — for the sake of argument — that the Germans *do* have a rocket program in place. We need more information. We have the capacity to take three-dimensional photographs now? Well, then let's take some more and build a model of Peenemünde. Show it to the P.M. See what he has to say."

There was an overwhelming chorus of *"Yes!"*

"All right, we'll convene next time with a model of the Peenemünde site to scale." Sandys saluted. "Good evening, gentlemen."

Duncan Sandys knew he'd been beaten in this battle. But he wasn't prepared to lose the war.

Chapter Fourteen

On the afternoon of December 27, Maggie and David ventured out into the mist to buy the nation's newspapers from the shouting boys in woolen caps selling them on the street. Chilled and damp, they returned to the P.M.'s map room to warm up and also read through each one, clipping out any mention of Churchill's speech. Everywhere, the Boss's Senate debut was rated a grand success.

"Oh, look!" Maggie exclaimed, as she used small silver scissors to cut through the inky pages. "David Lawrence says, *'He brought with him a tonic of reassurance and confidence that makes long-range planning for victory seem comprehensible in spite of the setbacks and defeats of the immediate future. Nothing compares with it . . .'* "

"Who's David Lawrence?" David asked, looking up from his desk.

"A columnist with the *United States News*

— he's also syndicated."

"Holy Hera!" David yelped, pulling out a section of the *Los Angeles Times*. There, in black and white, was a large photo of John in uniform, giving the V for Victory sign. *RAF War Hero John Sterling Arrives at the Beverly Hills Hotel,* blared the caption.

Maggie looked down at the photograph, stunned. John looked so familiar and yet at the same time almost a stranger. This was how the rest of the world saw him now, she realized. "But why is he there? Why wouldn't he tell us?"

But David, who probably already knew, had moved on and was going through more papers. "The Boss's in meetings all day today, and I'm nailing down the final details for his trip to Ottawa."

"Do you need me to go with him?"

"Let me guess. You're working on something else, right?"

Maggie nodded. She didn't know how much he knew, but she sensed it was nearly everything.

"Then you'll stay here, with the First Lady. I'll be accompanying the P.M., of course. And tonight they're showing *The Maltese Falcon* after dinner, if you're interested." David was an enthusiastic Dashiell

Hammett aficionado and knew Maggie was, too.

"I'm so sorry, but I'm afraid I'm —"

"Busy, right." Then, "Not with that mick, I hope. John told me about him."

Maggie rolled her eyes. "No, not with him. But is it your business?" With hands on her hips, she admonished, "And stop calling Tom a mick. That's just mean. We're in the U.S. It's nearly 1942, for heaven's sake."

David had the grace to look ashamed. "Your security clearance is higher than mine. I won't ask any more questions." He looked up, eyes bright behind his spectacles. "And I'll mind my own business about your love life from now on. I promise, Mags."

He does sound truly remorseful. Maggie impulsively jumped up and gave him a hug. "David, dear, I only wish I had something juicier to report. By the way, how's *Little Women* coming?"

"Amy just burned Jo's manuscript!" he reported, shaking his head. "What a witch! I don't know how Jo will ever forgive her."

Later, when David had been summoned to one of the meetings, Maggie looked up from her clippings. She rose, listening. No one seemed to be around, but one could never be sure.

Maggie made her way down the corridor, listening for any signs of people approaching. At the door to the President's private study, she hesitated, heart thudding. She tapped. Nothing. No response.

As assured as she'd ever be, she opened the door, scanned the room, and when she was certain it was empty, slipped into the President's private study. *If I'm caught, can I be hanged for treason?* she wondered as she stepped over the lion-skin rug, avoiding the sharp bared fangs. Leo the Lion's glassy eyes seemed to be watching her with suspicion as she made her way across the room to the President's desk. *Do the Americans use firing squads? Or perhaps the electric chair?*

The enormous desk was a mess, she realized, with file folders crammed with papers balanced precariously on top, books piled below. As she'd been taught, she gleaned as much information as she could before touching anything, memorizing how each item was placed.

She had made it through the files on top of the desk and was going through the first desk drawer when she heard a noise. She recognized the bold, echoing tread instantly; it was the butler, Fields.

Bugger, bugger, bugger! Heart pounding

in her ears, Maggie dove underneath the desk and curled up in the leg space. Like the President's *Resolute* desk in the Oval Office, this one had a small door built for the gap to hide his leg braces. Her breathing came quickly, and she struggled to slow it, as she'd been trained.

She peeked through the tiny gaps in the wood. Mr. Fields picked up a tea tray that had been left on the coffee table. He left, footsteps resounding in the corridor.

Maggie went limp with relief. Seated on the threadbare green carpet, she opened desk drawers, making her way up from the bottom. Nothing. Nothing useful to her, at least.

Victorian. The thought reverberated. Franklin Roosevelt was Victorian in his manners and tastes. Weren't the Victorians known for secret compartments? Could there be one in the President's personal desk?

Gently, she pressed on different wooden panels. Nothing.

She ran her fingernails into different carved pieces, looking for a hinge or a release. *Bugger.*

She got to her knees and opened the center drawer. Nothing, at least nothing relevant. Inside the drawer was a cubby for pens. She removed the fountain pens and pencils and pressed her finger on one side of the shallow tray.

It flipped open.

But the compartment was empty. *Oh, bugger.*

But hadn't she seen a desk like this one before? At one of the manor houses in Scotland where she'd trained? Maybe . . .

She pulled on the entire tray. It came up easily, revealing yet another secret compartment. This time, something was there. It was a small leather-bound appointment book. *1941* was embossed on the cover in gold.

Maggie flipped thorough the well-worn pages.

All of the entries were in code. *Bugger!*

The next morning, John Sterling removed his RAF cap and tucked it under his arm as he strode through the double doors and into the reception area. Framed and matted movie marquee posters lined the walls.

The receptionist, a young, very blond woman with large white teeth, glanced up. "Good morning!" Taking in his uniform, her eyes widened. "You must be Lieutenant Sterling."

"Yes, ma'am."

She giggled, a silvery bell-like sound. "Call me Cora, please. And it's miss — not ma'am." She blushed. "I'll let him know you're here. Please have a seat." She scooped up the telephone receiver and pressed a button. "Good morning, sir. Lieutenant Sterling is here."

She looked back to John, who didn't sit but paced the length of the room, uncharacteristically nervous. He stopped and turned when he heard a voice behind him.

"Dumbo was supposed to be on the cover of *Time* magazine this month, but then, well, Pearl Harbor was attacked. Now there's only one small black-and-white photo on the inside, but what can you do? I'm Walt" — the man said as he stuck out his hand, deep brown eyes shining — "Walt Disney. And you must be John Sterling. We've been waiting for you."

John shook it, taking in the man's appearance. Disney was shorter than John and trim, with black patent-leather hair, a thin mustache, and a narrow chin.

"Well, you're a long, tall drink of water, aren't you?" Disney scratched his head and broke into a smile. "I think I just might have to call you Stalky. Stalky, you know, after the —"

"Kipling character," they finished in

unison. This time both grinned more like schoolboys. *Stalky & Co.* by Rudyard Kipling was one of John's favorite childhood books. "I'd be honored, Mr. Disney."

"Now, now, Stalky, call me Walt. Everyone does. We don't stand on ceremony here." Disney escorted John into his office. Even with his longer legs, the younger man struggled to keep up.

"I know I probably sounded terrible, complaining about *Dumbo* with the war and everything going on. We're proud Americans here, I'll have you know! We've started making military-contract aircraft and warship-identification films. And my boys already have a new film in the hopper — not sure what to call it, but it'll probably be *Donald Duck in Nutzi Land* or, my favorite, *Der Führer's Face.* And we're working on a tax collection picture with Minnie. Dry as burned toast, but the old girl'll give it some shine."

Walt Disney's office was spacious, modern, lined with bookcases, and flooded with lemony California sunshine. Birds of paradise swayed outside the rectangular windows, which had views of a water tower and mountains in the distance. On the desk were figures from movies, some of which John recognized and many he didn't. Mickey and

Minnie dolls held a place of honor.

"Have a seat, Stalky." Disney jabbed a thumb at one of the chairs in front of his massive corner desk, then slid into the leather seat behind it. "Well, I'll be — Flight Lieutenant John Sterling, war hero — right here in my office. One of Churchill's 'the few.' Thank goodness Regina Wolffe sent you my way."

"Indeed," John said, crossing and then uncrossing his long legs.

"And look at you. You're like a movie star yourself! All the girls must be swooning. Have you had a chance to hit the Polo Lounge yet?"

"No . . ." John struggled to not say "sir" or "Mr. Disney." ". . . W-Walt."

"Well, you should. The ladies'll be all over you."

The subject made John uncomfortable. He repressed a vision of Maggie and a lacy negligee and said, "This is a beautiful studio."

Disney sat back and made a steeple of his fingers. "It's new," he said. "We just bought it. My brother Roy called me at one point and said we owed the bank four point five million dollars. Four point five mil, can you believe? And I just started to laugh.

"And so Roy said, 'What are you laughing at?'

"And I told him, 'I was just thinking back to the days when we couldn't even borrow a thousand dollars.' " Walt gave a hearty chortle.

John wasn't used to people discussing money at all, let alone so openly.

"Now —" Disney leaned forward. "Tell me about these Gremlins of yours, Stalky."

"Well, sir — Walt — Gremlins are rogues of the air." John realized who he was talking to and changed his approach. "Once upon a time, like all pixies, Gremlins lived in hollow banks beside rivers and waterfalls. Some of them migrated to the crags by the seashore and subsisted on pancakes made of tide foam. And now they've moved into the air."

John could see the spark of interest in the man's eye. "Gremlins and Alicias and Wonkers. Gremlins ride on RAF planes with suction-cup boots and drill holes in planes. Wonkers are young Gremlins born in a nest, and Alicias are the girl Gremlins — they're all cousins to leprechauns. They're having the time of their lives flying all over Britain, the Atlantic, and Germany in our Royal Air Force planes." He leaned forward. "But only pilots and gunners and people who work with planes can see them."

Disney leaned back in his chair. "Can *you* see them?"

"Well, of course," John said, his lips twitching into a smile.

The older man jabbed a thumb at a silver-framed photograph of two young girls. "My daughters. I like to show them what I'm working on, and when they saw your drawings of the Gremlins, they couldn't stop jabbering about them. Giggled their socks off. And I'll have you know, they're severe critics — 'That's *corny,* Dad,' they'll say." He pointed at John. "But they love your Gremlins. Love them!"

"Thank you." John decided against using any and all names.

"Would you like coffee? Or tea?"

"Er — coffee, please."

"Attaboy," Disney said as he pushed a button. "Cora, some coffee for Stalky and me. Thanks, hon."

He came out from behind the desk and perched on its edge, looking down at John. "Now, as I see it, we've got our work cut out for us. The first step is your story being published somewhere like *Cosmopolitan.* That's a fabulous introduction. Then we'll do a book."

"A book?"

"Yes, a book! 'For children and everyone young at heart.' " He stared into the middle distance, imagining it. "*The Gremlins: A Royal Air Force Story* by Flight Lieutenant John Sterling. You'll write it. I'll get the illustrator. Got to make those rascals more sympathetic, though — but we'll talk that through later. Then comes the merchandise — toys and games and hand puppets — jigsaw puzzles, comics, Charlotte Clark dolls. Then, we release the film."

"The film?"

"Yes, the film!" Disney exclaimed. "A movie! A motion picture!"

Cora came in with coffee and a heaping plate of doughnuts with rainbow-colored sprinkles, set it on a side table beside John, then left. Disney sat on the chair next to John's and poured. "Cartoon, but maybe some live action, too, all mixed together." He nodded, as if seeing various versions in his mind's eye. "That's what we do here, after all, Stalky. How do you take your coffee?"

"Black."

Disney poured, then handed John a steaming cup. "You know, Hitler and his boys hate me. Goebbels, especially. The Nazis hate what they call the Mickey cult. They think the idealization of a mouse is a sign of Jewish decadence. As early as 'thirty-three, they were saying things like 'Down with Mickey Mouse! Wear the Swastika cross!' And Hitler tried to ban Mickey in 'thirty-seven but had to give up. The mouse was just too darned popular."

John struggled over whether to take a doughnut or not. In the end, he reached for one and took a bite.

Disney nodded. "Let's work together. You'll move out for the next six months or so — work with us here in Los Angeles. Let's win this war, Stalky!" He lifted his coffee cup in a toast.

John blinked, his mouth full of pastry. Move to California? Los Angeles? Now?

Disney smiled, the waxed ends of his mustache pointing upward. "I'll give you a few days to make your decision. But mark my words, Stalky — the side with the best stories is going to win."

John Sterling left the Disney studio promising to think over the proposition and to return the next day, to see their presentation. After all, Churchill was convinced this meeting was necessary to the war effort. He decided to celebrate the offer with a swim back at the hotel. He went to his room and changed, then headed to the pool.

By the turquoise water, a man in a cabana was holding court with two pink telephones and a young blond secretary. In another cabana, there was an intense card game among four couples, fueled by pitchers of daiquiris. Men and women sunbathed, their bodies taut and coppery, while a few ladies of indeterminate age swam laps in the pool, careful not to get their elaborately coiffed hair wet.

John stripped off his shirt to his swim trunks and then unfolded his pale body in the striped lounge chair.

The woman next to him peeked over her sunglasses, large brown eyes with thick, dark eyelashes widening in appreciation. She was petite and brunette, wearing a bright yellow sun hat heaped with fake flowers, her even, white smile a tribute to the best of American orthodontia. "They're playing to see who's going to sleep with whom tonight."

"Sorry?"

She nodded at the couples playing bridge in the cabana behind them. "That's why they're so loud. The blonde laughs like a hyena."

"I see." John settled in his lounge chair and closed his eyes. Then, deciding he was being rude, opened them again.

She had picked up her drink but continued to appraise him over her sunglasses. "Your accent is simply divine, by the way. What brings you to town?"

"Business."

"Really?"

John, annoyed at feeling manipulated into a conversation he didn't want to have, yet unable to be impolite, countered, "And you?"

Once again, she flashed her perfectly straight teeth. "Divorce. I'm in Bungalow Seven until the papers come through."

The waiter arrived just in time. His skin was dark, but still shades lighter than that of most of the suntanned guests. "May I bring you something from the bar, sir?"

John was unexpectedly homesick for England. "I don't suppose you have Pimm's?"

"We do, sir."

"Then I'd like a Pimm's Cup, please."

"Excellent choice, sir."

As the waiter departed, John turned back to his neighbor. "These telephones," he said, nodding to the cabana with the man holding two receivers, "how do they work? Do you just bill the call to your room?"

"Here, use mine." She pushed a pink telephone toward him.

"I couldn't possibly —"

"No, really. I only get calls from my lawyer, which is too damn depressing to contemplate. Please. Go ahead."

"It's long-distance, I'm afraid —"

"My soon-to-be-ex-husband's paying for it. Talk as long as you want."

John smiled and lifted the receiver. When he got through to David at the White House, he said, "You'll never believe this. I'm calling you pool-side, old thing."

"I loathe and despise you" was David's prompt rejoinder. Then, "Well, if it isn't Hollywood star Flight Lieutenant John Sterling, taking time from hobnobbing with the rich and glamorous in Beverly Hills to chat with us hoi polloi." David was not hiding his annoyance.

His bitter tone confused John. "What?"

"We saw your picture in the paper. We know you're at the Beverly Hills Hotel."

So they knew where he was, but still not why. "And I miss you, as well. Is Maggie there?"

"Afraid not."

"I couldn't get her last night at the hotel, either. Is everything all right?"

"She's working." David's words remained clipped.

"With the mick?"

"Afraid so. They're on something for

354

Mrs. R. Can't tell you the details, but I do believe it's strictly professional."

"On her side, at least." There was a silence. "All right then, tell Maggie I called?"

"Of course."

John replaced the receiver.

"Everything all right?" the brunette asked.

The bartender arrived with John's drink, garnished with cucumber slices and strawberries, beads of water condensing and dripping down the icy Collins glass. He accepted it, took a sip, and leaned back in the chaise under the hot sun. "Grand," he lied. "Everything's perfectly grand."

Maggie's tea had long grown cold in the First Lady's office. She'd copied down the President's code for the day of Blanche's murder and a few other relevant dates, then returned the datebook to its secret hiding place. She wished she still had the miniature camera she'd used to photograph documents in Berlin.

Now she leaned back in her chair and rubbed at her forehead. She was starting to get a headache. She was trying to break the code of the entry on December 22, the day of Blanche Balfour's death. It read: R S F G H V N R Q U Q R X X M N V F.

From everything she could glean, it was a

substitution code — and so she tried letter frequency analysis, using the most frequently appearing letters in the English language in decreasing order of prevalence: E T A O I N S H R D L U.

No luck.

She did frequency analysis on the letters at the ends of words, the most common letters: E T S D N RY.

Again, no luck.

She tried a frequency analysis of pairs of letters — TH, HE, AT, ST, AN, IN, EA, ND, ER, EN, RE, NT, TO, ES, ON, ED, IS, TI. Then she tried it on letters that are often doubled: LL, TT, SS, EE, PP, OO, RR, FF, CC, DD, NN.

Still, no luck.

She decided to try crib dragging. Of course, the method worked best when the would-be code breaker had some domain knowledge about the likely content of the message. But Maggie knew she could also try matching letters against the most common words in English: "the," "of," "are," "you," "a," "can," "to," "he," "her," "that," "in," "was," "is," "has," "it," "him," "his."

And still . . . Was it a Caesar cipher? No. Or a Vigenère cipher? Hmm, maybe. A Vigenère cipher was really just a mathematical formula that could be viewed algebraically.

Maggie tried the words that first came to mind for President Roosevelt: "America," "freedom," "liberty," "justice." Then she used names of people she knew who were close to him — Fala, Eleanor, Harry Hopkins, Grace Tully — really anything and everything.

No luck. *Damn.*

David rapped at the door. "Children's Hour?"

Maggie shook her head. "Working. But thanks." Then, "David, you and John never discussed Britain's colonies in front of me before."

"Well, there's been this little thing called 'a war' going on."

"David!" Maggie rubbed her eyes and sat up straight. "But don't you think it's odd? With Mr. Churchill off to Canada, of course I've been thinking about the Commonwealth, and now with Singapore . . ."

"I love John like a brother," David told her. "I would walk through fire for him. But that doesn't mean I agree with his politics. And we decided a long time ago not to talk about certain topics, including India. Because we'd most likely end up beating each other senseless. You really didn't realize John was such a imperialist ass?" David asked.

"I always knew he was an ass," Maggie

said, remembering their first days together at Number 10, "just never figured him for one of those Empire-loving, chest-thumping sorts."

"He works for Winston Churchill!"

"Yes, but Mr. Churchill is" — she lowered her voice — "*old*. He's practically Victorian. But John's our age . . ."

"Plenty of men Mr. Churchill's age and older disagree with him on his handling of the colonies. So I don't think it's the Boss's age. I think it's truly his point of view. And John's, too. When it comes to this, to the concept of the British Empire, they are both absolute asses."

"You can see how, for an American, this doesn't exactly sit right?"

"I can," David said. "Which is why I think you should come along to Children's Hour. Even if your esteemed President is a trifle heavy-handed with the vermouth in his Martinis."

Maggie sighed. She looked at the piles and piles of papers and folders in front of her and stacked on the floor to each side. "I'm sorry, but I really do have to work —"

"If you throw him over for that mick — fine, *Tom* — do it gently. John may be an imperialist ass, but I'm fond of him."

"I'm not throwing John over for Tom, or

for anyone for that matter. It's actually nice to see an old friend." Maggie made sure they had absolute privacy, then looked to David. "You do realize that if you weren't 'like that,' it would be you."

"I know." He puffed out his chest, pleased. "Oh, I know."

"Have you heard from Freddie?" she asked, referring to David's "roommate."

"Just sent him a postcard — the Lincoln Memorial. I think he'll like it."

Maggie smiled. "Freddie's a lucky man."

"Oh, he is!" David agreed, nodding. "And, Mags, I'm about half-done with the book. Beth's terribly sick with scarlet fever . . ."

"Shoo," Maggie said, not unkindly. "I need to work."

CHAPTER FIFTEEN

Von Braun and Todt were in the concrete observation room at the base in Peenemünde, while around them, machines and control panels buzzed and hummed. This time, for this rocket launch, the room was empty. Everything rode on this demonstration; von Braun wanted no distractions.

"We have additional guidance for the rocket," von Braun said. "Rudders and such."

"The Führer doesn't care how you do it, as long as the rocket reaches its target."

Von Braun mopped at his face with a linen handkerchief. It was time. He pressed the large red button that would initiate the launch sequence, hoping Todt didn't see his fingers tremble. Stuffing his hands into his pockets, he leaned back on his heels as they intently watched the rocket on the monitors.

Once again, the orange flames blasted.

Once again, the ground shook, so hard it made their teeth chatter.

And once more, the rocket lifted from its launch pad.

This time, however, it flew up, then kept going.

Von Braun had forgotten to breathe. Todt's face remained impassive. The rocket flew higher and higher, until they lost sight of it on the monitors.

"Come on!" von Braun called, running for the stairs that led to the exit. "Let's see!"

The two men scrambled to the outdoors, where the frigid air still reeked of smoke. The rocket continued its trajectory, flying farther and farther, until it was a vanishing speck of black in the sky.

"I did it!" von Braun muttered, as if he didn't quite believe it himself. Then, louder. "I did it! Did you see?"

Todt smiled. "*We* did it," he corrected.

Von Braun couldn't stop rocking on his heels. "Do you realize what we've done? The spaceship is born! I've changed the world!"

"What I see is what will save us — a wonder weapon." Todt glanced around for his aide, who immediately stepped up. "Send the film to the Führer. He must know what we have, what we're capable of. He will want thousands! Millions!"

A shadow passed over von Braun's face. "But this is the only one that's worked so far."

"But it *did* work — don't you see? You get to keep your rockets program. We'll have a super-weapon. We're now in a race against time." Todt thrust his hand out, and von Braun grasped it. "We'll need as many rockets as you can make, as fast as you can make them! Point them to London, and we'll flatten it! With no loss of our men!" Todt looked von Braun in the eye. "This rocket, my friend, will decide the outcome of the war. Heil Hitler!"

This time, von Braun was able to answer with equal enthusiasm, "Heil Hitler!"

Clara had requested a copy of Noël Coward's play *Design for Living* from Lord Abernathy.

He'd delivered it a few days later with a quizzical expression on his face but no comment. The play was about the lovely young Gilda, a decadent aesthete, who finally settles on a relationship with two men — who are also in love with each other.

In the yellow drawing room, as Clara and Kemp drank after-dinner brandy before the blazing fire, she read aloud, " *'I love you. You love me. You love Otto. I love Otto. Otto loves you. Otto loves me. There now!' "*

Kemp uncrossed his legs. "So she's with one, then the other, then the two men are together. And then the three of them decide they only work as a trio — so they all live together?"

"It was a way for Coward to get around the censors. As long as there was a woman in the mix, the play wasn't about homosexuals."

Von Bayer, playing one of Bach's English Suites, stopped and went to the bar cart to pour himself a drink.

Kemp shook his head. "Degenerate English bunk."

Clara sipped her brandy and eyed him. "More or less. But with such witty repartee."

"I'm surprised you'd read something by an English author, let alone something so decadent. I don't believe our Führer would approve."

The blonde stretched and sat up. "Yes, but Herr Hitler's not here, is he? And all those rules were just for the workers, anyway — the bourgeois. And I'm so dreadfully bored. I want something to happen." She stalked back and forth on the carpet, like a lithe jungle cat in a cage. "I want something to *happen*! Even if it's bombs falling from

the sky. I can't stand the monotony anymore."

"Have another drink," Kemp urged.

Clara's eyes looked feverish. "Or the
plague!" She walked back and forth in front
of the fireplace, rubbing her slender arms
against the chill. "I don't put it past Hitler
to introduce the plague into Germany if the
Fatherland is ever invaded. Just imagine —
he takes half a dozen or so SS men and
makes them wander about somewhere at
the back of Aachen, spreading plague. If the
English and Americans catch it and don't
know how or from where, I wonder whether
they would stay."

"What a question!" Von Bayer stirred his
drink.

Clara leaned against the marble fireplace
mantel. She was wearing a clingy red-satin
evening gown. "Admittedly it would hit the
German people as well. But he's perfectly
capable of it!"

Kemp nodded. "Yes."

"He would, of course, inoculate himself
first, and then the rest of the vaccine would
go to the high-ranking members of the
party."

Kemp pulled out a silver cigarette case.
"Yes, it's really quite a good idea."

"Yes," the blonde mused. "To spring a

trap at the end, if everything is lost."

Von Bayer downed the last of his drink and poured another. "A 'good idea'?"

"Well," Clara replied, "as a last resort, before everything . . . Don't you think so?"

Von Bayer spoke as if to a small child. "But our own people would be done in by it, as well."

She sighed. "Yes, well, that's the rotten thing about it. What we ought to have are weapons to which all Germans are immune. Ones which will only hurt the enemy."

Von Bayer's good eye blazed. "This," he said enunciating carefully, "is why history will judge us and find us savages, despite our culture. We have sinned. This system has broken every moral code in the world. If you admit life is ruled by a great moral code, you must condemn yourself."

"I have no moral code." Clara fixed her gaze on von Bayer, one eye focused on him, the other just a little to the right. "We're all struggling to survive. That's what I do, I survive. It's Darwin's world now, not God's."

"You, my dear, have not seen actual combat."

"Yes, but those are very isolated cases," Kemp interrupted. "For which even the SS can't be blamed."

"You have no idea what you're talking about," von Bayer countered, "the atrocities perpetrated by the SS, the shootings, the mass executions . . ."

Kemp tapped ash into a heavy crystal ashtray. "I am the last to defend such actions, but you must admit that we were bound to take the most severe measures to combat the guerrilla warfare in the East."

"And what will they say when they find the mass graves in Poland?" von Bayer shouted. Kemp stood. For a moment it seemed the two men would come to blows.

Von Bayer kept talking, egging the other man on. "The worst thing about this is that we're to blame for the way things have gone," he persisted. "In the Great War, at least, we could say we were the decent ones and were dragged into it — we were cheated and deceived, and we fought decently. But in this war it's the other way round. We are the attackers, the instigators, and we have behaved like beasts. We *continue* to behave like beasts!"

"God, that's depressing." Clara sighed and poured more brandy into her teacup. "But your world is based on faith, on religion." She smirked as she poured. "Mine is ruled by blood."

Von Bayer blinked. "We have gone against

the laws of world order, Frau Hess — and, mark my words, we will be held responsible, by a world tribunal."

"The people simply gave vent to their rage." She reached out and stroked von Bayer's cheek with one long finger. "If one were to destroy all the Jews of the world simultaneously, there wouldn't remain a single accuser."

He drew back, as if burned. "One doesn't need to be a Jew to accuse us. We ourselves must bring the charge."

The slender blonde sank back down on the cracked leather and lifted her cup. "Oh, please. Do you think our Führer has nothing up his sleeve?"

"I'm afraid he might be out of aces," von Bayer said. "Spread himself too thin this time."

Clara looked up at him through thick lashes. "I am disappointed that they haven't started using the retaliation weapon yet."

"The rocket? That again?" Von Bayer snorted. "I can't believe in this rocket — if a rocket carried all the fuel it needed, it would never get off the ground. It's simple physics."

"The secret is liquid propellant," said Clara. "This rocket business," she mused. "I saw it once, you know, with my own eyes.

There's a special testing site on the Baltic Sea, a little place called Peenemünde. They've got these huge tubes. They go fifteen kilometers into the stratosphere."

"How do they aim them?"

Clara knit her brows, remembering. "You can only aim at a general area, but if you aim for somewhere densely populated, you're bound to hit something. Von Braun was there, and he said, 'Oh, next year the fun will start!' But it was all quite secret."

"So, why aren't we hearing anything about them?" von Bayer demanded.

Kemp rubbed at the bridge of his nose. "Yes, this rocket business is all very well and good, but why haven't we heard anything about long-range bombs here? We get the broadcasts, all the newspapers. . . . They couldn't hide something like that from us."

"Believe me, gentlemen," Clara said, "they're not using them yet — but wait until they do. These are weapons unlike anything you've ever imagined."

Kemp looked up. "If they prepare them in time, they could change the course of the war!"

Von Bayer nodded, longing in his eyes. "We could go back to Germany."

Kemp showed his teeth. "We could. We'd be heroes!"

Clara stretched and twisted her shapely legs. "We would."

Kemp began to pace again. "We could put this wretched chapter behind us once and for all. Move on."

"But what about the Jews? What about the witnesses?" Von Bayer cried.

"We'll kill them, too! We'll kill them all!" Kemp declared, throwing back the last of his brandy. The trio's gaiety was morphing into hysteria. "There won't be any witnesses — and then we can forget this all ever happened!"

Clara grabbed Kemp and kissed him hard on the lips.

Von Bayer cleared his throat. "I'll be going, then."

Clara looked him in the eye. "You don't have to," she said. She walked over to him, bent down and kissed him, gently at first, then harder, biting his lip. "You could stay if you want."

Von Bayer groaned.

Clara smiled at him, her catlike smile. "Do you want to watch?" she asked, slipping her gown's narrow straps off her shoulders. "Or do you want to be part of things?"

"Watch," von Bayer managed, gasping for breath.

■ ■ ■ ■

Up in the attic of Chatswell Hall, Arthur and Owen locked eyes. "Wait, is she with Kemp?" Arthur asked.

"No, she's with von Bayer! Wait, I think — both?"

Arthur dove to take the needle off the record. "We don't need to record this."

"No, wait —" Hank said. "I want to listen."

"Oh, good Lord . . ."

"Shut up!"

"I'm leaving. Go ahead, listen, if you want. If they say anything more about this rocket business, just don't be so distracted that you forget to record."

Edmund Hope had been watching. He'd been watching for weeks through the chink Clara had left in the blackout curtains.

He'd been watching the Tower of London, when Clara had been held there, through binoculars. He knew his wife had been sentenced to death. And, then, against all odds, he'd watched as she'd been transported away from the Tower.

But where? As a high-placed Bletchley code breaker and spy in his own right, he'd manipulated his way through red tape until he learned of Chatswell Hall, learned Clara was being held there.

And he'd taken the Tube to Cockfosters, walked to the Hall, then slipped in through a gap in the barbed wire. It was dark; no one saw him — no one knew. Why should they? The guards were concerned with prisoners getting out — not anyone sneaking in.

He'd watched Clara through the blackout curtains — watched her laugh and sing and flirt and smile. Now, when he saw her kiss the Nazi officer, he knew she had to die. And if His Majesty's Government wasn't going to do it, then he would kill that woman — for all of them.

For Britain.

The President and Mrs. Roosevelt had spent the evening dining with John Gilbert Winant, Ambassador to Great Britain, as well as Harry Hopkins and several other judges, politicians, and dignitaries. They said good-bye to their guests by eleven, and then retired to their separate bedchambers. But the First Lady couldn't sleep. In her nightgown, flannel dressing gown, and woolen slippers, she went to her husband's bedroom door. It was closed, but there was still a strip of light visible. She knocked.

"Yes?" she heard.

She pushed open the door. The President was in his blue-and-white-striped silk pajamas, sitting up in bed with Fala curled at his side. "Franklin, I know it's late, but —"

"What is it, dear?" he asked, putting down his book.

The First Lady walked into the room, stepping over piles of books and papers, then sat in a tufted chair next to the bed. Fala thumped his tail in welcome, and Mrs. Roosevelt reached out to stroke the wiry fur on his head.

The President favored her with one of his tremendous smiles. He smelled of peppermint toothpaste. "Now, that's an awfully long face, Babs," he teased.

"This is serious, Franklin," she said, her voice pitched higher than usual. When she withdrew her hand, Fala woofed in protest.

"All right, then," the President said, taking off his reading glasses. "Shoot!"

"I know you've been informed that a young woman who was in my employ for a short while, Miss Blanche Balfour, was found dead."

"Yes." The President's smile dimmed by a few watts. He nodded. "I was informed."

"It's come to my attention that she didn't

commit suicide, as we'd originally believed
— she was murdered."

Franklin gave his wife a sharp look. "How
do you know that?"

"Never mind how I know that, Franklin, I
just do. I think what is more important is
that a young woman is dead. Murdered! A
woman who worked in *our* White House!"

The President sneezed, then pulled out a
handkerchief and blew his nose. "It's tragic,
Babs. I'm so sorry."

The First Lady drew a deep breath.
"There was a letter." Her thin fingers worried at the edge of her dressing gown. "A
letter . . . about me. About me . . . and her."

A cloud passed over the President's face.
"No. There wasn't."

"But there *was,* Franklin. There was a letter at Blanche's apartment — one that
mysteriously vanished. And now, I've just
found out, there's yet *another* letter, one
that Miss Balfour had given to her fiancé,
Byrd Prentiss, 'in case anything happened
to her.' "

"So Prentiss says he has another letter,
hmm?" The President absently stroked Fala
as he watched red-and-blue flames dart in
the fireplace. Then he looked at his wife.
"I'll handle it, Eleanor."

"Maggie Hope says she destroyed the letter. I want you to know, there's not one shred of truth —"

"I said, I'll handle it, Eleanor!" At his side, Fala whined. The President reached down to comfort him.

"Franklin, I need to know, did you — did we — do anything that . . . I should know about?" The unspoken words hung in the air.

"No, Babs, I swear to you. And it will all be fine in the end."

"And Maggie Hope — Mr. Churchill's secretary — do you know anything about her being attacked after our going to Andrea Martin's talk at Metropolitan?"

"No!" His response was so loud that Fala gave a sharp bark. "Shhhh," he said, stroking the dog's fur. "No, of course not," he insisted. "And I'll look into extra security for her if you think she's in danger." The President turned his smile back on. "Now, you go to bed and get some sleep, Babs. It's going to be a busy day with Henri Giraud tomorrow."

"But, Franklin —"

"Go to bed now, Eleanor," ordered the President.

"Yes, dear."

When she had closed the door behind her, Roosevelt picked up the telephone receiver.

"Tell Frank Cole I need to see him tomorrow." He pinched the bridge of his nose, squeezing his eyes closed. "Yes, tomorrow. He'll know when and where," he said and hung up.

CHAPTER SIXTEEN

John returned, his nose sunburned, to the Walt Disney Studios the next morning.

This time, however, he was surrounded by other men in uniforms. U.S. uniforms. "The Army's moved hundreds of troops into the studio," Cora explained as she ushered John through. "The soldiers are part of the antiaircraft force that's stationed here, because of the aircraft factories. We're home to Lockheed Air, you know. And then we have troops training on the soundstages because they can close them up and the soldiers can do their war exercises in black-out conditions."

"How very . . . Hollywood," John murmured.

Cora beamed. "You made the gossip column, you know."

He sighed. "I know." He shuddered, remembering. He'd been brought up to believe a person's name should appear in the newspaper only three times — birth, marriage, and death.

"Your visit also merited a gushing mention in Hedda Hopper's column today."

"Who is Miss Hopper?"

"She's our resident snoop. Writes gossip for the *Los Angeles Times.* Everyone reads it."

"And what did this Miss Hopper have to say about me?" John braced himself for the indignity.

"She said you and a brunette soon-to-be-divorcée were looking *awfully* cozy by the pool at the Beverly Hills Hotel yesterday."

"I was merely being polite."

She smiled. "Of course."

They took a wide corridor to a conference room. It was a large, modern, high-ceilinged space with a gleaming wooden floor. An upright piano stood against one freshly painted wall. Bright sunshine streamed in through the open windows, while birdsong filled the air.

The walls were lined with bulletin boards, pinned with drawings of Gremlins. Cap under his arm, John went down the line, looking intently at each one.

"Perfect. Excellent," he said with a widening smile. Disney's artists had detailed his story of a Gremlin named Gus, who spots an RAF plane in the sky and wants to leave Gremlinland and see the world.

When the plane is shot down, he knows he has to help.

And so he and his trusted friends leave Gremlinland to try to find the RAF pilots. There they meet James — a tall, brooding pilot — who'd been shot down and injured and couldn't fly anymore. They give James new hope and swear to help him fly again and win the war against the Nazis.

"So, are we winning yet?" Walt Disney asked, joining them. "What do you think, Stalky? Did we do your Gremlins justice? You're the expert, after all."

John was inexplicably happy. For the first time in he couldn't remember how long, he felt joy. The visions he'd seen in his head, the visions that had gotten him through his time in Berlin and the escape, were now real, tangible. Others would see them, be entertained and perhaps inspired. "Yes, yes you did, Mr. — er, Walt."

"Come with me, Stalky," Disney ordered. They walked the wide corridors back to his office. "I want to acquire the rights to this story right away. I'm assuming we'll have to run that by the British Air Ministry."

John nodded. "And I'll have to talk to Mr. Churchill, as well."

"Of course, young man," Disney said, clapping him on the back. "Talk to Winnie, then get back to me. By the way, we'd like you to stay out here for a while. Enjoy our California sunshine, what do you say?"

"Awhile? What's 'awhile'?"

Disney gave his most inscrutable smile. "Who knows? You've got talent — I can see that! And you've got battle experience, too. We could use someone like you on permanent staff."

Maggie was working in the map room, opening and organizing mail for the Prime Minister that had been forwarded to the British Embassy and then sent in bags to the White House. Even though he was away, she could still smell the smoke from Churchill's Romeo y Julieta cigars. She wanted to get back to trying to break the code, but with the Boss and David on their way to Ottawa and John in Los Angeles, there was a lot to do. She typed up a summary of the P.M.'s mail to read to David over the telephone when he called in.

There was a sharp rap on the open door. "Miss Hope?" rang the First Lady's warbling tone.

"Yes, Mrs. Roosevelt?"

"When you have a moment, please come

to my office."

In the First Lady's sitting room, a wireless radio played Aaron Copland's *John Henry* as raindrops pattered at the windows.

"Close the door and then turn that down a bit, would you please, Miss Hope?" Mrs. Roosevelt requested when Maggie had entered.

She did as she was asked, then moved stacks of newspapers to take a seat on the fringe-trimmed brocade sofa piled high with colorful needlepoint pillows. She tucked one ankle behind the other.

"May I offer you a cup of tea, Miss Hope? I'm going to ask for one. And perhaps some cookies? Mrs. Nesbitt's made honeydrops."

"That would be lovely, ma'am. A cup of tea and a biscuit — er, cookie — would be perfect right now, thank you."

The First Lady pulled twice on a thick silk cord, then came to sit on a club chair beside Maggie. "Did you find anything?" she asked in a low voice, referring to Franklin's office. She was pale.

"I did," Maggie answered. "I found an appointment book in a concealed compartment. But it's in code."

The First Lady pursed her lips. After a moment, she asked, "Can you break it?"

"I was only able to copy down a bit, which makes it harder to crack. I'm working on it, though."

"Oh, I find mathematics impossible!" Mrs. Roosevelt said, throwing up her hands in frustration. "I fear we women aren't made to think that way."

"Not made to think that way? Or not *encouraged* to think that way?"

The First Lady shrugged. "I don't know. I was terrible at math in school, though — loathed it."

Maggie knew enough about the First Lady to venture, "But you didn't like public speaking at first, and look at you now!"

Mrs. Roosevelt gave Maggie a long, thoughtful look. "Yes, I see your point, Miss Hope. Practice, hard work, and tenacity are the keys to most things in life, aren't they? I'm sure math is no exception."

Maggie pulled a piece of paper from her skirt pocket. "Here," she said, handing it to the First Lady. "I copied this. It's the entry for December twenty-second — the day Blanche Balfour was murdered —"

R S F G H V N R Q U Q R X X M N V F

The First Lady looked at it, shook her head, then handed it back to Maggie.

"Now, it's all letters — no numbers or symbols," Maggie explained, accepting it. "So it's what's known as a 'substitution code.' I made one of these for my diary when I was a teenager at Boston Latin. It looks unbreakable, but it's not. To crack it, one can use a number of techniques — tricks, if you will."

Mrs. Roosevelt nodded, placing her chin on her hand.

"We can use what's called frequency analysis."

The First Lady winced as though she had a headache. "Oh, dear."

"No, no. It's just the way it sounds — there are letters of the alphabet, such as 'e,' that are used more frequently than others in English. So if a particular letter is used a lot, it's quite possible it's an 'e.' However, in this sample, the most frequently used letter is, alas, not 'e.' The sample size is just too small."

Mrs. Roosevelt attempted to look game. "All right, so then what?"

"So then we can look at repeated letters. There are only a few letters that repeat in the English language — 'e,' 't,' and 'd,' for example."

The older woman nodded.

"There's also a way people create code by

using a word or a name that's important to them or easy to remember. I've tried to break this particular one by using the names Eleanor, Fala, all of your children's names, grandchildren's names, previous Presidents . . ."

"He told me a long time ago that he changes it every once in a while." A thought occurred to her. "Try Lucy," the First Lady said, her mouth twisting with uncharacteristic bitterness. "Lucy Mercer."

"Lucy Mercer?" The name meant nothing to Maggie.

Mrs. Roosevelt shook her head. "Never mind — it's nothing. *She's* nothing."

If she's not important, why did you mention her? But Maggie resumed. "But, even if we don't know the key word, the code isn't unbreakable — we just have to keep trying different things." She took a deep breath. "And even if I crack the code, of course it doesn't necessarily mean we'll find anything incriminating."

"No," Mrs. Roosevelt agreed. "No, of course not." She rubbed her chin. "Code breaking is rather like life, isn't it? You just have to keep trying and trying, until you get it right."

Maggie beamed. "It is!"

There was a soft rap at the door, and a

maid entered, carrying a tray with a silver tea set, two cups and saucers, and a plate piled high with golden-brown cookies.

After the maid had left, Mrs. Roosevelt rose and walked to her desk. She picked up a manila file. "I want to show you something. I've only just received it."

As Mrs. Roosevelt checked the pot to make sure the tea was properly steeped, then began to pour into the delicate cups, Maggie opened the file folder and paged through. "Blanche's telephone records —" She breathed. She looked up at the First Lady. "Is this legal?"

Mrs. Roosevelt nodded, lifting her gold-rimmed teacup. "It is now, thanks to Congressman Sam Hobbs of Alabama. And with the country at war, Franklin's all in favor of legalizing wiretapping." She took a sip. "Ironically, the Southerners all favored wiretapping and making telephone records available to law enforcement. Attorney General Jackson said *'the only offense under the present law is to intercept any communication and divulge or publish the same. Any person, with no risk of penalty, may tap telephone wires and act upon what he hears or make any use of it that does not involve divulging or publication.'* "

Maggie stirred milk into her tea. "Why ironic?"

"Because one of the calls made from Blanche's phone that evening was to the Virginia Governor's mansion." The First Lady's hand went to the triple strand of creamy pearls around her neck. "I feel terrible doing this — with all that Benjamin Franklin said about how those who would give up freedom for safety deserve neither. . . ."

"So we can infer Blanche — or someone — was calling the Governor's mansion, the same Governor who isn't about to pardon Wendell Cotton —" Maggie said, too excited to taste her tea. "What number is this?" she asked, pointing to one dialed late that afternoon.

"That's to the Washington Office of the Governor of Virginia," the First Lady said. "It's where Byrd Prentiss works."

"Prentiss was her fiancé — it isn't odd at all that she would have called him. But is it possible to obtain *his* telephone records? I mean, as long as we're at it?"

Mrs. Roosevelt nodded. "I do believe we can manage that, Miss Hope."

Maggie went back to the file. "A call was made from Blanche Balfour's apartment, just before we arrived."

"A call to the Governor's mansion."

Maggie bit her lip. "There was a call to the Virginia Governor's mansion at around the time of Blanche's death. And there was another call made, well after that. A call to the White House."

"Let me see," the First Lady said, taking back the file. She peered at the small black print. "That number is for the White House's switchboard. But there's no way to tell who Blanche — or whoever — was calling."

"The call was made only twenty minutes before we arrived," Maggie said, putting the time line together.

"She was still alive then?" The First Lady looked horrified.

"No." Maggie shook her head. "According to the coroner's report, she'd been dead for hours. There must have been another person in the apartment that night," she said, her hands trembling. "Someone who had a reason to phone the White House."

After luncheon and several meetings — but before Children's Hour — President Roosevelt performed his water exercises in the White House's private indoor pool. It had been built especially for him in 1933, funded by the New York *Daily News* and the private donations of American citizens. The pool had been constructed inside the West Gallery, between the White House and the West Wing, in place of the old laundry rooms, which had been moved to the basement of the mansion. As Roosevelt swam, propelled by the powerful muscles of his arms and torso, gray light filtered in through the fan windows at the ceiling. The air was thick with steam and the smell of chlorine.

Frank Cole entered, the click of the heels of his black oxfords echoing off the arched ceiling. He stood on the blue tiles, clearing his throat when the President finished a lap and pulled himself to the pool's marble edge. Cole asked, "You wanted to see me, Mr. President?"

His eyes red from the water, Roosevelt looked up at the man. "Last night, Mrs. Roosevelt informed me that Blanche Balfour was murdered."

Cole spoke carefully. "I'm sorry to hear that, sir."

The President blinked. "Aren't you going to ask how it happened?"

"No, sir," Cole rejoined. "I have a number of other things on my plate right now."

"A young woman is dead!" the President snapped, his voice echoing off the tiles.

"Yes, sir," Cole said. "And I'm sorry. But

you know as well as I do who's also dead —
the 2,403 Americans at Pearl Harbor — not
to mention 1,178 wounded. Then we also
have the brave lost sailors of the USS *Reu-
ben James.* That's not even taking into account the Poles, the British, all those killed
in France and the Netherlands, and now
the Russians. . . ."

"All right, Cole," the President said.
"You've made your point. But still, a girl is
dead. A girl who worked for us."

"For your wife. She wanted to take down
your wife and, with her, your administration. And with your administration — the
entire Allied cause, which you and the
Prime Minister are struggling to create."

"Eleanor also tells me that a note was
taken. A note that could have compromised
her."

"As I said, sir, I regret that Miss Balfour
is dead. How it happened, however, doesn't
concern me. And neither does an alleged
blackmail note."

"There's a second letter," the President
said.

"No, there's not."

"Yes, there is." The President could see
the muscles of Cole's jaw tense. "According
to Eleanor, the late Miss Balfour's fiancé,
Byrd Prentiss, also has a letter from her that

casts . . . aspersions on the First Lady."

Cole shook his head. "It must be a fake."

"Maggie Hope allegedly destroyed it, Cole," the President said.

"I'll make sure of it, sir."

"What are you going to do?"

"Anything I need to, sir."

"Cole —"

"Sir, our nation has been attacked. We're bracing for war. Young men are joining up. They're doing what needs to be done. And I'm going to do what needs to be done as well."

The two men didn't look at each other, instead gazing up at the light trying to shine in from the high fan windows. "All right," the President said finally. "I don't need to know the details." He swam over to a ladder, then used his arms to pull himself out of the pool and into a sitting position, his withered legs dangling over the side.

President Roosevelt took the towel Cole offered, blotting his face. "Also, this Maggie Hope, the girl on the Prime's staff. I heard she was attacked."

"She's fine, sir." Cole gave a rueful smile. "That one can take care of herself."

"Keep her safe, Cole," the President admonished. He gestured for Cole to help him up and into his wheelchair. "God knows we don't need an international incident at this stage of the game."

Back in the map room, Maggie was still trying to crack the code and making no progress. She jumped when the phone rang. "Hello?" she said, expecting to hear David's voice.

"A Mr. Thomas O'Brian for Maggie Hope," said the White House operator.

"Yes, this is she."

"Please hold while I transfer the call."

"Hello!" Tom exclaimed. "I was wondering if you'd like to meet today."

There was a long pause. Maggie remembered their awkward encounter in her hotel room. "I'm working."

"So am I — but we both have to eat."

"True," she said. "I learned something new today, something I want to share with you, to get your opinion on. How's five?"

"Sounds good," Tom said. "I'll be by the statue of Andrew Jackson."

"*Not* my favorite president."

"All right, then by Lafayette's statue."

"I'll find it. See you then."

Lafayette Square had been named in honor of the Marquis de Lafayette, the young Frenchman who had befriended George

Washington and fought on the side of the colonials in the Revolutionary War. The seven-acre park north of the White House was designed in picturesque style with fountains and statuary, now shrouded in fog, cold and opaque. Overhead, the darkening sky was an eerie green, while black cumulus clouds gathered on the horizon.

Tom was already waiting on a bench by the statue of Lafayette in the southeast corner of the park when Maggie arrived with a brown paper sack of Mrs. Roosevelt's honeydrop cookies. She looked around. They had the park to themselves, except for the squirrels, chasing after acorns and scrabbling up and down the elm and sycamore trees in the wind.

She sat down beside him. "Do you think they work for the White House or the District's Chamber of Commerce?" Tom asked.

"Oh, the White House, definitely," Maggie said, throwing a crumb for one particularly bright-eyed squirrel who was cheeky enough to approach. "But are they Democrats or Republicans, do you think?"

"Democrats, of course," stated Tom. "They came in with the Roosevelts."

Maggie contemplated. "Well, the White House's staff doesn't change affiliations with the election of a president, so I doubt the squirrels have to."

"I have it on good authority that the red squirrels here are Communists — at least that's what J. Edgar Hoover says."

Maggie guffawed at that, startling one of the plump, furry creatures. "That's terrible, Tom."

"I know," he replied, looking pleased with himself, "but you *did* laugh."

"Thank you for that," she said. "The weather's so dreary, and then tonight . . ."

Is Wendell Cotton's execution. The unspoken words hung in the darkening air.

"I spoke with the First Lady," Maggie said finally. "And I saw Blanche Balfour's telephone records for the night she was murdered."

Tom looked surprised. "Is that even legal?"

"Apparently it is now. What's interesting is that three calls besides mine were made from Blanche's apartment that night. One to Byrd Prentiss's office. And then one, just around the time of her death, to the Virginia Governor's mansion. And then, hours later — well after Blanche was dead — there was a call placed to the White House."

"So there was someone else . . ." Tom whistled through his teeth. "No way to find out who took the calls at the other end?"

"No. Only that they reached the switchboard and were transferred from there."

Above them, the thick clouds rolled in. "Our friends the squirrels have taken cover," Tom noted as the wind picked up. "Maybe we should, too? I hear we're in for a real storm tonight."

"I need to get to Union Station," Maggie told him. "I'm taking the train to Virginia — I told Wendell and Andi I'd be there tonight, for support. I gave my word."

"I'll take you."

"Really," Maggie said, as she stood and brushed off cookie crumbs from her coat, "you don't have to."

"I'd be honored to drive."

"It's going to be . . . horrible."

"Then you'll definitely need a friend there with you."

CHAPTER SEVENTEEN

It was pouring. But despite the cold rain, protesters had gathered outside Thomas Jefferson Prison in the violet haze — those in support of Wendell Cotton and those against. Prison officers and police in rain gear with batons drawn were keeping the two groups separated. A train whistle blew in the distance.

On one side of the road were mostly colored protesters walking in circles, carrying signs reading, SAVE WENDELL COTTON! RACIST JURY! and THOU SHALT NOT KILL, singing Josh White's "Protest Blues." As they milled about under the streetlamps, their signs were becoming wet and unreadable. In the distance, a peal of thunder boomed.

On the other side of the road stood the supporters of the execution, some in white hoods and robes, drenched in the downpour. They'd tried to erect a huge wooden cross and set it on fire, but the rain had soaked the wood and the wind had extinguished their matches. Many carried signs — DIE WENDELL COTTON! VIRGINIANS TAKE OUT THEIR TRASH and GENESIS 9:6 WHOSOEVER SHEDDETH A MAN'S BLOOD, BY MAN SHALL HIS BLOOD BE SHED. But in the rain the ink and paint ran in rivulets down the handles, staining their robes. Singing the Ku Klux Klan's "Stand Up and Be Counted" under his white hood of anonymity, Byrd Prentiss marched with his brethren.

"Do you think it'll happen?" said one prison guard to another. Rain dripped from his cap's brim.

The other wiped water from his face. "It's gonna go down to the wire."

"It always does," the first said, nodding. "It always does."

Tom and Maggie were silent on the ride to Virginia and didn't speak as they passed by the protesters on each side of the road. Maggie gave their identification. They waved them into the dirt parking lot.

Maggie opened the car door and got out into the rain, sending her pumps plunging straight into a cold mud puddle. She sighed as the water bled through and soaked her stockings and feet.

"Sorry I don't have an umbrella today," Tom called from the other side, his voice muffled by the falling rain.

"It's fine," Maggie called as they sprinted to the prison doors, trying not to get drenched. "Tonight people have bigger things to worry about."

Inside, she patted at her hair and shook the drops off her coat. There was nothing she could do about her shoes. After signing in and again showing identification, she and Tom were led down a cement corridor to a holding cell. Maggie could see Wendell Cotton, looking younger than ever in a too-large white shirt and tie, behind thick iron bars. She recognized Mother Cotton and Andi, a white man in an expensive suit who she assumed was Wendell's lawyer, and a colored man in minister's garb.

Wendell and his mother clasped hands through gaps in the bars. The chains from his shackled wrists clanged against the iron. Andi looked up and nodded when she saw Maggie and Tom. Maggie went to her and grasped her hand. "Mrs. Roosevelt says she's praying for all of you."

Andi nodded, then swallowed, unable to speak.

A guard walked up. "It's time for you folks

to be leavin' now," he told them.

Andi fixed her gaze on him. "How can you do this? How can you be a part of this?"

"I don't believe in it myself," he replied, almost apologetically. "But it's the law."

"Then why? Why do it?"

He had the grace to look guilty. "Just followin' orders, I guess."

Wendell was breathing hard, doing his best not to cry. "Good-bye, Mama," he said to Mother Cotton. "I'll see you in heaven, you can count on it. And good-bye, Miz Andi. Thanks for all you done." He looked down at what he was wearing. "And thank everyone at the WDL and NAACP for the suit and tie. I never wore a tie before. I looks good," he said, trying to smile. "Course, they got me wearing a diaper, too, under all this — but at least you can't see it."

"It's time to go," the guard repeated. "Everyone out except the preacher man."

As Maggie, Andi, Mother Cotton, and the rest were shown out of the holding room, guards in gray uniforms entered, their boots polished to a high sheen. They all looked up at the long hands of the clock, then back down at Wendell, still breathing hard.

"Is the back of his head properly shaved?" the first one asked.

"Be not afraid . . ." quoted Reverend Johnson, locking eyes with Wendell.

"Stand up!" one of the others yelled to Wendell.

"Fear thou not, for I am with thee. Not only within call, but present with thee."

Wendell stood, the chains around his hands and feet clinking. He kept his eyes on Reverend Johnson's. *"Art thou weak? I will strengthen thee."*

"Lean over!" the officer said to Wendell.

"Art thou in want of friends? I will help thee in the time of need."

The officer inspected the back of the young man's head. "Yes, it's shaved."

Wendell's eyes never left Reverend Johnson's. *"Art thou ready to fall? I will uphold thee with that right hand which is full of righteousness."*

Wendell looked to the preacher. "I'm gonna die," he said, his voice cracking.

"Yes, my son," Reverend Johnson said, laying a hand on Wendell's shoulder. *"There are those that strive with God's people, that seek their ruin."*

"It's time to go, boy," the first guard said, his voice hollow.

"Let not God's people render evil for evil, but wait God's time," Reverend Johnson said as they began the long walk down the cor-

ridor to the execution chamber.

"Dead man walkin'!" called the guard in front. "Dead man walkin'!" His voice echoed against the cement. In the distance, thunder rolled.

Reverend Johnson strode beside Wendell, still speaking: *It is the worm Jacob — so little, so weak, so despised and trampled on by every body. God's people are as worms.*"

President Roosevelt looked at the clock on the desk of his upstairs office. It was ten, one hour before the scheduled execution of Wendell Cotton. His blue eyes were circled, and he rubbed at his nose with a handkerchief. Roosevelt fitted a Camel into his ivory cigarette holder and lit it with his customary long wooden match, drawing in heavily. The cigarette drooped, angled to the ground. He picked up the telephone receiver. "Get me Governor King in Virginia."

When the connection had been made, there was a crackle and then the Governor's honeyed tones. "Why, hello, Mr. President."

Roosevelt got right to the point. "Governor, we haven't necessarily been on the same side of things over the years. You've had your ways of seeing things and I've had mine. And I fully expect to see you take your shot at the White House when this war is over — and we've won." He was silent for a moment, as he watched the ash of his cigarette burn. "So, let's get down to it — whatever our disagreements, I know and you know that you want to be President when I'm gone. And you don't want me in your way. In fact, as a fellow Democrat, you'll need my support. We could achieve great things together, including winning this war — for God, and country, and decency everywhere. And then I'll give you my blessing."

He tapped the cigarette ash into a chrome ashtray; on it, the engraved image of a sailboat formed his initials. "But, Governor, I must say — call off your dogs."

"Why, Mr. President —" Governor King backpedaled, his tones sugared.

"Now, don't 'Mr. President' me," Roosevelt said. "You know what I'm talking about, King. This Wendell Cotton execution. You and I both know you have the power to stop it and save this man's life. And so, I appeal to you, as both your President and your colleague. We're all going to war now, Governor — both white and colored — but against the Axis, not against each other. We need to keep our eye on the endgame, not on disagreements on the home front. We can work on all that after we've licked the Japs and the Germans."

"Mr. President," Governor King drawled, "in representing the Commonwealth of Virginia, I must carry out the Commonwealth's wishes. This man, Wendell Cotton, murdered a man. A white man. And Cotton had a fair trial — he was sentenced by his fellow Virginians. Unless there is clear evidence for innocence — which there is not — I will not appeal the process."

There was a long silence. "Is that your final word?"

"It is, Mr. President."

Roosevelt hung up, slamming down on the connecting points with more force than was necessary. Then he used one finger to dial the extension for Harry Hopkins's room. "Get in here, old friend. We need to have a drink."

"Mr. President?" It sounded as if Hopkins had been woken out of a deep sleep. "Do you think it might be a bit late — ?"

"Harry, as your Commander in Chief I am *ordering* you to come to my office and drink with me. An American citizen is going to die in an hour — and I can't do a damn thing about it. The least we can do is drink to the poor bastard."

Maggie walked with Tom and the others to

the execution chamber. She shivered. Her feet were still wet; it was cold and damp in the corridors, and the chamber wasn't much warmer. The bulky wooden electric chair, on a platform like some macabre throne, had been positioned at the front of the room between a United States flag and the flag of the Commonwealth of Virginia.

The room was smaller than she had expected, with mismatched wooden folding chairs set up in rows on the wide-plank wooden floors. There was a section in front for the whites, and one, set apart, in the back for the coloreds. Fewer than thirty people filled the seats. Overhead, fluorescent lights gleamed from steel pendant lamps hanging from studded metal beams. Rain pelted down. The small glass windows, close to the low ceiling, were buffeted by the wind and rattled in their frames.

Maggie and Tom and the lawyer separated from Andi and Wendell's mother, as each went to her or his separate section. Women pulled their cardigans more tightly around them against the chill, while men in suits or in overalls and plaid work shirts worried the hats they held in their laps. All were silent. While it was easy to argue in favor of the death penalty or joke about Old Sparky with the buffer of distance and time — up close and personal, the electric chair was something different.

Above the door, a clock ticked. As the thunder roared again, one of the women gasped and gave a small shriek, then pressed a starched handkerchief against her mouth as though to stuff the cry back in.

Rain continued to drum against the tin roof as Wendell Cotton was led into the room by the guards. There were a few gasps and the scrape of chair legs as people stood to get a better look. Reverend Johnson put a hand to Wendell's cheek, whispered something Maggie couldn't hear, then went to sit with Mother Cotton and Andi.

Although he staggered when he first saw the chair, Wendell didn't falter. Instead, he walked straight to it and sat as each of the four guards began to clamp in his hands and feet, then his knees and elbows. One of the guards' hands was trembling too hard for him to fasten the leather straps, and Cotton said in a faint voice, "Take yo' time, Boss. Don't be in such a big hurry." There was a nervous snigger from the crowd, swiftly silenced by another growl of thunder.

A woman in the front row muttered, "Can't wait to see you die." Then, louder, "You killed my husband — and I can't wait to see you *die!*" It was Patsy Chandler, Billy

Bob Chandler's widow.

Wendell met her gaze. The widow was pale and painfully thin, her eyes puffy from crying, her face sallow.

"I's — I's sorry I killed your husband, ma'am." Wendell looked her in the eye. "But he was gonna kill me. Ain't no doubt about it."

Patsy Chandler surged to her feet. "Fry him up good, boys!" she shrilled. "Crispy, like bacon!" Her hate was palpable in the small room. "I'll dance around his body when he's gone!" A woman next to her shushed her and pressed her back into her seat.

Maggie thought her heart would explode in her chest. *They're just going to . . . do this? Murder a man? Right here in front of us all? They're all going to sit here and watch?*

The warden moved to a metal bucket filled with a saline solution, moistening a sea sponge. It dripped as he walked to Cotton. He placed the sponge in a metal cap, which was then attached to Wendell's head. Another sponge and electrodes were attached to his spine.

Wendell was breathing heavily, his chest heaving against the leather straps.

"One," called the warden. The man behind the curtain flipped a switch — marked THE

JUICE in crude writing on masking tape — that turned the generator up to full. The lights brightened, then dimmed. Maggie glanced up at the murky lights, realizing that all of the building's electricity had the same power source.

"God is angry," called Mother Cotton in a thin voice from the colored section.

Maggie felt sick. How could they just sit here and watch, while a man was killed? People should die fighting to protect others or in bed of old age — not in a chair as part of a grotesque spectacle.

The warden stood in front of the assemblage. "I will now read the warrant. Wendell Cotton, you have been condemned to die by the electric chair by a jury of your peers —"

Andi shot up to her feet. "That's a *lie*! He didn't have a jury of his peers! That's the point!"

A guard walked over to her, rubber baton drawn. Eyes blazing, she sat and crossed her arms over her chest.

"— sentence imposed by a judge of good standing by the Commonwealth of Virginia. Boy," he addressed Wendell, "do you have any last words?"

Wendell gulped in air. "I wanna thank everyone who is here for me," he said, voice shaking. "I think killing is wrong, no matter who. And I'm sorry I done killed a man. I think about it every day. And I wish to God I hadn'ta done it. But I did. And I'll answer to my Maker for that."

He looked again at Patsy, her teeth clenched and face burning with fury, seated in the front row. "I'm sorry what happened to your husband, ma'am. I truly is. But he drew his pistol first. And I drawed mine in self-defense. That's the God's honest truth."

He looked to the back of the room. "Miz Andi, please take care of my momma. I'm her only son. She ain't got nobody else." He took a deep breath. "My last words is — is that the system be rigged." Wendell looked to the guards. "Why don't you just lynch me and get it over with?"

The warden cut him off. "Any reason why this execution should not proceed?"

Maggie had many reasons. She had killed a man herself, in Berlin. And although it might have been necessary to her survival, and the success of her mission, she knew that he had been just a boy. She thought of him every day, just as she knew Wendell thought of Billy Bob Chandler. They had that in common.

She looked back up at the ceiling as the lights flickered again. They were slipping a black silk hood over Wendell's head. *No, I will not stand by while another young man is killed.* Quickly, she rose and walked to the back of the room. "Just say, 'It's God's will' — got it?" Maggie whispered to Tom.

Tom started and looked up. "What?"

"Just say, 'It's God's will.' And then get the lawyer to pull out every damn trick in the book."

Maggie ran from the room.

"Where're you going, miss?" a guard called as she ran into the hallway.

"Oh —" She stopped and looked up at him with big eyes. "It's just too much for me — I need to throw up. Please, where's the ladies' room?"

"Down the hall and to the left."

"Thanks." Maggie ran. She bypassed the ladies' WC and ran to the stairwell at the end of the hall.

"Wendell Cotton, electricity will pass through you until you are dead, in accordance with Virginia state law." The warden swallowed. "May God have mercy on your soul."

The room quieted, the only sounds those of Wendell's ragged breathing and the raindrops pelting the roof above. There was a flash of lightning and then an echoing crash of thunder. A few in the seats whispered, "Amen."

"God be angry," Mother Cotton called in a raw voice, louder this time.

Wendell continued to struggle for breath, his chest straining against the leather straps.

Maggie half ran, half fell down the stairs until she reached the prison basement. Her heart was in her throat, ears ringing from fear.

The walls here were brick, the ceilings low, and there were a few yellowing signs with danger printed in large red letters illuminated by only a few bare bulbs overhead. She dashed past low-hanging, rusty pipes and hulking machines, her heels striking against the concrete floor. It was damp in the basement, and smelled of mold. A low hum emanated from the machinery.

The concrete floor was covered in puddles from the leaking windows. *Great,* Maggie thought grimly. *Electricity and water, a perfect combination.*

In shadows, the huge Westinghouse generator hummed and buzzed as it increased power. The lamps on its control panel lit up, and the needle on the dial rose and fell until it reached 2,000 volts. *Oh, God, they're going to kill him.*

There was a loud bang behind her. "Hey, what're you doin down here?" The voice belonged to a bald, stocky man in denim coveralls, gripping a wrench.

Maggie spun toward him. "I was looking for the ladies' room, sir. You mean it's not down here?" Before he had a chance to respond, her elbow slammed into his forehead. He fell to the floor, unmoving.

Maggie shook out her stinging arm. "I guess not."

The warden gave the signal for the guard to pull the switch that would allow the electric current to flow to the chair. The guard raised the switch into position.

Electricity coursed through Wendell's body. He convulsed against the straps. Above, the lights flickered from the power surge and again dimmed.

The women covered their mouths and noses. There was a foul odor. Mother Cotton sobbed as Andi held her. The rain beat on the roof, and there was another growl of thunder. "God is angry!" Mother Cotton cried.

The warden stepped over to Wendell and took his pulse. He whispered something to the guards.

The crowd heard, and a whisper rippled through. *"He's not dead. . . . Not dead . . . Not dead . . ."* The soul of Wendell Cotton seemed to hover over them in the room, unable to stay, unable to leave.

The warden swallowed and hitched up his pants. He pulled out a handkerchief and mopped at his sweating face. He gave the order to turn the current back on, but the guard at the switch shook his head. The generator needed time to replenish its power.

Down in the basement, the lock on the generator was another problem. Maggie went at it with a hairpin, but it wasn't about to give. Her hands were trembling with fear. *Stupid hands.* Then she saw there was an iron key with a fraying red grosgrain ribbon on a hook by the door. *If you hear hoofbeats, it's probably horses, not zebras.* She dropped the hairpin and ran to get the key.

Above her head and to her left, a rusted pipe burst, spraying a fine mist. One of the lightbulbs sparked and then died.

She brought back the key and inserted it in the lock.

It wouldn't turn.

Upstairs, Wendell groaned. The warden

nodded to the guard at the switch. "On one," he said.

The guard flipped the switch, but nothing happened.

There was silence from the onlookers, then a gasp. There was the hum of electricity, and then the lights seemed to burn brighter. One of them flared, and the filament burned, raining orange sparks onto the heads of the onlookers. A woman screamed.

The warden looked to the guard. "What the hell's going on here?"

Prentiss had made his way from the Ku Klux Klan gathering, tossing his wet robe and hood in the mud, then bribing a guard to let him into the prison. He'd waited, standing in the back of the execution chamber, face hidden behind an open newspaper. He watched as Maggie and the reporter, Cotton's mother, and the Martin woman took their seats.

He was looking forward to seeing Cotton burn. The colored man's death meant Prentiss was one step closer to redemption. One step closer to being at the right hand of President King, when he was elected. One step closer to someday being President himself.

But when Maggie left her seat and whispered in Tom's ear, he knew she was up to something. He followed, a few paces behind, down the corridor, then the stairs, and watched as she took out the guard and found the key.

"Miss Hope," he said, just as she was about to turn the key to the cage protecting the generator's switch.

Maggie turned. "Who — who are you?"

He took long steps toward her, closing the distance. "Byrd Prentiss, ma'am. We haven't met formally. Although I must say you have a decent right hook." He pressed his fingertips to his jaw.

"You?" she said. "It was *you* outside the jazz club?"

"Who did you think?"

Someone on President Roosevelt's staff.

He performed a courtly bow, ignoring the water spraying from the broken pipe. "Governor King's right-hand man. Why hasn't your friend Tom O'Brian done anything with the letter I gave him?"

"Tom's investigating. *We're* investigating. And we're using our judgment on what's an important story — or not. We think solving Blanche's murder is far more important than hearsay about the First Lady." As the pieces fell into place just like a mathematical problem, Maggie blinked. "Oh, God. *You* killed her!"

"She committed suicide . . ."

"No, she didn't." Maggie's eyes narrowed. "She was drowned, and then her wrists were slit — to make it *look* like a suicide."

Prentiss gasped. "Surely you don't think . . ."

"Right now I'm thinking that your murdering a young girl and then setting it up to look like a suicide is the *real* story."

"You have no proof."

Water pooled on the concrete floor, reflecting the glowing dials of the generator. In the dim light, Maggie's lips curled into a half smile. "Blanche called you, probably to tell you she couldn't go through with it. You went to her apartment and killed her, making it look like a suicide. And then you called the Governor of Virginia moments after you murdered her."

A vein bulged in Prentiss's temple. "No!"

"You called the Governor's Mansion here in Virginia."

He took a step toward her, pushing a damp lock of hair from his forehead. "You can't know that. . . . There's no way . . ."

"Except I do. And I have evidence. Tapping telephones is legal now, and there was a tap on Blanche's. I saw the records myself."

"*Eleanor Roosevelt* is the story!" he insisted. "Eleanor Roosevelt is a *lesbian*. Eleanor Roosevelt has brought *shame* to the White House. She's brought shame to the United States of America!"

As the crowd murmured, Andi stood. She locked eyes with Tom, who gave her a slow nod. Then she made her way out the door and down the corridor.

The warden and the guard at the switch exchanged glances. The guard nodded. *"One,"* the warden repeated.

Still, nothing. Only the pelt of rain and a low roar of thunder.

The warden looked out over the horrified crowd and then tugged at his collar. "We're having some problems with the electricity, folks, but that's all. I'm sure we'll have it fixed in no time."

Overhead, the rest of the lightbulbs blew out with a series of loud pops and a shower of sparks. Then the assembled group sat, silent, in the darkness.

Andi found Maggie and Prentiss in the prison basement.

"You killed her!" she heard Maggie say

over the hum of the machinery and the gurgle of the rushing water.

"*That's* not the story!"

"You did, didn't you? You son of a bitch!" Sparks from the overhead lights fell into the standing water, spluttering as they flamed out. Maggie saw Andi from the corner of her eye and turned.

"What's going on?" Andi said. "What are you doing down here?"

"Trying to save Wendell," Maggie said. "Oh, and by the way, it was Prentiss here who killed Blanche."

"No, I didn't," Prentiss insisted. "You're crazy. You're trying to make it look as if I murdered my own fiancée —"

"You *did*!"

Prentiss laughed, an ugly sound. "You don't have a shred of proof."

"Oh, but I do."

"You have proof that a murder occurred and that a phone call was made to the Governor's mansion. That's nothing. Nothing!"

"The note — Blanche's suicide note. How would *you* know she left a note if you weren't in the apartment that night? You told Tom there *wasn't* a note at the scene!"

A muscle under Prentiss's eye began to twitch. "Fucking bitch —" he muttered.

"*This* is the story, the real story," Maggie said. "You sent Blanche to the White House to seduce the First Lady. Then, when Mrs. Roosevelt didn't take the bait, you two decided you were going to lie about it, to frame the First Lady for so-called indecent behavior anyway. But Blanche got cold feet — didn't want to go through with it. So you killed her — made it look like a suicide and left the note that you knew would spread the scandal you and Blanche had planned for.

"But someone from the White House, someone who had tapped Blanche's phone, knew something was wrong when she didn't show up for work that day." Maggie was piecing it together even as she spoke. "They saw her body. And took the note."

"No —"

"So then you had to forge *another* note —"

"No!" Prentiss snarled, his voice distorted by hate and desperation.

"You knew there was a note framing Eleanor Roosevelt," Maggie insisted. "You couldn't know that if you hadn't been there. The phone call to the Governor's office was made immediately after Blanche died. You were letting Governor King know it was done."

"King didn't know any of the details!" Prentiss cried out. "He didn't know!"

"But I know. I know you killed her, and now Andi knows you killed her. And someone at the White House who suspected you before I even arrived in Washington knows you killed her — 'White House Secretary Murdered by Virginia Governor's Aide' — *that's* the headline. What do you think, Andi?"

Prentiss lunged. But Maggie twisted away from his grasp, ducking past the spray of water from the broken pipe to reach the back of the generator. Andi grasped a handful of wires.

"Don't!" Maggie cried to Andi. "You'll electrocute yourself!"

As Andi tore the wires from the machine, neon blue sparks flew up into the air.

The execution chamber went black. Tom blinked in shock. *Just tell everyone it's God's will,* Maggie had said. But what was she doing? What was happening?

And suddenly, up in the execution chamber, he knew. "It's God's will!" he cried into the darkness. "It's God's will that this execution be called off," he said, his voice gaining strength. "Mother Cotton's right — God is angry. He's *angry*! And He wants us to stop!"

"Lower your voice," the warden rasped. The smell of fear was palpable in the room, along with the stench of smoke. There was a ripple of nervous whispering from the crowd. A guard cursed.

Tom whispered in the ear of Wendell Cotton's lawyer and the man nodded. "This is an Eighth Amendment violation!" the lawyer called to the warden, rising to his feet. "This is *torture*! It's cruel and inhumane!" Around him, the crowd's whispers turned increasingly urgent and bewildered.

One of the guards brought in a kerosene lantern. The flame wavered and cast long shadows that climbed up the walls and hovered near the ceiling like the outlines of dancing angels and devils. "That's not for you to say," the warden called back to the lawyer. "Or for me. Or for any of us. The jury has made its decision. The Commonwealth of Virginia has made its decision. And we're here to see that it's carried out."

More lanterns were brought in, their golden light flickering, tossing surreal shadows. "No," Cotton's lawyer insisted, "no — you had your chance. Now it's for the courts to decide. The *courts*, not us. Continuing this farce of an execution is a direct violation of Wendell Cotton's protections under the Eighth Amendment. We must delay — until Virginia can assure proper administration of this electric chair."

"We must stop this execution!" Tom cried. "It's the will of God!" He turned and spotted Mother Cotton. The two locked eyes in the dim light and nodded.

"It's the will of God," Mother Cotton called out.

The crowd took up the chant: "It's the will of God!"

Prentiss made a wordless, animal sound of rage and dove after Andi, ignoring the stream of icy water that doused him. Andi dropped the wires and ducked away from his hands. As he spun, his coat flared out and touched the edge of the glowing wire. An arc of blue-white electricity sparked from the generator and to his body.

There was a *crack,* and then Prentiss's body dropped to the floor like a puppet with its strings cut.

"Praise Jesus!" Mother Cotton cried in the execution chamber, struggling to rise. Tom ran to her in the colored section to help her stand, then kept a protective arm around her. "Praise Jesus!"

"Amen," he answered.

The warden went to Wendell and ripped off the hood. The boy was still alive, although barely conscious. "Get him out of this damn thing," he called to the guards. The four men who had strapped Wendell Cotton in now worked at the same leather restraints to save him.

The men carried Wendell up the same long hallway, but this time toward the infirmary and life.

Andi and Maggie watched in horror as Prentiss's body fell to the floor with a loud splash. "Oh, my God —" Andi leaned against the wall, unable to stand. "I think he's *dead*."

Maggie assessed the situation — the generator, the growing pools of water, the dead body. "We've got to get out of here. Come on." She started climbing up the stairs, then realized Andi wasn't following. The young woman stood as if frozen, unable to tear her gaze away from Prentiss's body, trying to comprehend what had happened.

"Andi, come on!" Maggie cried. She didn't move. Maggie grabbed Andi's hand and pulled. *"Andi!"* Together, they ran up the stairs.

■ ■ ■ ■

Tom gave Maggie and Andi a sharp look as they returned to the execution chamber. "Now, don't tell me you were clutching your pearls and fainting away like a Southern belle and Miss Martin brought you the smelling salts."

"What happened while we were gone?" Maggie asked.

"They tried to execute Wendell, but he lived through it," Tom said. "The chair short-circuited, or something. Then they tried again, but the generator couldn't create enough power. Wendell's safe, for now, at least. Maybe now the Governor will do the right thing — give him a real trial. Or let him serve in the military."

Andi shook her head. "I don't trust them as far as I could throw them. They could try to execute him again as soon as the rain stops and they fix the generator."

"No," Tom responded. "The lawyer's brought up all sorts of Eighth Amendment issues that will keep them busy for months if not years."

"So, at least he has more time." Maggie's body drooped with relief.

Andi's face relaxed for the first time since

Maggie had met her. "And maybe now he has a prayer for justice."

Hours later, Tom pulled up to the Mayflower Hotel. It was dark, and the streets were slick with rain.

Maggie felt so much — relief that Wendell was still alive and might have a chance at escaping the death penalty. Fear at how close to death she and Andi had come. Disgust at a madman intent on poisoning the country with scandal. And an almost unbearable grief as she contemplated humans and the pain they inflicted on each other.

"A man died tonight," Tom said. Maggie had told him about Prentiss.

"Yes, and another man lived," Maggie replied. She felt a deep and terrible exhaustion, from all the horrors of war. She was wet and cold, and yet her forehead felt as if it were burning. And when she swallowed, she could feel a tickle in the back of her throat. *I don't have time to be sick,* she thought.

"I don't know how I'll ever sleep," Tom said. "Not after all that."

"I know." Maggie put her arms around him. "So, don't. After — Well, I just don't want to be alone, either."

"All right then," he murmured, returning her embrace. "I'll come up."

When they reached Maggie's room, she used her key to open the door and then flipped on the light switch.

There was a man sitting in the wing chair. His coat was slung over the back of it, his fedora on the table next to it. And he had a gun in one hand trained at Maggie's heart.

"Miss Hope — and Mr. O'Brian. I assume I'm not interrupting anything? We have business to discuss."

Chapter Eighteen

Edmund Hope had prepared.

This time he'd driven to Chatswell Hall, and in the trunk of his car were all the materials he knew he'd need. It had taken him three trips from his parking spot in the woods, hidden by darkness and shrubbery, to get everything to the Hall itself, but he'd done it.

Now, it was time.

He put an eye to the chink in the blackout curtains. There she was — Clara — drinking and laughing with two men. There she was — kissing one. And then the other. Taking off her gown.

He lit a match. It burned red in the darkness. "Good-bye, darling," he whispered. He lit the fuse and hurled the first of the Molotov cocktails through the window.

Glass shattered. Lit bomb after lit bomb rained into the drawing room. Clara, Kemp, and von Bayer scrambled to their feet, shocked and stunned as the velvet drapes burst into flames.

"We've got to get out of here!" Clara shouted, pulling up her gown's straps. "Now!"

The trio made it to the front hall and had begun to pound on the doors when they heard the crash of more breaking glass and the eruption of ancient fabric into flame.

Clara struggled to open the thick double doors. "Oh, God!" she cried. The three went on pounding, screaming for help.

Upstairs in the M Room, Arthur and Owen were listening. "Damn! What the hell happened?"

"Sounded like an explosion!"

"They're still in the drawing room!"

Arthur ran to the window, pulled aside the blackout curtains, and looked out. Flames danced from the drawing room windows. He could just make out a dark figure against the fire. "We're under attack! Call down to the guardhouse! We've got to get the prisoners to safety!"

"Oh, please —" Owen said, also going to the window. A match flared in the darkness, and more flames ignited, outlining the figure of a man splashing a canister of what looked to be gasoline everywhere. "*We've* got to get to safety."

The two young men scrambled down the narrow servants' stairs and bumped into Naumann, who was making his way up.

"Thank goodness you two are all right!" he exclaimed. "Come on!"

"The prisoners —" Arthur gasped.

Naumann nodded. "We'll go out through the kitchen, then circle round to get them. Hurry!"

They made it from the drawing room to the front hall, the acrid smell of smoke filling the air.

Kemp and von Bayer were trying to pry open the thick doors, but the handles on the outside were chained together and locked. Even if they could break through the bolt, the links would never give.

A lit Molotov cocktail crashed through the glass of one of the hall's mullioned windows. Instantly, flames licked up the elaborate curtains. "Fuck!" Clara snarled, her eyes darting.

Then the door caught on fire. The trio ran desperately to the wide hallway, but it seemed as if every window was now swallowed in growing flames. "The windows are barred anyway," Clara said, trying to think. "We must get to the servants' quarters."

"That's locked and barred, too!" von Bayer panted, his eyes watering from the thickening fumes.

"Oh, for God's sake, we have to try!" Clara said. The two generals looked lost in fear and smoke. "Good Lord, look at you two — it's no wonder we're losing the war! Come on!"

Outside, Arthur, Owen, and Naumann reached the front doors of Chatswell Hall only to see them awash in flame. "There's no way for them to get out," Arthur groaned.

"Well, it *is* a prison," replied Owen. "Are we really going to worry about a bunch of Nazis burning to death? I say we get the listening equipment out while we still have time."

"They're in our custody — we can't let them die," Naumann insisted. "No matter how odious we may personally find them."

Owen took in the chaos, mouth agape. "Jesus, it's like the bloody Blitz all over again."

Arthur was thinking. "Who would have done this? Surely not any of our people — they know we've been getting good information out of these idiots —"

Naumann began to shout through the

broken windows, "Oi! Oi!" He tried to get closer but was pushed back by a wall of heat.

"That's not going to help," Owen called over the roar of the flames. Sirens sounded in the distance.

"Look!" Arthur said to Owen.

In the garish light, a figure was running away from the burning building. As the two younger men gave chase, Edmund, still holding one of his homemade bombs, stumbled. The bomb ignited, setting him on fire. Bright flames danced around his silhouette.

Edmund screamed. The unholy sound echoed off the walls and beams of Chatswell. Arthur and Owen tackled him, rolling the blazing man in the grass until the flames were extinguished.

"We need to get him to hospital," Arthur told Owen, over the injured man's screams. "Help me carry him."

Inside the house, Clara and her cohorts were having no luck with the servants' door, which was dead-bolted from the other side. Shadows cast by the fire danced up the vaulted ceiling. Suddenly Clara turned, then ran up the grand staircase.

"Where are you going?" Kemp shouted, breathless from his exertions. He and von

Bayer began to follow, even as sirens wailed from the drive.

Clara didn't answer, her heels clicking on the marble chessboard floor.

"The windows . . . are barred —" von Bayer panted.

Clara didn't stop. "The original part of this house predates the sixteen hundreds," she gasped.

"So?"

"England was newly Protestant then," she panted. Reaching her room, she slammed her palm into one of the wooden wall panels. The oak gave way, swinging with an agonizing creak.

"This was here all the time and you never told us?" Kemp said, eyes wide.

"You're going to complain about that *now*?" she hissed.

The three entered a dusty brick room with no windows and a low ceiling.

"What's this?" asked von Bayer, peering into the darkness.

"It's a priest hole," Clara said. "It's where the damn Catholics used to hide their damn priests during Protestant Elizabeth's reign." Her hands pressed at the other walls, hoping to feel something give. "Sometimes they were attached to the servants' quarters, so that a visiting priest could make a quick getaway."

The two men began pressing on the walls as well.

"Of course sometimes," Clara continued, panting, "the family was arrested, so the priest was never found and eventually died of suffocation or thirst."

"And this is your grand plan?" Kemp snapped.

Clara glared. "Do you have a better idea, General Kemp?"

"Yes. I'm going downstairs. I'll take my chances with the firemen with the axes and the hoses, thank you."

Von Bayer nodded. "I agree. I'm not going to roast to death in an Elizabethan priests oven."

"But this is our only chance of escape! *Real* escape. If we go back down, they'll just take us right back into custody again!"

Kemp was already on his way out. "Custody wasn't so bad," he called over his shoulder. Von Bayer followed.

"Fine," Clara said. "But don't give me away, boys?" She managed a seductive smile even as the house burned down around her.

While von Bayer shook his head, Kemp put a hand to his heart. "We lost you in the smoke and confusion," he told her. "I give

430

you my word as a Prussian and a gentleman."

And then Clara was alone, in the dark.

"Shut the door." Frank Cole gestured with
his gun. His different-colored eyes glittered
in the shadows. "Where's the letter?"

Don't panic — remember your training.
"Wait," Maggie urged. "Which letter?"

"The letter Prentiss forged. The one he
said Blanche gave to him 'just in case.' "

"I burned it," Maggie said. "At Mrs. Tao's
restaurant. It's long gone."

Cole relaxed visibly, then stood and stuck
his gun in the back waist of his trousers.

"But what about the *first* letter?" Maggie
asked. "The one that Prentiss left in
Blanche's apartment? We never found that
one."

"No," Cole said. "No, you wouldn't have.
You didn't miss anything, either. As you
probably guessed, Miss Hope, I disposed of
that one."

"Prentiss was forging them," Tom said.
"He could have any number of copies —"

"I took care of that, too. His townhouse
has been, shall we say, thoroughly cleaned."

"Oh, my God," Maggie exclaimed as the
heat came on and the radiator pipes began
to bang. "We're all on the same side here."

"Sorry about the gun," Cole told them. "Had to make sure you both gave up the letter without incident."

"I was never going to use it," Tom said. "I didn't believe it. Never did."

Cole appraised him. "I know. But it's my business to take care of those things."

Maggie nodded. She knew men like Frank Cole. She'd worked with them before. "We won't hear from Prentiss again."

"My sources tell me that Byrd Prentiss died in a freak electrical accident at Thomas Jefferson Prison. I don't suppose you had anything to do with that, Miss Hope?"

Tom gave Maggie a sharp look. "Did you?"

"I wish I could claim credit, really," Maggie said. "But it was, as they say, 'an act of God.'"

Cole nodded. "How did you know about the note in Blanche's apartment?"

"The First Lady and I went by on the evening of the twenty-second — we found the body and called the police. Before I left, I took the blank notepad. I did a pencil rubbing to reveal the note."

"And what happened to that copy?"

"I burned it. In Mrs. Roosevelt's fireplace."

"Good," he said, reaching for his fedora.

Maggie blinked. "It was Prentiss who tried to attack Andi and me outside of the Music Box," she said to Cole. "He confessed to it. But you were there, too, weren't you? You've been following me, haven't you?"

"Yes, I was there, as well," Cole answered. "Watching from a parked car. The President asked me to keep you safe." He gave a grim smile. "And I would have intervened. But you seemed able to handle yourself."

Maggie thought about all the times she'd kept watch for the shadow in the fedora, how frightened she'd been. "I do wish you'd introduced yourself, Mr. Cole."

He walked past her to the door. "In most cases it's best the client doesn't know. Happy New Year, Miss Hope, Mr. O'Brian." He let himself out.

Maggie bolted and chained the door behind him.

Without words, she walked over to the bed and took off her shoes. Then she climbed in.

"Well, that was —" Tom began.

"Yes." Maggie tried to say good night, but fell asleep before she could form the words.

"Maggie —"

She heard a voice, far away, through swirling fog and smoke and rushing water. She stirred, realizing she was still wearing her clothes from the night before. She opened her eyes. Tom was there, sitting on the edge of her bed. "Good morning," he said, switching on the bedside lamp.

She clapped her hands over her eyes against the light and groaned. "You'll get used to it," he promised.

"We —" she began.

"Didn't do anything. Besides sleep," he finished, reading her thoughts.

"What time is it?"

"Early," he said, tying the laces of his oxfords. "Almost six."

Maggie groaned again, then yawned and stretched. Going to the window, she pulled aside the chintz curtains and dealt with the blackout shade. The storm had passed. The street below was still wet from the previous night's rain, and dead leaves blown down by the wind littered the street. The sky was cloudy, but slivers of pale blue were visible and the bare branches of the trees danced in a gentle breeze.

"It's a beautiful day," she said, her breath catching in her throat. *And life goes on.*

Tom switched off the lamp; they didn't need it anymore. "I have to get to work."

They were suddenly shy around each other. "Me, too," Maggie said. She put a hand to her hair. "I mean, I need to change. And then get to the White House —"

"Yes," he said. "Well. Um, I'll — see you later?"

"I think so. Er, yes — definitely."

When Maggie reached the map room in the White House, she unpinned her hat and took off her gloves. Her hair was freshly washed and twisted into a bun; she was wearing a wool suit and a crisp white blouse. She felt like a different person than the woman who'd battled Byrd Prentiss only the night before. Prentiss was dead. Wendell was still alive. And the First Lady's name was still unblemished. The British-U.S. alliance would continue, unimpeded by scandal.

David and Mr. Churchill were still in Canada, with the P.M. giving a press conference at Government House in Ottawa. As Mr. Fields brought her a slice of buttered toast, a soft-boiled egg in a cup, and a pot of lukewarm coffee on a tray, Maggie listened to the exchange over the wireless, watching squirrels scamper across the damp lawn.

"Do you think Singapore can hold on?" one of the Canadian journalists asked.

"I do," the P.M. replied.

435

"Have you received any offers of peace from the Axis powers?"

Maggie could only imagine the expression on the P.M.'s face. *"We have had none at all,"* he answered, *"but then I really think they must be hard-pressed for materials of all kinds, and would not want to waste the paper and ink."*

"How long will it take to achieve victory?"

"As I said in the States, if we manage it well," the Prime Minister retorted, *"it will take only half as long as if we manage it badly."*

When the press conference was over, Maggie distracted herself by going through the morning newspapers. She was glad to see the Red Sox's Ted Williams had been voted baseball's Man of the Year — making up for the fact that he'd lost Most Valuable Player to Joe DiMaggio. She sipped her coffee as she read how the New York Film Critics Circle had voted *Citizen Kane* picture of the year, and that Wallis Simpson, now the Duchess of Windsor, had been voted number one on the annual list of the ten best-dressed women in the world. *Hah,* Maggie thought. She hoped that awful woman was enjoying her exile in the Bahamas.

There, in the *Los Angeles Times,* was yet another photograph of John with the same brunette, soon-to-be-divorced socialite.

Horsey, Maggie decided. *Too many teeth.*

She rolled her eyes and flipped the pages to the real news. Mohandas Gandhi had stepped down as the head of the All-India Nationalist Congress because of his commitment to nonviolence. India, where opposition to British colonial rule was brewing, conditionally supported England. Some there wanted to leverage support for England in exchange for independence, but Gandhi would have none of it. *"I could not identify myself with opposition to war efforts on the ground of ill will against Britain. If such were my view and I believed in the use of violence for gaining independence . . . I would consider myself guilty of unpatriotic conduct."*

Maggie started when the First Lady rapped at the open door. "Miss Hope, I'm glad to see you. Come into my office, won't you?"

Maggie followed her into the now-familiar room and sat on the fringed sofa.

"I just heard from Miss Martin," Mrs. Roosevelt said, smoothing out nonexistent wrinkles in her tweed skirt. She was wearing a matching jacket, sky-blue silk blouse, and her usual triple strand of pearls. "It seems as if there were technical problems last night at the Thomas Jefferson Prison."

"Yes," Maggie replied, folding her hands

in her lap. "The storm knocked out the power."

The First Lady raised an eyebrow. "Sounds like it was quite an evening. I also heard from Frank Cole. He . . . well, he explained everything to me."

"Excellent," Maggie responded. "But have you heard anything on Wendell's condition? How's he doing?"

"Andi told me the prison doctor says he's recovering and he'll be just fine."

Maggie lifted an eyebrow. "And are they going to try to kill him again — after they patch him up?"

Mrs. Roosevelt shook her head. "No. Or, at least, not soon in any case. In fact, that attorney has them tied in Eighth Amendment knots so tight that I have the feeling Governor King might ship Mr. Cotton off to Japan or Germany just to be rid of him. It seems that the Governor's associate, Mr. Byrd Prentiss, was found dead in the basement of the prison."

"Oh?" said Maggie.

"So the Governor's in a weak position to bargain. It looks as though Prentiss himself was trying to stop the execution — then was caught himself in a horrible accident. We'll never know the real story, most likely." She gave Maggie a sharp look. "And that's fine with me."

Maggie gave an involuntary shudder, remembering.

"Miss Martin told me, 'It was God's will.' Although she added that she also believes 'God works in mysterious ways.' " The First Lady looked directly into Maggie's eyes. "And personally, I believe He helps those who help themselves."

Maggie kept her face blank. "Yes, ma'am."

"You know," Mrs. Roosevelt said, almost to herself, "you're damned if you do, and you're damned if you don't. So you might as well try to help others and hope God joins in. And, no matter what you do — or how you live your life — people are going to say the most horrible things about you, Miss Hope."

Her eyes went to Lorena Hickok's open door. "So you might as well do what you want. No one can take away your self-respect unless you give it to them." Mrs. Roosevelt smiled at Maggie. "I think, I hope, that in your life you'll remember that, dear. Because I have the feeling you're going to do quite a bit in this war and not everyone will like it. By the way, I have something for you."

The First Lady handed Maggie a page of what looked like code.

"Mrs. Roosevelt?"

"More notes from Franklin's calendar," she explained. "You said you hadn't taken enough of the code to be able to break it. So here's some additional material." She colored slightly. "Oh, I know it's terrible that I went through his papers, but ever since I found those letters from . . . that woman . . . in his suitcase —"

Maggie didn't know what the First Lady was referring to, but remembering the way the President had bestowed his grin on Princess Martha, she could imagine.

"There's code for the entire month of December — that should give you enough to work with." She gave a wan smile. "I couldn't solve it." Then, "You're going to the ball, yes?"

"The ball?"

"The New Year's Eve Ball — day after tomorrow. We're having it here, in the East Room. Oh, it's one of those things to raise money for the war effort. We're going to need a lot of money, I fear, before this is over. I'm on the committee, so I must go. I don't like these social events, but they *are* necessary." She grinned. "I'd love it if you'd come, too."

"Thank you, Mrs. Roosevelt. I'd be honored. I'll just see if Mr. Churchill can spare me."

That evening, Mr. Churchill, David, and the rest of the entourage returned from Ottawa, triumphant. As they congregated in the map room, the P.M. called for drinks all around, which Mr. Fields procured — to accompany oysters on the half shell, pâté de foie gras in aspic and crisp toast points, and a silver bowl of smoked, salted almonds. When everyone had a glass of champagne or the equivalent, the Prime Minister raised his own tumbler of Johnnie Walker and soda. "To the Americans!" he intoned.

They all toasted, "To the Americans!"

"What's all this?" It was Harry Hopkins, with Mrs. Roosevelt right behind him.

"We're toasting the citizens of your wonderful country," Churchill declared, beckoning them in.

"Well, then I must also make a toast," the First Lady said in her quavering soprano as Churchill poured and handed her a glass and the First Lady raised it to Maggie. "To the British!"

"What's going on here?" It was the President, wheeling himself in.

"We're toasting, Franklin!" Churchill replied. "Get the man a glass!" he bellowed, waving a hand.

"Oh, how grand!" The President gave one of his electrifying grins, and when he had a glass, he raised it high. "To the Allies!" he said. "The U.S. and Britain together at last!"

"To the Allies!"

As the toasting continued, Maggie edged toward David. "Are you all right? You don't look well at all."

"I was up all night with *him.*" He gestured to Churchill with his chin. "The Boss had some health problems up north, I'm afraid. But we brought his doctor with us, thank goodness."

"He looks wonderful now," Maggie said. And so he did, smiling and clapping people on the back.

"He's been through a lot," David murmured. "And looks can sometimes be deceiving."

Maggie regarded the President, in his wheelchair, something hidden from most Americans and the rest of the world. *They're men,* she realized. *Mortal men.* She thought of Churchill's Victorian ideas of imperialism. *And flawed.* "Did you read about Mr. Gandhi this morning?"

David nodded. "I did."

"I adore Mr. Churchill," Maggie said. "I really do. But I don't always love what he

442

does as Prime Minister."

"But other people need to believe men like him and FDR are heroes. Especially if we're going to get through this war."

"The men behind the curtain," Maggie mused. "To the public, they're the Wizards of Oz. Or that's the story, at least. But they're really just flawed men, when you pull away the curtain, aren't they?"

The smile returned to David's face. "Does that mean I'm the little man who guards the gates of the Emerald City? With that horrible green fur hat? And the enormous mustache? *Who rang that bell!*" he mimicked. *"Well, bust my buttons, that's a horse of a different color!"*

"Oh, David," Maggie said. "What would I ever do without you?"

"Oh, I almost forgot, Mags. I'm terribly angry with you."

Maggie was taken aback. "Why?"

Behind his glasses, David's eyes were wide. "Beth is sick," he whispered.

"Beth?"

"Beth March? *Little Women*? She has scarlet fever, you know."

Maggie realized what part of the book he was up to. "I know," Maggie said, in soothing tones.

"They didn't have antibiotics back then."

"No."

"Maggie, you have to tell me — what's going to happen? Is Beth going to get better?"

"David, you know I can't say. You're going to have to keep reading."

At Barnet Hospital, Edmund Hope was admitted for second- and third-degree burns. "Take his clothes off," the doctor instructed. His blond hair was turning gray, and large liver spots marked his face and hands. "We need to treat all his burns."

The nurse did as the doctor asked, removing the rest of Edmund's clothes. Naked, he seemed small, his body covered in wisps of gray and ginger hair, his skin sagging and his stomach bulbous. The burns on his torso were raw and oozing.

But when she took off Edmund's socks, the nurse gave an involuntary scream. She jumped back, her hands clapped over her mouth.

"Control yourself, Nurse!" the doctor admonished. But even he winced at the stench emanating from Edmund's feet. They were rotting.

"Diabetes. Left untreated for God knows how long. Goodness knows how he was even able to function, with his body disintegrating away on him like that." The doctor shook his head. "We'll have to amputate."

At this, Edmund opened his eyes. "Wha-what?"

"Sir," the doctor said, in a gentle voice, "you've sustained major burns to almost a third of your body. We're going to treat you with antibiotics."

Edmund blinked.

"Sir, you were in a fire. You've been badly burned. We're going to treat you for the burns — and we're going to amputate your feet."

The injured man groaned.

"Sir, your feet are severely infected. The infection has spread to the bone. If we don't remove your feet and part of your legs, the infection will enter into your bloodstream and cause sepsis — probably death."

"No!" Edmund tried to struggle, but the pain was too great. "No," he moaned. "You're not cutting off my feet!"

"Sir," the doctor insisted. "You have diabetes. You must have had diabetes for quite some time now. If you'd seen a doctor earlier, perhaps we could have prevented the infection, or at least stopped it, early on. But when it's allowed to fester . . ."

"Please save my feet," Edmund whispered. "I'll do anything. I have money. I can pay you," he begged.

"I'm afraid it's too late now, sir," the doctor said. "There are some things even money can't buy."

Edmund turned his face to the wall. "It's hate."

The doctor looked to the nurse, confused.

"I've let my hate fester. I've lived on it, consumed it — and now it's consumed me." He moaned. "I tried to burn her out of my life and only ended up burning myself. All the hate — years and years of hate — has poisoned me, rotted me from the inside out . . ." His eyes rolled back in his head as he lost consciousness.

"Prepare him for surgery," the doctor told his nurse.

John Sterling had resigned himself to not getting back to Washington in time for the new year. Walt Disney had invited him to a party that was being held at the Beverly Hills Hotel. He dressed, then realized he was early, so decided to have a drink first at the famed Polo Lounge.

"Macallan, neat," John said at the bar, with a mural of Persian polo players. A buxom cigarette girl with a tray full of cellophane-wrapped packs made her way around the tables.

"Yes, sir," the colored man behind the bar replied. He returned with the whiskey.

"Thank you," John said. He waited, then took a sip. It was perfect. He gazed around the bar. There were genial conversations going on — he caught snippets of them, on topics such as film, books, and horses. At a nearby table, the unmistakable Marlene Dietrich was complaining to her manager about how tedious it was to be known as the woman with the world's best legs. "Then wear pants," the man snapped.

"I might just do that," she retorted.

A tiny man known as Buddy the Page — all of four feet tall, with frizzy orange hair, a brass-buttoned green jacket, and striped pants, marched through the lounge yelling, "Ca-ll fo-ooh Loo-ten-ant Stur-ling! Ca-ll fo-ooh Loo-ten-ant Stur-ling!"

John, embarrassed, raised a hand. "I'm Sterling."

Buddy winked at him as he plugged in a pink telephone, then handed over the receiver. "Then this call is fo-ooh you."

"Thank you." John put the phone's receiver to his ear. "Hello?"

"Stalky, is that you?"

"Hello, Mr. Dis— er, Walt."

Disney's voice boomed. "Couldn't wait until the party to tell you — I've been talking to your boys at the Air Ministry. They're a tough bunch — even demanding final script approval — but in the end, I decided to go for it. I've bought the rights to the Gremlins, Stalky. We're going to make a movie! So, what do you say, Stalky? We have a deal? I'll need you to stay here, work with us for a while. We can keep you at the Beverly, if you'd like."

"I'm honored, sir," John said, overwhelmed. "But I must insist that my share of any profits be shared with the RAF Benevolent Fund."

"Fine, fine," Disney said. "We'll let the lawyers work all that out. So, we have a deal?"

John took a deep breath. "I must discuss it first with Mr. Churchill."

"Do what you need to do, Stalky! But do it fast! Show business is just that — *business*. This town waits for no man, including Winston Churchill. Give me a call tomorrow after you've talked to him."

"Yes, sir. Happy New Year, sir."

When he replaced the receiver, Buddy came over. "Yoo-ah all done there?"

"Can I call out on this?" John asked.

Buddy opened his arms to take in the Polo Bar, the hotel, all of Los Angeles. "This is Hollywood, Loo-ten-ant. The land where dreams are made. Yoo-ah can do anything you want."

"I'd like to call Prime Minister Churchill," John said. "At the White House."

"Yes, Loo-ten-ant. Right away, Loo-ten-ant."

It took awhile for all of the various lines to connect and for someone to hand the telephone receiver to Mr. Churchill in the Rose Bedroom, but at last they were speaking.

"Lieutenant Sterling!" the Prime Minister boomed. "Just returned from Ottawa. Lovely country, Canada, lovely country."

"Sir, I —"

"Just thinking of you. I have another mission for you, should you choose to accept it."

John twirled the pink telephone cord between his fingers as the bartender brought out a silver bowl of macadamia nuts. "Sir?"

"This is a secure line?" Churchill was shouting to David. "Are you *sure* we're on a secure line, Mr. Greene?" When the P.M. was sufficiently reassured, he turned back to the telephone and his conversation with John. "We've uncovered what we think are Nazi rocket launchers, on the coast of the Baltic Sea."

"What?" John was shocked. He'd known

there'd been talk about a possible Nazi rocket program, but as far as he knew it was as real as his Gremlins.

"It's true. We've had RAF pilots fly over and take reconnaissance photographs. We've also had the rocket information confirmed by some of the prisoners of war we're holding. But because we're so sorely lacking in resources, we want to make absolutely sure what we're bombing before we drop anything."

"How can I help, sir?"

"We need more pilots. I know you're itching to get back in a plane. This would be your chance. Only this time you would be shooting with cameras, not guns. Special cameras, with special film, made to take photos in three dimensions." There was a pause as the Prime Minister's voice echoed on the line. "But I know you're doing important work there in Los Angeles for us —"

"Yes —"

"This is your decision, my boy. I won't interfere."

"Yes, sir."

"However, I'd prefer you to stay in Hollywood, if that Disney chap will have you. Propaganda is one of our biggest weapons in this war, and don't you forget that. The

450

handsome young RAF pilot, making a Disney movie — that's something we can't replicate without you. In other words, I can probably find another pilot, but I can't find another you."

"Sir, I feel my duty —"

"John," Churchill said, using the young man's Christian name for the first time. "Do you remember that Charles Laughton movie of Henry VIII?"

John was confused. "Sir?"

Ice cubes clinked; the P.M. was probably taking a swig of his whiskey and soda. "Do you remember the scene with Henry going into the bedroom with Anne of Cleves? And then he turns and says, 'Ah, the things I've done for England'?"

"Yes. . . ."

"Well, that's what you've got to do, young man. Do what you must for England."

"Yes, yes, sir. Then —" John knew his next words would change his life, perhaps forever.

CHAPTER NINETEEN

One New Year's Eve day, the White House was bustling with preparations.

During the night, the East Room's chandeliers had been lowered so that each crystal globe and gasolier prism could be washed and polished, and then rehung. They glistened, casting dancing rainbows on the wooden floors, rubbed to the highest sheen.

Maggie had asked for her dress to be sent over from the Mayflower and changed in David's room. She was wearing her old pale blue gown trimmed in black velvet, the one she hadn't been allowed to wear the Christmas before at Windsor Castle because "only the Queen wears blue." It was also the dress she'd worn when John had once proposed to her — which now seemed a very, very long time ago. She dabbed on a bit of lipstick, then slipped into her satin slippers and picked up her beaded clutch. It was time to go.

When she opened the door, she saw David standing there, just about to knock. They both gasped, surprised, then laughed. He wore a black dinner jacket and black tie. A sprig of red holly berries adorned his lapel. His face lit up when he caught sight of Maggie. "There you are!" he said. "You look dazzling, as always."

"You clean up well, too," she retorted as he caught her gloved hand and bowed to kiss it. Maggie realized there was music spilling out from the ballroom — a small orchestra, from the sound of it. "Shall we go?"

David offered his arm. "Your wish is my command." But before they could, the telephone rang. He returned to the room and picked up the receiver. He was momentarily taken aback but then handed it to Maggie. "It's for you," he told her. "I'll give you some privacy."

"Hello?"

"Happy New Year!" came John's voice.

"Happy New Year!" Maggie echoed. "How are you? I've missed you."

"I'm good," John said, "great, even. But I wanted to talk to you. I have some news."

Maggie felt her stomach drop and wrapped her free hand in the telephone cord. "Oh, really?" she asked, affecting nonchalance.

John strained his voice to be heard over the sound of the crowd. "Well, apparently, Walt Disney himself likes my Gremlins. He's made an offer to buy the rights, and wants me to stay in L.A. until the project is up and running."

"That's fantastic, John! Congratulations!"

"Thank you."

"For how long?" she asked, heart humming. "How long do you think you'll stay in L.A.?"

"Six months, at least. Maybe more. The Boss has given his blessing. Says I'm more use as a storyteller than a fighter pilot — I'm saving him a front-row seat for the premiere. I figure I can completely recover here, then go back to the RAF when this winds up. Although I'm not sure when that will be."

"I see."

"What I want to say, Maggie, is that I don't want you to wait for me. I know you'll be in Washington, or back in London — or wherever. And I don't want you to stop living your life."

"Because you haven't?" Maggie asked, her tone sharp. "With that divorcée who was in the paper with you?"

There was a long pause, and in it Maggie

could hear the crowd at the bar singing "Auld Lang Syne."

"That's not — No, I'm just saying, Maggie, that life is short and —"

She didn't want to hear any more. She didn't want to know. "Good-bye, John." Swallowing back a sob, she hung up the telephone.

Outside, in the hallway, David was waiting. "Are you all right?" he asked, seeing her face.

"I — I think John and I just broke up," she managed.

"I'm sorry, love — and I'm sorry about the timing of this request, but the Boss would like to see you."

"Now?" Maggie said, wiping away a stray tear with her fingers.

"Afraid so."

"I noticed there was a suitcase in your room," Maggie said, trying to change the subject. "Are you running away to join the circus?"

"I have plenty of circus right here, thank you, but I am off to Florida, with the Boss."

"Florida?"

"Yes," he answered. "Somewhere on the coast." David brightened. "I've never been to Florida. I hear it's warm enough to swim in the ocean there at this time of year! But, by the way," he added, looking as petulant as possible, "Beth died. *Died*. And Jo doesn't marry Laurie. He marries the awful Amy and Jo marries Professor Bhaer, who's old and ugly, and chews with his mouth open."

Maggie nodded. "I know."

"It's a *dreadful* ending!"

"A novel set in wartime. Not everyone's going to get what she wants." Maggie kissed his cheek. "Thank you for everything, darling David. I do adore you, you know."

He bowed low, and offered his arm. "It would be quite impossible not to, I should think."

As Maggie and David passed the door to the Rose Bedroom, they spied the Prime Minister's doctor packing up his stethoscope in his leather satchel. *Mr. Churchill's heart? Is there something wrong with his heart?* Maggie and David exchanged looks, then peeked inside. The P.M.'s face radiated exhaustion, and he was already in his pajamas and dressing gown — highly unusual. Even on an ordinary night, the Boss often stayed up working until one or two in the morning. Now, on the night of an important ball, he was already in bed.

He waved an unlit cigar from his supine

position. "Miss Hope, come in," he began, as the doctor let himself out. "Not you," he barked, pointing at David with his cigar. "Just Miss Hope."

When she had closed the door behind her, he said, "I know you and Mr. Greene must be on your way to the ball. And I know you young people don't have much of a chance to enjoy yourself these days, and I am sorry." This admission was huge coming from Mr. Churchill, who rarely acknowledged life outside of his own sphere.

"It's fine, sir. How can I help you?"

"Sit down, sit down," he growled. "Excellent work on the Prentiss situation."

"Yes, sir." She took a seat on a pink silk chair. "Thank you."

"First, some good news, Miss Hope. As you so cheekily requested, as a condition to work for me again, we've located your half sister."

For a moment, Maggie couldn't breathe. "Is she — is she alive?"

"She is. She's at Ravensbrück concentration camp, as a political prisoner. We're working on the best way to extract her."

"Thank God," Maggie said, breathing once again. "And thank you, too, sir."

"Although, she won't tell them what they want to hear — won't give up her fellow resistance fighters." He gnawed at the cigar. "Elise Hess may be German, but she's no Nazi. And she seems to be on the side of Right." He picked up his monogrammed silver lighter. "Miss Hope, you should be proud of her."

Maggie was indeed proud of her. She wondered if her sister would ever be proud of *her*. "Yes, sir — but if she's being held at Ravensbrück . . ." Maggie had heard of what went on in the camps. "She may not be alive for much longer."

"Exactly. Which is why I have some of your fellow Baker Street Irregulars in Berlin standing by. If things go as planned, Miss Hess will be out of the damn camp soon. And she will be able to meet you in London."

"London?" Then, "When? When can I see her?"

"You leave tomorrow," he told her. "I've had Mr. Greene make travel plans for you. The SOE officers will be coming with Miss Hess as soon as they can." He waved her away. "I'm tired now. I'll see you in London, Miss Hope. And Happy New Year."

"Happy New Year to you, too, sir. And thank you."

"He looks terrible," Maggie whispered to

David, when she caught up with him downstairs.

"I know," David said. "But the doctor's been looking after him. And Florida will do him good. And, as Mr. C probably told you, I've arranged a train trip for you tomorrow from here to New York, then a seat for you on the Boeing 314 Clipper, from New York to Lisbon. You'll be traveling with a group of American entertainers — singers, dancers, comedians, and the like en route to entertain our troops. You'll fit right in."

"Oh, ha-ha and ha."

David smiled. "From Lisbon, we'll get you on a jump flight to London. Gubbins at SOE is glad to hear you're coming back. He has a particular job in mind for you."

Maggie quirked an eyebrow. "What is it?"

"There are secrets in this world, even from me," David intoned, eyes lifted heavenward. "You'll find out when you get there."

"And Elise will meet me in London?"

"We're doing everything in our power to get her out of Germany and safely to London. You know we can't make any promises —"

"I know — I know. And thank you." The music from the ballroom swelled. "Would you like to dance, David?" she asked impulsively.

"I would like nothing better."

Camera flashbulbs exploded, lights gleaming on ladies' satin gowns and heavy jewels. When Maggie reached Mrs. Roosevelt in the receiving line, the First Lady favored her with a wink.

The East Room seemed magical — illuminated by chandeliers and candles, decorated with red roses and poinsettias. An orchestra played on a stage as couples twirled and spun to the music. There were small linen-covered tables set up around the dance floor, and people sat and drank champagne as uniformed waiters, colored men all, passed hors d'oeuvres on silver trays.

"I hear this is where President John Adams's wife, Abigail Adams, hung the laundry to dry, back in the day," Maggie said to David.

He chortled. "I've always suspected you Americans were odd birds — now I know for sure. Can you imagine our Queen hanging laundry in a ballroom?"

Maggie thought about the current Queen Elizabeth, how strong she had been during the early days of the Blitz — refusing to send the young Princesses to Canada or to leave the King. "I can, actually, if it would help the war effort."

David was scanning the crowd. "Your favorite mick is here," he said, catching sight of Tom.

"Be nice," Maggie warned. "He's been through a lot in the last week."

"As have we all."

She gave a harsh laugh. "As have we all."

Tom reached them, bowed to Maggie, and shook David's hand. "May I have this dance?" he asked Maggie.

"Do you mind?" she asked David.

"Go, go," he said with mock annoyance.

She smiled as she took Tom's arm. The conductor raised his baton, and the orchestra segued into a dreamy rendition of "Winter Wonderland." Light sparked off the lead singer's sapphire drop earrings as she took a deep breath and began to sing. Her creamy alto voice was vibrant and rich, reminiscent of Ella Fitzgerald's, and Tom was an excellent dancer. For a moment, Maggie relaxed as they turned around the floor in a slow fox-trot.

"Maggie, I'd like to step out with you."

She couldn't help it — a laugh burst from her throat.

"What's so funny?" he demanded, spinning her around. "It's not exactly the response a red-blooded American man about to go to war wants to hear. I'm making you a sincere offer. In fact, I'd like to take you out to dinner tomorrow night." He dipped her and, when he pulled her back up, continued. "*Not* Chinese, either, I'll have you know."

"I adore Chinese," Maggie said, breathless. "But I'm sorry, Tom." She did her best to collect herself. "It's all so implausible! First of all, I'm leaving tomorrow to go back to London. And you're leaving for basic training — and then goodness only knows where we'll be and what we'll be doing."

"All over this country, people are doing their duty. But that hasn't stopped them from asking a special girl to hold a place in her heart. Maybe write a few letters."

"I'm happy to write to you, Tom, but you do remember I'm not Catholic, yes?"

"Yes." He spun her around again. "But you could always convert."

Maggie rolled her eyes. "Unlikely. Maybe, someday, something along the lines of Thomas Jefferson's beliefs."

Tom shuddered. "Relativism incarnate! That's not real religion, you know. You might as well join a country club."

Maggie thought of Elise, who had once wanted to become a nun but quite liked young men. "I do know of someone who'd be perfect for you. Maybe — just maybe — after this blasted war is over, I can introduce you. Her name is Elise. Elise Hess."

"How do you know her?"

She's my half sister. "We met in Berlin. But she's meeting me in London. At least, I hope she is."

"And she's Catholic?"

Another twirl. "Quite."

"Oh, Emma Woodhouse. . . . I don't want a matchmaker. But tell me — this Elise . . ." This time, a dip. "Is she pretty?"

Maggie looked up at him. "Beautiful."

"Not as beautiful as you, though."

Maggie blushed pink.

Tom put his hand to the small of her back and guided her to one of the gilt chairs. "By the way, I have something for you." He took out a rolled, thin book from his jacket's front pocket. It was tied with a blue ribbon.

"Oh, my goodness," Maggie said. "What's this?"

"Merry Christmas — open it and see."

Maggie untied the bow and unrolled his gift. It was a comic book.

"It's brand new," Tom told her. "The first book in a new series with a girl, er, woman, as the hero. Heroine. You know what I mean. Wonder Woman is an Amazonian warrior princess who fights for justice, love, and peace. Like someone else I know."

"Wonder Woman!" Maggie exclaimed. "Thank you, Tom!"

They kissed. It was a perfect kiss, absolutely perfect. As they pulled apart, Maggie remembered what John had said. And he was right. "Life is short," she said to Tom.

"It can be," he replied.

"I'm serious. Life is short — anything can happen. At any time. *Carpe diem.*" She kissed him again, longer this time. "And *carpe noctem,* as well. Would you like to go back to the Mayflower with me for a nightcap?"

"Why, Miss Hope, I thought you'd never ask."

CHAPTER TWENTY

"I don't know how 1942 will end," Tom said as he came out of the steamy bathroom, wrapped in nothing but a towel, "but I do know it started wonderfully well."

Maggie, who had already bathed and dressed, caught a glimpse of him in the mirror as she put on lipstick. She whistled.

Tom put on his clothes, then went to the window. New Year's Day was a grim gray. "Not exactly a great omen," he said.

"What are you going to do today?" Maggie asked.

"Roosevelt's declared a Universal Day of Prayer — thought I'd go."

Maggie nodded. Newspapers across the country had contained full-page ecumenical ads asking Americans to go to the church of their choice. She flipped open the *Washington Post* on the dresser and read the President's words to the nation as she put on her pearl earrings.

The year 1941 had brought upon our nation, as the past two years have brought upon other nations, a war of aggression by powers dominated by arrogant rulers whose selfish purpose is to destroy free institutions. They would thereby take from the freedom-loving peoples of the earth the hard-won liberties gained over many centuries.

The new year of 1942 calls for the courage and the resolution of old and young to help win a world struggle in order that we may preserve all we hold dear.

We are confident in our devotion to country, in our love of freedom, in our inheritance of courage. But our strength, as the strength of all men everywhere, is of greater avail as God upholds us.

Therefore, I do hereby appoint the first day of the year 1942 as a day of prayer, of asking forgiveness for our shortcomings of the past, of consecration to the tasks of the present, of asking God's help in days to come.

We need His guidance that this people may be humble in spirit but strong in the conviction of the right; steadfast to endure sacrifice and brave to achieve a victory of liberty and peace.

"And then later today," Tom said, "representatives from twenty-six Allied nations are meeting to pledge their support for the Atlantic Charter by signing the Declaration by United Nations." He grinned. "I'll be there. With my camera, of course."

"Of course," Maggie said. "Look, my car will be here shortly. I'd rather we say our good-byes here, if you don't mind."

He walked to her and wrapped his arms around her. "Take care, Maggie Hope," he said, bending down to kiss her lips before going to put on his hat and coat. "And you never know, maybe I'll see you in London."

Maggie wiped away a wayward tear. "I hope so, Tom. And wherever you're sent, please be careful. And, in the meantime, I'll write to you at Fort Bragg."

Before she left the White House, Maggie had one more call to make.

"Andi?"

"Maggie!"

Maggie was relieved she'd caught her. "I just wanted to see how you're doing — we didn't have much time to talk that night."

"That *crazy* night."

"It was pretty crazy, wasn't it? And I've seen my share of crazy." Maggie cleared her throat. "Anyway, I just wanted to make sure you're all right. What you did —"

"What I did was the right thing," Andi finished, her voice strong. "I'm not ashamed. I may have" — she lowered her voice — "I may have pulled the wires out, but he's the one who stepped toward us. As far as I'm concerned, he did it to himself."

"If you ever want to talk . . ."

"No." Andi sounded adamant.

"Well, if you ever do, I'm ready to listen. And how is Wendell?"

"He's still in the hospital, but his momma's going every day, to make sure he's all right." Andi sighed. "I don't know what's going to happen, but he's safe, at least for today."

"The other reason I'm calling" — Maggie wrapped the coiled telephone cord around her wrist and took a soft breath — "is to say good-bye. I'm going back to London."

"Good-bye?" Andi sounded shocked. "But you just got here!"

"I know, but do you remember my telling you about my sister — my half sister?"

"The one who wanted to be a nun?" Andi chuckled. "Yes, of course."

"Well, it turns out she may be able to get to London. So I'm going back. I want to be there to meet her."

"Well, I understand — if she were my

468

sister, I'd do the same. I must say, it's been interesting, Maggie. And I hope we'll meet again someday."

"I do, too, Andi. Maybe in London? We could actually go to places together there. Britain's not perfect, but on that count they're more civilized than most Americans."

"When this damn war is over, we'll celebrate with tea at the Ritz," Andi said decisively. "And then go dancing at that jazz club you mentioned."

"The Blue Moon Club! All right, I'll write you a letter as soon as I get back to London."

"Please do — we need to keep in touch. Bon voyage, Maggie Hope."

"*Àbientôt,* Andrea Martin."

As the blue-and-white streamlined passenger train *Southerner* made its way from Union Station in Washington, D.C., to Penn Station in New York City, Maggie stretched in her seat. She gazed out over the Chesapeake Bay, watching the gray clouds begin to melt away. The sky turned lighter, a filmy white, and then, finally, the deep blue of the American and British flags. It had been twenty-five days since the attack on Pearl Harbor and ten days since she'd arrived in the United States.

Maggie reached into her handbag for the paper with the code. Even with Mrs. Roosevelt's additional material, she didn't have enough to break it, she realized. Then she remembered that name Eleanor Roosevelt had mentioned in passing: Lucy Mercer.

She tried it as LUCYMER, to eliminate the repeated letters, making the code alphabet L U C Y M E R A B D F G H I J K N O P Q S T V W X Z for the usual A B C D E F G H I J K L M N O P Q R S T U V W X Y Z.

The hairs on Maggie's arms lifted as she realized she'd cracked the code. And so R S F G H V N R Q U Q R X X M N V F became O P E R A T I O N S N O W W H I T E or OPERATION SNOW WHITE. Could it refer to Blanche? It had to . . . The day was the same — and *blanche* meant white.

On the day of Prentiss's death, she decoded the entry J B C P M B Q V N Q L to read D U C K H U N T I N G. *Duck hunting.* She knew for a fact that the President wasn't duck hunting that day. Could it be a code for a shooting? Shooting a Byrd, perhaps?

And what were the larger implications? That the President had a personal intelligence service beyond J. Edgar Hoover. That his intelligence officers had discovered a plot to discredit the First Lady.

Prentiss had killed Blanche and left the note. But what if he hadn't? What would Frank Cole have done that night? And what was he planning to do on the night of the execution?

Her head was spinning. Maggie tore the paper with the code and her decryption into tiny pieces. Then she opened the window and threw out the pieces. They were picked up by the wind, scattering over the stony Maryland shore.

She took a deep breath. The First Lady had not been dishonored. The Roosevelt Administration was stronger than ever. And the United States and Britain stood together with a newly created organization of two dozen other nations to take down the Axis.

A woman, Blanche Balfour, had been murdered. A man, Byrd Prentiss, had died. And a young man, Wendell Cotton, had been saved.

Maggie leaned against the headrest. She was thinking about her love of math. How clean it had always seemed, how elegant and pure. *But it isn't like that anymore, is it, Hope?*

And really, it never had been — that was just how she'd seen it when she was younger. She'd once believed math was tidy and predictable — with right and wrong answers. Now modern math and physics and quantum mechanics — and modern life — seemed to be more in line with Heisenberg's Uncertainty Principle. Uncertainty was a fundamental part of nature, and what people knew — what people *thought* they knew — was imprecise at best. It all depended on who was telling the story.

She had returned to the United States hoping to find out where she belonged — the United States or the United Kingdom. But now it struck her that a woman without a country, without a husband, without parents, and without religion was in the perfect position to be a spy. To be on her own, not answering to anyone.

She was free.

The train pulled out from a dark pine forest and careened along the rocky Atlantic shore, patches of sun skidding across the indigo water. It passed beneath the dappled clouds as it traveled in and then out of the shadows.

In the leather seat in front of Maggie, a young mother held her pink-cheeked baby wrapped in a paisley shawl over her shoulder; he appraised Maggie with bright blue eyes. Maggie waved. The baby gave a gummy grin back, then bit down on his chubby fist, kicked his feet, and laughed. Maggie laughed along with him.

She was thankful that the groundwork for victory had been laid. She was looking forward to returning to London. She couldn't wait to see her friend Sarah and to reunite with her cat, Mr. K. She was looking forward to seeing her sister again, to explain things to her, and to try to salvage their relationship. And she was also looking forward to returning to work for the SOE — and learning what her next mission would be.

Epilogue

The red sun was setting over the north London countryside. Through the smoke, Chatswell Hall was still standing, although it had sustained an immense amount of damage from the fire.

As the day drew to a close, one of the firemen leaned on his shovel. "I'm sorry, sir," he said to Naumann. They were surrounded by still-smoking ruins. "But there's no way any prisoner could have survived."

Naumann sighed. "At least we got the men out. They're back in custody in the Tower." To the firefighters, white-haired men with lined faces — too old to serve in the military but still spry enough to do their duty — he said, "Thank you, gentlemen. You've all worked valiantly. It was an old manor house, with plenty of wood. You did your best." He kicked at a smoking ember, the remains of a Tudor beam. "Sometimes you can't save them all."

"What about the loon who set the fires?" another asked.

"He's in hospital," Arthur answered. "Last I heard, he survived. But barely."

"We've got enough problems 'ere — bloody fool has to make more?"

"*There is more in heaven and earth . . .* Well . . . however the damn thing goes." Naumann looked at the men. They'd been working for over twenty-four hours. "What's the local here?"

"The Green Dragon, sir."

"All right, then," Naumann said. "First round's on me."

It was after midnight, more than twenty-four hours since the fire had started, when Clara emerged from her hiding spot.

There were no voices, no sounds of men battling flames. All that was left were some stonework and a few still-smoking beams. Clara opened the paneled door to what remained of her cell. She made her way down the central staircase, stepped over the remnants of the charred front door.

She looked up at the glittering stars and took a greedy breath of cold, smoky air.

And then she began to make her way to the road that she knew would take her, eventually, to London.

It is the duty of the older generation, if possible, to leave an authentic record of their experiences during World War II for the benefit of future generations. Without it, history would simply be hearsay.

— Peter Hart, M House secret listener

HISTORICAL NOTES

This is a novel. It is a work of fiction. If you want to read history, I suggest reading a nonfiction book or, better still, a library of them. However, in the course of writing this book, I consulted many nonfiction books and documentaries, and I'm delighted to share my reading and watching list.

First an overall thank-you to the extraordinary filmmaker and documentarian Ken Burns. Yes, I watched almost all of his series, concentrating on *Jazz, Baseball, The War, The National Parks,* and, of course, *The Roosevelts.* What a terrific overview of life in the United States before and during World War II through many lenses.

In terms of researching Winston Churchill and Franklin D. Roosevelt's meeting of December 1941 at the White House, I relied on many sources, including: *Franklin and Winston: An Intimate Portrait of an Epic*

Friendship by Jon Meacham; *One Christmas in Washington: The Secret Meeting Between Roosevelt and Churchill That Changed the World* by David Bercuson and Holger Hedwig; *Franklin and Winston: A Christmas That Changed the World* by Douglas Wood; and *December 1941: 31 Days That Changed America and Saved the World* by Craig Shirley.

For Eleanor Roosevelt, I relied on *My Day: The Best of Eleanor Roosevelt's Acclaimed Newspaper Columns, 1936–1962* by Eleanor Roosevelt.

For researching the White House and Washington, D.C., I studied *White House Butlers: A History of White House Chief Ushers and Butlers* by Howard Brinkley; *The White House: The President's Home in Photographs and History* by Vicki Goldberg in cooperation with the White House Historical Association; *The Willard Hotel: An Illustrated History* by Richard Wallace Carr and Marie Pinak Carr; *National Geographic*'s *Inside the White House: Stories from the World's Most Famous Residence* by Noel Grove with William B. Bushong and Joel D. Treese; *Washington, D.C.: Then and Now* by Alexander D. Mitchell IV; *The White House: Its Historic Furnishings and First Families* by Betty C.

Monkman; and *The Mayflower Hotel: Grande Dame of Washington, D.C.* by Judith R. Cohen.

For an overall look at the United States during that pivotal time, I am indebted to *The American Home Front: 1941–1942* by Alistair Cooke.

I also consulted the following documentaries: *National Geographic*'s *Inside the White House;* Smithsonian Channel's *White House Revealed;* Smithsonian Folkways' *White House Workers; Inside the White House;* PBS's *Echoes from the White House; American Experience:* "Eleanor Roosevelt"; *Biography:* "Eleanor Roosevelt: A Restless Spirit"; Richard Kaplan Productions' *The Eleanor Roosevelt Story;* Team Productions' *FDR: A Presidency Revealed;* and *Biography:* "FDR: Years of Crisis."

To learn more about President Roosevelt and wiretapping as well as his personal secret security detail, I relied on Joseph E. Persico's *Roosevelt's Secret War: FDR and World War II Espionage.* While Frank Cole is a fictional character, he's based on journalist John Franklin Carter, FDR's associate.

Yes, the British did put high-ranking Nazis up at various manor houses outside London and monitored every word they uttered, recording and transcribing the relevant ones. I relied on *Tapping Hitler's Generals: Transcripts of Secret Conversations 1942–45,* edited by Sönke Neitzel; Helen Fry's *The M Room: Secret Listeners Who Bugged the Nazis;* and the documentary *Secrets of the Dead:* "Bugging Hitler's Soldiers."

And, yes, the British did have a secret weapon of 3-D photography, with which, in tandem with information from the bugged German officers, they discovered Hitler's rocket program. Sources were: *Spies in the Sky: The Secret Battle for Aerial Intelligence During World War II* by Taylor Downing; *Operation Crossbow: The Untold Story of the Search for Hitler's Secret Weapons* by Allan Williams; *Nova:* "3D Spies of WWII"; *National Geographic War and Military Collection:* "Nazi Secret Weapons"; *Top Secret Weapons Revealed:* "Nazi War Machines"; *Top Secret Weapons Revealed:* "In Search of the Smart Bomb"; and *Nazi Mega Weapons:* "V2 Rocket."

John Sterling's progression from wounded RAF pilot to children's storyteller is inspired by the career path of Roald Dahl. Yes, he sold an idea for a book and movie about RAF Gremlins to Walt Disney! I relied on

The Irregulars: Roald Dahl and the British Spy Ring in Wartime Washington by Jennet Conant. For period details about the Beverly Hills Hotel, where Roald Dahl stayed, courtesy of the Walt Disney Company, I consulted *The Pink Palace: Behind Closed Doors at the Beverly Hills Hotel* by Sandra Lee Stuart. For an insider's look at the Disney Studios, I referred to *Walt Disney and Assorted Other Characters: An Unauthorized Account of the Early Years at Disney's* by Jack Kinney and *The Disney That Never Was: The Stories and Art of Five Decades of Unproduced Animation* by Charles Solomon.

People will probably say that a mixed-race, lesbian, possibly transgendered person couldn't possibly have had access to Eleanor Roosevelt, let alone eventually become a practicing lawyer — and they'd be wrong. Andrea (Andi) Martin is based on the indomitable civil rights lawyer and feminist Pauli Murray. Andi's also inspired by actress-model-writer-traveler Anita Reynolds, who spent significant time in Paris in the 1930s.

The fictional character Wendell Cotton is based on Odell Waller, a black sharecropper sentenced to death by an all-white, poll-tax-paying jury in Virginia in 1941 and championed by a young Pauli Murray. The real

Odell Waller, alas, was executed.

To research American history and race, I spoke with my late mother-in-law, Edna MacNeal, who lived through it and discussed her own experiences with me (usually over a glass or two of red wine). I also relied on the books *Defying Dixie: The Radical Roots of Civil Rights, 1919–1950* by Glenda Elizabeth Gilmore; *Freedom's Daughters: The Unsung Heroines of the Civil Rights Movement from 1830 to 1970* by Lynne Olson; *The Case of Odell Waller and Virginia Justice, 1940–1942* by Richard B. Sherman; *American Cocktail: A "Colored Girl" in the World* by Anita Reynolds; *Proud Shoes: The Story of an American Family* by Pauli Murray; and *Dark Testament and Other Poems* by Pauli Murray.

RECIPES

PRESIDENT ROOSEVELT'S MARTINI
Franklin Roosevelt did mix drinks at Children's Hour and reportedly enjoyed making Martinis. As far as I can tell there's no exact recipe, but we know from his personal secretary Grace Tully's memoirs that they were heavy on the vermouth (which was considered old-fashioned). He was also known to add a few drops of Pernod, orange blossom water, or olive brine for flavor.

Here's my best approximation of his Martini. Enjoy!

2 parts gin (according to some he preferred
  Plymouth; according to others, Beefeater)
1 part dry vermouth
splash olive brine
2 olives for garnish
crushed ice

Shake gin, vermouth, and olive brine in a

container half-filled with chipped ice.
Strain into chilled cocktail glasses.
Add garnish.

WINSTON CHURCHILL'S MARTINI

Winston Churchill's enjoyment of spirits was legendary, but, by all accounts, he preferred his drinks unmixed. According to various sources he was appalled at the copious amount of vermouth in President Roosevelt's Martinis, but drank them, in the name of diplomacy.

gin (according to some he preferred Plymouth, according to others, Boodles)
crushed ice

Shake gin in a container half-filled with chipped ice.
Bow respectfully toward France (where dry vermouth is produced).
Strain into a chilled cocktail glass or coupe. Garnish with lemon peel if desired.

ACKNOWLEDGMENTS

I'd like to thank posthumously my mother-in-law, Edna "Miss Edna" MacNeal. Miss Edna grew up in Harlem during the World War II years, and we had a great time talking about the blackouts in New York City, trying to find Pearl Harbor on a map of the world, and her neighborhood regulars, like the ice-delivery man, the milk-delivery man, and the knife-sharpening man. I'll miss our discussions of the adventures of Maggie Hope and I'm grateful that she was able to read so much of the manuscript of this book.

She had funny comments, too, such as "I personally don't like this 'African American' nonsense. 'Black' is fine — but to tell the truth I was fine back in the day with 'colored.' " She was also a huge fan of the Roosevelts and loved reading all the research books with me, and discussing the President and First Lady (as well as Lucy Mercer).

487

An enormous thank-you to Kate Miciak, my fearless editor and Maggie Hope's fairy godmother at Penguin Random House. I'm grateful for her support and guidance and good humor. Also to the Penguin Random House family, especially Lindsey Kennedy, Maggie Oberrender, Victoria Allen, Robbin Schiff, Julia Maguire, Kim Hovey, and Vincent La Scala, and, as always, the intrepid sales force. Hats off.

Thank you to Maggie Hope's other fairy godmother, Victoria Skurnick, aka Agent V, and the team at the wonderful Levine Greenburg, especially Lindsey Edgecomb.

I'd like to thank Noel MacNeal for his love and support; he took care of so many things so I could write — and also drew John Sterling's Gremlin. And thanks also to Matthew MacNeal, who was always supportive of my writing schedule and trips.

Kudos and huzzahs to reader and all-around goddess Idria Barone Knecht.

Special thanks and gratitude to reader and editor, the lovely Phyllis Brooks Schafer, Londoner and Blitz survivor.

Gratias tibi ago to historian Ronald J. Granieri for guidance and edits — and answering many, many odd-sounding questions without blinking.

Hugs to Blake Leyers, for reading, as well

as to Lauren Barone, and fellow scribe Scott Cameron. Thanks to electrician Neil Poulter, police officer Rick Peach, and lawyer Michael T. Feeley, as well as to medical doctors Mary Linton Peters and Meredith Norris.

I'm grateful to Frank and Geri Serchia; John, Melissa, Jeremy, Cassidy, Jack, and Riley Kreuzer; Mary Linton; and Stephen Peters for their gracious hospitality and the space and time to write.

Special gratitude to my Jungle Red Writers sisters: Rhys Bowen, Lucy Burdette, Deborah Crombie, Hallie Ephron, Julia Spencer-Fleming, and Hank Phillippi Ryan.

And high-fives to "wicked smaaat" MIT alumni, code-breaking experts Wes Carroll, Doug Stetson, Erik Schwartz, Steve Peters, Emily Prenner, M. L. Peters, and Monica Byrne.

Finally, a mention of Thomas Bluemle and David O'Brian, both men from Buffalo, New York, whom I had the privilege to know, and who both died much too young. The character of Tom O'Brian was named in their memory. I know if they'd lived during World War II, they'd have been among the men storming the beaches (or breaking the codes).

Tom and Dave, I think of you often and thank you for the example you set.

ABOUT THE AUTHOR

Susan Elia MacNeal is the *New York Times* and *USA Today* bestselling author of the Maggie Hope mystery series, including *Mr. Churchill's Secretary, Princess Elizabeth's Spy, His Majesty's Hope,* and *The Prime Minister's Secret Agent.* She is the winner of the Barry Award and was shortlisted for the Edgar, Macavity, Dilys, Bruce Alexander Memorial Historical Mystery, and Sue Feder Memorial Historical Fiction awards. She lives in Park Slope, Brooklyn, with her husband and son.

www.susaneliamacneal.com
Facebook.com/Susan Elia MacNeal,
Author
@SusanMacNeal

The employees of Thorndike Press hope you have enjoyed this Large Print book. All our Thorndike, Wheeler, and Kennebec Large Print titles are designed for easy reading, and all our books are made to last. Other Thorndike Press Large Print books are available at your library, through selected bookstores, or directly from us.

For information about titles, please call:
(800) 223-1244

or visit our Web site at:
http://gale.cengage.com/thorndike

To share your comments, please write:
Publisher
Thorndike Press
10 Water St., Suite 310
Waterville, ME 04901